W9-BGE-769

Andy McNab joined the infantry as a boy soldier. In 1984 he was 'badged' as a member of 22 SAS Regiment and was involved in both covert and overt special operations worldwide. During the Gulf War he commanded Bravo Two Zero, a patrol that, in the words of his commanding officer, 'will remain in regimental history for ever'. Awarded both the Distinguished Conduct Medal (DCM) and Military Medal (MM) during his military career, McNab was the British Army's most highly decorated serving soldier when he finally left the SAS in February 1993. He wrote about his experiences in three phenomenal bestsellers: *Bravo Two Zero, Immediate Action* and *Seven Troop*.

He is the author of the bestselling Nick Stone thrillers. Besides his writing work, he lectures to security and intelligence agencies in both the USA and UK. He is a patron of the Help for Heroes campaign.

Also by Andy McNab

Novels featuring Nick Stone
REMOTE CONTROL
CRISIS FOUR
FIREWALL
LAST LIGHT
LIBERATION DAY
DARK WINTER
DEEP BLACK
AGGRESSOR
RECOIL
CROSSFIRE
BRUTE FORCE
EXIT WOUND

Andy McNab with Kym Jordan
WAR TORN

Quick Reads
THE GREY MAN
LAST NIGHT ANOTHER SOLDIER

Non-fiction
BRAVO TWO ZERO
IMMEDIATE ACTION
SEVEN TROOP
SPOKEN FROM THE FRONT

For more information on Andy McNab and his books,
see his website at www.andymcnab.co.uk

ZERO HOUR

Andy McNab

BANTAM PRESS

LONDON · TORONTO · SYDNEY · AUCKLAND · JOHANNESBURG

TRANSWORLD PUBLISHERS
61–63 Uxbridge Road, London W5 5SA
A Random House Group Company
www.rbooks.co.uk

First published in Great Britain
in 2010 by Bantam Press
an imprint of Transworld Publishers

Copyright © Andy McNab 2010

Andy McNab has asserted his right under the Copyright, Designs
and Patents Act 1988 to be identified as the author of this work.

This book is a work of fiction and, except in the case of historical fact, any resemblance
to actual persons, living or dead, is purely coincidental.

A CIP catalogue record for this book
is available from the British Library.

ISBNs 9780593064986 (cased)
9780593064993 (tpb)

This book is sold subject to the condition that it shall not,
by way of trade or otherwise, be lent, resold, hired out,
or otherwise circulated without the publisher's prior
consent in any form of binding or cover other than that
in which it is published and without a similar condition,
including this condition, being imposed on the
subsequent purchaser.

Addresses for Random House Group Ltd companies outside the UK
can be found at: www.randomhouse.co.uk
The Random House Group Ltd Reg. No. 954009

The Random House Group Ltd supports the Forest Stewardship
Council (FSC), the leading international forest-certification organization. All our
titles that are printed on Greenpeace-approved FSC-certified paper carry the FSC logo.
Our paper procurement policy can be found at
www.rbooks.co.uk/environment

Typeset in 11/14pt Palatino by
Falcon Oast Graphic Art Ltd.
Printed and bound in Great Britain by
CPI Mackays, Chatham, ME5 8TD

2 4 6 8 10 9 7 5 3 1

Mixed Sources
Product group from well-managed
forests and other controlled sources
www.fsc.org Cert no. TT-COC-2139
© 1996 Forest Stewardship Council

PART ONE

1

Wednesday, 5 September 2007
22.39 hrs

The Arab guy at the keyboard was so small his feet only just touched the pedals. His shirt collar was far too big for him, and so were his green suit and matching bow-tie. It looked like the management had ordered a dozen the same size and tough shit if you didn't fit. Tonight's menu had been dished up along much the same lines, but at least the place had air-conditioning.

Diane perched herself on the stool next to mine. She was dressed up for a night out. Everything was covered, but she'd overdone the makeup. She crossed her legs and leant towards me. The pack of B&H glinted in the bar light.

I picked up my orange juice with a shake of the head. 'No thanks, I don't.'

'Quite right too.' She tapped a long red nail on her disposable lighter, took her first deep drag and reached for her G-and-T.

'What do you think of it so far, Nick?'

'My kind of party.' I checked my G-Shock. Less than nineteen minutes to go.

Her half-emptied glass went back on the bar. She studied me as she took another drag. 'Your first time?'

I gave her a grin. 'Thought I'd give it a go.'

'This is my second.' She swivelled to face me, losing herself for a moment in a cloud of cigarette smoke. 'The first time I didn't really want to come. It was so soon after my divorce. But all my friends— Well, everybody has their own lives, don't they? Kids and mortgages. Too much going on, I suppose.'

'Same here. I was left at a loose end. My mates have better things to do than play around with a single lad. Or maybe their wives won't let them out in case I lead them astray. I've always wanted to come here, so when I saw the ad I thought, Why not?'

She took another drag and raised her drink again. We clinked glasses, toasting our exclusion from the world. She sucked an ice cube into her mouth and crunched it.

'How long were you married, Nick?'

'Not long. Couple of years. You?'

'Fifteen.' She made it sound like we were cellmates comparing stretches.

'Long time . . .'

She downed the rest of her gin a bit too quickly. I sensed her life story was about to swamp me. I pointed at her glass and mimed a scribble to the barman.

She kept going. 'You're right. A very long time. We didn't have any kids. He left me for a younger woman, of course. He's got a little girl now.'

A fresh glass appeared. The first sip went down very smoothly.

'What about you, Nick?'

'Only one.'

'How old?'

'She was sixteen.'

Her face fell. 'I'm so sorry.'

'It was a long time ago.'

'How did she ... pass away ... if you don't mind me asking?' Her hand slid across and gripped my arm.

'An accident. In London. She was ... run over.' I didn't care if she thought I was lying or not. 'Anyway, I'm knackered – I think I'm going to head back.'

'Oh, please, I didn't mean to upset you. Please stay.'

'It's not that.' I smiled at her. 'You know what? Maybe that's why I'm here. The women in my life don't tend to stick around for long. I tend not to get that involved, you know what I mean?'

The bill arrived. I made a move for my wallet but she gripped me more tightly.

'I think you and me are exactly the same, Nick. The last thing I want is an ... attachment.'

I freed my sleeve and counted out some notes. She was getting ready to leave too. 'So, Nick, maybe we could go back to the hotel and have a quiet drink there, away from the rest of the gang?'

She nodded over at the restaurant area, where a table of eight or nine was still waffling about today's highlights.

'Thanks, Di. But I think I'll just get my head down.'

I grabbed my nylon day sack and slid off the stool. I turned for the door as she finished off her drink. She wasn't giving up. 'Nick, if you can't sleep, call my room. I'll only be reading. Or I'll be downstairs with the others. Anything but sleeping. It's just so ... hot ...'

She wasn't wrong. I pushed open the doors and walked out of the Jisr al-Kabir into the heat of the night. The restaurant was only a stone's throw from the landmark suspension bridge that spanned the Euphrates in the north-eastern city of Deir el-Zor, but there was no cooling breeze off the river. Deir el-Zor meant 'monastery in the forest', Baltasar had told us. I'd have to take his word for it. All I'd seen was rugged mountains and desert, and farmers tilling the fields on the banks of the river. Not much went on here unless it had to do with the newly

9

invigorated tourist trade. All the action was eighty miles downstream, in neighbouring Iraq.

There were untold numbers of ancient cities around here, our guide had continued. They'd survived Romans, Jews, Ottomans and even the French, who ran the country until 1946. Just about the only natives we'd come across were street vendors trying to flog us camel-hair blankets or sacks of cardamom or coriander. What the fuck was I going to do with any of those?

It was here that we'd be staying for the next three nights of our ten-night run-around of Syria's religious and cultural sights and antiquities. Our tour group was a mix of born-again singles looking for the Promised Land, history-buff singles who wanted to follow the routes of Crusaders and sad-fuck singles like me and Di.

The hotel was the other side of the river. I wandered past the teahouses that lined the road down to the bridge. The pavement tables overflowed with old guys, their hookah-pipes bubbling away as they spun the shit. You name it, the topic was taboo in Syria, but the night was the coolest time to get out and get waffling to your mates, so here they were. And the open air was just about the only place they could be confident the secret police's ears weren't flapping.

I smiled to myself. If everything went to plan in the next two hours, these lads were going to have a lot more to talk about. And they weren't the only ones.

2

As I crossed the suspension bridge I couldn't help another little smile. We'd been here earlier today with our ever-enthusiastic guide. Baltasar was a squat, energetic little man with an enormous moustache. He kept twirling the tips as if they were waxed, but they weren't. Seconds after each twirl, the whole arrangement would collapse again in the heat.

He was so devoted to his mother-country that he claimed just about everything you could think of originated from here. Even Jesus spoke Syriac – which was probably the only fact he'd given us that was actually true. As we'd gazed out across the mighty waters he'd told us the Euphrates featured strongly in the prophecies of the Book of Revelation. 'Where it is written that the river will be one of the scenes of Armageddon . . .' He'd raised his hands to the skies like a prophet. 'The sixth angel poured out his bowl on the great river Euphrates, and its water was dried up to prepare the way for the kings from the east.'

Tonight it wasn't going to be kings coming from the east. It was going to be loud bolts of thunder roaring in from the west, in the form of seven F-15 fighter jets armed with AGM-65 Maverick missiles and 500-pound bombs.

The hotel lay a block beyond the far bank. The rectangular

concrete monolith had had a few licks of green paint and a bit of a dig-out to cater for the tourists, but that was about it. The air-conditioning, like Baltasar's take on history, was beyond repair.

The security guard at the front door had a blue sweater on over his blue overalls. There wasn't as much as one drop of sweat on his ancient face. I went into the lobby. The small bar area and a couple of soon-to-be-threadbare sofas were taken up by faces from our *Road to Damascus* tour. I hadn't bothered to find out all their names. Baltasar was at the centre of the group.

'Ah! Mr Shepherd! Are you not coming to join us?' He gave his whiskers a tweak. 'I was explaining about the archaeological remains at Dura-Europos and—'

I kept on walking. I pulled out my BlackBerry and waved it. 'I'll maybe come down later, mate. I've got to make a call.'

There weren't any lifts. The stairway was encased in mustard-coloured walls and a musty, smelly brown carpet that kept me company up all six flights. I'd asked for a room at the top. I wanted the view over the city; I didn't mind what it cost.

I let myself in with a large key. The room was basic, but at least it was clean. There were two sheets and a pillow, a thin green blanket and no TV. A two-litre bottle of water and a small glass took the place of a mini-bar. I used it to clean my teeth each morning, then got the rest of it down my neck before buying another from Reception for the day's sightseeing.

I shoved my earphones into place and hit the icon that looked like a date and time application. It took a second or two to load, and when it did I tapped in Cody's number.

There was a long tone, followed by a short break. Cody Zero One was beginning to receive the call. The green padlock icon on his illuminated screen would be telling him it was in secure mode. He wouldn't have to shove anything in his ear. He'd just press a button and take it on loudspeaker.

Cody Zero One was my new mate in Air Combat Command at Nellis Air Force Base. He was in the CAOC (Combined Air

Operations Center) but this was a Coalition operation. The US might be controlling things from Nevada, but it was British boffins at GCHQ who'd contributed the technical and electronics expertise, while the Israelis were providing and flying the weapons-delivery platforms, the F-15s. All three empires were all taking part.

Nellis was about eight miles from the centre of Las Vegas. I knew it well. I'd been there a number of times when I was in the Regiment. We came with RAF Tornado crews to practise splashing targets with lasers so they could come in and bomb them. After a day on the ranges, we'd get down and hit Vegas for as long as we could. Not so much for the gambling – what's the point? – but for the big bowls of shrimp they gave away free to keep you at the slots and tables.

The tone sounded another two times before a familiar Texan drawl came online. 'This is Cody Zero One. Identify yourself. Over.'

The signal strength was fine, but sound quality wasn't that good and there was a delay of about one and a half seconds. He sounded like he was doing lengths in a swimming-pool. The software was very much first-generation. It had to take what I was saying, bounce it off whatever satellite they were using, encrypt it, bounce it down to Cody and back to me once Cody started gobbing off. We had to follow radio voice procedure.

I pictured Cody in his air-conditioned bunker twenty metres under the Nevada scrublands, with his desert camouflage uniform starched to fuck, and his perfect teeth and white walled haircut. Alongside him would be a jug of coffee and a box of Krispy Kremes, and in front of him a set of massive plasma screens projecting real-time satellite pictures of the target about twenty miles from my balcony.

The al-Kibar complex was a nuclear reactor. Specifically, it was a gas-cooled, graphite-moderated reactor, a carbon copy of the Yongbyon plutonium reactor in North Korea. As you'd expect, the Israelis were unhappy about having one of these on their doorstep, especially one that was tooling up to produce nuclear weapons for a country they had technically been at war with for sixty years. To make things worse, North Korea and Iran were both implicated. Iran was going to use al-Kibar as a secondary facility for its own nuclear programme.

Tonight's operation was going to take less than an hour from start to finish, but it had taken nearly a year to confirm and plan. Luckily for me, it was the UK that had put one of the two final nails into the coffin of al-Kibar. I was holding the shitty end of the stick, but that didn't matter to me: I was here to fly the Union Jack. Fucking about in another country, getting things done and, more importantly, getting away with it, that was the juice for me.

My iPod earphones sparked up again.

'This is Cody Zero One. I say again, identify yourself, over.'

'Cody Zero One, this is James Zero Two. Over.'

I couldn't wait for the day when the software was so smooth you could just talk.

Cody came back after a couple of seconds. 'Roger that, James Zero Two. Fifty-nine – I say again, fiver-niner. Over.'

I did a quick calculation to make sure I wasn't about to fuck up. 'Roger that. Fifty-nine, fiver-niner. That's minus fifty. Minus fiver zero. Over.'

I wanted to make sure I got this right first time. I'd only have one chance to confirm it. The password was nine. To get 59, you had to take off 50. If he had said 02, I'd have said plus 07.

'This is Cody Zero One. Ra'am is not airborne. Acknowledge.'

'Roger that, Cody Zero One. Ra'am not airborne. Out.'

I wasn't cutting off the phone. I was just making sure he didn't rattle on with the commentary until I needed to know.

Pilots all over the world like to give themselves nicknames. There are Lightning Strikes, Cobras, Hell Hawks, Flying Buccaneers – all sorts going on. 69th Squadron of the Israeli Air Force called themselves Ra'am – the Hebrew for thunder.

It was hard not to take the piss, but then again, I wasn't an Israeli with a fucking great mushroom cloud taking shape right on my doorstep. Nor was I a Yank with worries about what the fervently anti-American Iranians were up to. I was just a Brit low down the food chain doing a job, and that was the way I liked it.

I unzipped the day sack. First out was my very Gucci Nikon digital camera, together with the world's supply of lenses and all the leads and bits and pieces to download pictures onto my Sony notebook. I'd had to explain to Security that I used the extending umbrella with the silver-coated interior as a reflector to help with my photography. These three bits of kit were all I was going to need to do my bit of the job.

The Brits had confirmed that al-Kibar was a nuclear plant. Up until then, the Israelis had had no concrete evidence of its use – or who was helping build it. All they knew was that the Syrians received high-ranking military delegations from North Korea. Mossad was convinced that they were intent on upgrading Syria's military capabilities. North Korea had already helped Damascus develop medium-range ballistic missiles, and chemical weapons such as Sarin and mustard gas. So were they now taking them to the next level?

If that was the case, Israel would retaliate exactly the same as it had in Iraq in 1981 – when they flew over the border and bombed the fledgling Osirak reactor near Baghdad back to the Stone Age. There was no fucking about. They asked no one. They just went and did it. They broke international law, but nobody gave a shit. The only victim was Saddam. The fact that they themselves had nuclear weapons didn't come into the equation. A lot of people belonged to that club. Even Pakistan and India were members. But the line in the sand had to be drawn at Axis-of-Evil countries, like Syria and Iran.

The Israelis suspected what was happening at al-Kibar, but they lacked hard intelligence. And Syria was a different kettle of fish from Iraq. Washington wouldn't back an attack without the int. But then things changed. In November 2006 Mossad came to the Brits for help. A senior Syrian official was staying at a big fancy hotel in Kensington that cost £1,600 a night. The Security Service went in and had a mince around. The guy had been incredibly careless. He'd gone out for the night and left his laptop in his room. MI5 opened up the back and inserted a Trojan horse program. Over the next couple of months, they drained out the construction plans for al-Kibar, together with hundreds of emails and photographs.

The photographs did the most damage. They showed the complex at various stages of construction since 2002. The main building looked like a tree-house on stilts, with pipes leading into a pumping station on the banks of the Euphrates. It was going to need a lot of water to create fissile material. As the building grew, it sprouted concrete piers and roofs, which could only have one function – to camouflage the place from above. Al-Kibar's core design, they could now prove, was the same as North Korea's Yongbyon reactor, even down to the number of holes for fuel rods.

The clincher was a photo that showed an Asian guy in blue tracksuit trousers standing next to one of the Arabs who'd been working there all the time. The Brits quickly identified the Asian as Chon Chibu. He was the chief engineer behind the North Koreans' plutonium reactor at Yongbyon.

The Israelis were wetting themselves with this int, but it still wasn't enough for the US. Washington thought it would be years before the Syrians were capable of producing a bomb. They could be fucked up without the US getting drawn into another war.

Things might have stayed that way had not a high-ranking Iranian decided to switch sides. General Ali-Reza Asgari was a massive catch. Head of Iran's Revolutionary Guard in Lebanon in the eighties, he'd become Iran's deputy defence minister in the mid-nineties. His fall from grace had come after the election victory of hardliner Mahmoud Ahmadinejad in 2005.

Asgari had branded several of those close to the new president as corrupt. He was living on borrowed time.

The Iranian general was an intelligence goldmine. He confirmed that Tehran was building a second, secret, plant in addition to the uranium enrichment plant in Natanz, already known to the West. And that Iran was funding a top-secret nuclear project in Syria, launched in co-operation with the North Koreans.

Finally, the US had to sit up and take notice. The UK would be standing shoulder to shoulder with them, and sharing blood. That blood, of course, was going to be mine if I fucked up. From swanky executive suites in Kensington to high-profile defectors larging it in Washington, the operation had now come down to Cody munching doughnuts in Nevada, and me sitting in a dingy hotel room checking my watch.

In exactly fourteen minutes, a bright flash would light up the night in the distant desert, followed by the sound of thunder that would signal Armageddon.

3

I plugged the laptop into the wall socket, let it sort itself out, and unfurled the umbrella. I extended the handle, pulled off the small plastic knob at the end and lifted the cap beneath it to reveal a USB slot. I placed what was now a satellite dish on the floor by the open window.

Six floors below me, giggly Brits headed back to the hotel against the hum of traffic. Long fluorescent tubes dangled outside a line of shops to show off the goods on display. Above me hung a huge blanket of stars. In the middle distance, between the stars and the city, lay the inky blackness where the desert took over. Out there somewhere, oblivious to what was on its way, was al-Kibar.

The 200mm zoom lens was much heavier than the others. It housed a lithium battery that could power the device on its own or become an instant backup if the local grid cut out. I ran a lead from it into the USB slot in the top of the umbrella. Another USB wire ran from the camera to the laptop. Its screen was now displaying thumbnails of the hundreds of pictures I'd been taking to make my cover story stand up.

I hit the blue circle icon to open the programme.

'This is Cody Zero One. Ra'am are airborne – Ra'am are airborne. Acknowledge.'

'Roger that, Cody Zero One. Ra'am airborne.'

I checked my G-Shock: 23.26. I fired up my countdown display. GCHQ had pre-set it at eighteen minutes.

The F-15s had taken off from Ramat David Air Base, just south of Haifa on the Mediterranean coast. It was also near Megiddo, which, according to Baltasar and the Book of Revelation, would be one of the sites of the final battle between good and evil. That seemed appropriate. The attack on al-Kibar was certainly going to be Biblical.

Ten fast jets would take part in the initial attack, though only seven would be coming my way. For now all ten headed west, out into the Mediterranean. It was a decoy manoeuvre. Both the Turks and the Syrians would be tracking them. Everybody wants to know what the Israelis are up to 24/7 in this part of the world.

The screen displayed an empty bar chart. The Tefalheads at GCHQ who'd put this together must have realized that I needed everything to be as simple as possible. I turned off the lights and picked up the umbrella so that the inside and the shaft pointed out of the window. I moved it up and down and side to side until the bar chart was about three-quarters full of green. It was the best I could do and all that was needed.

I propped the umbrella on a chair and anchored it across the handle with my pillow.

'This is Cody Zero One. Ra'am first wave ready to go active.'

I adjusted the dish. 'Roger that, Cody Zero One. I am seven-five, seventy-five per cent. Over.'

'Roger that, James Zero Two. Seven-fiver. Good to go. Stand by.'

Someone somewhere counted down Ra'am's first wave on a radio. It was slow, guttural and very Israeli. 'Five – four – three – two – one – go, go, go.'

'This is Cody Zero One. Ra'am first wave active. Acknowledge.'

'Roger that, Cody Zero One. I'm still seven-fiver.'

Three of the ten F-15s had peeled off and headed east-north-east towards the Syrian border. They were going to attack the radar site at Tall al-Abuad with their Maverick missiles and 500-pounders. The moment that happened, the stakes would be raised. Every unit near the border would hear what was going on, and the Syrian military would start flapping big-time.

All I could do now was listen as Cody gave the running commentary. I needed a picture in my head of what was happening. So did the other guy listening in. Ehud Olmert, the Israeli prime minister, was taking personal responsibility for the Ra'am part of this attack. I was sure his surroundings were a little more comfortable than mine.

'This is Cody Zero One. Ten seconds to contact.'

I counted them down on my second-hand.

'First attack – ordnance deployed. Contact, contact, contact. Second attack . . .'

There was a pause.

Cody was waiting for the Mavericks from the second wave to deploy as he watched the target on his screens. He'd be looking for the splashes all over the night-vision thermal imagery as bombs and missiles hit the radar installation.

'Ordnance deployed. Contact, contact, contact. Third attack . . .'

Another pause, shorter this time.

'Weapons deployed.' For Cody, it would have been like watching a video game. 'Contact, contact, contact.'

That was the radar defences fucked up.

'Ra'am second wave now active . . . James Zero Two, acknowledge.'

'Roger that, Cody Zero One. I still have seven-fiver.'

The seven remaining F-15s were now screaming towards the Syrian border to break through the secure corridor that had been opened by the attack. From the moment they hit Syrian air space, it was exactly eighteen minutes to target.

Cody couldn't help himself now. There was excitement in his voice. 'Ra'am second wave – now in the combat box. James Zero Two, all yours – acknowledge.'

'Roger that, Cody Zero One.'

I hit my countdown timer. My eyes were glued to the screen. I wasn't sure what to do if the bar percentage dropped. Fuck about with the umbrella, I supposed.

The F-15s would be virtually hugging the ground to avoid being illuminated. Now the border had been attacked, ground-to-air missile systems would be searching the sky. They wouldn't know what the fuck was going on, but they'd know there had been an attack on their air defences, and that meant there was going to be an air incursion. But what type? Jets? Ground troops? A combination? There'd be nothing for them to latch onto just yet, but Ra'am couldn't hug the desert for ever. They were going to have to gain height in excess of 8,000 feet in order to assume their attack profiles. That was where I came in: if I didn't fuck up the Russian-made Tor-M1 and Pechora-A2 surface-to-air missiles that were protecting al-Kibar, they were going to fuck up Ra'am, and it really would be Armageddon.

Everything fell silent. Cody, me, Ehud Olmert – we were all holding our breath. Even the noise outside was blocked as I kept my eyes glued to the screen and the bars fluctuated between 73 and 75.

I checked the timer. Fourteen minutes fifteen seconds to go. I turned back to the screen. My laptop was linked by satellite to America's Suter airborne-attack system. This package could feed enemy radar emitters with false targets, and even directly manipulate the Tor-M1 and Pechora-A2 sensors so they closed down completely. And that was what was happening now – or, at least, I hoped it was. I was directly attacking the micro-processors within the Syrian missile systems. It was easy enough. The chips had had kill switches programmed into them. When I hit the go button, I'd be sending a pre-programmed code to those chips, enabling Suter to override and tell the system what to do.

Syria's missile systems might have been built in Russia, but the chips inside them hadn't. Russia had been in shit state for years after the collapse of the Iron Curtain. Bizarre as it seemed, they plugged the gap by buying microchips off-the-shelf from Taiwan and the West. Washington and London weren't slow to catch on. As soon as they found out what was happening, they mobilized their Tefalheads. Microchips bound for Moscow and other unfriendly states were either repro-grammed or built from scratch with back doors or kill switches installed. Until they twigged, the West would be at liberty to disable whole weapons systems at will.

It wasn't the first time the Russians and their various mates had been at the sharp end of this particular conjuring trick. In 2004, the CIA inserted a software Trojan horse into computing equipment bought from Canadian suppliers to control a trans-Siberian gas pipeline. A three-kiloton explosion tore the pipeline apart; the detonation was so large it was visible from outer space.

The radar systems on the border were old Soviet-era kit and didn't have the kill switches, so they had to be hammered the old-fashioned way. The Syrians also had the newer, state-of-the-art Russian Pantsyr-S1E missile systems, but luckily for us they wouldn't be operational for a month. I guessed that was a reason we were pushing ahead with the attack.

There was a distant rumble in the sky. It could only mean one thing. The F-15s' engines were on full thrust to push them up from the sand. At 8,000 feet they'd acquire the target and scream down towards it at forty-five degrees. That was when they were at their most vulnerable. If I fucked up, they could be illuminated.

I didn't even bother looking out of the window. They were miles away in the darkness.

I looked at the timer. Fifty-eight seconds until the first attack.

There was a loud thump.

Then another.

I glanced at my watch as the door took another pounding. There was nowhere to run. I had to stay and make sure this shit worked.

'Nick . . . ?'

I gave a low groan. 'I'm sleeping.'

Cody sparked up in my earpieces. 'First attack – ordnance deployed.'

'Shorry . . . Nick . . .' Her voice was slurred. It sounded like she had her face pressed against the door. 'I was wondering . . . if you fancied a drink. Maybe I could bring a bottle up?'

'*Contact, contact, contact.*'

There was a distant flash of sheet lighting, then another, from the strip of darkness between the city and the stars. A few seconds later, the pressure waves from the first series of explosions rumbled over the rooftops.

Cody continued his commentary as the next Ra'am rolled down into the target.

'Nick? Did you hear that? What was that?'

'Thunder . . . There's a storm out there.'

The screen still showed 73–75 per cent. There were more flashes and rumbles as the seven F-15s kicked away at the target.

Cody gobbed off in my ear and the thunder continued to roll. I muted the BlackBerry. 'Tell you what, Di, give me ten minutes and I'll see you down at the bar.'

She rattled on the door with both hands to mimic the explosions. 'Better bring that umbrella of yours.'

Another lightning bolt flashed on the horizon, then faded with her laughter as she headed back along the corridor.

PART TWO

1

Tuesday, 9 March 2010
12.50 hrs

It wasn't supposed to be this way.

I leant against the triple-glazed floor-to-ceiling windows of my penthouse apartment and tried to look out over Docklands, but the stabbing pain in my head played havoc with my vision. It felt like I was swimming through a pool full of razorblades.

The glass-and-steel monolith had had its final lick of paint the day Lehman Brothers had gone belly-up and the owner was no longer flashing the cash. 'Their crunch is your lunch,' the overly pushy estate agent told me, with a megawatt grin and flash of racing-car cufflinks. 'If you've got cash on the hip, you can really clean up at times like this.'

I'd been penniless through every other recession in living memory, so it seemed like a nice idea. And I'd loved everything about this place, from the dual-aspect reception room opening on to the roof terrace to the secure underground parking space; from the granite worktops to the limestone bath with integrated TV; from the private balcony and walk-in wardrobe that hadn't yet been filled, to the guest bedroom with the cantilevered glass pod sticking out over the dock.

It was like something out of a Bond film. The photochromic glass frontage darkened when the sun got too bright during the day, and the night-time views across to the Canary Wharf towers and the glistening river beneath were so fantastic I never closed the blinds.

Before the headaches had begun I'd just sit there with a brew, mesmerized by the aircraft warning lights. If I needed a change of scenery I'd wander over to the other side of the apartment and gaze past Tower Bridge towards the mishmash of South London estates that used to be my manor. As a kid I'd looked back across the water and thought the disused warehouses and crumbling tenements along this stretch were even worse than the shithole I called home, but Docklands was a very different story now. And so was what had been happening inside my head for over a week.

'You OK, Nick?'

Julian was sitting on one of my fancy leather armchairs, working his way through my supply of coffee capsules.

I didn't look round. 'Yes, mate.'

I wasn't about to tell him the truth. I didn't like people worrying about me. It made me uncomfortable. No one had given a fuck about me when I was a kid, and I'd got to prefer it that way.

The forest of tower cranes standing over Millwall Dock was a blur, but the one with Christmas lights still draped across its boom was starting to come back into focus.

'This isn't good for you, stuck away up here, keeping yourself to yourself. You're turning into a recluse. You've got to get back out into the real world, do the things you do best.' He hesitated. 'I'm worried about you.'

I knew he wasn't just concerned about my social life: he had a job for me. I'd tried to blank the pain instead of dealing with it these last few days; trying to stand there and take it until it gave up for a moment and went away. Maybe it was working. I'd always gone that route during my time as a deniable operator, and before that when I was in the Regiment. I'd done it as far back as I could remember.

I'd taken whatever my stepdad had dished out and not given him the satisfaction of knowing I was about to cry. I'd just stepped up to the plate, taken the punishment and dared him to have another crack. Which he always did. Me not reacting the way he wanted had pissed him off big-time: the slaps had got harder, and so had I.

So, no way was this shit going to get to me.

I turned back to Jules. He was dressed immaculately as usual, in a crisp white shirt and black suit, shiny shoes, perfectly knotted fancy red tie. He looked more like a Calvin Klein model than the first black section head of the Security Service, MI5.

We'd become quite good mates, as far as the mates thing went for me. He wasn't coming over from his Edwardian apartment in Marylebone and banging on my door for brews the whole time, but he was a regular visitor, and always called first. Maybe that was why I liked him so much. Or maybe it was because he was the only mate I had left. Everyone else seemed to have got themselves royally fucked up or dead.

'Listen, mate, I keep telling you I'm not interested. Why the fuck would I want to go and work again? Take a look at all this.' I waved a hand around the apartment, then wiped it down the side of my face as if it was about to magic the pain away. 'Waste of a morning, mate. I'm shitting money. I don't need any of yours.'

He put down his mug. 'Ah, yes – your grandmother's inheritance . . .'

'She put it away for a rainy day – bless her.'

Pinpricks of light still swam across my retina, but I could now see well enough to get the full benefit of his ironic expression. Julian knew exactly where the cash had come from.

I took a seat beside one of the three glass coffee-tables scattered around the massive room.

Op Sec triggered MI5's answer to Catch-22: they could only tell you what the job was once you'd signed up for it – but you wouldn't want to do that until you knew what you were letting yourself in for. Not even our friendship could change that.

It was another of the reasons I liked him. He was one of the good guys, straight down the line. Truth, integrity, defence of the realm and all that shit: he radiated it.

I realized I was a bit jealous. I might have the penthouse, the knockout view, the Porsche downstairs, but this lad had things money can't buy.

Jules leant forward, his elbows on his knees. 'They want you back, Nick.'

'After all those years of getting fucked over from both sides of the river, all of a sudden your lot can't do without me?' I laughed, and that made my head start hurting all over again.

Jules shifted uneasily in his chair. 'Are you sure you're OK, Nick?'

I managed to dredge up a smile from somewhere. 'Never better, mate. Never better. Although that fucking "Chinese" we had the other night has given me the odd dodgy moment.' I pointed a finger. 'I blame you.'

He leant back in his chair. 'You should be thanking me. No wheat, no dairy, no toxins – Vietnamese is probably the healthiest food you've eaten in your life.'

'But don't you get bored eating that Ho Chi Minh shit all the time?'

He smiled. 'When I do I'll go somewhere else. You still coming on Saturday?'

'I'll call you.'

Ten minutes later he headed for the lift and I made it to the toilet just in time to bulk up another gutful of coffee-flavoured bile.

2

Wednesday, 10 March
11.34 hrs

The wind gusted down Harley Street, throwing pellets of rain against the window. The nurse had disappeared fifteen minutes earlier, after announcing that Dr Kleinmann was just checking a few things. She'd done her best to look encouraging, but it wasn't working.

A dark blue Bentley coupé pulled up across the road. I'd spent a great morning test-driving a green one a couple of months ago, but decided it was just too wide for my parking space. An overweight driver leapt out with a multi-coloured golfing brolly and held it over a couple of equally large Arab women as he ushered them into the clinic opposite.

The row of gracious old houses where grand families had once played charades by the fire and drunk to the health of Queen Victoria now hosted hundreds of offices and treatment rooms, turning over cash-paying patients seven days a week.

I was waiting in one of the drabber ones: the consultation fees hadn't stretched to a can or two of Dulux in the last couple of decades, and they hadn't been chucked in the direction of the central heating either.

A pitted brass chandelier hung from a sepia moulding above my head, casting enough light over the carpet and furniture to make it painfully obvious that they could have done with a bit of a steam clean. Shabby or chic, it didn't seem to make much difference to the bill. Whatever you were there for, you came out a few hundred quid lighter. A clock on the mantelpiece ticked away the minutes, and the pounds.

Fuck it, I wasn't exactly spoilt for options. The NHS needed all sorts of details that I'd got out of the habit of providing, and BUPA weren't much better. The Firm had never provided health insurance for people in my line of work, and without a bank account I was willing to divulge, I couldn't set up my own. My credit history was non-existent. I'd slipped out of the frame years ago, when I'd left the army; I hadn't paid tax since I'd picked up my discharge payslip. So I had to come to places like this, pay cash, and get on with it. I wasn't complaining. The less anyone knew about Nick Stone, the better.

'Sorry to keep you waiting, Mr Stone.' The accent was East Coast, but it would have been equally at home in LA or Jerusalem. Dr Max Kleinmann carried a large brown folder with my name splattered all over it, but he didn't look happy to see me.

His expression was as grim as the weather and made sterner still by his black-framed glasses. Was he suffering under the usual burdens of marriage, mortgages and school fees, or was he just pissed off not to be on Rodeo Drive?

His dark, tightly curled hair was thinning on top, and a patch of stubble sprouted from above his Adam's apple where he'd failed to zap it with his razor. The combo made him look a bit ridiculous, and that cheered me up for some reason. Perhaps it would help me take what he was about to say to me less seriously.

'I just wanted to be sure I was seeing what I was seeing . . .' He came and sat opposite me, on my side of his desk. 'I wish I had better news for you.'

I turned back towards the window.

'You OK, Mr Stone? You still with me?'

Of course I was. I just didn't know what to say. I came out with the first thing that hit what was left of my mind. 'That's me fucked, is it?'

He didn't even blink. 'This is where the hard work starts. Let me show you . . .'

I followed him over to a light box on the wall. He hit a switch and it flickered into life. He slid the scan under the retaining clips.

He pointed to the tiny shadow on the right side of my brain. 'This lesion, I'm afraid, is the problem. We know it as a glioblastoma multiforme, a particularly virulent type of astrocytoma. It's a high-grade tumour, which tends to grow quite quickly. It's the most common type of primary malignant brain tumour in adults. I'm surprised the symptoms aren't worse. You have headaches, nausea, drowsiness?'

'Yeah, all that. Listen, Doc, I don't need to know all the technical bollocks. Just – can you zap it?'

'With treatment it can be made bearable.' He breathed in slowly. 'Mr Stone, have you anyone waiting for you downstairs?'

'No, there's no one. No one to call, no one to worry about.'

At last Kleinmann was looking a little happier. He wouldn't have to trot out the usual bullshit, shepherding me and my loved ones through the emotional labyrinth that led from here to fuck knew where. He could just get down to business.

He pushed his glasses further up his nose and leant forward to take a closer look at the tumour, in case it had changed into something nice like a Teletubby in the last few minutes. I found myself doing the same, examining the scan as if I knew what the fuck I was looking at.

'You say it'll keep growing?'

It was hard to believe that something so insignificant was going to finish me off. I'd always imagined it would be something a bit bigger, something more like the diameter of an RPG, a rifle butt or at least a 7.62mm round, but this little fucker was no more than pea-sized. Checking out like this? It felt so . . . *pedestrian* . . .

I tried to smile. 'I always wondered what a death warrant looked like. Does it have a use-by date?'

I turned away and went back to my chair. I didn't need to see any more. Looking wasn't going to change anything.

Kleinmann followed me. 'Like I said, Mr Stone, this is where the hard work starts. Chemotherapy and radiation treatment, that's going to help, and there is—'

'But will that nail it?'

Kleinmann sat down opposite me. 'No.' He flicked his coat over his legs like a woman adjusting her skirt. 'It could keep you going for six months, possibly longer. But without any treatment? Two months, maybe. We can't stop the pressure on the brain increasing. Of course, if you need a second opinion—'

'Don't worry, Doc, no second opinions. It's there, I've seen it.'

'What about the treatment? Would you like to go ahead with the chemo and radiation? The pain is going to get worse. There could be weight loss, maybe incontinence, vomiting still to come. But I will give you some drugs to help you in the short term.'

I got up and headed for the coat hooks. 'Thanks, I'll take whatever Smarties you're offering. But chemo and all that gear? I don't think so.'

Kleinmann sprang to his feet. 'There are far more advanced treatments available in the US – or Italy, if you want to be closer to home. I could recommend some excellent clinics . . .'

I bet he could. With a nice little kickback if I took him up on the offer. 'I think I'm going to handle this my own way.'

'Let me give you some details of support groups, counselling—'

'I don't need any of that.' I shrugged on my coat, then paused. 'Out of interest, any reason I got it? Just one of those things?'

'You have an unusual amount of tissue scarring. You appear to have taken a great deal of blunt trauma to the cerebral cortex over a number of years. Are you a boxer, maybe?'

I shook my head.

'When the grey matter is shaken about over a sustained period of time it can cause irreparable damage – and in extreme cases provoke conditions such as yours.'

'Thanks for that, Doc.' I gave Kleinmann a slap on the shoulder. 'I hope your next appointment's a nice boob job.'

I made for the door, not knowing quite what I felt. It wasn't fear. Fuck it, we've all got to die some day. It was more frustration. I didn't want to end on a dull note. Better to burn out than fade away, I'd always thought. Better to be a tiger for a day than a sheep for a year; to die quick standing up than live for years on my knees. All the shit I'd seen on soldiers' T-shirts the world over actually meant something today.

'No, no – wait, Mr Stone. You're going to need to control the pain as the symptoms worsen.' He disappeared for a minute or two and came back with a large bottle of shiny red pills. 'Take two of these every six hours.'

I nodded.

'And please, take this information.' He waved a brown A4 folder at me, stuffed with leaflets and flyers. 'It's all in there – treatments, support groups, help lines. Read them, think about it.'

I took the folder and stuffed it in the nearest wastepaper basket, then headed back towards my 911 waiting faithfully in the rain.

3

16.15 hrs

The storm pounded against the triple glazing.

For about the hundredth time in the last hour, I reached for the mobile, twisting and turning it in my hand before putting it back down again.

What the fuck was I going to say to her?

Did I need to say anything?

It was only six months since I'd first held Anna in my arms. Even then I'd had the feeling I'd known her all my life. We were standing among the wreckage of an aircraft full of dead men and drug dollars I'd shot down in Russia. We'd met at an arms fair press conference in Tehran two weeks earlier. I was working undercover for Julian; she was investigating a corrupt Russian's links with Ahmadinejad and the Iranian ayatollahs.

She said she wouldn't have touched me with a ten-foot pole if she could have sorted it on her own. Then she gave me the kind of smile that makes your knees go funny. I'd first set eyes on her when she was giving the Russian a hard time in front of the world's press. She was a dead ringer for the girl from Abba with blonde hair and high cheekbones. I'd fancied her big-time. I used to sit in the NAAFI as a sixteen-year-old boy soldier with my pint of Vimto and a steak and kidney pie, waiting for *Top of the Pops* to hit the screen. 'Dancing Queen' had already been number one for about five years, and I took my seat in front of the TV every week hoping her reign would be extended.

This amazing woman had helped me choose furniture for the flat, and in between writing investigative pieces and flying around saving the world she'd come and stay. Only a few days at a time, mind, but for me that was almost long-term. The only thing we'd fallen out over was her smoking. She wasn't about to be sent onto the balcony to do it.

I headed for the kitchen sink, swallowed a couple of Kleinmann's Smarties and stuck my mouth under the designer tap. I clicked the kettle on and told myself I had to bite the bullet.

Did I really want to do this? Did I really need to do this?

I had to. I didn't want her standing in the wreckage with me again. She deserved so much better.

I twisted and turned the mobile in my hand. Why drag her down with me?

My arse rested against the stainless-steel cooker. It would always be this shiny. I had all the toys now, but I was never going to turn into Jamie Oliver.

Finally, I stabbed a finger at the keypad and dialled.

'Jules, mate? Count me in for Saturday.'

4

Saturday, 13 March
14.00 hrs

Chelsea were at home to West Ham. Kick-off wasn't for another hour, but I still had to park so far from the ground I might as well have walked all the way from Docklands. I still preferred it to taking the tube, especially the way I was feeling.

I passed the Vietnamese restaurant on the corner by Fulham Broadway where Jules came to be deprived of wheat and dairy practically every night. Fuck that. I went into the station and came out again with two big frothy coffees.

I walked the last couple of hundred metres up the Fulham Road and flashed Julian's spare season ticket at the turnstiles. The concourse was buzzing with blue-shirted fans clutching plastic pint glasses of lager, and overseas visitors taking pictures of each other eating expensive hot-dog baguettes. I made my way through them to the Block A steps. The stadium gradually came into view as I climbed. It was huge and, apart from a few bored-looking stewards in fluorescent orange jackets, virtually empty.

Julian was in his usual seat in row twelve, studying the

programme with the kind of concentration he'd normally save for a PhD thesis.

'Oi, mate . . .'

He turned round, all smiles. I made my way along the row and handed him his coffee.

'Nightmare parking, as usual. If you were a true friend you'd support a team closer to my home.'

'I don't know why you don't use the tube.'

'No way, mate. After a lifetime of being poor, it's the 911 everywhere for me, including the corner shop. You posh lads think it's good to cycle and take public transport, and I'm glad. There aren't enough spaces as it is.'

Jules shook his head and smiled. It was the same banter every time, but he didn't care. On the phone, he sounded like he'd shared a school desk with David Cameron. In the flesh, his closely cropped hair, clean shave, sharp suit and glowing ebony skin made him look like he should have been out there with Drogba on the pitch, not watching from the stands.

Posh lad or not, I enjoyed his company. I certainly wasn't here for the football. The last time I'd gone to a game more than twice in the same year, I was a twelve-year-old bunking over the fences at Millwall. I didn't really like it even then – I just went for a laugh, a pie and a can of Fanta. But it was no picnic at Millwall: it always ended with a brawl.

I fished in my pocket for the season ticket.

He shooed it away. 'You'll be needing it for next time.'

This was the third time this had happened. 'How much do these things cost?'

'Enough to make my eyes water.'

'Another burden on the bleeding taxpayer.'

'When was the last time you paid tax?' Julian flashed his perfect white teeth. 'Come to that, when was the first time?'

I gave him a 500-watt grin, even though I suddenly had a head full of pain. I palmed two Smarties and swallowed them with a gulp of Pret A Manger's frothiest.

We both stared out over the pitch.

'I've been giving that job a bit of thought.'

Julian glanced behind us. People had started to fill the nearby seats but there was nobody within earshot. His eyebrow arched towards his immaculately sculpted hairline. 'What about Granny's nest egg?'

'She always wanted me to work for a living . . .'

Jules pulled out his BlackBerry and hit the secure speech icon before dialling. That was a good sign. His spare hand covered the mouthpiece like he thought I'd added lip-reading to my CV.

He closed down and put it back in his pocket. 'OK, you're on. But you'll need to give me a lift in that penis extension of yours.' Jules got to his feet. 'We have an audience with the top man. He'll meet us in three hours. The Blues will have to win without us.'

'Not a chance. West Ham will kick the shit out of them. Three–nil, I reckon.'

5

GCHQ Cheltenham
17.23 hrs

I came off the M5 at junction eleven and followed the A40 east towards Cheltenham. Just before the town, I turned off at a roundabout. Jules switched the radio to medium wave to tune into Talksport.

They were waffling about football and, of course, I'd been way off the mark. Chelsea had won 4–1.

We pulled onto Hubble Road. GCHQ had been the most secretive of Britain's three intelligence services since way back, and I always reckoned they chose this location on the edge of a spa town in rural Gloucestershire just to add to the mystique. While MI5 and MI6 gathered human intelligence, GCHQ's main mission was soaking up the signals equivalent, via the interception of phone calls, faxes, emails or any other electronic means. They monitored the airwaves for any vital snippet that might stop a terrorist attack in the UK or help the military in Afghanistan. They were also tasked with protecting the government's communications against attack by enemy codebreakers.

This was Boffin Central, where some of the world's most

powerful computers played tunes for people with brains the size of a planet. I smiled to myself as I remembered the TV commercial for Tefal. A group of white-coated boffins with extra large heads hovered over a new kettle or iron, making sure it was perfect for the likes of me. They must have filmed it right here.

The man we were going to meet was Julian's new boss. The whole of the British intelligence community's new boss, by the sound of it. Tresillian had been made *über*-chief of all three services – MI5, MI6 and GCHQ – a position that had only just been created.

'There's a thread of continuity at last. If GCHQ picks up a whisper, he can give the order for SIS to take immediate action. None of the old red tape.'

'Or the old checks and balances?'

I slowed. There was a barrier across the road ahead, manned by two guys in uniform. The first layer of security. Jules flashed his pass and we were waved through.

'Seriously new broom. Actually – new broom, old handle. His family go back to before the Domesday Book.'

I nodded. The most powerful people the world over are the ones we'll never hear about. Like those who are so rich they make sure they never feature on Forbes' List or the *Sunday Times* Richest.

'That's nice for him. But is he any good?'

'Shit-fucking-hot, if he says so himself.'

I was so surprised I took my eye off the road. I'd never heard him swear.

He directed me to the car park at the front of the huge steel building. Everyone called it the Doughnut. Viewed from above, that was exactly what it looked like.

I drew level with a black BMW 5 that was three up.

Julian nodded. 'Tresillian's already here.'

'Hope he's got the kettle on.'

The driver was still behind the wheel, in weekend clothes.

The engine was running. He was watching a DVD on a windscreen-mounted player. The two in the back were in suits that looked just a little too small for them. They were waiting for their principal to finish his meeting with us so they could take him home.

The driver's window came down and Jules said hello.

As I got out, I recognized a scene from *The Transporter*. I nodded. 'Great movie.'

I got no reply. The window slid back up.

A sign by the main doors said cameras, mobile phones and recording equipment or similar electronic devices were forbidden in the main building.

Jules handed the woman at Reception some ID that looked like a credit card and she swiped it through a reader. 'Good evening, Mr Drogba.' She passed him a form to sign, checked it, and passed me a red badge. 'If you could hand that back in when you leave, Mr Lampard?' She didn't bat an eyelid.

We hadn't even got past the main reception area before we hit another layer of security. This time it included the electronic equivalent of a full body search. We carried on and followed a circular walkway that ran inside the building. Everyone called it the Street. It felt a bit like being in an airport terminal, with open-plan offices leading off both sides. Glass cases displayed exhibits from GCHQ's history, including the radio set used by the Portland spy ring to send messages back to Russia in the fifties and sixties.

'I don't know what the layout was before, Nick, but now the linguists and analysts work on the upper floor. They've had to squash up to accommodate CSOC.'

The cross-governmental Cyber Security Operations Centre was another new one on me. It had recently been set up to deal with any threat Britain might face from the Internet – and to carry out some cyber attacks of its own.

All the guys on the upper floor spent their time studying intelligence on everything from terrorism and nuclear proliferation to serious organized crime and counter-espionage. It was no place for the likes of me. Neither was the basement. I remembered the huge halls with endless rows of blinking computers. In all there were about ten thousand square metres of the things. They generated so much heat they needed a cooling system that used a lot of local water. During the floods in 2007, the mains were cut and special supplies had to be tankered in.

We passed something I didn't remember from past visits: a small memorial honouring the number of GCHQ staff who had died in service. More had been dropped in Afghanistan in the past few years than anywhere else.

6

I followed Jules from the bright, fluorescent corridor into a room where the only light seemed to come from the glow of plasma screens mounted on a walnut-veneered wall.

As I closed the door behind me, the hum and chill of air-conditioning took over. A dozen solid walnut chairs sat around a huge oval walnut table. The room was carpeted with Axminster's finest, and it smelt like it had only just been laid. I wondered if it was the fruit of some kind of government initiative to boost local industry or Tresillian cocking his leg and marking out his territory. If they'd given Anna the cheque-book and an hour in Ikea she could have saved the taxpayer thousands.

At the far end of the table, below a vibrant plasma screen, I saw the world's most pissed-off face. There were far too many wrinkles in it for a man in his early fifties. His hair was thinning on the top and swept back. Either it was wet with sweat or he'd stepped straight from his office shower.

Charles Tresillian looked like he'd sprung from a grainy black-and-white of Shackleton's final expedition and spent his Saturdays running from office to office, encouraging the troops. The set of his jaw certainly suggested he had a country to protect, and he expected to lead from the front.

A map of Moldova, wedged between Romania and Ukraine, north of the Black Sea, was spread across the screen behind him.

For fuck's sake – these guys must see me as a one-trick pony.

Tresillian kept his brooding gaze on me as I crossed the carpet. He slid two files across the table at no one in particular. I went to the right and Jules to the left.

'You're our man, are you? Are you as good as Julian says you are?' His voice was deep and clipped. His finger provided the punctuation. 'He tells me you're shit-fucking-hot.'

People expected the shits and fucks to tumble from mouths like mine because they assumed we wouldn't know the difference between a thesaurus and a brontosaurus. But from a posh well-educated lad like Tresillian they somehow carried the same gravitas as one of Churchill's soundbites.

I nodded. 'Yeah, I am.'

'Well, I'm the shit-fucking-hot man with the big picture. Sit.'

Jules and I took chairs facing each other. I leant forward and dragged one of the buff-coloured folders towards me.

'Gentlemen, shall we?'

Tresillian opened his folder and we followed suit.

'This is the situation, Mr Stone. It is one that you will endeavour to make good. Hector Tarasov is a friend of the UK in Moldova. Our sources in-country tell us that his daughter has gone missing. We want to find her for him, in as covert a way as possible.'

'What does he do?'

'He's an industrialist.' He tapped the printout of the map. 'Here, in Transnistria.' His finger stayed on the narrow sliver of land to the east of Moldova. 'When it was part of the Soviet Union, Moldova had its share of factories, many of them military. With independence, in 1991, the eastern strip of the country, known as Transnistria, east of the Dniester River, seceded.'

I tried a smile. I wasn't comfortable with the Mr Stone business, and even though my head was starting to pound again, I wanted to see if I could lighten the tone a bit. 'Sounds like one of those lunatic names the head sheds give a country during battle training.'

It wasn't going to happen.

'If only, Mr Stone. Transnistria was Moldova's most industrialized region, as well as its most Russified. Moscow intervened to stop a civil war over the secession, and since 1992 Russian troops have watched over what is being termed a "frozen conflict" that has left Transnistria isolated, unrecognized by any nation but Russia, and Moldova divided.'

He raised a finger at the plasma screen. 'The reason our friend is very important to us is because this strip of land is a major producer of Russian arms for worldwide export. It has the largest steel-production plant that the Russian Federation has access to.'

'What does Tarasov's factory make?'

'Tons of mind-your-own-fucking-business.' His lips pursed and his frown added another ten years to his age. 'This operation is about the daughter.'

I looked down at an eight-by-five colour picture of a young woman with dyed blonde hair that reached her shoulders. The roots showed through in the centre parting. She'd gone for the Goth look; her pale, almost translucent skin made her look like she belonged in a teenage vampire film. A bare male arm hung loosely round her neck. She was trying hard to smile into the camera, as you do at family events when you're having a shit time. The image almost filled the page. There was no information about where or when it might have been taken.

'Her name is Lilian Edinet. She's twenty years old. This picture was taken approximately seven months ago. We have, of course, checked on all social networking sites to see if we could get any information on her whereabouts or any more recent photos.'

Another image was pasted over the map on the screen – the wide shot her face picture had been lifted from. She stood in front of a T55 tank mounted on a stone ramp surrounded by plaques: a monument to the great wheat harvest or whatever. The arm belonged to an older man, who looked a lot happier than she did. He was in his mid-forties and had very dark, almost jet-black hair and a dental plan that only money, not God, could give you. Peas out of the same pod, they looked like a double act. Behind them was a massive chunk of boring grey factory. Red signage proudly covered the top third of the building.

Tresillian looked up. 'That is Hector Tarasov.'

He turned to Jules. 'I don't care too much for Facebook myself. I can't see why anyone would want to make so much information freely available. It's out there for ever. Good for us, though, eh?'

My head filled with questions. 'Can I make contact with Tarasov? Find out what he knows? What about her mother?'

'On no account must there be any contact with Tarasov.'

'He must be taking steps of his own to—'

Tresillian was dismissive. 'More from Julian later. As I said, it's the girl we're interested in. She is the sole reason you're here.' His eyes searched mine to make sure I was getting the message.

I nodded. 'Lilian – she doesn't look that happy, does she?'

'On the contrary. By all accounts this young woman is quite a feisty little piece. However, she is missing, and you will find her at all costs. UK plc does everything within its power to help its friends.' He paused. 'Do you understand?'

'Of course. You want leverage to score some big Brownie points off the Dadski.'

He didn't answer or smile. Nick Stone was too far down the food chain to make funnies. He reminded me of some really good officers I'd come across in the army. They weren't your best mates, but you knew where you stood with them, and exactly what was required. If you didn't fuck them over, they might not fuck you over. But it still all depended on what side of the bed they got out of that morning.

48

'Exactly, Mr Stone. We're not a fucking charity, are we?' He turned his head. 'Isn't that right?'

'Exactly, Mr Tresillian.' Julian's teeth gleamed in the subdued lighting. 'We have a job to do.'

He turned back to me. 'I cannot impress on you enough, Mr Stone, that this matter is of national and international importance. It is critical that this young woman be found and delivered to us. When you find her, a contact and safe-house will be available until arrangements are made to bring her back to the UK. She will never leave your sight, and only when she is physically under the contact's control will the task be complete.

'If you find her and she's dead, I still want the body. However, you will not kill her to make your job easier. Nothing and no one must be allowed to stop you achieving your aim. Nothing. No one. Is that understood?'

I nodded. Hector Tarasov must be one powerful player. Tresillian even wanted bragging rights delivering the body.

He nodded back. 'That's very good. One last thing. This situation is very fucking delicate. Only the three of us in this room and eventually the contact will ever know that it's happened.'

I nodded again.

'Good. Has Julian completed your financial requests?'

'We haven't discussed that yet, but finance—'

'Good.' He slammed the palms of his hands on the table as he stood up. 'Very good.'

Julian and I pushed our chairs back and stood up. Tresillian advanced on me with the relentlessness of a large armoured vehicle. 'Julian will brief you now. The next time we meet will be to congratulate you on a job fucking well done.'

As he gripped my hand I smelt tobacco. A splash of Old Spice and an anchor tattoo on his forearm and he could have been a ringer for my granddad.

He went out, leaving his folder on the table.

7

We sat back down. The gentle hum of the air-conditioning replaced Tresillian's growl.

I pointed at the now vacant chair below the screen. 'He seems a lad. I bet he's changed more than just the carpet.'

Julian carried on extracting sheets of paper from his folder and lining them up on the table. All I got from him was a wry smile.

'She attends Moldova State University in Chisinau, the capital. Do you know Moldova?'

Not much. Particularly with a splitting headache. I'd never operated there. 'Only bits and pieces. It's best known for arms smuggling and people trafficking. What about the police – is anybody liaising? Is there someone in the British embassy I can rely on?'

'Out of the question, on both fronts. The local police are either useless or corrupt. If it turns out she's been kidnapped they might even be part of the problem.'

'When did she go missing?'

'Ten days ago.'

'Who's been looking for her?'

'Only the father. He's frantic, according to our sources. He's hoping he either gets a ransom demand or she'll be back in touch. Kids that age drop off the radar all the time without thinking of the implications.'

I pointed up at the screen and the green-glossed T55, its barrel facing forward, ready to attack. 'He's an "industrialist", right? The tank outside the factory provides a bit of a clue. Any known enemies in the arms world?'

'None. He manufactures for the Federation so he's one of the bad guys but, as I understand it, he's our friend and we want to keep it that way.'

I focused on the picture of the girl. 'She speak English?'

'Probably of the cable-TV variety, same as any other kid anywhere.'

'And you have nothing at all from the networking sites?'

'She closed her Facebook page two weeks ago. She's not on any other site.'

'You've checked flight manifests out of Moldova?'

Julian nodded. 'And visa applications that come into the Hungarian embassy in Chisinau – they deal with all applications for Schengen countries.'

'Tell me about the name.'

'Edinet was her mother's maiden name. She died when Lilian was little. It helps her keep a low profile. We don't think anyone at the university knows who she is – it reduces the kidnap risk.'

'Can you give me addresses?'

'We don't have her latest details. Like a lot of students, she's floated from flat-share to flat-share. The last sighting was at the university a couple of weeks ago.'

'What about Tarasov himself?'

'He can't go to the police, of course, because they're too corrupt. Alert the Mafia and all of a sudden he's facing a massive ransom demand if they find her. He's bound to be looking. But stay away from Tarasov, Nick. He's strictly off limits – Tresillian wasn't joking.'

Fair one. 'What's she studying?'

'Sociology.'

'Does she have any medical conditions?' If she needed insulin injections or whatever, I had to know. And if she'd been kidnapped, she might be dead already.

Julian shrugged.

Something else really puzzled me. 'Why is this an MI5 job and not the Firm's?'

'With Tresillian at the helm of both, the demarcation lines are blurring.'

I swallowed another couple of Smarties as he glanced back down at Lilian's picture.

'As Tresillian said, nothing must stop you finding her. Of course we're going to deny anything to do with the operation, but you will have secure comms with me at all times. I'll help you as far as I can, but we cannot be seen poking around in-country. It wouldn't help our relationship with Lilian's father, and certainly not with the powers that be.' He gathered up the paperwork. 'Why don't we get some coffee while I give you the lowdown?'

I followed him to the door. Bright light flooded into the room.

I couldn't help smiling to myself. I was back at work. One last kick at life.

And I now had a really good reason to phone Anna.

PART THREE

1

Monday, 15 March
10.47 hrs

The International Airport Chisinau is the biggest in the
Republic of Moldova. It's a member of Airports Council
International (European region), the massive posters in the
revamped terminal proudly proclaimed, as well as the Airport
Association of CIS Civil Aviation and the ALFA-ACI
(L'Association des Aéroports de Langue Française Associés à
l'Airports Council International). What was more: *The main
priorities of the personnel's activity consist in providing a high-level
of flight safety and qualitative services.*

But for all its fancy new associations with the West, old
habits died hard. I was held by three Customs guys in a side
office ten seconds after they saw a European passport and no
mates tagging along. There was a special tax I needed to pay.
Since I was only carrying a day sack, they pegged it at thirty
dollars.

I'd now been waiting for Anna's flight from Moscow
Domodedovo for close to five hours – the last two because her
Air Moldova flight was delayed. This was probably the eighth
time I'd gone back to the coffee shop in Arrivals, treated myself

to a milky Nescafé instant, and soaked up the propaganda as I sat and sipped it.

I'd even resorted to reading the warnings on the packet of Nurofen I dug into occasionally. Long-term kidney damage wasn't high on my list of concerns, so I popped another couple out of the blister pack, grabbed some more Smarties and washed them all down with a swig of coffee.

I'd transferred my two-week supply of shiny red pills into a plastic Superdrug case. It was easier to shove into my pocket than a big fuck-off bottle. Also, the label had my name on it and I couldn't be arsed to scratch it off.

It had taken me seven hours from Heathrow with a Munich connection. Normally that wouldn't have been much of a problem; I was used to living in airports. You just find some seats, lie down, read posters, drink brews. If you're lucky, you go to sleep. But that wasn't going to happen. My head was pounding – but I think it was mostly about seeing Anna again.

Fetch up in Moscow, with the biggest collection of billion-aires on the planet, and you can't move for fancy foreign labels. Moldova's old split-level Soviet-era airport had had a major refurb, but Starbucks and all the high-end brands had still given it a miss. Jules had told me that its earning potential outside the small capital was the same as Sudan's, so I guess it was no surprise.

Despite Julian's briefing, I wasn't exactly sure where Moldova stood in relation to the rest of the planet. Some guys immersed themselves in demographics and GDPs and could tell you the ten most popular names for girls and boys wher-ever they fetched up, but I never saw the point. This place was land-locked, and had a population of five million. The indus-trial strip, whose name I kept forgetting, ran along its eastern border. That was all I knew, and all I needed to know. All I had to do was find the girl, grip her, and hand her over.

I took out my new BlackBerry and checked for messages. The Tefalhead at GCHQ who'd briefed me on the encryption system and then got Mr Lampard to sign for it had been very pleased with his toy. Apparently it contained both a hardware *and* software-based secure communications solution that protected GSM cellular communications with a unique authentication service and advanced end-to-end encryption software. I hoped it worked better than the one I'd been issued with three years ago.

'Combined with a secure mobile authentication solution it is capable of ensuring that all mobile voice and SMS communications, as well as data-at-rest within the device, are fully protected. It offers security against any attempt to intercept active communications both from inside a telephone network as well as over-the-air.'

That was all well and good. I just needed to know that, when I switched it on and pressed the security app icon, Jules and I could talk without anyone else listening in.

The security technology was based on encryption algorithms as well as a user/device authentication process, the Tefalhead explained. I could pretty much grasp that. But I got lost when he started talking ciphers and 128-bit block sizes.

'Your BlackBerry uses these algorithms simultaneously as well as a 4096-bit Diffie-Hellman shared secret exchange to authenticate each call/device/user, in order to provide multiple layers of security and an effective fall-back inside the crypto-system design.'

I'd nodded enthusiastically and his face lit up. 'So, to recap . . . I press the app icon if I want secure speech. When a call comes in I wait for the app to give me the go-ahead, and both sides can talk in real time?' I can't have been the brightest pupil he'd ever had.

I took another sip and looked around. Moldova might be in shit state but at least they were trying to get out of their hole. Most of the arrivals coming in from other flights were suited. Most of the guys with wheelies and mobiles stuck to their faces gobbed off in Russian, but I picked out a few European and

American voices. A couple of the local papers sitting in the newsstands were English editions. They'd binned visas for people like me and I didn't even have to show a return ticket. Anything to get new money into the country. But for all that, the staff still mooched about like throwbacks to the old order. They'd brightened up the buildings and forgotten to refurbish the employees.

At long last the Moscow flight flagged up as landed. It was show time. I suddenly worried that I should have cleaned myself up a bit in the last five and a half hours.

I got up and walked over to the sliding doors that stood between Customs and the arrivals hall. I knew she'd be one of the first out. Like me, she travelled light. The rest she'd buy when she needed it.

I felt my stomach flutter. At first I tried to blame it on the drugs. But I couldn't escape the fact that I was excited – for the first time in as long as I could remember.

Then the real world kicked in. She'd agreed to come when I'd finally got round to phoning her, but only after I'd waffled and begged and lied about needing her help with a K and R. Perhaps she was only here to find yet another poor girl ripped out of her world, drugged up, beaten and fucked on the other side of the planet. That was the sort of thing that made Anna get up in the morning. I just happened to be along for the ride.

As the first wave of wheelie bags swept past, I almost had to stand on tiptoe to look beyond them. The doors half closed, then pulled back again to reveal a blonde in a black woollen coat, with a haircut that looked like a German helmet.

I locked on to her eyes but she seemed to look right through me.

2

I tried to read her expression as she came through into the hall. She scanned the faces beyond the barrier, trailing a wheelie behind her. When she finally spotted me, there was no instant smile or greeting.

I blurted out the first thing that came into what was left of my head. 'You've had your hair cut.'

'I thought I'd ring the changes. More practical for my next job. Well, the one I *was* going to take.'

She'd been approached by CNN to cover women's issues following the rise of Islamic fundamentalism in some of the former Soviet republics. She knew the subject matter and this part of the world like the back of her hand. CNN must have liked the hairdo: they'd granted her a two-month deferment.

She let go of her wheelie and it toppled over. She left it where it was, finally treated me to the smile I was hoping for, and ran the last four or five paces towards me. She threw out her arms, wrapped them around me and held me tight. I did the same. I really couldn't get enough of this girl.

Her hair brushed the side of my face. 'Mmm . . . Nice smell.' I took in another lungful of Bulgari. I'd bought her some in London during her last visit.

She moved her head a little so she could get her mouth closer to my ear. 'I love it.' She kissed me on the cheek. 'You know what, you idiot? I missed you . . .'

The pain in my head leaked away, along with the tension in my shoulder muscles. Anna's perfume was more effective than any number of Kleinmann's Smarties. I hadn't been able to gauge her mood on the phone. She'd immediately offered to help, but didn't overcook things on the emotional front. I understood that. I was the same. Unlike me, she wanted to save the world. Maybe you could only do that if you kept yourself just detached enough from it to stop all the shit stuff swallowing you up.

On past performance, I knew that anyone I got involved with wouldn't stick around too long. Now I also realized that a tiny part of me hoped she might be able to save me too – or at least give me the chance to avoid flushing the last couple of months of my life down the toilet as well as the rest.

She took half a step back and gave me a long, hard look. 'You have the picture for me?'

I righted her wheelie and she took my arm as we walked towards the coffee shop. I opened up my secure BlackBerry and clicked on the blow-up of Lilian. I left her studying the image at the square plastic table as I went and bought more Nescafé instants with hot, sweet milk. They cost twenty lei each, but the woman was more than happy with a couple of dollar bills. Hard currency still said more about you than the local stuff ever could.

Anna's eyes were still fixed on the screen when I came back to the table. 'Does Julian know I'm here?'

'What he doesn't know won't hurt him. And it won't hurt us.'

She turned the BlackBerry screen towards me. 'She's very pretty, beneath all that anger. Trafficking has to be the strongest possibility.'

'But she binned her Facebook account before she went AWOL. And she's a uni girl, switched on, not some pointy-head from the sticks who'll fall for the nearest scam.'

Anna smiled like a mother whose kid has just said something naïve. 'You know nothing about this country and its people until you understand about trafficking. I'll take you to see someone who will help you understand.'

'Have you ever come across the name Hector Tarasov? He's her father. He has a factory in Transnistria. A factory with a tank outside.'

She shook her head and reached into her coat pocket for her iPhone. 'I can Google—'

'No need, mate. I've already had a look. Nothing. It doesn't matter, just background.'

She sat back, not touching her brew, and tilted her head to one side, studying me.

'What?'

'I'm still trying to work out why you're here, Nicholas.' She'd started calling me that recently – told me I deserved all three syllables, especially now I'd got a penthouse and a Porsche. I knew she was taking the piss, but I rather liked it. 'You should be enjoying your life. You have no more reason to do this sort of work.'

I thought we were made of the same stuff: she wasn't going to hang up her Crusader's shield any time soon. I was surprised she felt the money might have changed things for me. 'I *am* enjoying my life. But I don't want to just fade away.' I laughed slightly uneasily. 'I want to die with my boots on.'

She gave me a puzzled look. 'I know you've taken some punishment over the years, but you should be able to survive a straightforward K and R job . . .'

I took another sip of coffee and decided that eight cups was already more than enough. I couldn't quite bring myself to look her in the eye.

'Except that this isn't a K and R job, is it, Nicholas? When have you ever been involved in the commercial world?'

I'd known it wouldn't be long before she rumbled that one. Recovering kidnap victims is quite a business. If the victim is recovered alive, you can cop a percentage of the premium that would have been paid out by the underwriters in the event of a death, or on any ransom demand. It wasn't entirely risk free, but Anna was right – it was a long way from being on the receiving end of an RPG.

'I'm doing it for Jules.' I shifted my chair closer to hers. 'I couldn't tell you over the phone.'

She lifted a hand and stroked my face. 'You look really pale, Nicholas. You sure you're feeling OK?'

'Sure. Too many planes, that's all.'

She got to her feet. 'Why don't you fix the car? I'll phone and check the hotel reservation, then call Lena. I'll wait for you outside.'

'Lena?'

'There's nothing Lena doesn't know about trafficking.'

I walked away with a bit of a spring in my step. The only negative so far was that there weren't any hotels at the airport. If we did find Lilian, we might have to hole up somewhere with her until Tresillian sorted out the safe-house. The beauty of an airport hotel is that all you have to do is scan the departures board, see which plane's leaving next, and leg it to the sales desk.

3

It was only fifteen Ks into Chisinau. There were a surprising number of shiny new BMWs and Mercedes weaving their way between the clapped-out trucks and tractors, but the road still wasn't exactly choked with traffic.

The fields on each side of us looked absolutely knackered. As with most of the old Eastern bloc the heavy use of agricultural chemicals, including banned pesticides like DDT, had ripped the heart out of the land. And severe soil erosion from diabolical farming methods had fucked whatever chance these places had of being self-sufficient.

Anna grimaced as we passed a police car. 'I've been to more than fifty different countries and I've never seen cops as corrupt as the ones here.'

'They certainly don't hang around. I had to cough up a fistful of dollars to get through Customs.'

'I was stopped here twice in two hours once, both for completely invented offences. They target locals the same. They don't even wait for people to do something wrong. The moment they've finished fleecing one victim, they flag down the next.'

Anna was on a roll.

'And it's not just about driving. Their favourite trick on a slow night is to stop foreigners at random for "looking suspicious". Two hundred lei is the standard fine. If we get stopped on the street you'll be asked for your passport. The law says that foreigners have to carry them at all times. Photocopies aren't good enough. If you're alone, keep saying you don't speak Romanian or Russian. There are no guarantees, but if you're lucky they'll be too lazy to pursue it.'

We hit the city proper. Many of the people on the streets looked pretty well turned-out, particularly the young guys.

I nodded at a fancy-looking restaurant. 'I thought we were supposed to be in Europe's poorest country. Who can afford to eat in a place like that?'

'You don't want to know. Moldova's the same as everywhere in the old Soviet Union. There's a handful of haves and a whole nation of have-nots.' She stared out of the window at the wide concrete esplanades. 'Most people in Moldova don't live like this. They scrape by on less than three dollars a day. Away from the towns, work is scarce. I wrote a piece about a small village a few kilometres from Chisinau where every male had sold a kidney to the West. In lots of villages, only children and grandparents remain. Over a million have left the country to find work. That doesn't include the numbers who've been trafficked.'

'I take it Tarasov is one of the haves?'

'For sure.'

'And how do we explain all the Mercs and Hummers?'

'The Moldovans like to claim Transnistria can't function independently. They say it doesn't have the industry or infrastructure – but they do, and not just through weapons manufacture. There's a 480-kilometre border with Ukraine and it's not controlled. As well as the sale of old Soviet military machinery, extortion of businessmen and money laundering, there is huge trafficking in arms, drugs and, of course, human beings. About two billion dollars are being laundered every year in Transnistria and no one wants to give that up without a fight.

'But what should really have the rest of the world sitting up and paying attention are the dozen or so companies that produce arms around the clock. They've turned up in Chechnya, Africa, all over – even in Iraq in Saddam's day and now Afghanistan. International organizations don't accept that Transnistria even exists, so they can't visit and investigate. There, Nicholas – next right.'

Anna directed me off the main. A couple of turns later, we pulled up outside another drab Soviet-era monolith a dozen storeys high. 'Forget the arms business. Everyone should just have shares in ready-mixed concrete.'

The Cosmos was pretty much in the centre of town. I could see a bank with an ATM, a shopping centre, restaurants, and a Western-style supermarket with a multi-storey attached.

I parked in a guest space and walked towards the entrance, my day sack over my shoulder. She trundled her wheelie a step or two ahead of me.

'To be fair to Stalin, the city had to be totally rebuilt after the Second World War. The little the Germans left standing was flattened by an earthquake.'

As we approached the reception desk she stopped for a moment. 'I stay here a lot. They know me. That's why we're in separate rooms.' Her eyes suddenly sparkled. 'Besides, we're working. See you back in the lobby in fifteen minutes. Lena isn't that far away.'

4

Lena Kamenka's office was in the basement of a run-down apartment building south-east of the city centre. An old woman scrubbing her doorstep with a brush and bucket pointed us to a staircase. There was a look of disapproval on her wizened face. Some things, it said, are best swept under the carpet and left there.

I followed Anna down the metal steps and stood behind her as she pressed the buzzer.

The girl who answered the door was in her early twenties. She had the kind of jet-black hair you can only get from a bottle.

'Welcome. Please come in.'

She led us along a corridor, past a battered sofa and coffee-table. The walls of Lena's office were lined with archive boxes. She sat behind a small desk strewn with files, waffling away at warp speed on the phone. She greeted Anna with a smile and a nod.

'You would like coffee?' The girl smiled shyly.

'Thank you.'

She left the room and Lena gestured to us to sit down. She carried on her conversation for another ten minutes in about three different languages. When she finally hung up, she threw her arms round Anna and greeted her like a long-lost sister.

I guessed Lena was about thirty. In a stylish blouse, grey cardigan and sharply tailored trousers, she looked more like a lawyer or businesswoman than a social worker – or she would have done if it hadn't been for her short, spiky blue hair and long, silver-painted fingernails.

She joined us at a small table covered with yet more files and loose-leaf binders. Photocopied head shots of young women stared up at us from their covers. Most were teenagers. One looked no older than twelve. None of them looked like Lilian.

Lena was a repatriation specialist. Her main task was bringing trafficked Moldovan girls home. Nearly all of them had been sold into prostitution abroad.

'You are lucky to catch me in.' Lena sighed. She spoke English like it was her first language. 'I have to go to Odessa today to collect a girl off the ferry from Istanbul. There's usually somebody on it for us. As for the airport, sometimes I think I should just take my bed up there and move in.'

Brothel raids in countries like the UK, Germany and Holland produced many of her clients. Her number was on the walls of police stations all over the world.

Lena tapped her cell phone. She'd positioned it carefully in front of her and kept checking the signal every minute or so. 'I never switch it off. Sometimes they're just metres from the pimps. I might have only seconds to get their details. Often they don't even know what country they're in.'

'What do you do then?'

'I tell them to look out of the window. A road name, a bus number. Sometimes I'll get caller ID, but I can't call back unless they tell me to. It's too dangerous.'

We needed to cut to the chase here. 'Anna told you my paper is interested in trafficking into London, yeah?' I leaned in. 'What's the chain, Lena? Does it start with a kidnapping?'

'Sometimes, yes. They drug girls, take them from the fields. Sometimes they drag a drunken city girl off the street and bundle her into the boot of a car. But they don't need to go to all the trouble of beating them up and smuggling them out of the country if the girls are happy to travel of their own free will. Sometimes they even pay their own fares. The gangs call it "happy trafficking". These ones are even given fake passports if they want to get away to start a completely new life, away from the poverty – or whatever else it is they're trying to escape from. The gangs prefer these girls. If they're not bruised and battered they'll earn more as prostitutes.' She sighed. 'It's only when the person who meets them has taken away their passport that they discover the broken promises, and by then it's too late. The ones with fake ID are lost for ever.'

She looked up as the black-haired girl came back in with a tray carrying three steaming cups. She put the tray down on Lena's desk and busied herself with an ancient fax machine. Then she lit herself a cigarette and joined us.

'There isn't anything happy about happy trafficking, is there, Irina?'

The girl stared at me for so long I thought she was never going to speak. Then I realized she didn't quite know where to begin.

'I was seventeen. I was at college. I was training to be a teacher. English teacher. One day a girl I went to school with came to see me. She was working at an expensive restaurant in Greece, she said. She was making a good salary. She could get me such a job if I wanted. I needed more exams to graduate, but also I needed money. My mother was ill.' Irina took a drag and blew a stream of smoke at the ceiling. 'I agreed to go with my friend. She organized everything. She drove us to Odessa, and came with me on the ferry to Istanbul. Then she put me on a plane to Athens. She said she would join me later.

'Another "friend" met the flight. He told me the waitress job was finished. He said he could take me to Italy. There was work in Italy, he said. On the journey, he asked me strange questions. "Do you have any scars? Will your parents come looking for you?" We arrived in Milan and there was no restaurant. That was when I found out what my school friend had been working as. And to buy her freedom and get back to Moldova, she had promised to recruit a new girl.'

She inhaled again, more deeply this time. She was bracing herself. 'In Italy, the "friend" took me to meet some men in an apartment. Russian men. They said I had to help them repay their investment. I said no, so they beat me. They said they would kill me if I didn't do what they said, and give them what I earned each day.

'I kept saying to them I must go back to Mother. My mother was sick. She needed medicine. They didn't listen. I had to work seven days a week, from the afternoon to early morning the next day. Twelve hours every day, except when I had my period. The Russians took everything. They said if I tried to escape, the police would bring me back to them. The police were their friends.

'There were three other girls. We were all locked in the same room until a customer came. We had to wear big T-shirts. For six months, I did this work. The customers paid fifty euros for half an hour. Sometimes I made a thousand euros a night. I got nothing.

'And then, at the end of each night, the Russians had a game. They would come into our room and they would rape us all one by one. One of the girls cried so much they said the neighbours would hear. They crushed her toes under a door as punishment.

'Escaping was not easy. You cannot just jump out of a window and be free. And we had no money. Some of the regular customers were policemen. Our visas were renewed even though we were prisoners. But we talked about it a lot.

'The apartment was in a big old building. In the winter it was cold. We used to put a blanket in the big gap under the door to stop the draught. I was doing that when I suddenly had an idea. The door was locked from the other side, but they always left the key in. It was a big old-fashioned key. I pushed about a metre of the blanket underneath, and I used an eyebrow pencil to push the key out of the lock. It fell onto the blanket and I pulled it to our side. The others were too scared to come with me, but I ran.

'I ran and ran. A lady waiting for a bus gave me some money. I took a bus to another city.

'I went to a church and the priest telephoned Lena. She made all the arrangements and she was at the airport for me. Not my family. They were too ashamed. When I went home, the police came to my house two days later. They didn't want information about the Russians. They didn't want to know anything about my friend or her friend in Athens. All they wanted was sex. I said no. They said they would tell the Russians where to find me. They knew who they were. I called Lena and she rescued me – again. Now I help her with her work.'

Irina looked exhausted from retelling her story, but also defiant. 'I still work twelve hours a day, seven days a week. But now it is with Lena, helping others like me. We will stop the trafficking one day.'

The way she said it convinced me she'd succeed – or die trying.

5

Irina went to make more coffee. Lena offered me a cigarette. I shook my head but Anna was straight in there. They both lit up.

'Who are these guys? Old-fashioned Mafia?'

Anna waved a hand at the case files that surrounded us. 'Or the Russian, Albanian and Ukrainian gangsters who run mixed cargoes of women, drugs and arms? Take your pick. But one thing is certain: they'll do anything to turn a profit. Lena told me about those speedboats being intercepted in the Adriatic. The traffickers threw the women overboard to distract the police and protect the heroin and the hardware.'

Lena nodded. 'But it must have hurt them. I'll tell you a sad statistic. After weapons and drugs, human trafficking is now the third most profitable criminal enterprise in the world. Tens of billions of dollars a year. Obviously, trafficking on this level requires organization and cross-border networks. But at the Moldova end, things aren't so structured. Many of the recruiters are amateurs who see an opportunity and grab it. Friends betray friends. Even a family member sometimes, in exchange for a couple of hundred dollars. Maybe worst of all, it can be the person the girl shares her bed with.'

Anna and I exchanged a glance.

'Anna told me when she called that she's helping you research a piece on girls who end up in the UK – is that right? In which case, there's something you have to understand about Moldova. More than a quarter of the economically active population have migrated in search of work. A third of our GNP – a billion dollars – is money sent home from abroad.

'Irina and I go around the country, giving out our numbers and showing films. But it's an uphill struggle. Nobody wants to believe us. On TV, they have their noses rubbed in glossy images of life abroad. Maybe they only have to look next door to see a neighbour's new clothes or mobile phone. An unemployed girl who's starving isn't going to be put off by our warnings.'

That made a lot of sense, but our girl was bright and from a rich family. I was about to ask about university kids, but Lena hadn't finished.

'Moldova is important to the traffickers as a source, but the trade isn't centralized. There are local recruiters, but nearly all Moldovan girls are sold to non-Moldovan gangs. It isn't a vertical business model. Once they're out of the country, it's almost impossible to pick up the trail. We have to wait until the victims contact us.'

'Where do they end up?'

She shrugged. 'All over. The Balkans were the big destination until about ten years ago. Now it's Russia, Turkey, Israel, Dubai, any European city . . . The methods have changed, too. Traffickers have become smarter. Like I said, nowadays it's mostly happy trafficking. Victims are only allowed to go home when they've worked off "debts" and "fines" invented by their pimps or, like Irina's friend, if they undertake to send back one or two replacements.'

'What about the authorities? Supposing a girl is reported missing, what happens? Do the parents go to the police?'

She shook her head, and for a moment I thought she was going to burst out laughing. 'No. Nobody goes to the police.

We never share information with them. The most powerful gangsters are nearly always former cops – and so are their *kryshy* . . .' She looked at Anna, lost for the right word – the first time in an hour.

'Roofs.'

'Yes, their roofs – their protectors. These men are at the highest level of the police and the Ministry of the Interior. Before they'll even open a case they demand sex or money.'

A phone rang, and stopped. Irina went over to the fax machine. She had to bend down to read the first few lines as the paper curled back on itself. 'From Spain . . .'

Lena's mobile rang. She picked it up and signalled for quiet. She listened, then spoke quickly and urgently into the mouthpiece.

She looked at me. 'I'm sorry. I have to go.'

Irina handed her the sheet.

'A girl has just been found during a raid in Barcelona. I have to speak to her mother.'

I snatched a glimpse of the picture. The face was bruised, but the girl it belonged to wasn't Lilian.

6

Str A Mateevici
15.15 hrs

We were parked on the wide avenue that divided the university from the park in the north-west of the city. The university was Lilian's last known location, which made it a good place to start.

The trams had looked tired and their wires had sagged across the cobblestoned streets as we drove out of the centre, but my first impressions of the city had been wide of the mark. It might have been in shit state, and there was quite a bit of rust about, but there was also a lot of civic pride. Mateevici was clean. The trees both sides were well tended. At first glance we could have been in any town in Connecticut, had it not been for the US embassy building about six hundred metres down the road.

The State University campus was a sprawl of trees, grass and concrete paths. Most of the buildings were ugly lumps of post-war concrete, part of Stalin's rebuild after the annihilation. A couple of grand Hapsburg Empire-type buildings had survived. They looked like giant Battenberg cakes.

The students walking past the car had come straight from

Central Casting. Some were lanky; some were overweight. Most were scruffily dressed. Their day sacks were stuffed with books. Some shared jokes; some walked on their own with headphones or mobiles stuck to their ears.

'Hard to think that only in April last year these kids were rioting on the streets.'

I'd been away on a job at the time and must have missed the coverage. 'What about?'

'Moscow. Young Moldovans didn't like their leaders embracing the Kremlin. The president, Vladimir Voronin, was a Communist, very pro-Russia. For the past four years the Kremlin had mounted a charm offensive to woo him away from the EU and NATO with offers of subsidized gas and closer economic ties. It paid off. Voronin refused to join Brussels's Eastern Partnership programme. He called it "a plot to surround Russia".

'Then came the elections. The trouble started as soon as the result was announced. The Communist Party had won a suspiciously large proportion of the vote.

'Ten thousand demonstrators massed in the city centre, most of them students. They carried Moldovan and European flags and shouted anti-Communist slogans. They gathered outside the government building and made their way down the main boulevard to the president's office. The police used tear gas and water cannon but they couldn't stop the crowd breaking in. Windows were smashed on two floors and fires started.

'Voronin called it an attempted coup d'état and pointed the finger at Romania, a NATO and EU member. Moscow backed him up. The Kremlin were shitting themselves. Imagine – protesters overrunning Moldova's parliament and ransacking its president's office. The scenes must have been horribly familiar to them. It's only five years since young pro-Western protesters toppled Moscow-friendly regimes in Georgia and Ukraine.'

I nodded. I'd been to both after their 'colour' revolutions.

Russia's power in the region was at an all-time low. At home, the Kremlin kicked back by stamping out foreign-funded NGOs, abolishing local elections and setting up special 'youth groups' so they could keep an eye out for anything similar happening inside Russia. Abroad, the Kremlin's new priority was to assert its influence and fight against increasing Westernization. Moldova's unrest would have been a test of Russia's ability to project power and protect friends.

'What happened?'

'What always happens when the people take on the state. The police came in mob-handed and arrested more than two hundred.'

'Could Lilian have been involved?'

'A sociology student? Does a bear shit in the woods?'

'Russian bears shit wherever they want to.'

She grinned. I liked it when she did that. 'Ready?'

I nodded. I was in her hands. I didn't speak the language, and I wasn't the world's leading expert on universities.

'They'll think we're parents visiting, or here to find out about evening classes or something. We'll just wander round a bit, try to find out what bars she went to or groups she hung out with. Then we'll take it from there.'

We left Mateevici and followed one of the concrete paths that snaked through the grass. Anna had been on Google in the car. There were twenty thousand students, spread across twelve faculties.

We stopped at a blue and white signpost that must have been really useful if you could read Cyrillic.

'OK. Philosophy's in that direction. Sociology must be close by.'

She put her arm through mine as we followed her hunch. 'These kids are hungry for knowledge, Nicholas. They know it's the way out of poverty. You people in the West, you have it so easy. You think education is a right, not a privilege that must be earned. You have a welfare system to catch you if you fall, or if you just don't give a shit. These people have no safety net. They have nothing without an education.'

I could see through the windows that every lecture room was packed. We came to a newer building, lots of brick and glass. I held the door for her. Wherever you are in the world, an institution smells like an institution: a blend of body odour, wood polish, boiled cabbage and bleach.

She led me down a wide corridor lined with posters, wall charts and notice boards. My boots squeaked on the tiles. Students young and old leant against walls and talked sociology shit, or maybe just shit.

Anna stopped an older guy in a brown and grey patterned sweater. He looked Scandinavian rather than Russian. He pointed in the direction we were already heading. I smiled my thanks and got a very dark look in return. Maybe my jacket didn't have enough herring-bones and snowflakes.

'Where are we going?'

'I thought we'd start at the administration offices. Maybe I'll say I'm an aunt on a surprise visit from Moscow, hoping to pick up her phone number or address.'

We came to a line of benches that would have been more at home in a park.

'Wait here, Nicholas. It might be better, just a woman on her own. And we'll have a problem explaining the fact you don't speak your niece's language.'

It sounded fine to me. I took a seat as she disappeared into the office.

7

I was surrounded by display cabinets bursting with trophies, framed certificates and photographs of bigwigs handing them over, shots of social and sports events, class and year portraits. It got me thinking. I decided to have a closer look.

It took a few minutes, but it was worth it.

A group of students dressed like Victorians stood, bathed in sunshine, outside the building; a party maybe, or some kind of commemoration. Lilian was in three of the pictures. She was alone in one, poking her tongue out at the camera. In another she looked almost shy, alongside three or four other girls. It was the third that interested me. The lad she was with had eaten a few too many pies. He had a mop of fuzzy brown hair and bum-fluff on his chin. He and Lilian had their arms around each other. Their eyes were swivelled towards the camera and they seemed to be enjoying a very un-Victorian kiss.

I was about to move on to the next display when Anna rushed out of the office. 'We need to go.'

I kept scanning the photos. 'Hang on, look at—'

She grabbed me. 'Now, Nick. *Now.*'

Sweaterman was piling down the corridor towards us with a posse of six or seven very pissed-off mates.

'What the fuck's happening?'

The office clerk came to her door. She shouted and waved her arm to move us on.

'No questions.'

I started walking fast beside her. We went back the same way we'd come in, with Sweaterman's posse in hot pursuit.

8

Anna didn't turn a hair as we drove away. There was no need to flap. They hadn't jumped into vehicles and followed us. All we had to do was make some distance.

I watched in the wing mirror my side as we rumbled across a cobbled junction. Trams, buses, cars, carts – all tried to head in a dozen different directions at the same time. Once we were clear I glanced behind us.

'What the fuck was all that about?'

'They thought we were secret police.'

I turned back but kept an eye on the wing mirror. A dark blue Beamer with the new shark-eye headlights and low-rider sills was shadowing us, but keeping its distance. The front fairing made it look like a hovercraft. It was having a hard time with the cobbles and potholes.

'So teachers now stand up to the police round here, do they?'

'The people united will never be defeated. Haven't you heard?' She allowed herself a smile. 'Or, as they've been saying more recently, the people with Twitter will never be defeated.'

'Like the green revolution in Iran?'

'They had it here first. As soon as they heard the result, the students started tweeting, trying to mobilize opposition. There was also a rush on Facebook and videos on YouTube. Suddenly everybody knew what was going on. It gave them a sense of power. Something they'd never experienced before.

'The police wanted to get in there and grip everybody, of course. The first people to arrive for a rally outside the government buildings found their cell phones were dead. The network had been switched off. But somebody had Twitter, and they used it to give live updates over the GPRS networks. The authorities won that round, but it could be the beginning of the end of totalitarianism. It's fascinating, don't you think – what started as social networks becoming the tools of political change? I might do a piece on it—'

I cut in. 'Chuck a right.'

She didn't ask. She just did.

We turned onto a single-carriageway street lined with shops and apartment blocks. A group of cyclists, all women in black, wobbled over the cobbles in front of us. Anna had to slow down. She glanced in the rear-view. 'The BMW?'

I didn't turn round. I smiled and moved my hands as if telling her a funny story. 'He still with us? He's been back there a bit too long.'

She turned her head and smiled back. 'The registration is C VS 911. That's a Chisinau plate. Four men. Very short hair. Not smiling, not talking.'

I nodded as we eased past the women, still jabbering away with no awareness of the vehicles trying to get past in both directions. Anna changed up and we accelerated.

'Take the next right.'

The indicator clicked away. The Polo lurched across a pothole as we hit a small side road. I sat back and waited for Anna.

'They've come with us.'

'Any of them talking on a phone or radio?'

'No.'

'Good. They're not setting an ambush. As long as we keep moving we're OK for now. Every time we turn, see if they communicate.'

'Who do you think they are? Secret police? Uni security?'

'Did you get as far as mentioning Lilian's name in the office?'

'No. The woman was on the phone, face like thunder. She was probably getting the good news from the guy in the sweater.'

'Could it be the university warning us off, or trying to find out who we are? Might be police, I guess – maybe somebody saw me checking out Lilian's picture. They may be doing the same. Whatever, we need to bin them as fast as we can.'

'How am I going to do that? Are we going to drive around in circles until we run out of fuel?'

'Head back towards the hotel. Remember the supermarket across the road? Drive into the car park.'

We overtook an old guy with ladders roped to his bike as she worked her way back onto the main.

'They're with us.'

'Normal speed. Nothing we can do about them. We've got to concentrate on that lard-arse in the photo. We need to find out who he is. Maybe she's done a runner with him. It could be something as simple as that. Falling in love and all that sort of shit.'

'How are you going to go back and check that out, Nicholas?' She sounded annoyed. 'You going to disguise yourself as a normal human being or something?'

'Give Lena a call and tell her we're on our way.'

I pulled out her iPhone and dialled the number. She was waffling away in Russian as we approached the multi-storey.

'We want one on the ground floor if we can. In between a couple of parked cars.'

She drove under the height bar and into the gloom.

'There, to the right – straight in.'

Anna swung the wheel. The Beamer followed us in and rolled to a halt. They only had two options: back out, park up and come back on foot, or come past us looking for a space.

They couldn't park close by because we'd have eyes-on. With luck, they'd have to carry on up to the next floor.

Anna slipped in between two minging old Skoda-type estate cars. The Beamer's tyres screeched on the painted concrete as it carried on up the ramp.

She turned off the engine and started to get out. I gripped her arm. 'Bring everything. This car's history. We're not coming back.'

We made for the pedestrian exit. There was no point checking behind. It was all about making distance and getting as many angles between us as we could.

We'd soon find out if they were following. I hoped not. There were a lot more of them than there were of us. And they were big fuckers.

9

17.05 hrs

Irina sat behind the desk. Lena collated documents and pictures for her visit to the mother of the girl in Barcelona. She was still trying to trace her. The address they'd been given was wrong. I could barely see them. The women were all smoking their cigarettes like they were one step away from the firing squad.

Anna brought them up to speed. 'Nicholas heard rumours about one of the traffickers in London. His source said he was moving girls to the UK and had a contact at the university.'

'Contact?' Irina rested her hands on the mountain of box files in front of her. 'What is his name?'

I shrugged. 'I wasn't given his name, but I was shown his picture. There's a shot of him outside the faculty office.'

Lena was still gobbing off on her mobile.

'We got chased out before we could find his name.'

She didn't bat an eyelid. 'I'll go and have a look.'

'You sure?'

Of course she was. She'd done things that were a lot more dangerous.

'When?'

'As soon as possible. Now?'

'Lena can drive me.'

'OK. He's overweight, with big frizzy hair. In one of the photos he's kissing a girl. She's blonde, dyed blonde.'

Lena closed down her mobile. 'No problem. I'll drop you off.' She'd been listening to every word. She pulled another cigarette from her pack and stabbed it at us. 'You want to stay here?'

'If that's OK.'

'Of course.'

They started towards the door, arm in arm. Lena's mobile kicked off again. She dug in her bag. 'But please don't leave. The office must never be unattended.'

Anna and I sat back and enjoyed a moment's silence.

Eventually I stood up and went over to the stack of files on the desk.

10

We spent nearly an hour flicking through them. There wasn't anything to check on a PC because there wasn't a PC.

I was feeling rough.

Anna read my mind. 'Up the stairs, you can't miss it.'

I followed her instructions and dry-swallowed a couple of Smarties. Fuck the water: I didn't trust anything out of a tap in this neck of the woods.

Anna was kneeling by the fax machine when I got back, sifting through sheets of paper. 'Maybe the police don't want them to be online. It would make Lena's job too easy.'

I picked up a box file labelled 2005 and discarded it. Our target wouldn't have left school by then.

'I bet it's Lena who doesn't want to be online. Cell phones are giving the police enough information already.'

Anna brought another pile of documents to the desk for me to rifle through. 'You OK, Nicholas?'

'Fine. I was knackered from the flight and we haven't exactly been dossing around since then, have we?' I paused. 'All this smoke's not helping.'

Anna scrutinized the desk top. 'I've been thinking, Nicholas. Maybe we could go away together . . . Spring is so beautiful in Moscow.'

'What about CNN?'

'CNN can wait. Maybe I could show you the White Nights in St Petersburg.' Her face lit up. 'It's such high latitude the sun doesn't sink below the horizon. You can walk along the river in daylight, even at two in the morning.'

'Sounds like an insomniac's paradise.'

We sat in silence for a while. I didn't know what more to say. Did I look that bad? Was it that obvious?

'Nicholas . . . Why are you *really* doing this job? You don't need to. It's not a game, you know.'

'Part of me has always tried to pretend it *is* a game. But not this time. I don't want to go all dewy-eyed on you, but I'm worried about this girl. I don't want to let her down. I've been there before, and I didn't like it.'

Her iPhone rang. 'Hello, Irina.' She grabbed a pen and paper with her spare hand. I watched her write just two words.

Viku Slobozia.

They spoke a little longer, and then she closed down.

'That's him. He's a post-grad. Irina's already called Lena. Neither of them has heard of him. Lena's picking her up.'

I'd been hoping his name would ring bells. They'd know who he was and where he lived, and we'd go down to his flat and come out with Lilian. What now? I picked up a file with a photocopied picture on the cover, and a light bulb flicked on in my head. 'You know what, Anna? Lilian might not be on Facebook any more, but this boy might be.'

11

'Found him!' She held up the iPhone. 'He's quite the Mr Lover Man. At least, he seems to think so.'

She expanded the first picture with her thumb and fore-finger. Viku Slobozia was giving it some in a bar, in full eighties porn-film gear. He clearly thought he was Daniel Craig. He'd not held back on the hair gel, but the frizz remained defiant. The dickhead even had Aviators on indoors.

She scrolled down. 'Here we are.'

It was the photo I'd seen at the uni, the one where he'd mistaken Lilian's face for a pie. She scrolled some more. Lilian was only one in a cast of dozens. Mr Lover Man had many 'chicks'. There was a different girl in every picture. He either had a giant appetite, or they didn't stick around long. I couldn't blame them. Maybe Tresillian was right about all this social-networking shit. It made you look a dickhead, and for ever.

She pointed at a caption. 'It says: "Viku loves the ladies."'

I bet he did. But I still couldn't believe the ladies loved him. I went back through his gallery of conquests. Lilian included, they all looked younger than him. Maybe that was his secret. He was a post-grad who only hit on first and second years.

The next three pictures had me worried.

I expanded one of Slobo sitting in an old-style silver Merc convertible, one of the little two-seater jobs with a steel roof that folded back and tucked into the boot. A machine like that should have been way beyond his student grant.

What he cradled in his hands concerned me more. He posed side-on to the camera, gangster-style, the barrel of a chrome-plated Desert Eagle semi-automatic pistol aimed at the ground about ten feet away. There was no mag in it, but that didn't matter. The thing was still so heavy he couldn't hold it straight. Fully loaded, it would hold nine .50 rounds to fuck people up with. The weapon fitted his profile, of course. As a bad-boy brand it was up there with Mercs and magnums of Cristal champagne.

'Why don't you email him, Anna? Get a date. Looks like he'd give a warm welcome to a new girl in town. Just stay away from his mouth.'

Her brow furrowed as she scrolled to the end of Slobo's picture library. 'Don't you think there might be an age issue?'

'We'll worry about that when the time comes. He's not going to know until he meets you, is he? By then it'll be too late.'

She hesitated a few seconds while she gave it some thought. Then the thumbs got moving again. 'This guy's so vain he's got to be checking his page ten times a day.' She smiled. 'I bet he replies inside an hour.'

'What makes you say that?'

'I don't think Mr Lover Man will turn down what I'm saying is on offer.'

12

We could hear Lena gobbing into her phone from half a street away. That thing never left her ear.

She swept in like a tornado, grabbed the first available piece of paper and started scribbling. Irina was just behind her. She looked down at the coffee-table and saw no mugs. 'You haven't had coffee?'

'Didn't even think about it. We were checking files. We thought we'd have a look in case our guy was tucked away in there somewhere.'

She looked almost offended, like we'd spurned her hospitality. 'I'll make some.'

Lena accepted one of Anna's cigarettes and they both lit up. She finally finished the call as Irina came back with the brews and placed her mobile carefully on her desk. 'The mother broke down with joy. I'm trying to arrange a call between them. The mother has no phone. They're poor. They have nothing. But, hey . . .' Her hands went up in the air to signal a change of subject. 'So what do we know about this Viku Slobozia?'

She listened intently as Anna tried to explain how we'd found him on Facebook. Her eyes narrowed. She wasn't having any of it. 'This doesn't ring true. There's more to it.

Why didn't you tell us you were going to the university? Irina could have gone in for you straight away. We're here to help.'

There was no way I was going to let Anna bring up Lilian's name. I jumped in. 'It was my fault. I'm trying to protect people in London. I didn't want anybody here to know what we were doing. And then I met you two. I didn't want to affect what you're doing, or add to your workload. But I realize now that I could have messed things up.'

Irina took a sip of her brew. 'What next?'

'I'm waiting for a reply.' Anna looked up from her iPhone screen and grinned. 'I'm an innocent seventeen-year-old today, new to the city. He's in for a shock, isn't he?'

They didn't like the joke. They both looked concerned. 'He might have contacts in London, but who cares about them? It's the contacts he's got here you have to worry about.'

I shifted in my seat. 'It's the only way, Lena. He likes linking up with young girls. But don't worry, I'm not going to put Anna in danger. I'll take over before he gets his tongue out.' I didn't mention his Desert Eagle.

Anna's iPhone kicked off. 'I told you.' Her face fell the moment she opened it up. 'Shit. He wants my Facebook page.'

'Tell him you haven't got one.'

Lena cut in: 'No, tell him your parents wouldn't let you have one. But now you're free of them and in the city, you want to put one together. You want to get as many friends as possible. Maybe he can help you do that. If he's a trafficker or he's moving you on, he's going to take the bait. It's perfect for him. No Facebook, no trace. None of your friends are going to be worried about you because you haven't refreshed your page.'

Anna thumbs bounced around and she hit send.

We had less than a minute to wait. The phone vibrated again. Anna wasn't impressed. 'Now he wants a picture.'

Irina stood up, pulling back her hair. 'Use me.'

'No.' I shook my head. 'You don't want to go that route again.'

Lena gave a sad smile. 'It's all right. It won't be the first time Irina's posed as a potential victim to flush these fucks out.'

Irina nodded. 'Nick, it's not a problem.'

'That's all well and good, but if he wants to meet, it's going to be Anna or me standing there. What happens then?'

Irina smiled for the camera. 'That's easy. I'll meet him for you.'

Anna hesitated before pressing the button. She looked at me. 'Too dangerous. He's got a weapon.'

Irina walked back to the desk. 'Where do you think you are, Nick?' She dug around in her small black leather handbag and pulled out a .38 revolver. 'Meet this country's only reliable policeman.'

Then Lena pulled aside her grey cardigan to reveal a shoulder holster. I didn't recognize the weapon from the grip but I knew it would still go bang and kill people. 'In our business you need these things. If Irina wants to go, let her. She knows what to do.'

Irina was back in pose mode, still waiting for Anna to do her David Bailey number.

I pointed at her bag. 'Have you used that thing?'

'Three times. And if I ever see the friend who sold me, it will be four.'

13

The border crossing into Transnistria was at a place called Bender. It would get us into Tiraspol, the capital of this breakaway state, just thirty minutes later. As Viku said when he replied to Anna, he was chilling out at home for a while. Why didn't Anna come and spend some time with him, see some sights?

That was exactly what a much younger Anna was going to do tonight. Irina had taken over the communication on Anna's iPhone. She said she was new at the university. She was coming in from Moscow and was suddenly getting cold feet because she had no friends in Chisinau. She'd come across him on Facebook and wondered if he'd help her out. He looked a fun kind of guy.

Anna had been at the wheel of Lena's Skoda estate for the best part of an hour.

Irina bounced around on the back seat. The roads were unsigned, potholed and totally unlit. We'd had close shaves with tractors, pedestrians and livestock. Anna's eyes were glued to the small pool of light in front of us as yet another minibus taxi overtook us on a blind corner, packed to capacity with people and suitcases.

'You have the presents?'

I patted the four hundred US dollars' worth of lei in my jeans, two hundred in each pocket. Irina had changed some for us both. She'd lost ten per cent on the deal because her USD bills weren't in absolutely pristine condition.

The headlights picked out a sign that said we were coming to the border. Anna slowed. A pool of light bathed the rutted tarmac about two hundred metres ahead.

'Look bored, Nick. Who knows? They might just let us through. Irina, be asleep.'

Six or seven guys were sitting in the middle of the road on fold-up chairs. One got slowly to his feet as we came into view. He indicated for us to park up behind them.

'Shit.' Anna wasn't impressed. 'We're visiting a friend in a bar, remember. Use his real name, Irina.'

I nodded. I'd leave it to her to explain why her boyfriend was British and didn't speak a word of her language.

Two older guys stepped forward. They had parkas with the hoods up, and orange armbands to show they were official. One of them came round to her side of the vehicle. Anna powered down the window and tried being short, sharp and aggressive.

They didn't buy it.

Irina produced an ID card. Anna pulled her passport out and I followed suit. My guy had a grey beard but I couldn't see much else of his face. With his hood up, he looked like something out of *South Park*. I smiled as he took it away. I couldn't tell if he'd smiled back. I doubted it.

He walked round to the front of the wagon. I hated this. I hated losing control of a passport, even for a few minutes.

We were held as a couple of people-carrier buses screamed straight through. The bearded one was joined by his mate. They had a chat about the passports. He came back and gobbed off in Russian at Anna. He handed Irina back her ID card, but he pointed at me. Then he pointed at the bonnet.

'Give me two hundred, Nick.'

I passed over the two notes from my right pocket and the passports were slipped back through the window. Transaction complete. Simple as that.

Up went the windows and we moved off.

'All that nonsense just for a bung?'

Anna manoeuvred between two trucks. 'They said it was a car tax to cross the border. That's a new one on me. Normally it's a fine for some kind of driving offence.'

'Why do they sit in the middle of the road? They got a death wish or something?'

Irina's head appeared between us. 'Moldova refuses to build an official checkpoint because it considers Transnistria a break-away province. But at the same time they're not too thrilled about having their eastern border wide open. So . . .'

No sooner had Anna accelerated than she had to slow down again. We entered a massive concrete anti-tank chicane.

Irina stayed in tour-guide mode. 'These were put here by Transnistria in case the Moldovans came across again. It gives the one thousand Russian "peacekeepers" time to get to the border to help.'

Anna prepared her passport for another outing. We emerged from the chicane to see two uniformed Russians in camouflage parkas and furry hats, AK47s slung across their chests. They looked severely pissed off at being on stag at this time of night.

'They're part of the Fourteenth Army, the so-called "secret Russians". You can't move for them over here.'

Ahead of us, on a straight bit of tarmac, there was another pool of light. More lads sat outside on chairs, but this time there was a Portakabin close by.

'This one's trickier. Same story. Visiting a bar.'

More Russian soldiers milled about. They'd pulled in a few of the newer-looking wagons but the rest screamed through. The Transnistria flag, ripped and tattered, flew above the door.

It was just the old Soviet red duster with the hammer and sickle in the top left-hand corner and a green stripe across its centre.

We joined a queue. Three Russian soldiers took our passports and Irina's ID. Their condensed breath hung in the air. They ordered us out and pointed to the Portakabin. Vehicles honked their horns and the smell of diesel fumes filled the cold air.

A trestle table groaned under a pile of brown-paper forms. Anna picked up a pencil. 'I'll do it.'

My passport was causing quite a stir. Maybe they'd never seen a British one. They were probably working out how much they could get for it on eBayski. Word had got around. The commander made a special guest appearance, a high-peaked hat cocked on the back of his head and a cigarette clamped between his lips.

He beckoned Anna over. The two of them exchanged pleasantries, and then they got down to business. Whatever it was he'd asked for, she wasn't going to give up without a fight. Finally they seemed to agree.

I dipped into my left pocket. She held up her hand. 'He wants four hundred. He's going to let us stay until two a.m.'

'It's by the hour?'

'Welcome to Dodge.'

I handed over the money, and fished another two notes from my wallet. He accepted the cash before getting one of his underlings to stamp the form about six times.

Anna took it and we got back into the car. None of us said a word as we left the checkpoint and almost immediately crossed the three-hundred-metre-wide Dniester River into Transnistria. I expected to see Checkpoint Charlie at any minute.

The roads here were even worse than Moldova's – stretches of concrete and tarmac that looked like they'd been carpet-bombed. Maybe they had. We passed the burnt-out shell of a building, crumbling walls stained brown where its rusting iron skeleton poked through.

Anna shook her head. 'This place depresses me so much. It's like the Wild West. There are no international aid agencies here. Why would they risk their people? It's bandit country.'

With one hand on the wheel she flipped open a cigarette pack, lit two and passed one back to Irina. 'Have you heard of Viktor Bout?'

'The world's biggest arms trafficker? He still in jail in Thailand?' I powered down my window to lose the smoke. She smiled and did the same.

'He operated out of Tiraspol. Same as the Russian and Ukrainian Mafia. They come here to hide. The police are a joke. Even when families are afraid their daughters may have been trafficked they don't report it. They just don't trust them.'

For the next two kilometres, we passed factory after factory. Even at night, some were still online and belching fumes. Minging cars filled the parking lots, along with the occasional Merc. There was plenty of foot traffic. The young lads sported cheap tracksuit tops, jeans and trainers and wore their hair white-walled around the sides. The occasional whore patrolled a street corner. Ancient Trabants kerb-crawled alongside them. I could almost see the hot breath on their windows.

'Whatever they manufacture here, they do it away from the prying eyes of the international community.' Anna flicked her butt out into the darkness. An old guy at the roadside looked tempted to go and pick it up. 'The border with Ukraine is only a kilometre or two away. It's unmarked and unguarded. All sorts of goods are smuggled across, from cigarettes and alcohol to serious weapons.'

Irina nodded. 'Smugglers load up and head for Odessa. From there they can ship whatever they have to the rest of the world. This place is—'

'Anna! *Stop!*'

She braked hard and pulled over to the side of the road.

'Over there . . .'

I stuck my hand through the open window and pointed. The tank was mounted on a ramp in front of the factory.

'That's the building.'

'You sure?'

'I've seen a picture of it.'

She tilted her head to get a better look at the sign on the wall. 'Well, he isn't making tanks.'

14

I reached for the door handle. Anna grabbed my arm. She knew exactly what was on my mind. 'We only have twenty minutes.'

Irina's head reappeared between our seats. She looked confused.

I smiled. 'This is where one of the girls used to work. Maybe they can help. I'll pop in and find out.'

'At this time of night? There won't be—'

'Do a circuit and I'll meet you here in fifteen, OK?' I fastened my jacket and stepped out into the drizzle. I didn't want Irina to get rattled, or Anna asking what she should do if I wasn't here when they got back.

Light leaked through the narrow slit windows that ran the length of the building. Trucks were parked up in what looked like a large loading bay to my right. Apart from one slow-moving vehicle in the distance, there was very little sign of life. The main entrance, to the right of the tank, was a gate in the chain-link fence. I approached the security area. A body, fat and bored, sat reading a paper. I veered away to the left.

Fuck knew what I was going to achieve in the time. I wanted to find out what Tarasov was making in there. Tresillian might have sounded like a straight talker, but that didn't mean what he was saying was straight.

I climbed the three-metre fence. It was simple enough. I was soon kneeling on the wet verge the other side. The factory didn't have high security or cameras. Crimes against property would be almost non-existent in a place like this. Thousands of Russian troops were based in this narrow strip. If they couldn't catch a thief and deal with him, the local Mafia would. Anybody intent on doing some nicking probably drove across the border for the night.

The building had large steel air ducts. Steam escaped from a jumble of smaller pipes that looked like a gang of eels clinging to the blockwork. Two cars were nosy-parked against the wall. I rattled in between them for cover.

One of the windows above me was open. I gripped the brackets holding the air ducts. The steel was cold and slippery. An uncomfortable film of sweat gathered on my back as I climbed. I checked my G-Shock. I had less than ten minutes left. I had to get a move on.

A vehicle turned the corner below me. In a couple more seconds its headlights would catch me in their glare. I hauled myself up level with the window and scrambled through.

The corridor had a glass wall that ran the length of the building and overlooked the works area. There was movement down there: three or four people in blue nylon boiler-suits, with hoods and gloves and white wellies. They all had full-face masks attached to a filter hanging from their belts. The place was quiet, apart from the hum of the heaters. There was no clunking of machinery, and not a spot of oil in sight. You don't need oil when you're soldering microprocessors onto motherboards.

Further along, the rectangles of silicon and pressed steel were being packed into green, foam-lined aluminium boxes. White stencilling on the sides probably indicated wherever they were bound. I couldn't be sure – it was all Greek to me.

I pulled the BlackBerry from my jacket, checked the flash was off and activated the zoom. Then I inched forward until I could hold it against the glass. I angled it downwards, and took five shots in a panoramic sequence.

A third vehicle had pulled up beneath the window. Its lights were off. I pulled myself over the sill and onto an air duct, then scrambled back down the pipes to the ground. It was a 3 Series Beamer. That wasn't a big deal. We'd seen plenty of them. But this one had the low-rider trim. And its registration was C VS 911.

15

Tiraspol
20.15 hrs

The Cold War had never stopped in this city. I'd seen more
government propaganda billboards than in Cuba and North
Korea combined. There were still more statues of Lenin than
you could shake a Red Flag at. Yet another tank was mounted
on a ramp beside me, the third T55 I'd seen as a monument to
Communist glories since we'd crossed the border.

Heavily armed police loitered on every street corner,
twiddling batons and pushing up their peaked caps. Old
women in headscarves and long, threadbare coats shuffled
past. Rainwater dripped from gutter pipes that disgorged their
contents straight into the street.

Irina and I sat double-parked on Constitution Street, staking
out Manik. Anna had gone in to check if Slobo was already at
the bar. The right-hand side of the road was pulsating with life.
On the left was the inky blackness of the graveyard where
some of the fifteen thousand dead from the USSR's eight-year
war in Afghanistan lay. A massive billboard hung above the
gates. This one featured the hard-line president, Igor Smirnov,
shaking hands with Dmitry Medvedev, the president of the

Federation. It looked like an ad for a sci-fi convention. With his big eyebrows and bald head, Smirnov was the spitting image of Ming the Merciless, Flash Gordon's nemesis, and Medvedev was a ringer for Captain Kirk.

Neon lights splashed the bar's name across the night. It was one of dozens along this stretch. Tinted-glass frontage had fucked over the ground floors of the faded ex-Soviet stucco buildings. It sounded like each bar was trying to out-music the last. The noise poured out onto the cobbled street like a demonic DJ's mix.

BMWs and Mercs waited outside with their engines running. Each of the new Mafia élite who piled out of them had a couple of heavy-looking lads to keep an eye on them. This was where some of the millions of dollars changed hands each night that made it a dangerous town.

A lone figure moved down the road towards us, leaving a trail of smoke in her wake. The tip of her cigarette glowed with each inhalation. Her blonde helmet and long dark coat began to take shape as she got closer.

Anna opened the passenger door and jumped in. 'I felt like a grandmother in there.' She shivered as I powered down her window. She got the hint and threw out what was left of her cigarette. 'He hasn't shown yet.'

Brake lights glowed, then sidelights, in the middle of the line of cars nearer the bar. I fired up the Skoda's engine to take the space before anyone else. I glanced at her. 'Now we wait, yeah?'

Anna kept her eyes glued to the bar entrance. Irina leant forward. 'I hope Mr Lover Man hasn't stood me up.'

I pulled into the kerb and closed down the engine. 'Maybe he had second thoughts. Maybe you're too old for him.'

My reward was a punch in the arm.

We settled down and watched in silence.

I opened my window a few inches to cut the condensation. I could feel the bass notes pounding through the darkness.

Lights flashed and bodies gyrated in the bar's murky interior.

A group of men came past us, leather-jacketed and smoking. They made their way up the three concrete steps and through the double glass doors.

'Don't take any chances, Irina. This guy has a weapon.'

'That makes two of us.' Irina stretched her legs along the rear seat. 'Don't worry about me. I will do my part and we will nail him together, yes?'

A flash of red bounded up the steps. I had a glimpse of knee-length coat, fat face and a mop of frizzy hair. 'We've got a possible.'

I kept focused on the entrance. 'Where did he come from? Anyone see his car?'

Neither of them answered.

Irina was already reaching for her door handle. I leant back and gripped her arm. 'Anything that isn't right, just walk. OK?'

She nodded, but not convincingly enough for my liking. 'Let's hope our friend likes what he sees.' She slipped out of the car, along the short stretch of sidewalk and disappeared inside.

I peered at my G-Shock. A quarter of an hour later, she was still nowhere to be seen. I unpeeled a stick of gum and popped a couple of Smarties down my neck at the same time.

'Anna?'

We both kept eyes on the bar.

'I've been thinking about what you said ... You know, Moscow and St Petersburg ... Sounds a good plan.'

She looked at me, waiting for the catch. 'That would be ... lovely. How long for?'

'I don't know – a month or so?'

I wanted to keep on talking, to tell her everything, but felt like I was standing in front of the phone in the kitchen all over again. I knew what I wanted to say, but I couldn't get the words out.

Irina came out of the bar. Thank fuck for that. Slobo was close behind her, downing the last of a beer before tossing the bottle over the wall. He looked very happy with himself. They turned towards the Skoda. He was porkier than his pictures suggested. His baggy jeans were hardly baggy at all. But you had to hand it to him. He certainly knew how to make the best of a bad job.

They were both laughing. She slipped her arm through his as they passed us, flirting away in Russian.

They crossed the road and walked under the *Flash Gordon* meets *Star Trek* billboard, then through the gate into the Afghan graveyard. The darkness swallowed them.

Anna and I jumped out of the car. I locked both doors the old-fashioned way and handed her the keys.

We fell in behind the two of them, close enough to hear their murmurs and giggles, but far enough back not to breathe down their necks.

16

They carried on past a row of slate slabs surrounded by gravel, then slowed and stopped. It looked as if Slobo had picked the spot for his big moment.

Anna was still a few steps behind me. I moved just near enough to make out their silhouettes. I wasn't going to jump in and fuck things up. Irina knew what she was doing. All I hoped was that she'd know when to call for help.

Slobo turned to face her. I watched his hands reach inside her coat. He grabbed her arse, pulling her towards him. Irina put her hands on his waist. They kissed briefly, and then she pulled back, toying with him. I could hear her murmuring gently as Slobo's hands moved up inside her coat and fondled her breasts. She kissed him again. She was holding him static, waiting for me.

This was as good place as any to grip him and get it over with. We could be heading back across the border within the hour.

I took a few paces towards them. They had stopped kissing and Slobo was now almost dragging her along the path. The tone was still playful but it was starting not to look like much fun. I checked behind. Anna was with me.

They moved beneath a dim light suspended over another

gate. Beyond it was a narrower street than the one we'd parked in. It, too, was lined with cars. There were no neon invitations on this one, just grey apartment blocks that looked even greyer in the drizzle. A lot of the rendering had given up the struggle, exposing the blockwork beneath. TVs flickered behind net curtains and watery light seeped from windows steamed-up from another night of cabbage-boiling.

We watched from the shadows as they left the graveyard and crossed the road. Slobo kept a hand on Irina's arse. He seemed to be steering her towards the cars. One of them was the old-style silver Merc convertible.

'Fuck it – I'm going to have to take him now. Let's go.'

As they neared the car I broke into a run.

Not straight towards them, but diagonally across the street.

He was more concerned with her arse than his own security. I couldn't see him getting any keys out and there was no flashing of indicators.

I reached the pavement as they slid between the front of the Merc and a knackered van. The entrance to the apartment block was less than three strides away. She stalled him some more with a kiss. I didn't know if she could see me or not. He fumbled around with some keys, trying to get one of them into the lock while still copping a feel.

They tumbled into the hallway. I ran forward as soon as they were out of sight and jammed my foot in the closing door. I waited for Anna to catch up and then followed.

We eased past a rusty old pram, a bike and a pile of bulging bin bags. The stench caught in the back of my throat. Maybe it was garbage day. Or maybe it was just a hangover from the bad old days: the belief that though anything inside your four walls was your responsibility, everything else was the state's.

The clatter of footsteps, punctuated by the occasional giggle, echoed down the dank stairwell – Irina's way of letting us know where she was. There were about twelve steps up to a landing where the flight turned back on itself. We hit a set of fire doors that had long since come off their hinges. TVs blared and families screamed at each other somewhere down the corridor.

I heard the jangle of keys as I reached the next landing. I took the stairs two at a time and ducked my head quickly around the corner. She had him pinned against the wall, trying to kiss him again, but Slobo had done with foreplay: he wanted her inside.

He shoved her away so hard she banged against the opposite wall. He pushed open the door to his apartment and gripped her by the arms. The laugh wasn't friendly any more. He had her where he wanted her. He twisted her around and pushed her through the entrance. Fuck that. Playtime was over. I ran towards them. He still had his back to me as I crossed the threshold. He was totally focused on the prize. She stood to my right by a small table and a couple of plastic chairs. Her hand reached into her handbag as he advanced on her.

I barged into the room.

I grabbed his shoulder, spun him round and swung my open palm across his face. The sound of the blow was as loud as his scream.

He crumpled, both hands on his cheeks. I pushed him down onto his arse on the dark blue carpet with my boot. He looked up, wide-eyed with shock. A good slap can be far more effective than a punch. It takes you straight back to your childhood, to the time your dad let you know who was top dog. Most kids don't step up to the plate and risk any more. They withdraw, feel sorry for themselves. They take the pain and never want it to happen again. That was the way it was for Slobo. From the look of anguish on his face, I reckoned his childhood must have been much the same as mine. No fighting back, no retaliation, just withdrawal. But I knew that wouldn't last for long.

I kicked into his back. I wanted to keep his jaw in one piece. He keeled over completely. I searched him as Anna handed the car keys to Irina and signalled that it was time for her to leave. She'd wait for us in the car.

Irina stopped for a moment and stared down at Mr Lover Man with a look of the purest hatred. She patted her handbag. He might not have known what it contained, but he got the message loud and clear.

A split second later, as the door closed behind her, the subservience had gone. He gave it full revs with the Russian abuse. I didn't have to be a UN interpreter to understand his I'm-going-to-kill-you-you-will-pay-for-this shit.

I kicked into his chest to shut him up and put my boot firmly on his neck. I powered up his mobile. Scrolling down the list of contacts, I found 'Lilian E'. I pressed dial. There was nothing. No ring tone; no message service. I memorized the number and checked the call log. Only a handful of local numbers and one international. I memorized that too.

I leant down to make sure we had eye-to-eye. If he spoke English I'd soon know.

'Tell him if he stays still and answers my questions I won't hurt him.'

His eyes were fixed on mine. I could see what he was thinking. What the fuck was an American, Brit, Australian or whatever doing here? I moved behind him, out of his direct sight. I hoped it would make him flap a whole lot more.

17

Anna spoke gently to him. She sounded almost motherly. The only word I could make out was 'Lilian'.

I got the impression she was casting me as the bad guy. She was the good one, the one he could trust and confide in, the one who wouldn't rip his head off his shoulders. But his shoulders still tensed as she reached into her coat pocket. They relaxed again as she pulled out her cigarettes and lighter. She tapped out a couple and offered him one.

As she lit hers, I saw the reflection of the flame glisten on her cheek. She was crying. As she talked to him now, there was a sadness in her voice that almost made me reach for a Kleenex.

Slobo sucked down a lungful of smoke.

I turned away and started ripping the place apart. The flat might have been small, but he had an expensive iPod dock and flat-screen TV. The stack of well-thumbed DVDs next to it would have taken a month to work through. Mr Lover Man must have kept them for a quiet night in. I didn't think German farmyard stuff and hard-core bondage was the way to a girl's heart.

The wardrobe was stuffed with clothes that reeked of tobacco and cheap cologne. I glanced round. He was listening intently to Anna, but looked more interested in her cigarettes than in keeping us up to speed on Lilian's travel plans.

'How's it going?' I tipped out a shelf full of rip-off Armani underwear.

'He's telling me nothing.' She said it matter-of-factly, as if we were discussing the weather. 'He just keeps saying that he saw her a couple of weeks ago and hasn't heard from her since.'

I opened the bedside cabinet nearest the bathroom door. The drawer was stuffed with packets of condoms and lubricants, four or five chunky square watches and a pair of handcuffs that Irina would no doubt have been treated to if he'd had his way.

I found his Desert Eagle in the cupboard on the other side of the bed. I lifted it out and pulled back the top slide to check if there was a round in the chamber. There wasn't. I hit the magazine release catch with my thumb. The empty mag fell into my hand. The weapon was a bit of a metaphor for this dickhead. All bling, no substance.

He'd probably bought the Israeli-made pistol before he discovered he couldn't get hold of the ammunition. Or maybe he thought it went nicely with the handcuffs. Perhaps it was a sex thing, the closest he could get to a hard-on.

I showed Anna the weapon. He turned and looked at me. He was worried, but not yet fearful. He knew it wasn't loaded. He said something, but it sounded like he was still trying to weasel his way out.

'Anything?'

'Still the same story.' Her tone was starting to change.

I dropped the weapon onto the black, imitation-satin sheets. I knelt down and pulled a large clear plastic storage box from under the bed. Inside it was a small digital camera, Kodak printer, and a carton of photographic paper. I picked out six or seven five-by-eight pictures. The face had been cut neatly out of every one, but I could see that they were all of the same girl. I recognized her shape and the pale, almost translucent tone of her skin. I also recognized the background. Lilian had been posing against the battleship grey wall of the room we were in. I stood up with the pictures in my hand. 'Anna . . .'

She took one of them, knelt down and thrust it at him.

Slobo's head jerked back and he spat in her face. She didn't flinch. She rose slowly and stood over him as he fired off another volley of Russian. She shook her head and went through to the bathroom to clean up.

'Bring back a towel.'

I picked up the handcuffs. Slobo guessed what was about to happen and started to get up. He'd finally realized he was going to have to take me on. I wasn't about to encourage him. I dished out another hard slap across the head and took him down with a kick in the solar plexus. I crunched my knee on his neck to keep it on the floor, grabbed his hands and snapped on the cuffs behind his back.

I grabbed him under his elbows and dragged him to his feet. I didn't say a word. I didn't need to. He had to comply or he was going to be in huge pain.

I turned him round and shoved him, back first, onto the bed so his cuffed wrists were beneath him.

I ripped the case off a pillow and shoved it over his head. He wriggled and cursed. I gave him a punch to the side of his face. *'Shut the fuck up!'*

He fell silent. He might not have known the words but he got the message loud and clear.

I left him there. He wasn't going anywhere except maybe back on the floor. I went over to the sink and opened the cupboard underneath. The biggest pan I could find held about three litres. Home cooking obviously wasn't part of Slobo's seduction routine.

Anna emerged with a striped bath towel. She saw me filling the pan from the tap.

'No, Nick, not that . . .'

I walked towards her with the full pan. 'If we don't, we're going to be here all day.'

'You might kill him.'

'I've had it done to me. I know what I'm doing. You just *think* you're dying.'

18

I put the pan down beside the bed and dragged him round by his shoulders so his head hung over the edge. I jumped onto his chest. He tried to fight me but with his arms behind him he was fucked. I reached across and picked up the pan. 'Put the towel over his face. Hold it firmly either side.'

She hesitated.

'Anna, we have to crack on. No one has ever lasted more than a minute with this. That's the way it works.'

She placed the towel over his face but wasn't really holding it.

'It's got to be tight. We want to find her, don't we? This won't kill him. It'll just . . . give him some motivation.'

She wasn't at all happy with it, but pulled down either side on the towel. He tried to writhe from side to side. I gripped his face with my left hand under his jaw. 'Pull harder, for fuck's sake!' The towel tautened and became almost like a strap around his head.

I started to pour, making sure the water fell evenly and constantly over his nose and mouth. It wasn't long before he was gagging. The reflex was automatic. There was nothing he could do to stop it.

'Anna, hold it tight.' I controlled him with my weight. 'Hold it, keep it there!'

The gurgling and choking continued under the material. He couldn't breathe. His body went ballistic, kicking out, trying to buck free of me. He thrust out his elbows in a frantic attempt to pull free of the handcuffs. He was probably ripping his own skin. I certainly had when it had been done to me.

I motioned for Anna to lift the towel. I peeled back the pillowcase far enough to expose his nose and mouth. He coughed up a mixture of water and alcohol-rich vomit.

I gripped his head with both hands and nodded at the pan. 'Go and fill it up. *Hurry. . .*'

Slobo couldn't see anything because the pillowcase was still over his eyes. His chest heaved up and down for oxygen. His brain couldn't work out that he was getting all he needed. Waterboarding is guaranteed to get the victim telling everything he knows, and even some things he doesn't – anything to keep breathing. Physically, it's like being trapped under a wave, but that's fuck-all compared to the psychological hell. Your brain screams at you that you're drowning, that you're going to die.

Anna returned with the water. 'Get ready with that towel again.' I pulled the pillowcase back over his mouth and took the pan from her.

He'd be telling himself to keep calm. But he'd know that he couldn't. He'd already had one taste of this. The second was going to terrorize him.

I started pouring. His body jerked like he was being Tasered. Then, suddenly, as if someone had thrown a switch, his strength ebbed. He had nothing left to fight with. He knew that death was just seconds away. He'd given up.

I let Anna take the towel off and pulled up the pillowcase. He puked water and bile.

'Ask him where the fuck she is.'

Anna bent closer to his ear, still talking slowly and gently. His chest heaved beneath me.

115

I could make out the word 'Lilian' again, and then something like 'Christmas' or 'Christine'.

It was just starting to get interesting when there was a thunderous crash at the door.

I looked up. Another of those and it was going to part company with its frame.

19

I rolled off Slobo's supine body. 'Anna! The bathroom! Go in the bathroom!' Anything to keep her out of the line of sight of whoever was about to bomb-burst into the room.

She dived over Slobo and scrambled across to the other side of the bed.

I rolled onto the floor and jammed the web of my right hand onto the butt of Lena's revolver in the waistband of my jeans.

Two crew-cut monsters exploded through the door, pistols drawn down, heads swivelling, trying to work out what to do next.

I sucked in my stomach, wrapped my thumb and three fingers round the grip of the revolver and pulled it out.

The boy to my left turned and brought his weapon into the aim. My eyes didn't move. My hand came up and his face blurred as my foresight became pin sharp. I squeezed the trigger as hard as I could to overcome the double action of the hammer. The round kicked off.

The other one dropped to a semi-squat as the back of his mate's head splattered against the grey wall behind him. He started firing. I had no idea what at.

Where was Anna?

I focused on my foresight once more. The hammer was back

in the full-cock position. He brought his weapon round. It completely obscured his face. It didn't matter. I pulled my trigger and he went down.

'Anna! Anna!'

She piled through the bathroom door as I got up.

Slobo was writhing on the bed. He'd taken some rounds. Our second uninvited guest must have seen the Desert Eagle within his reach and decided not to take any chances.

Anna looked at the two bodies. 'The BMW?'

'Tarasov's guys. The car was at the factory.'

Anna looked at Slobo. 'Oh, God . . .'

His chest was still heaving, but not enough to keep him alive.

'Do you know where she is?'

'Yes.'

The noise from the corridor was even louder now. TVs had been cranked up to full volume so Slobo's neighbours could say they hadn't heard a thing.

'Did you get her new name?'

'No.'

'She must have one. The photos – they've got to be passport photos.'

His eyes rolled. 'Tell him we want her new name. Tell him he's not in good shape, but I can save him if he gives us the name.'

I eased his head up to help him speak. This time, Anna didn't fuck around. Slobo was definitely on his last legs. We needed the answer fast.

'Tell him I can save him—'

'Sure, Nick, I'll tell him you're Florence Nightingale. Now shut up.' Her earlier tone had disappeared completely. She was giving Slobo the good news with both barrels.

He slurred a few words. Saliva dribbled from his mouth. His head went limp and his eyes stayed open.

'Did you get it?'

She nodded.

I let him go.

I stepped over the bodies and checked down the corridor. There was nothing that would slow us down.

I came back and looked her in the eye. 'Take a breath. Are you ready?'

She nodded.

'Good.' I gestured towards the first one I'd dropped. 'Check him for car keys.' I frisked the other guy's long leather coat and came up with the Beamer's.

We headed out into the corridor, the weapon still in my hand in case we had a drama. We ran down the stairs and out into the street. I pointed Anna to the right and I headed left, eyes peeled for a glint of blue.

She called out to me.

I turned to see her pointing at a vehicle that I couldn't see. Too many others were in the way.

I ran towards her, hitting the key fob until lights began to flash. 'You drive.' I threw her the keys. 'Lena's. *Go, let's go!*'

20

Anna turned about four corners before we hit Constitution Street again. I kept a look-out for any major drama on the street.

'I hope Irina's OK.'

Anna swerved to avoid an old guy on an unlit bike. 'You think they might have got to her first?'

The Skoda was where we'd left it.

She slowed down. Through the rain-slicked windows I could see the silhouette of a body in the driving seat. It wasn't moving.

I powered down my window. Irina raised her head and wound down hers.

Anna leant across me. 'Irina, he was a trafficker.'

She got it straight away. 'Was?'

'We need to split up now. I'll keep Lena's weapon. I'm going to dump it. Will you be OK making your own way back?'

She gave me a dazzling smile and fired up the Skoda's engine.

'Nobody saw us or knows about us, OK?'

Irina nodded. She came out of her space and stayed behind us until the next junction. Then she peeled off to the right.

I quizzed the Beamer's dash. 'Half a tank. Will that get us to the ferry?' We had to get out of this place, but I wanted to avoid the airport. Ships are less secure and easier to get onto than planes.

'It's two hours maybe, not far.'

'We'll give the hotel a miss.'

'I'll call them later and they'll bill me. What about the Polo?'

'We just leave it.'

An oncoming vehicle's headlights splashed across her face as she concentrated on the road. The rain was heavier now. The wipers sounded like a drumbeat.

'And the pistol?'

'I'm going to keep it as long as I can – at least until Odessa.'

We hit a pothole and the Beamer's skirting scraped the tarmac.

'What did Mr Lover Man say about Lilian?'

'She's gone to Copenhagen. A place called Christiania. Have you heard of it?'

'No.'

'It's a commune inside the city. Slobo said she needed to get away for a while. She was pissed off with her father.'

'Does that mean he knew who Tarasov is?'

Anna kept one hand on the wheel while she fished in her pockets for cigarettes. 'I don't think so. He just said "her father". But he cut off her Facebook, and he moved her along with a new ID. She may think she's taking a break in Hippie Land, but I think Slobo had other ideas.'

I powered down my window a quarter of the way as she lit up. Spots of rain peppered my face. 'Do we have an address?'

'He didn't know it. Or if he did, he wasn't telling me.'

I sparked up my BlackBerry. 'What's her new name?'

'Nemova.'

'How did she travel?'

She took a drag of her cigarette. 'He didn't say, but I didn't ask. It wasn't exactly coffee and chat.'

My screen lit up and showed four bars. I hit the time and

date app. It took a second or two to load. I tapped in Julian's number. There was a long tone and a short break as he began to receive the call. The green padlock icon would signal secure mode. It rang three times.

'Nick?'

'She's been trafficked. She's in Denmark. Some kind of commune, maybe. She's got a new name. Lilian Nemova. I'll spell: November – Echo – Mike – Oscar – Victor – Alpha. Worth checking the visa applications again?'

Julian didn't answer immediately. He was probably still writing it all down. 'I'll get somebody on it. Then I need to inform Mr Tresillian.'

A deep growl cut in. 'Already here, Julian. Now listen to me, Mr Stone. Excellent work. Go to Denmark. Find her. A contact and a safe-house will be arranged once you've discovered where she is.' There was a pause. 'A commune? A fucking commune? I didn't even know they still existed. Do these people think the world owes them a fucking living?'

Jules and I weren't sure who was meant to answer.

Tresillian filled in the gap. 'Anyone got anything useful to say?'

'I wouldn't mind dropping out myself one day.'

The jokes still weren't welcome. 'Not on my watch, Mr Stone. Next time we hear from you I trust it will be good news.'

The phone went dead. Obviously Julian didn't have anything to say. Or if he did, tough shit.

Before closing the BlackBerry down I shifted the cursor to the camera icon and clicked on 'View Pictures'. I spent a few moments willing the minute Cyrillic script to magically translate itself into plain English and leap out at me. 'I took these of the shipment stacked inside Tarasov's factory. You see the stencilling on the nearest case? Can you read what it says?'

She zoomed in on each photograph in turn. 'Just a series of numbers and letters – the product serial ID, maybe.' She looked up. 'Why not run them by Julian? He'll be able to blow them up on a big screen.'

She wasn't wrong. I thought of the one on the wall behind Tresillian's head. And I thought of the look on Tresillian's face when I'd asked about Lilian's dad. 'My orders were to steer well clear of Tarasov. And if the boss of bosses is listening in to Jules's incoming calls . . .'

She squinted harder at the BlackBerry's tiny display. 'I can't – no, hang on . . . here, in the corner . . .'

'What?'

'Some kind of shipping label.'

'Russia?'

She zoomed in further. 'Yes and no. It's shipping to Moscow but it's marked "for onward transit". There's an end-user company mentioned. I don't recognize the name – but I know somebody who might.' She pulled out her iPhone. 'Is there anything else about Tarasov I should know?'

I couldn't tell her. I didn't know myself.

She pressed the speed dial. It didn't sound like there were any pleasantries. The exchange was short. 'He'll call back when he's done some digging.'

21

'Anna?'

'About an hour and a half, I think.'

'No, not that. I was thinking about you, back in the flat. Those tears, the way you brought them on like that. What was that all about?'

'It's what I do, Nick. I get people to talk. I told him I was her sister. I told him I didn't care what he was doing, why he was doing it, who he was doing it with. I just wanted her back.' She flicked the stub of her latest cigarette out of the window. 'Not that it got me far this time.'

The city was way behind us now. The arc of the BMW's full-beams cut into the darkness ahead.

'How do you manage cry-on-demand? Do baby journalists have to go to acting school or something?'

'Sort of. I learnt the trick from an American reporter in Bosnia. It came in handy sometimes at road-blocks. She used to think of something really sad. Her mother's death, maybe.'

'And you?'

'I'm sure you can guess.'

A grim silence filled the car. The pulse in my neck quickened. I pictured a twenty-one-year-old kid on a mortuary slab with the back of his head removed by a tumbling missile fragment. I was just going on what she'd told me, but the image was astonishingly vivid – maybe because I was no stranger to scenes like that.

It was 1987. They were young. They were in love. They'd started dating when she was just sixteen – a schoolgirl. He was almost nineteen and in the Soviet Army. And then he'd gone to Afghanistan. She waved goodbye to him at the station, and the next time she saw him he was in a coffin. Even now, she still went to the station sometimes when she wanted to remember him.

'Grisha was an idealist.' I remembered the sadness in her voice as we'd walked along a windy Moscow *prospekt* and she'd told me the story. 'He loved poetry. That's how we met. His family lived in the same apartment block as mine. One evening when I came back from school I found him sitting on the front steps. He was reading Pushkin. I love Pushkin . . .'

They'd got talking. He wanted to go to university to study literature, but his family didn't have the money or the influence to send him – in those days you couldn't do it any other way. He would have been conscripted anyway, to fight in Afghanistan, so why not get a university education from the army as well? It meant signing up for five years, but then he'd be free of it. He wanted to become a teacher.

Anna's father didn't approve of the relationship. But, then, he didn't approve of anything much. He was an alcoholic. The Soviet system had killed his love of life. He worked in a factory that made machine tools. He hated it. Anna's mother was scared of him.

Anna was his only child. He wanted her to make something of her life, and study, study, study, he said, was the only way to achieve it. She had to see Grisha in secret. He had a motorbike, so they could escape every so often for a few hours on their own.

When he'd joined the army, Grisha had gone away for almost a year. In that time Anna saw him only once. He didn't talk about his training, but she could see that it had affected him deeply. It was only after the Chechen war, years later, when she'd helped families who'd tried to discover what had happened to their dead or missing sons, that she'd found out what they did to recruits. There was systematic abuse. Punishments had nothing to do with performance. If the officers and the NCOs in charge were having a bad day, they beat you. If they were bored, they beat you. When Grisha had come home that summer he was a changed man. He didn't want to talk about the army, just kept telling her that it wouldn't be long – another four years – and then he'd be free of it.

It was Grisha's father who had bought the motorbike, a beaten-up old thing from the Great Patriotic War, and restored it for him. The only times she had seen Grisha happy that summer were when he and his father had worked on the bike and when he had taken Anna out on it.

It was her eighteenth birthday while he was still on leave so they had decided to hand in their application to get married. Russians didn't have engagements and rings. They applied to ZAGS, the department of registration. But the wedding had never happened. He was sent to Afghanistan before ZAGS had given them a date.

Grisha used to write a lot when he was in Afghanistan. In February 1989, the month the war ended, so had the letters. The army told her he was missing, presumed dead. She wrote requesting further information, but the authorities had never replied. It was like he'd never existed.

Almost a year after they'd lost the war, Grisha's father had got a call from a man who claimed to be from the military forensic medical laboratory that had performed an autopsy on his son's body. He wanted to meet; there was something he needed to ask. But Grisha's father was too scared. This was Soviet Russia.

Anna had said she would go. 'I had nothing to lose. I'd left school and was waiting to go to university. I met this man –

this colonel – at a café. He told me about himself – told me that he had served in Afghanistan and what an utter, godforsaken waste of life it had been. People like Grisha, he said, deserved better. Then he showed me some pictures.

'The autopsy had been carried out at a medical laboratory in Kazan. They'd flown the bodies there, the bodies of everybody who'd been in Grisha's armoured personnel carrier. The first picture showed him almost as I remembered him: face up, eyes closed, like he was sleeping.

'The colonel told me the carrier had been hit by an anti-tank rocket. A fragment had pierced his eye, hit bone and tumbled. In the next picture, I saw the exit wound. There was nothing left of the back of his head – just a big black congealed mass of blood, brains, bone fragments and matted hair.'

It was a Soviet missile. The army had found a whole cache of them soon afterwards. The boxes had identified the manufacturer. Someone had sold them to the *mujahideen*.

Grisha's father worked for the Soviet Union's biggest arms manufacturers. Weapons that he had helped to build had killed his son. Grisha's death drove them both – him, until his death, to unearth arms trafficking; her, to champion the underdog at every turn.

I turned my head. Anna was weeping, and this time the tears weren't on demand.

'Walking through that graveyard made it easy. Those places always make me cry.'

'Pull over, Anna, I'll drive. You navigate.'

She bumped to a halt. Three trucks thundered past us, just metres apart. She hardly noticed. She had both hands on the wheel, head down.

'I try to move on, Nick, I really do. But it's . . . hard . . .' She turned to face me. 'Do you understand?'

I put a hand gently on her shoulder.

22

About half an hour out of Odessa, Anna glanced towards me again. 'When you asked about the tears, Nicholas, what were you trying to tell me?'

Jesus, this girl didn't miss a thing. 'Nothing really. I was just—'

She pulled into the side of the road again and swivelled in her seat. 'OK, we can play this one of two ways.' She took a deep breath. 'Either you carry on treating me like one of your army friends – and we pretend there's nothing wrong – or you tell me why you look like shit and what those little red pills are for.'

I didn't say anything for a moment. 'Anna, I thought . . . I thought . . . if you still can't hold back the tears every time you think about Grisha, then what right have I to—'

'You don't really understand this at all, do you? Grisha's story is about the importance of telling the truth, however painful it might be.'

Her beautiful, sad eyes bored into me, and stripped me back layer by layer. And for the first time since I could remember, I didn't cut away. I told her about the headaches and the visit to Kleinmann. I told her about his prognosis and the Smarties and the fact I had binned all the other treatment on offer. Finally, I told her about sitting in the flat, desperate to make a call to her, but being unable to do it. I told her I was too scared of her reaction, that I didn't want her to bin me.

Then I sat, arms folded, not daring to look at her, and stared out into the darkness.

I felt her fingers gently brush my cheek.

'You idiot . . .' She was shaking her head. 'I would never walk away. Surely you know me well enough to know that?'

I nodded, letting my hands drop, and tried to smile.

A tear had formed in her eye, and I watched it roll down her cheek. I'd done that. Her first chance of moving on and I'd fucked it up for her.

'You can understand, can't you? I wanted this one last kick at it before I go. Wouldn't you do the same?'

'The treatment – we can fight this . . .'

'It'll just delay the inevitable.' I pulled the Smarties out of my jeans. 'At least I can take these in front of you now.' I flicked it open and stared at the shiny red pebbles inside. I let the silence lengthen. 'I don't want to be a lump of dribbling jelly, depending on you, making your life as miserable as mine would be. You don't deserve it. Fuck it, better to burn out than fade away, eh?'

She moved her mouth closer to my ear. 'You stupid, stupid idiot.' She kissed me on the temple, then took two Smarties from the case and gently popped them into my mouth. 'We'll do this whichever way you want. But promise me one thing: be open to the idea of getting involved. It feels just as scary to me.'

We held each other close. A wave of happiness washed over me. She murmured in my ear, 'I'm glad you told me. I want to be with you.' She kissed me on the cheek again. 'And it doesn't matter for how long.'

Bulgari was still there, on her neck, though much weaker than this morning. Or maybe it wasn't there at all, and I just wanted it to be. Fuck it: it still felt comforting, reassuring and safe.

She was the one who pulled away. 'We have to get back on the road, Nicholas. Let's move, or we'll never get to see those White Nights.'

She spun the wheel and we carried on heading south.

PART FOUR

1

Copenhagen
Tuesday, 16 March
11.15 hrs

The Turkish Airlines Boeing 737 was on its final approach. The three-hour flight from Istanbul wasn't full. Anna found herself a spare row of seats and slept all the way, cuddling her pack of 200 duty-free Camel. We were dressed in the same clothes we'd been wearing when we'd left the Cosmos yesterday morning and the Bulgari was a distant memory.

Less than two hours after I'd called him, Julian had come back to confirm that Lilian had obtained a visa under the name of Nemova and flown to Copenhagen ten days ago. She had booked the ticket in person at a travel agency on Nicolae Lorga Street in Chisinau. The Malev Hungarian flight was the cheapest available, departing Moldova at 05.45. It arrived in Copenhagen at 09.15 after a one-hour stopover at Ferihegy in Budapest.

Lilian had asked for a window seat. She hadn't booked in conjunction with anyone else. Nor had she checked in with, or asked to sit next to, anyone else. She'd paid cash for the US$693 return fare.

The return was booked for one week later, but she'd never checked in. Her mobile hadn't been used since the night before her departure and couldn't be traced. It had disappeared off the face of the earth, just like her.

Shortly after Julian's call, Anna heard back from her contact. The company in Moscow that Tarasov's shipment was bound for specialized in radar technology. He didn't yet know who the end-user was. For that last piece of the jigsaw puzzle, he would have to dig some more.

We'd arrived at the port in Odessa to discover that the ferry to Istanbul only sailed on Saturdays and Mondays, and took a couple of days. We'd rerouted ourselves in the direction of the airport and spent the rest of the night in the car. I dropped Lena's pistol into a river and ditched the Beamer, then walked the last two K to the terminal.

We took the Aerosvit Airlines 07.00 flight to Istanbul, arriving at 08.35. We caught the connection to Copenhagen, leaving at 09.00, by the skin of our teeth. There wasn't a problem with visas. Brits and Russians don't need them, and Anna smoothed over the minor hiccup caused by the absence of both a Moldovan exit stamp and a Ukrainian entry stamp with a story about us taking the wrong road out of Transnistria and missing the border post. The immigration guy accepted the explanation, together with all the *lei* that Irina had exchanged for us. This was another former Soviet republic, after all.

While Anna slept, I'd thought about Lilian.

She'd bought herself a return ticket, but that might not be significant. She was bright enough to know she'd have problems at Danish Immigration if she couldn't show an intention to leave. I bet Slobo had told her that.

Anna had told me that citizens of the Republic of Moldova can't just rock up at the check-in desk and jump on the first plane to the EU. Pre-2007, they'd had to report in person to the Danish embassy in Bucharest, in neighbouring Romania, for a tourist visa. Post-2007, an EU Common Visa Application Centre had been set up in the Hungarian embassy in Chisinau to simplify travel to Greece, the Netherlands, Belgium and twelve other 'Schengen treaty' countries.

The Schengen visa was designed to make travelling between its fifteen European member states – which aren't the same as the EU countries – much easier and less bureaucratic, but they're still not issued on the spot. They take ten days to process.

Travelling on a Schengen visa means that the holder can travel to any or all member countries, avoiding the hassle and expense of obtaining a new one for each country. This might have been good for Lilian, but it could be a problem for us. She could have landed in Copenhagen, but then been moved on to Austria, Germany, Belgium, Finland, France, Greece, Iceland, Italy, Luxembourg, Norway, Portugal, Spain, Sweden, or the Netherlands.

There was something else Julian had got from the Hungarians: a scan of all three pages of Lilian's Schengen-visa application form. Besides all the usual personal details, she had had to state the main purpose of the journey (she'd put tourism); duration of stay (up to thirty days); whether her fingerprints had been collected previously for the purpose of applying for a Schengen visa (no, they hadn't); intended date of arrival in the Schengen area (3 March); intended date of departure from the Schengen area (10 March); and surname and first name of the inviting person(s) in the member state(s). If that wasn't applicable, then the name of hotel(s) or temporary accommodation(s) in the member state(s), and the address and email address of the inviting person(s) / hotel(s) / temporary accommodation(s). She'd put Hôtel d'Angleterre, 34 Kongens Nytorv. Was the cost of travelling and living during the applicant's stay covered by the applicant himself / herself? Yes. Means of support? Credit card.

None of her responses meant very much. Plenty of people

bluff in their visa applications and she'd had Slobo helping her on her way.

At the bottom of the form, she'd had to sign that she was aware of and consented to the collection of the data required by this application form, the taking of her photograph and, if applicable, of her fingerprints.

Julian had already checked. They hadn't taken her fingerprints, but she had supplied a photograph; he sent it to my BlackBerry. She looked more or less the same as she had outside the factory. Her hair was a bit longer, that was all. Or it had been. It might be short again by now.

So all we knew was that she had landed in Copenhagen. Julian had been able to confirm she hadn't taken an onward flight. But that also meant jack-shit. She could now be on a train or a car to anywhere in Europe. The only good thing about her being trafficked rather doing a runner was that someone, somewhere, knew where she was.

We didn't have a choice. We had to find the next link in the trafficking chain, then follow whatever we could wring out of him.

2

The moment I saw the Hôtel d'Angleterre I knew we weren't going to be finding Lilian's name anywhere on the register. A big, imposing building overlooking an elegant square in the heart of the city, it was clearly a five-star establishment with fuck-off rooms that would cost at least two thousand kroner (three hundred dollars) a night. When she'd seen she needed a name for her visa application, she must have done a quick Google and chosen the most distinguished. Maybe Slobo had told her it carried a lot more weight than a B-and-B in the hippie quarter.

I parked up.

Anna had gone to book us into an airport hotel while I got a serious wad of kroner from an ATM, organized the car, bought a city guidebook and cajoled a shedload of coins from the shopkeeper. Once we'd checked in, I'd gone to the hotel business centre and bluetoothed Lilian's picture to a printer. Fuck the shower and shave: we'd buy new kit later.

We now had an A4 colour copy each, as well as a map of Christiania downloaded from the Internet and printed off.

The d'Angleterre was as grand inside as out. It wasn't the sort of place to have pictures of its clientele on the wall, but I knew from Anna's Googling that everyone from Winston

Churchill to Tony Blair had stayed there when they were in town.

To the left was a cocktail bar. Reception was to the right. The uniformed guy behind the desk greeted us with an efficient but not over-friendly smile. 'Equality is entrenched in the Danish psyche,' Anna told me. 'Staff don't go out of their way to establish rapport with customers, in any sort of business.'

And there was me thinking they were just miserable.

I produced Lilian's picture and passed it over. 'Have you seen our sister? She would have checked in here ten days ago. We haven't heard from her and – well, we're getting a bit concerned, to be honest. She's travelling alone.'

He studied it hard. He was in his twenties himself. A guest as attractive as Lilian would have registered. I watched his eyes not his lips as he replied. He didn't recognize her. I could have asked if there was anyone else I could check with, but there didn't seem much point. If all other avenues ended in dead ends, we'd come back here and start all over again.

We went back to the car.

'I've been thinking about your treatment.'

'Lack of it, you mean.'

'Why not in Moscow? We would have more time together.'

'More time dribbling and shitting myself. What's the good of that? I don't want it. I certainly don't want you exposed to it.'

'Isn't that my choice?'

'Maybe. But the way I see it, I go on until it's too painful or just too much for us both. Then I take a couple of bottles of pills, we lie down and only you wake up.' I hit the key fob. 'What do you think?'

She opened her door and stared across the roof at me. 'Brilliant. And I get left to clean up the mess.'

3

Christiania was a short distance away. While I drove, Anna scanned the guidebook. In 1971, the abandoned eighty-five-acre military camp at Christianhavn, on the eastern edge of the city, had been taken over by squatters who proclaimed it the 'free town' of Christiania. The police tried to clear the area, but it was the height of the hippie era and people looking for an alternative lifestyle poured in from all over Denmark. The following year, bowing to public pressure, the government allowed the community to continue as a social experiment. About a thousand people had settled in, transforming the old barracks into schools and housing and starting their own collective businesses, workshops and recycling programmes.

'A thousand people on an eighty-five-acre site.' I glanced across at her. 'Where would a concerned sibling start looking?'

'She'll have turned up needing somewhere to stay. There's nowhere you can pay to stay in Christiania. I think Slobo promised to help her do the runner, told her this was the perfect place to hide, and finished off with the oldest trick in the trafficking book: saying he had a friend who would help her and even get her a job.'

'Whatever, she'd also have needed to eat and drink. Even if she's already been moved on, someone must have seen her.'

She ran her finger down the page. 'Car-free Christiania has a market, some craft shops, and several places where you can get coffee and something to eat. The main entrance is on Prinsessegade, two hundred metres north-east of its intersection with Bådsmandsstræde. You can take a guided tour of Christiania. There's a Pusher Street information office next to the Oasen café.'

'Can you get us to that intersection?'

'We're almost there. Left in four or five blocks.'

'Does Pusher Street mean what I think it means?'

She nodded. 'Since 1990, the story of Christiania has been one of police raids on Pusher Street. The police, decked out in riot gear, have patrolled Christiania regularly, staging numerous organized raids leading to some ugly confrontations and arrests.'

She went back to the map page. 'This is the one. Left here.'

I found a space on a street full of bars and cafés just off Prinsessegade. I pushed enough coins into the machine to last us a few hours and stuck the ticket on the dashboard.

We walked a couple of hundred yards to an alleyway. A short way down it, a big wooden sign announced, 'You are entering Christiania.' On the reverse, for our benefit on the way back, it said, 'You are entering the EU.'

An information board told us that guided tours left from there at three in the afternoon. Another showed a camera with a red slash through it. The dealers had never gone away, Anna said. No dealer likes a camera in his face.

We walked between walls plastered with graffiti and murals. A familiar smell hung in the air. The slightly sickly, pungent scent of cannabis thickened the further we went. A woman cycled past us on a bike with a huge wooden box on the front containing a pair of muzzled Rottweilers.

A young guy with dreadlocks stood guard by a fence, radio comms in one hand, oversized spliff in the other. I guessed the system worked like the one the Amish had in the film *Witness*.

One call and the community came running – or, in Christiania's case, the dealers. The guidebook had said that the narcotics police, backed by the Riot Squad, had raided Pusher Street several times, arresting any of the dealers who didn't pack up and run fast enough.

'Does it say why they don't just close the whole place down and be done with it?'

'There would be riots. The hash market turns over millions a year.'

Anna read some more from the guidebook as she walked. Perfect. It made us look like tourists in search of a 'sanctuary for anyone who is tired of the consumerism and routine of everyday life'.

It must have sounded idyllic to a girl raised in an environment of chaos and gangsterdom after the fall of the Iron Curtain. Slobo wouldn't have had to sell this one too hard.

'Turn on, tune in, drop out – whatever. Lovely until the money runs out and you realize you have to get a haircut and some work clothes and earn a living.' I grinned. I was starting to sound like Tresillian.

Graffiti covered every inch of wall.

Living to lower standards for a higher quality of life.

Loud music bounced out at us from somewhere out of sight.

A guy in a sweater full of holes ambled towards us.

'Pusher Street?' Anna showed him the map.

He pointed wearily. Christiania was Copenhagen's second biggest tourist attraction after the Tivoli Gardens and every one of them probably wanted to be able to tell their friends back home they'd dared visit Pusher Street.

'Have you seen this girl?'

Anna produced her picture but he'd already gone.

4

We came to a small market. Three or four stalls sold T-shirts, hats and scarves. Anna showed the stallholders Lilian's photograph but none of them recognized her. I wondered if they would have recognized their own mothers. Everybody looked slightly dazed.

Anna spotted a bar. 'As you said, she had to eat and drink . . .'

We went in. The big airy room was full of guys with wispy beards and woolly hats with earflaps. It was us who looked weird. We did what any concerned family member would do. We went up to the bar and held out Lilian's picture. The girl had pierced eyebrows and a nose-ring. Her hair was bleached.

'Have you seen this girl?'

'I'm sorry, no.'

'Do you mind if we ask your customers?'

'Be my guest. But please buy something.'

I ordered a couple of beers and handed over a fistful of kroner. We left the bottles on the bar and started to circulate. The first table responded to the photo with shakes of the head. So did the next. People did look, but I got the feeling they wouldn't have told us even if they had seen her. I put it down to rage against the machine. 'This is shit, Anna. Let's try that information centre.'

As we turned to leave, a ruddy-faced man in his sixties hauled himself to his feet, as if to follow us out. Then he seemed to think better of it and sat down again. Maybe he was just too stoned or pissed. He had long white hair that needed even more of a wash than we did and a beard that Gandalf would have been jealous of.

I caught Anna's eye and we headed back to his table. She sat opposite him, and I stood alongside. He concentrated very hard on his glass. Everything about him suggested he'd downed a good few whiskies before he'd got to this one.

He nodded at the pictures. His watery eyes seemed to loosen in their sockets. 'Your . . . child?'

'No, my sister. She's run away. She came here, maybe ten days ago. You've seen her?'

He pulled out a packet of Drum and some papers but seemed in no hurry to open them. Anna took the hint and pulled out her readymades. He feigned delighted surprise and helped himself to three.

'You know, many people say that this place saved them when they were at their lowest ebb and had nowhere else to turn.' His English was accented but faultless. 'I'm one of them. I left home when I was fifteen and drifted until I found Christiania.'

He paused to light the first of his recently acquired Camels and sucked in the real deal with the kind of pleasure that only smokers know. Me, I wished we were still in the EU where this shit was outlawed. Anna sparked up too, adding to the pollution.

Gandalf waved his free hand around the commune as if it were his kingdom. 'In the early days we built our own houses in the woods or renovated the old barracks. We had a right to build as we chose. This place is all I know.'

I wasn't sure if the smile that lurked behind the hair was

143

fuelled by happiness or cannabis, but it showed off the three or four yellow tombstones that still clung to his gums in all their glory.

I stuck a finger on Lilian's chin. 'Her name is Lilian Nemova. You seen her?'

'Russian?'

'Moldovan.'

His eyes wobbled as they moved down her picture once more, but only for a fleeting second. 'You do not sound like a Moldovan, brother.'

Anna was getting as pissed off with him as I was. 'He's helping me find her.'

He took a swig from his glass.

I kept an eye on people coming in and leaving the bar. You never knew.

'We were hard-working people here. Artists, socialists, anarchists – people who drank and smoked too much, but we had rules. We have bad people preying on the weak and lonely.' He waved in the vague direction of the free town outside. 'It was the dawn of a new era. A new way of living. Then it all changed. We've even had a murder here – *here, in Christiania!*' He pointed a wrinkled finger at the sugar bowl in front of him like it was the root of all evil. 'It's wrong. It wasn't supposed to be this way.'

He necked the last of his drink.

'But have you seen her?'

He shook his head; he didn't want to look at the photo again. 'These are sad days. Turkish gangs, Palestinian and Balkan gangs, Russian gangs. They are all here.'

I crouched down, elbows on the table, trying for eye-to-eye. 'One of the gangs – the Russians maybe – would they have her?'

He stared into his empty glass and kept shaking his head. He started to cry. Saliva dribbled into his beard.

'Fuck him. Let's get out there. The more people we hit, the

better the chance that whoever lifted her will front us.'

Anna wasn't too sure. 'You think that would be the best thing to do? We might get very dead, very soon.'

'Got a better idea? People aren't exactly falling over themselves to help us, are they? We could be here for days waiting for this twat to get sober.'

5

Back on the street, I studied my map. 'That way.'

There were no signs to tell us we'd arrived, but it wasn't long before we found ourselves on Pusher Street. It was like we'd crossed the border between the fairy kingdom and the land of the trolls. The atmosphere changed abruptly. These were mean streets. Cannabis fumes hung more heavily in the air. Aggressive-looking skinheads, some hooded, stood round flaming metal barrels, furtive and menacing. I watched a young guy approach one group and be steered down an alley. Their job seemed to be to direct buyers and keep an eye out for police.

Everywhere I looked, pit-bull terriers wandered unleashed.

'It's an old Russian trick.' Anna nodded at a dog that should have had tattoos on its front legs. 'They're trained to whisk the stash away from a police raid.'

Large canvas parasols covered makeshift stalls. I stepped under one and eyed the merchandise. Lumps of cannabis and bags of skunk were displayed on a tree trunk and a wooden barrel. I showed the stallholder Lilian's picture and asked in English if he'd seen her. He was about her age. He was dressed in grimy old German Army gear that hadn't been washed since Stalingrad.

As he started to answer, a skinhead with a black sweatshirt strode over from one of the braziers. *'Fuck off!'* He yelled it straight into my face and gave me a shove. I nodded and retreated, hands raised. Too many hard faces were glaring at me to play it any other way, too many pit-bulls at their heels. So much for the Summer of Love.

My anxious sister clasped my arm and guided me away.

I tried my best to look scared, and part of me was. 'If she's shacked up with one of those arseholes, Anna, we could have a problem.'

6

There were hundreds of buildings in Christiania and Lilian could have been holed up in any or none of them. Almost all the businesses, shops and restaurants were located in Christiania City. A network of footpaths and bridges connected the sprawling residential sectors. North of where we were, the town gradually gave way to woods.

The main barracks had been converted into an apartment building called the Ark of Peace. It was the largest half-timbered house in northern Europe, and housed more than eighty people. Then there were another eighty-five acres of old army buildings, run-down trailers and modern self-build wood and brick cottages. Even if everyone was at home, it would take the two of us days to cover the ground.

'We're going to have to split up, Anna. Are you OK with that?'

'No problem.'

I unfolded my map. 'Why don't you start at this vegetarian restaurant, the Morning Place, and the after-school centre, the Raisin House, and carry on down the road into the green residential area? I'll do the bars and clubs round Pusher Street. If we get jack-shit, we RV back at the bar at last light anyway.' I touched her face. 'Any drama, just run.'

Anna gave me a hug and I watched her disappear down the street. Just a few yards away, two roaming dogs suddenly had a turf dispute that erupted into a full-blown fight. Their owners ran over with chains to subdue them. I was in no doubt of what kind of welcome we'd get if we did track Lilian down.

7

The Opera was a music-venue-cum-community-centre in an old brick-layered building at the top end of Pusher Street. The Café Oasis was on the ground floor. Above it was the information office.

I went inside and tried the girl at the till. 'She might have cut her hair. She might have dyed it.' I doubted Lilian would have spent her hard-saved cash on a visit to the stylist, but if she had fallen foul of a trafficking gang there was no telling what look they'd have opted for, and I needed to get people's brains in gear. I scanned the other customers while I was talking. You can concentrate so hard on looking for the next person to quiz or the next bar to go into that the target could walk straight past without you noticing.

The girl shook her head.

I stuck my head inside the music venue. A high ceiling supported by tall, decorated wooden pillars and a red and white dance floor in the shape of a starburst gave it a circus feel. Sofas and armchairs were arranged living-room style along the furthest wall, in stark contrast with the shit and rugs outside. The place was deserted.

I went upstairs to the information office. I drew a blank there too, but at least the guy suggested pinning up a photocopy. I hadn't brought any. I thanked him and said I'd come back later if I'd had no luck.

The Children's Theatre and the Jazz Club also shared the building. Nobody was in either of them. Immediately across the road was a clothes and ethnic handicrafts store, and Marzbar, an Internet café. I visited them both, keeping my eyes skinned.

A long, three-storey grey-stone building that had once been the garrison's arsenal now housed the music venue, Loppen – the Flea – along with a restaurant, a gallery, some hobby workshops, a youth club, and, down by the entrance, the Infocafé and the Christiania post office. It took me more than an hour to cover every option with Lilian's picture.

Back out on Pusher Street, I went into the Sunshine Bakery, the laundry, and behind these, the community kitchen and a bar called the Monkey Grotto. Nothing. I just hoped that people would be starting to hear about the two dickheads bouncing about trying to find a girl. Maybe it would get to the gangs before we started turning up the temperature tonight.

I dropped into another bar, Woodstock, a bit further on, and the tattooist opposite. I bought a grilled-vegetable sandwich in a small gallery and eating-place next door. I moved on to Nemoland, a café and outdoor music venue, with a bar inside and outside, bench tables and parasols, an outdoor stage, and a bistro serving Thai food. There were palm trees, Greek- and Chinese-style decorations, lots of blue bench tables, but not one sniff of recognition of Lilian from the locals.

I began to think it might be time to take another route. Plan B was double-edged. It might lead us straight to Lilian – or fuck us up so completely that we'd never get anywhere near her.

8

I headed for the RV just before last light. Noisy revellers, a lot of them already the worse for wear, were streaming into Christiania for a night of music, drink and drugs. Outside in the city, the street-lights would be burning. Here in the free town, bare bulbs hanging behind windows struggled to do the same job.

Moving as fast as I could without drawing attention to myself, I jinked down a series of lefts and rights, stopping only once to check the map. I ran into Anna on the way.

'Anything?'

'Nothing. But I did get a call from Moscow. He's found out the end user.'

'A company?'

She shook her head. 'A country. The radar is for the Pantsyr-S1E and heading for the Iranian military. You know what an S1E is?'

'Yeah – ground-to-air missile. Tarasov's making the boards for the missile systems.'

We carried on towards the RV arm in arm. Guys with radio comms and roll-ups the size of RPGs lingered in the shadows, their pit-bulls snarling at their heels.

We eventually got bored with pushing our way through

groups of dithering tourists and local teenagers toking their heads off and darted down a side street.

A figure stepped out from the shadows, a white guy in his early twenties in a black leather jacket and old army cargoes. His head was shaved. Even in this light I could see his eyes were bloodshot and out on stalks.

'You want cannabis?'

'No.'

'Cocaine? Heroin?'

It sounded like a threat rather than an invitation to sample tonight's special.

We didn't break step. 'No.'

Walking backwards just ahead of us, he gestured towards the rear of a nearby building. 'Come with me, come down here. I can get you anything. Ice? Ket?'

I shook my head. 'We don't want anything.'

'If you don't want to buy, what are you doing here? You cops?'

Anna was just as sharp with him. 'We don't have money.'

He flexed his fist. 'Yeah, right, and I don't have a dick.'

We kept going.

He slid his right hand into his pocket. 'I'll cut you both. Buy some stuff or fuck off, cop.'

It wasn't a knife he tugged from his pocket, but a radio.

Anna pulled out the picture. 'Have you seen her?'

He didn't even bother looking. 'Fuck you.'

We carried straight on past him. He wasn't going to follow us onto the main. Darkness was where he lived. 'Fuck you, bitches – got no money. Suck my dick and I'll give you a freebie. Hey, everybody, look out – cops.'

We were opposite the entrance to the alley that led back to Prinsessegade. We were going against the flow. People were pouring past the sign that told us we were entering the EU, three or four abreast.

9

Gandalf was in the corner where we'd left him. It looked as though his glass had been refilled a good few more times. An ashtray was piled with roll-up ends. The one in his mouth had gone out and its ash had taken up residence in his beard.

He looked up blearily to see who had come into the not-so-busy bar and went straight back into waffle mode, as if he'd only finished his last sentence to us a few seconds ago. 'Gangs. Violence. It's the government's fault. We used to sell the best hash in Europe here, right here in Christiania. But then the *politi* bust the trade. Then the gangs . . .'

Anna sat down at his table. 'Maybe you could tell us a little more about the gangs. Where are the Russians? Do you know where we can find them?'

I sat beside her as Gandalf continued his rant. His eyes wobbled and bounced like a one-armed-bandit display but never made contact with either of us.

'We are citizens of Denmark. We pay our taxes—'

I thought he was going to end his sentence but he started a new one instead.

'Our music halls and art galleries have contributed to Denmark's culture and commerce. We have a free health clinic. We shelter and look after addicts, alcoholics, even homeless . . .'

He raised a nicotine-stained index finger to make sure we understood the full weight of the next category. '. . . and *madmen*. The cops still do nothing but hassle us. But do they do anything to the gangs? No! We are used by them – what can we do?'

Anna pulled out a pack of Camels and offered him one. 'Do you know where the Russians are?' She pulled out Lilian's picture again. 'Where can we find them?'

He refused the cigarette. 'Why do you think I would know? I know nothing.' He was angry or scared, it was hard to work out which.

His fist went down hard on the table; hard enough to make the glass rattle. *'Nothing.'*

His head went down again. Tears rolled from his eyes. 'I just cannot take any more . . .'

We left him to it, and ordered coffees and open salmon sandwiches at the bar. Money upfront, of course.

'I think we're going to get a big fuck-all tonight. She may already be drugged up and fucked up, but we won't find her on the street. Those lads out there on Pusher, they're the low end of the market. They're not catering for the kind of customer who's looking to drop his Armani trousers, and they're not traffickers. We won't get near the Russians via them. We'll just rub them up the wrong way and find ourselves on the receiving end of a pit-bull.'

Anna was waiting to see where this was going. 'So?'

'So, get your mobile out.' I closed my eyes, trying to visualize the international number on Slobo's call register.

'Check the code for Demark. Is it four five?'

Her thumbs clicked away as I got my head in gear. It wasn't exactly instant recall, but it didn't need to be. I tended to remember the shapes of numbers rather than the numbers themselves.

'Yes – plus four five.'

'Slobo had one international number on his mobile. It began with four five.'

'Couldn't Jules have traced it?'

Our brews arrived and I waited for the bartender to put some distance between my mouth and his ears.

'Anna, Jules has given me the all-singing, all-dancing BlackBerry, but it doesn't mean I want to get in touch with him and Tresillian every time I need Directory Enquiries.'

I buttoned my lip as the sandwiches appeared.

'The other thing you should know is that I think Jules is a good guy – but I don't know Tresillian well enough to trust him, so until I find out what this shit is really about, I'd rather tell them both as little as possible.'

I reached for Anna's iPhone as she started to eat and tapped out the number on her keypad until its rhythm felt right in my head.

'This call could fuck up Lilian for good. I don't know for sure what we'll find at the other end. But I do know that we've already rattled a few bars on a few cages – and maybe one in particular.'

'Do it.'

I dialled and waited for the ring tone. It sparked up a few seconds later.

Nothing for three rings.

Anna raised a hand. 'Hang up.'

I did as she asked. I knew she'd have a good reason.

'Now dial again.'

I dialled and she waited until the ring tone sounded in my ear, then pulled the phone away. The nineties Nokia ring tone fired up across the room. This time it woke Gandalf up enough for him to reach into his pocket.

'*Hej?*'

I closed down. He gave his mobile a shake, had another listen, then shoved it back into his coat.

Then he looked up and saw us both staring at him from the bar, Anna's iPhone still in my hand.

He knew he'd fucked up. He got to his feet and headed for the door.

Anna made to follow but I held her back. 'He won't get far. We don't run. We walk.'

The dim lighting in the street was still effective enough for a quick scan to reveal Gandalf's whereabouts. He might have thought he was doing a Usain Bolt, but his ageing legs and pissed-up brain were letting him down.

He took the corner as we started to push our way through the crowds. It took no time to catch up and push him onto a muddy patch between two barrack blocks.

I pulled him up from the shit by his arms.

'Please, please . . . Kill me – yes, please kill me. I cannot take any more guilt. They make me do it . . . Kill me, please. I beg you, end it . . .'

I shoved him against a rotting wooden panel, which shut him up long enough for Anna to start questioning him.

'Where is she? Where did she go?'

He looked at me, wild-eyed. 'I don't know. They took her. I don't know where she'll be now.'

'Who took her? *Who?*'

More tears fell. He clasped his hands together in prayer. 'It wasn't supposed to be like this. I just meet the girls, that's all. I meet them and escort them. They make me do it. I have no choice. Please, I can't take any more. Kill me now . . .' His hands parted and he brought them up to cover his face.

Anna moved in closer. 'Who are they?'

'Russians.'

'Where do you take them?'

'To the green house – the house near Loppen.'

I grabbed Anna's arm. 'I know it. Let's go, fuck him.'

He fell to his knees and grabbed me as I turned. His arms tight around my legs, he sobbed into my jeans. 'All those young girls. The lost, the hiding. They sell them. They fill them with drugs and they sell them.' His shoulders heaved.

I pushed him off me and he fell back into the mud.

'I have nowhere to go. They would throw me out of

Christiania. I wanted to tell the *politi*, but what would they do? I had to do what they told me.' He looked up at me, still pleading. 'Please, please, kill me. I am dead now anyway. I am so tired. Those girls, those poor girls . . .'

He curled into the foetal position. I bent down and rolled him onto his back.

Anna tried dragging me away. 'Nick, no – don't!'

I shook myself free, wrenched aside his beard and gripped his neck. My hands started to tighten.

'Thank . . . you . . . I am so . . . sorry . . .' His voice rasped, but there was relief in his eyes.

I leant closer, my mouth alongside his ear. 'Fuck you. You're living. You can remember every girl you've handed over to those arseholes. You had a choice, and you took the easy way out. But not this time.' I fished in his pocket for his mobile before letting go of him. Then I took Anna's hand and headed back out into the street.

10

I followed Anna up the flight of broken wooden steps and onto the veranda of the house with flaking green paint, keeping a few paces behind her as a good BG would. I'd quizzed the call register on Gandalf's phone before binning it, not expecting anything much. He was either more switched on than he looked, or – more likely – his trafficker mates weren't taking any chances.

The house was long past being a home. A rusty fridge sat discarded by the front door. The wood under the peeling paint was rotten. The place looked more like a crack den than the HQ of an international business enterprise.

I stayed close as Anna banged on the glass panel in the top half of the door. Light filtered weakly through the minging net curtains that hung behind it.

Footsteps echoed on bare boards. The curtains twitched and the door opened just enough to show a chin unevenly coated with bum fluff. Its owner nodded at whatever Anna said, but still went to close the door on us. Anna's foot shot into the gap. She bollocked him in fast, aggressive Russian. The runt gave up. He nodded and closed the door.

Anna waited, not looking back at me as more footsteps thundered towards us. I could hear voices, then saw movement and shadows through the netting. She had told me that these guys were greedy. That, above all, they were businessmen. A sale was a sale. We were about to find out if she was right.

The door opened. Two, maybe three, bodies filled the hallway. The first one's hands reached out. Anna tried to duck out of the way but was too slow. He grabbed her by the hair and dragged her in, a pistol jammed into her neck. There was nothing I could do now, except follow.

She stumbled through the entrance. The runt already had a weapon on me. A second body reached out and gripped my coat. He shoved the muzzle of a weapon into my neck and pushed me down onto the floorboards as the door slammed shut behind me.

All three extra bodies were well into their thirties and wore black North Face parkas with fur-lined hoods. Anna went ballistic at them and they couldn't give a fuck. I heard the rustle of nylon as they went about their checks Russian-style. She kept up the bollocking, as you would if you were in the business. I tried to look completely unconcerned as my jeans pockets were pulled out and the BlackBerry was lifted.

There was an old wooden staircase dead ahead, uncarpeted, dimly lit by a bulb with no shade. A dank smell filled the air, strong and sickly, as if the house hadn't been aired for years.

The biggest of the North Face boys got his dibs on Anna. He leered at his mates as he ran his hands over her body. She glared back at him. The stream of Russian that poured out of her told him that she was ready to bite. He seemed to like whatever she was saying, though, and gave her breasts an extra frisk so he could hear more.

The runt was obviously in charge of storage. He stood there enjoying the show, with both of Lilian's pictures, our maps and mobiles clutched in his hands.

I heard movement at the top of the stairs and looked up to see two wide-eyed teenage faces. The girls were on their hands and knees, trying to hide from view, but captivated by the

aggression on the floor below. Apart from oversized T-shirts –
one from a Guns N' Roses concert, the other a plain grey that
had once been white – they were naked. Their hair was a mess,
but pushed back far enough for me to see that both had thin,
painted eyebrows that made them look like dolls.

They almost jumped out of their skins as Mr Big caught sight
of them. They shot from sight as he dragged himself away
from Anna's breasts and double-stepped it up there, shrieking
like the world's angriest parent.

Anna and I were hauled to our feet and pushed against the
wall. These guys were big and aggressive, but what was more
worrying was their air of who-gives-a-fuck. They looked like
they'd just as easily kill us as offer us coffee.

Anna took the lead. She began to talk to the runt. It sounded
like she still wanted to meet the boss. Her tone was measured,
persuasive and even – despite being punctuated by screams
and shouts from upstairs as the girls got a good slapping. She
had to speak up to be heard, and managed to show no interest
whatsoever in the drama unfolding above us.

The runt pointed towards the back of the house, but it was
clear I wasn't invited.

She didn't budge. She turned and pointed at me. This time it
sounded like she was telling them to fuck off. Her words were
quick and aggressive. The slaps and screams stopped and the
girls began to beg.

The runt asked her something.

Whatever she answered, it seemed to work. He strode off
down the corridor. Anna hadn't looked at her hired help once
since we walked up to the building. She was playing it well.
She gave me an order in Russian and signalled what I was to
do. I stayed behind her along the short stretch of corridor and
as we went through a doorway at the rear. Our footsteps
sounded unnaturally loud on the bare boards.

The kitchen was large and filled with smoke. A man smaller
than even the runt – but clearly infinitely more powerful – was

sitting with a brew, drawing hard on an untipped cigarette. The girls and Mr Big were now directly above us. I knew I couldn't show the slightest interest in the sounds. We were buyers: we knew these girls needed to be kept in hand.

The odd glimmer of makeshift street-lighting managed to fight its way through what was left of the blind. It was obvious now why they kept their coats on. It was colder and more miserable in here than it was outside. There was no heating. This was a meeting place. People weren't here all the time.

The only thing that looked like it might work was a Nespresso machine like the one in my flat. It sat among the general shit by the sink, next to its discarded packaging.

Anna didn't wait to be asked. She went over to the table and sat opposite him. Bed springs started to squeak above us. I heard a muffled sob.

Anna ignored it all and kept talking, cool and calm. In case he wasn't getting the message, she leant over and helped herself to a cigarette from the pack that sat next to an old dinner plate piled high with butts. She lit it with a plastic throwaway that lay next to his mobile.

He gave me a cursory glance, out of boredom more than anything. I looked away. He would have expected nothing less. I was Anna's BG. My total focus was on my principal, not on trying to establish eye contact with anyone else.

Mr Big was really getting into it. His breathless shouts were followed by a couple more slaps and an anguished scream.

Anna was playing a blinder. She exuded confidence. She sounded like she really was here to buy herself some girls.

I looked around. A small bread knife lay beside half a loaf near the coffee machine. That was the only weapon I could see. The corridor was blocked by the North Face crew, who were leaning against the wall, maybe waiting their turn upstairs. The door behind Anna was bolted. If the shit hit the fan, all I could do was to hold them off long enough for her to unbolt it and run.

The springs stopped squeaking and grunts were replaced by sobs. I still didn't move a muscle, but I made myself a promise then: for as long as I lived, I'd track these fuckers down – and their mates – and kill them.

Anna sparked up another of the boss's cigarettes and put the lighter back on the table. The smoke curled from her mouth and nose before she spoke. The only words I recognized now sounded like names of countries. He was still calm. He lit himself another cigarette too and took such a mega-drag I could see the paper burn down like a fuse.

Anna sat and waited while he thought about what she'd said. But she didn't wait for long. She stood up before he'd delivered his answer: she'd had enough of this bullshit.

I turned towards the North Face guys. I wanted them to know that we intended to leave in one piece. Fuck the mobiles and the other stuff. I moved into the corridor just in time to see Mr Big give his mates a very satisfied grin and put his coat back on.

The small guy started talking. Anna stopped, turned back, went to the table and sat down. She helped herself to another cigarette from his pack.

He gave an order to one of the North Faces. I heard the front door open and close.

We waited in silence. The two of them smoked. The boss checked his mobile now and again for messages as Anna sat back, picking tobacco from her lips. The sobbing above us gradually subsided.

After three or four minutes the sound of clubland laughter echoed down the hallway and a new body appeared. Dressed in a brown overcoat over a black polo neck, he was so slim his head looked as if it really belonged on someone else's shoulders. Everything about him was immaculate. His nails were manicured, possibly even polished. Not one dark brown hair from what was left on his head was out of place. He didn't give Anna or me as much as a glance as he headed for the small guy's side of the table.

He jerked his head. 'She speak English?'

He was no Russian: his accent was Scouse, deep, strong and quick.

The small guy shrugged.

The Scouser took a seat next to his mate.

Anna stubbed out what was left of her cigarette on the plate and frowned impatiently, wanting to get on with business. 'Who are you?'

'I'm Santa fucking Claus. What the fuck's it to you? Why have you come to us?'

He wasn't exactly cross-eyed, but they looked ever so slightly inwards. He reminded me of someone I'd known back in my battalion days. Robot was permanently AWOL. He'd always either gone to a Millwall match, or got arrested after one. His big pleasure in life was smashing up shop fronts or battering other teams' fans with a hammer. Being in the army had messed up his social life.

I always kept clear of Robot. He was as crazy and unpredictable as he looked. One day he walked into someone in the cookhouse by mistake. Instead of 'Why don't you look where you're going?' the guy said, 'Why don't you go where you're looking?' It cracked us up, but Robot didn't see the funny side. The squaddie he'd collided with was in hospital for weeks with a fractured jaw.

Anna relaxed back into her chair. 'I want girls. I'm expanding into Italy, France, Germany. I want to pick them up from here, and do my own distribution.'

The Scouser leant over and examined the last cigarette in the pack. With a curl of the lip he extracted a silver case from an inside pocket. He flipped it open, selected an untipped cancer stick of his own and bounced it up and down in his lips as he spoke. 'What's your name?' He reached for the lighter.

'Anna.' Her tone was assured. She was going for it.

The Scouser dipped into his coat and pulled out Lilian's

pictures, along with our mobiles. 'What the fuck's this shite about?'

Anna didn't miss a beat. 'She is one of mine, from Moldova.'

He smiled. 'Not any more.'

Anna sat back and accepted the news with a slow nod. 'Is she upstairs?'

'Not now. Those two are just perks for the lads.' He waved an arm towards the doorway. 'Can't be all work, no play. Know what I mean?'

She didn't bother answering. 'The hard part is getting the girls into Europe. If you can do that, why don't I just come to you? It will make my life easier.' She retrieved the pictures from the table and screwed them up. 'Do you have girls for sale, or am I wasting my time?'

'That depends.'

She pointed a finger at him. 'I want young ones. No crack whores or ugly pigs the Turks have already finished with. I want the ones you get fresh from here. No scars, no skin ink.' She draped an arm coolly over the back of her chair.

He put cigarette and lighter to one side. 'Who wants them? Who sent you?'

She laughed. 'Why? Are you with Animal Welfare? You want to make sure they go to good homes? Now, do you have some for me to see, or what? I want a good price. If I get that, we can do business. A lot more business. But young. No more than twenty-one, twenty-two.'

The Scouser flicked a speck of ash off his coat, then studied her through the cloud of smoke that still hung over the table. He finally shrugged and put his hands in the air. 'Tell you what, give me a number. Maybe I'll call you.'

'No. Fuck you.' She stood up, grabbed our mobiles and turned, ready to leave.

He waved an arm. 'For fuck's sake, calm down. Sit down a minute.' He pulled out a pen and wrote on the cigarette packet.

She came and stood beside me. She wasn't going to do fuck-all of what he said.

He threw the empty packet at her. 'Be at that address tomorrow. I'll see what I can do. Wear one layer of clothes. That coat. And have a fucking bath, will you? You smell and look like shite.' He pointed at me. 'And no fucking ape.'

She had what she wanted. She turned towards the door, confidently expecting the North Faces to part like the Red Sea.

PART FIVE

1

Schiphol Airport, Amsterdam
Wednesday, 17 March
09.25 hrs

The flight from Copenhagen only took ninety minutes and landed on time. We'd followed our new mate Robot's advice and bought new gear and day sacks to carry it in, then gone back to the hotel for a shower. Of course Anna had kept her coat.

I reached into my brown-leather charity-shop bomber jacket and pulled out my passport. I'd put it into the right-hand inside pocket so I had to use my left to take it out. The action was awkward enough to remind me I was doing something unusual: that I was Nicholas Smith, not Nick Stone. Julian's guys hadn't exactly pushed the creative envelope there, but it fitted my alias business cover. Nick Smith was an unemployed satellite-dish engineer. He'd only ever worked for small outfits. You never used a well-known company like Sky or BT as cover. If you did and got caught, they'd go ballistic. Apart from anything else, you'd be putting their genuine personnel at risk. They could become a target for reprisals.

In my well-worn jeans, bomber and Timberlands I was just

one of the thousands of Brit workers moving in and out of Schiphol and other EU airports every day. They spilt out of the no-frills flights from Gatwick and East Midlands, day sacks and wheelies in hand so they could bypass the luggage carousels and get to work. With a couple of days' growth, I really looked the part. Nick Smith was in good company as he approached the Immigration desks.

Being unemployed is always good cover. You don't have to go into detail about who you work for and risk having it checked. Chances are, you won't be questioned going from one EU country to another, but you never know. All I needed was enough to get me through the first layer of security.

Anna was four or five places behind me in the queue. My cover didn't sit well with her in tow, and that was one of the reasons why we weren't together. The other was that the meeting Robot had lined up for this morning was our best and maybe only chance of getting hold of Lilian. If for any reason we got lifted together, that chance would evaporate.

My passport was now in my right hand. I flicked the picture page open with my thumb, ready for the scanner. The flat screens beyond the desk by the luggage carousel showed newsreels of yesterday's suicide bombings and Taliban attacks in Kabul. The caption said the death toll had reached double figures.

I recognized the square near the war victims' hospital, just down the road from the Iranian embassy. It now had a massive hole in the ground where one of the car bombs had kicked off, and the buildings around it were in ruins. It was the way of things now. Back in the studio, they rounded off the piece with some new accusations that Islamabad trained and funded the Taliban, and Pakistan had refused to use US technology in their nuclear-energy systems.

I'd been there before too – and I didn't blame them. Word had got around after the al-Kibar adventure. President Zardari and his mates didn't fancy the Americans tripping the kill switches at Zero Hour and making free with their airspace.

The kill switches in the al-Kibar ground-to-air defences really did work. There was no illumination of Ra'am's F-15s as they went into their attack profile. But the real reason the Americans approved the mission was to send the Iranians a clear message. Which had to be why they were getting their kit direct from Tarasov, these days.

It was my turn to approach the desk. One glance at Nick Smith's photograph and the Dutch immigration officer waved me through.

2

I picked up the keys for a Fiat Panda while Anna headed for the Radisson, opposite the terminal. It would be easy to park in highly congested streets, and it wouldn't draw too much attention to itself. It would blend in even more once I'd installed the baby seat that the very tall blonde woman at the Budget desk passed over with a smile. I liked the Dutch. They spoke perfect English and even looked like us. Maybe that's why the Costa del Clog had taken over from Spain as every self-respecting Brit villain's hideout of choice.

I handed her Nick Smith's MasterCard. It had about £2,000 left out of its £5,000 limit. You can't do without credit cards. They're uncomfortably easy to track, but you need them for things like car hire and flights. Try to pay cash and you'll be flagged up as a possible terrorist or, in this neck of the woods, drug-dealer or criminal.

Half an hour later, we were following the A10 north, day sacks tucked alongside the baby seat. There hadn't been time to go to the room. All the earlier flights had been fully booked, and the clock was ticking.

Anna was navigating with the map Budget had given us. The place was heaving with blue motorway signs and glass-fronted office blocks – we could have been driving along the

M4 into London. I even passed a service station with signs for BP and a Wild Bean coffee shop.

Anna told me we had a while before we hit the city exit. 'Do you know Amsterdam? Do you know where this—'

'Used to. When I was a young soldier in Germany, I used to go to the Dutch camp to buy stuff because everything was cheaper. A tank unit was billeted there – good lads. We played football with them and went downtown as a gang, that sort of thing. We even went on a couple of trips to Amsterdam with them, doing what young soldiers do. We out-drank them, of course.' I gave her a grin. 'But only just.'

'What is it with soldiers?' She wasn't impressed. But she probably knew I was trying to keep her mind off the meeting and what went along with it.

I suddenly realized I had a bit of a lump in my throat. That sort of carry-on had stopped years ago, but until the day I'd walked into Kleinmann's consulting rooms the memories of those times had always brought a smile to my face. Thinking about them now just made me miserable. Not the events them-selves, but the thinking about them. Was this what happened when you knew the clock was ticking?

The sun was bright, even though it was starting to spit a little with rain. I pulled the visor down to protect my eyes and Anna handed over a couple of Smarties.

As I swallowed them, something weird happened. I started to think about the people I'd fucked over. Not work people, but the real ones – women mostly, who I'd messed around through naïvety, stupidity, or just not giving a shit. What had happened to them all? Did they think of me? What did they think of me? I didn't even know where my ex-wives lived, let alone anyone else, but should I go and say sorry, like an alcoholic starting out on the Twelve Steps?

Was I good or bad, all things considered? Was there a heaven and a hell? If there was, I knew which of the two I'd be heading for.

For the first time ever, I found myself thinking about what happens when you die. Maybe you discover all the secrets of the universe in a nano-second. Or maybe an old man with a long white beard presses your off button and then there's oblivion. Part of me wanted there to be something that went on afterwards – even if it was in a place where you had to meet all the people you'd fucked over and try to be best mates with them. I rather liked that idea. There were a few times I should have been a better person and done the right thing, rather than what I was getting paid to do. Actually, more than a few.

I was starting to scare myself here. Fuck this. I made myself cut away. I'd always preferred action to thought. Maybe that was why I'd wanted this job: it was the one thing that could stop me thinking about that kind of shit. The fact was: I was going to die. Getting shot at, you know you stand a chance of getting killed – but you don't *know* it for sure. And every second you were still alive was a bonus. I was on Death Row now, with the date of my execution pretty much in the firing squad's diary.

I closed my eyes for a second, as if that was going to block everything. I turned the radio on, but the Dutch presenter sounded like he was clearing his throat after every syllable.

Anna had been busy with her iPhone. She was inputting the meeting place so her sat-nav app could tell us the best route.

'This is our exit.'

I peeled off the motorway, thankful that I had to start changing gear and going round roundabouts, anything to keep the weird stuff at bay. The architecture changed from glass and steel extravagance to boring two-storey rectangles.

The coalition government had just collapsed and it was election time. Huge billboards had been erected so the competing parties had somewhere to slap their posters. The only face I recognized was the smiling blond-haired right-winger, Geert Wilders, whose anti-Islamic views had barred him from the UK.

174

They had the same arguments over here as we did about the war in Afghanistan, but ours hadn't yet brought down a government. The Dutch had about 2,500 troops over there and had taken a lot of casualties. Now it looked like they were all coming home. Their mums would be pleased, but I wasn't sure the boys themselves would be: they were good lads and wouldn't want to leave the job half finished.

The iPhone's GPS was up and running.

'Another thirty minutes, depending on traffic.'

The address Robot had given her was a café on Herengracht, one of the three main canals. It was close to the city centre, and deep in *Van der Valk* country.

3

We crossed a bridge and turned left onto Herengracht. The houses looked too large for families to live in. A lot of them were offices for banks, lawyers and architects.

Anna put her phone down. 'It's down towards the other end. On the junction with Bergstraat.'

'Got it.'

'As soon as we get there we turn left.' She checked her watch. 'We've still got twenty minutes. All good.'

'I'm going to try to park on the side road. You need to be set up and waiting for him. If anything spooks you, get up and walk. Don't take any chances. Last night was bad enough.'

Her eyes stayed on the road.

'Any fuck-ups and we get separated, we meet back at the hotel. No one knows about it. It's just ours.'

'There – up on the left, by the junction.'

I slowed down, which made a couple of cyclists very happy, but really because I wanted to give us better eyes on the café. It was bang on the junction.

Five or six people were braving the chill to eat their breakfast at tables outside. The canal was less than ten metres away on the other side of the road.

I took the left up Bergstraat. The street was much narrower, with houses on both sides. It was bollarded all along. There was no parking. Behind a window in one of the houses, a woman sat on a stool in her underwear. I looked at the next house. Her neighbour was in the same line of business.

I drove the fifty metres to the end of the street and turned left. I found a pay-and-display space. I did a three-point turn so I'd be facing her.

I wanted to make sure that what I'd said had registered. 'You must keep your back to the canal, OK?'

She nodded.

'If anything doesn't feel right, you get up and walk.'

I got no response.

'Don't fuck about, Anna. We don't know what we're up against. Anything dodgy, just walk away and we'll sort it out some other way.'

She nodded again.

'Make sure he takes a seat facing the canal so I can get a good look at him.'

She tucked her phone into the glove compartment and got out of the car.

I gave her a couple of seconds, then went off and bought a ticket. The guy at the *bureau de change* hadn't been happy to change so many of my kroner into euro coins, but I'd insisted. I crossed the road and walked along the canal. I stopped to admire the view. I could see Anna was already at a table. She'd taken the one right on the end by the pavement. She had her cigarettes out and a waitress had already pounced on her.

I strolled to one of the seats by the canal, about seventy metres from Anna's back.

The street was full of young mums with their kids. Even the dogs had shiny hair. Everything was pleasant and ordered. The air smelt of coffee and grilled cheese.

Anna's brew turned up and she smoked, drank and waited. As I soaked up the atmosphere, I checked for anyone else doing the same, staking out the meeting place before Robot's mate turned up.

I sat and waited for another ten minutes. A bald head in jeans appeared from the direction of the bridge we'd crossed. He looked like a bouncer or a Russian billionaire. He wasn't fat, but he could have done with losing a stone. Beneath his black-leather bomber jacket his gut strained against his shirt. He spotted Anna and went straight over. She gestured at the bench opposite her but he wanted to sit alongside.

He was going to search her.

Not a drama, but I'd wanted him facing me so I could do a walk-past, maybe grab a picture or some video footage with the BlackBerry for Jules. I would now either have to get up and walk straight towards them, or wander down Herengracht and then come back. Either way, I'd stick out like a sore thumb.

I could still walk past, then do a full 360 round the block, but I wasn't going to leave Anna unprotected for that long. It was better to stay put and give up on the photo. Maybe there'd be a chance to follow him after the meet.

They spoke with their faces inches apart. Both of them smoked. He refused a drink when the girl appeared.

After two or three minutes he got out his mobile. He said something to Anna and she nodded. Then she stubbed out the rest of her cigarette.

My view was suddenly blocked by a crimson Lexus 4x4 with darkened windows that had emerged from Bergstraat and pulled up right next to them. I got to my feet and walked towards them.

I crossed the road in time to see her blonde hair and the bald head ducking into the back of the wagon. I couldn't see if she was doing it voluntarily or under duress.

I was close enough now to hear the door shut, even see my own reflection in the side windows as the Lexus made a left.

I turned up Bergstraat, keeping to a slow tourist amble. But as soon as the Lexus was out of sight, I broke into a run. The women in the windows looked at me like I was a madman.

I jumped into the Panda and hit the ignition, narrowly missing a cyclist as I pulled out. I gunned it towards Herengracht and turned left.

The Lexus had gone.

4

I had to put my foot down and risk running someone over – there was no other way. My eyes were glued to the road ahead. I braked hard at every junction and stared down it for a second or two before continuing. The Panda's engine screamed its complaint. So did the people on the pavement.

I reached the top of the street. If I went left, I'd be going into the centre. If I went right, it would be to the harbour bay and then out of the city. If I was going to top her, where would I go? I threw it right, jumping a red light. Horns honked. Fuck 'em.

I snatched up a gear as the rev counter hit red. The traffic lights were suspended on wires across the junction ahead. They were on red too. A long line of vehicles tailed back towards me. There was nothing I could do. I was stuck.

The honkers from the last junction caught up with me and stared daggers. I jumped out and climbed onto the Panda's roof. The steel buckled beneath my feet, but I caught a hint of crimson near the front of the queue, in the right-hand lane. The Lexus was aiming for the northern, industrial, side of the city.

The lights went green. I jumped back in and pushed forward, willing them not to change again before I got through. I was flapping even more now.

I saw the Lexus turn right as the lights went to amber. I was two cars back from the junction. The one ahead of me stopped. I glanced behind me for bikes and mounted the kerb. I eased my way past. It wasn't a popular move. Every driver in Amsterdam stood on his horn.

I bumped my way back down onto the road and edged into the traffic heading right. There were two lanes. I pushed into the outside one, trying to get my foot down as I wove between vehicles. The Lexus was maybe four or five ahead. I had a better view of it now we were starting to go downhill. We were heading under the bay.

A sign for the next turn-off showed a graphic of a factory with a smoking chimney and the words Noord 5.

I went into the tunnel, still in the outside lane. About halfway through we all passed a police car on the inside lane. I didn't know if we were speeding but the Lexus and the rest of the traffic didn't seem concerned. Nobody slowed. I went for it.

The Lexus manoeuvred across the lanes, reaching the inside as we emerged into daylight. He was taking the turn-off. I glanced over my shoulder as I moved over. The police car was coming up behind me.

The Lexus took a right at the top of the hill just as the lights turned red. I checked my mirror. The police car was right up my arse. I had to sit there. The signs to Noord 5 now showed more little factories with smoking chimneys, this time with boats parked up alongside them.

The lights changed and I turned right. The police car came with me. I stuck to 60 k.p.h. We had left *Van der Valk* country far behind. The buildings here were local authority two-up, two-down monstrosities surrounded by muddy swathes of what might once have been grass. There were little Dutch touches like dormer windows, but the streets weren't lined with milkmaids with blonde pigtails and clogs. All I saw were black or South East Asian women, and many more of unknown origin completely burqa'd up. The weather had changed too:

Noord 5 seemed to have its own micro-climate. Everyone was wrapped in a long coat to fight the cold and the dark clouds that were gagging to dump on them.

I paralleled the long side of a rectangular market covered with plastic sheeting. Cheap clothes hung on rails next to stalls piled high with big bottles of cola and shampoo. Nearby houses had boarded-up windows and numbers painted on the brickwork because they'd fallen off the doors. Kerbs were choked with rusty, minging old cars. Sink estates are the same the world over. The only difference here was that Iranian or Turkish flags hung from every other sill.

I took the first option at the next roundabout. The police car carried straight on. The Lexus must have come this way, but I didn't know which of the three exits it had taken.

I headed along the southern end of the market towards another, smaller, roundabout with another three exits. Where now? I had multiple options to cover. All I could do was cruise with my eyes peeled.

I went with the flow. Everyone I saw was in shit state. It was as if they'd been dumped here and forgotten.

I slowed to a crawl and stared down every side street.

Nothing.

I drove on.

5

An hour and a half later, I was flapping more with every passing minute. I kept telling myself she was a switched-on girl. She knew how to handle herself. She'd dealt with the Russians. But that meant fuck-all. I wanted to find her. I *needed* to find her.

For the last thirty minutes I'd been parked up by the market, as close as I could get to the stretch of dual carriageway that ran between the small roundabout and the big one – the last known location I had for the Lexus.

Last light was in twenty minutes. After that, I'd go back to the RV, the hotel, and hope that she'd turn up.

I was on the far side of the bay. North-west of here was the canal that connected it with the North Sea and the commercial waterways of Europe. That was why Amsterdam was a hub for trafficking drugs and women.

I was tucked into a line of vehicles. Kids on mopeds screamed up and down, helmets perched on the top of their heads and leaning so far back they could have been auditioning for *Easy Rider*. Women trundled past, laden with plastic shopping bags. Not one of them gave me a second glance. They were all too busy keeping their own shit together to worry about anyone else's.

A crimson shape came into view, heading towards the small roundabout. It was definitely a Lexus. I wanted to start the engine and be ready to roll but had to wait until it had gone past and committed to an exit. Everything had to look normal. He mustn't see me reacting. I guessed he was going to take the third option, towards the larger roundabout, and then right, back through the tunnel.

I couldn't see anything or anyone through the windows as it passed. It surprised me by taking the second left, into the housing estate by the market.

I followed, engine screaming. No way was I going to lose this fucker now, until I knew if she was inside. If she wasn't, I would have to take action with the bald head and his mates, and get them to tell me where she was. Fuck finding Lilian. That could wait.

The road widened. Some of the shops already had their lights on. The Lexus's brake lights glowed. It looked like he was about to pull over. I slowed, ready to abandon the car at the kerb if they got out and walked.

He wasn't pulling over. He was making a turn. He swung the vehicle right round until he faced me head on.

I was going to have to let him pass before I reacted.

I pulled up outside a kebab shop next to a rank of clapped-out taxis. Lads leant against the bonnets, smoking and chatting, wrapped up against the cold. The Lexus had stopped. The rear door opened and I caught a glimpse of her jeans as she got out. The passenger window came down. I pulled out my BlackBerry and started driving. I went past slowly, the phone to my ear, trying to make it look like I was chatting away to someone as I tried to get a clear shot of Anna's new best mate.

She finished her exchange with the bald guy and crossed the road towards the taxi rank. I stopped to let her past as he powered up his window and drove off.

I dropped the BlackBerry into my lap and carried on for a couple of hundred metres before swinging round by a dark-grey stone building. It looked like an old government institution, maybe a library or a theatre. Its big glass windows were filled with posters in Arabic. It must have been a mosque of sorts. Shoes were stacked on racks outside a side entrance.

Anna was talking to the driver of the taxi at the head of the queue. She saw me, gave the guy a thanks-but-no-thanks, and turned to walk down one of the side streets. I followed and pulled up alongside her. She looked around and jumped in. The expression on her face said she was ready for her bollocking.

'What the fuck are you doing? I told you, didn't I? Anything spooks you, get up and walk. Didn't I say don't take any chances?'

She listened to me as she fastened her seatbelt. 'Nick, watch the road. I've found Lilian.'

'Alive?'

'I think it's her. There were twelve girls, some of them fresh off the plane. I can show you. Go back to the roundabout.' She lowered her window and lit a cigarette.

She took a drag. 'It was dark. But there's one who could defi-nitely be her.'

'What about Baldilocks – you get his name? Anything?'

She shook her head. 'He's a Brit, but he doesn't sound like you. He's like the one in Christiania. The one who gave us the address.'

'A Scouser?'

'I don't know what that means. But he sounded the same.' She took another drag. As we turned onto the roundabout I let down my window too.

'Take the second exit – follow the signs for the docks.'

I checked the blue plate high up on the first building past the roundabout. The street was called Distelweg.

'Follow the road. It twists and turns through this housing estate, and then you cross a canal. After that, it's a dead straight line down the centre of the docks.' She turned her head to blow out another cloud of smoke. 'I told him I'd buy the lot, thinking that maybe I could get them all out quickly. We could find the money, couldn't we, Nicholas? Five thousand euros. Five thousand each. They're young . . .'

'Brilliant. When do we have to deliver the cash?'

'We don't.' She sighed. 'Turns out they've already been sold and are due to leave this Thursday. He just wanted to show me how fresh his merchandise is.'

As we drove over the bridge and into almost total darkness I had the same feeling I'd had at the Bender border crossing into Transnistria – like I was crossing into East Berlin. In my rear-view, the canal shimmered under the street-lights. We passed four or five ropy-looking boathouses. Just forty metres later the world was pitch black.

Anna tossed out her cigarette and climbed into the back without being told. She crouched in the foot-well as I turned onto the dead straight tarmac road that bisected the dock. Potholes lined the verge where it surrendered to the mud, and stacks of wooden pallets sat outside a parade of industrial units. Watery pools of security lighting surrounded a similar group of buildings in the distance. A few trucks and vans were parked up here and there, but there was no sign of life. This wasn't a 24/7 part of town.

All signs of habitation petered out about four hundred metres further on and were replaced by a run of steel railings. To reinforce the Checkpoint Charlie experience, it started to rain.

Anna rested her head on the baby seat. 'OK – now we're at the wasteground. The place I was taken is on its own, set back from the road. There's a tower on the left-hand side.'

The Noord 5 area was on the far side of the water. Piles of rubble and twisted steel reinforcing rods glistened in its ambient light.

We passed a double gate secured with a shiny new padlock and chain.

'That's where we drove in.'

Droplets of rain bounced through the open window and onto my cheek. I studied the dark silhouette of the target: an imposing rectangular structure with a tower at the left end. I couldn't see a single light.

'I think it's a grain silo – or, at least, it used to be. There was flour over everything. It smells like a cake shop when you go in.'

I carried on for another hundred metres or so, to a point where the road turned sharp left and then almost wound back on itself. We passed a ferry point, not much more than a slipway, too small for vehicles, just for pedestrians and cyclists. I drove back towards what I hoped was the Berlin Wall canal. With luck we'd be able to cross it and get back onto Distelweg via the estate.

The bay was immediately to my right. On the other side of it was the Amsterdam I remembered. Spires were silhouetted in the neon glow. Navigation lights glided up and down the waterway between us as tonight's passengers tucked into a romantic canal-cruise dinner.

'Describe the building for me.'

'It has concrete floors. The door we went in through is on the right-hand side of the building. Inside is a hallway with four doors into offices, two on each side. The first on the right is where the girls are kept. They're in sleeping bags on mattresses.'

'Did you see inside the other three rooms?'

She shook her head. 'We went straight into the first on the right. There is a staircase on the left. I could hear voices coming from the first floor. Dutch voices. I didn't see them. There were definitely two captors, maybe three or four.'

We crossed the canal and found ourselves in another estate – narrow roads and prefab houses, painted white.

'Did they open the main door for you, or did the bald guy have a key?'

'It was locked. He made a call and they unlocked it from the inside. They locked themselves in again when we left.'

'What about the gate? Was it open when you got there?'

'I couldn't tell. The driver got out, but I don't know if it was locked. They might have unlocked it after the call. I just don't know.'

'Anything else?'

She climbed back alongside me and thought for a while. 'It all happened so fast and I didn't want to be obvious. When we met at the café, I told him I wanted to see what condition the girls were in. If they were good, we could do business. These guys are greedy, they always are.'

'Well done, mate. Brilliant.'

She laughed. 'But . . . ?' She knew what was coming.

'Anna, you're a nightmare.' I looked at her. 'Don't do that sort of shit again.' I stopped the car. 'You drive back.'

We swapped seats and I checked the BlackBerry footage I'd taken earlier to make sure Anna wasn't visible. The quality was OK – a bit dark, but they'd be able to get a few decent sightings of the face.

Anna followed signs to the A10.

I hit the secure button and waited for the app to do its stuff. I pressed send, then dialled Jules's number. 'I've found a possible.'

He sounded surprised. 'Is she OK?'

'I've uploaded a video for you. He has the possible. I've got three days max before she's being moved on. The lad's got a Lexus, a crimson four-by-four hybrid thing. I don't know if it's his. I don't even know the plate. All I know is that face. Can you find out who he is? The quality ain't great, but the Tefalheads should be able to sort something out. If not, fire them.'

'How difficult will it be to get to her?'

'Hard to tell. The girls are protected.' I repeated Anna's description of the target. 'All I know is, there are twelve of them, and one's a possible. I'm going to get in there and confirm.'

Tresillian jumped in from nowhere. 'Well done, Mr Stone. I'll organize a safe-house and a contact. Call back in two hours. In the meantime, start planning to get in there, find the possible, and if she is our target, get her out. We need this to be done as quickly as you can. Do you understand me?'

'Loud and clear.'

'Stand by.'

He cut us off.

We reached the slip road onto the A10, southbound to Schiphol.

'We'll drop you off at the Radisson and I'll take the car.'

'Drop me off?'

'I've got to go on and do the job. You're not going to come to the safe-house, are you? They can't know you're here. So wait out in the hotel. It'll be safer for both of us. If the shit hits the fan, it means I've got somewhere to go, a safe RV. And if I've got Lilian, it means she's got somewhere to go as well.'

'But can't I drive for you or something like that?'

'No.' I squeezed her hand. 'You have to be on the safe side of the fence. For both of our sakes.'

6

Back on the A10 from the airport, I ignored the city centre turn-off. I crossed the North Sea canal. The smoking-chimneys sign warned me to turn off in one K. I downed a couple more Smarties and a swig of Coke.

Anna was pissed off with me. She didn't want to sit in a hotel room until I'd finished the job. But there was no alternative. The less my contact – and therefore Tresillian – knew about what I had up my sleeve, the better. In any case, the job would be done and dusted within a couple of days. Then we could sample some R-and-R, Moscow-style. And find a way of not talking about how long I might have to go.

I'd follow Tresillian's most recent set of instructions, then get back on target tonight. Who knows? I might even have her out of there by first light.

It wasn't long before I was paralleling the market. The place was closed but a lot of the kebab joints and corner shops in the vicinity were still open. Brightly coloured lights glistened in the rain slick that coated the Panda's side windows.

It had been good spending time with Anna. And I wouldn't have got here so quickly if it wasn't for her. But now I had to perform, and when push came to shove, I preferred to work alone. I was in control of just one person. If anything went wrong, I only had one person to blame.

I ignored the first two exits on the small roundabout, including Distelweg, and took the last option. I hit the road that doubled back on itself, eventually turning left onto the street I'd been given. Papaverhoek was narrow, and paved with concrete cobblestones.

Down at the far end, maybe two hundred metres away, sat a baby cargo ship looking like a road-block. I slowed right down. Cars parked both sides. A long blue wooden building with yellow awnings on my right. Blinds – also yellow – closed, but a sign hinting at the pleasures within: 'FilmNoord XXX'. Foyer open, but no customers in sight.

I passed a run of concrete prefab garages with corrugated-asbestos roofs. Some didn't have doors, just the arse of a rusty car sticking out. To my left, and stretching for sixty to seventy metres, was a two-storey office block: brick with white metal windows; precise, uncluttered, well-kept, Germanic. Numbered '1–3', it wasn't the one I wanted.

The next building along was connected to it, with its far end overlooking a patch of wasteground. A large wooden door that might once have been varnished stood to the left of a metal shutter. 'Dickinson (NL)' was stamped on a faded white plastic nameplate.

I parked nose-in to the shutter and left the engine running. The windows above me on the first floor were barred and grimy. There was no movement or light.

I retrieved my day sack from the passenger seat and got out. There was nothing in it I'd particularly need if I had to do a runner: it was just good drills to keep all your gear with you.

I looked for cameras as I walked towards the entrance but couldn't see any. A couple of street-lamps further back towards the main cast an intermittent glow, but that was about it. Nothing much happened down here. The only reason for anyone to venture this way after hours would be to work late for the Germans or stock up on some porn. I wondered if FilmNoord XXX had contributed to Slobo's collection.

My head was clear. I realized I'd forgotten about the pain as soon as Anna had gone missing. I decided to ease back on the Smarties and see if I could start to grip this thing on my own.

The door had three locks. I rang the bell. The intercom crackled alongside it.

'It's Nick.'

'Bradley.' His tone was crisp.

'OK, Bradley. Fifty-five.'

He was silent for a moment. 'Subtract forty-six.'

'OK. Let me in?'

The intercom closed down and an electric motor to my right began to whirr. The shutter groaned and shrieked its way upwards. I went and sat in the Panda while it finished torturing itself.

Only two of the four fluorescent tubes hanging from its ceiling were working but they were enough to show that the Volkswagen Golf to the right of the loading bay was disguised as a compost heap. Its wiper blade had somehow managed to cut an arc through the shit on the rear windscreen but reversing was still going to be a challenge.

I pulled in beside it as soon as there was enough clearance, then got out and hit the green down button. The floor was covered with dust and the kind of tyre prints they get very excited about on *CSI: Miami*. Beyond the cars there was an empty space where whatever came into or out of this building was stored, and a set of steps that led up to a gallery.

'Mr Smith . . .'

A man in jeans and a leather jacket came down them to greet me. His voice was accentless but educated and his smile was ironic. He thrust out a hand, allowing me a glimpse of cufflinks in the shape of miniature shotgun cartridges, and we shook.

Bradley's hair was short and blond, and casual dress wasn't

his thing. He reminded me of my estate agent, and the kind of officer I'd done my best to forget about since leaving the Regiment. He had a blue plastic folder tucked under his arm. 'Shall we go inside? I have your briefing pack.'

He led me back up to the gallery and through a thick wooden fire door. A narrow concrete stairway went up the centre of the building, past a landing with a push-bar fire escape, to a corridor which ran the length of the top floor. Three doors, all of them open, led into empty offices that over-looked the road. A couple of old wooden filing cabinets was all that remained of the furniture, but indentations in the carpet marked where desks had once stood, and worn areas traced the most popular routes between them.

'What is this place? Who does it belong to?'

He checked his stride, as if he couldn't walk and talk at the same time. 'It was built just before the Germans invaded. The Resistance used it as a hide for downed Brit air crews.'

'Who else knows I'm here?'

He looked disappointed that I'd needed to ask. 'No one apart from Mr T and Julian. Did Julian tell you he and I knew each other at Marlborough? I joined the army and he . . . Well, he's done all right for himself, hasn't he?'

'Don't know, mate. Never set eyes on him. Where do the Dickinsons fit in? Do they know what's going on?'

'My mother's family. They were the ones with the money. Her grandfather started in paper packaging in 1936. He ended up with businesses all over Europe. My father took over the group when my mother inherited, and they both died just over ten years ago. A boating accident . . .' The blood rushed to his cheeks. 'It was only then that I discovered he was bankrupt. I managed to keep a little of the empire, and this is part of it.'

'Are you in the service?'

He smiled. 'I like to think so. The company has had links with HMG since those Resistance days. During the Cold War, my father gave the Firm any titbits he picked up while on business in the East. I'm more a sort of roving ambassador myself – one foot in the import/export world, the other with you guys, whoever you are. I don't need to know. We're not exactly a new breed, I suppose. Private enterprise doing its bit to defend democracy.'

He gave me a smile that didn't go anywhere near his eyes.

'What about the road? Any movement?'

'Virtually none. The office block next door had less than ten-per-cent occupation even before the recession. Now everyone has gone. The whole area is due to be redeveloped.'

'What about the porno shop?'

'They don't get out much. Must be allergic to sunlight. They'll be forced out eventually, though. The natives are getting restless.'

I followed him into a narrow, box-like room at the back of the building. He turned on the light. Varnished wooden pigeonholes with rusting metal card-holders covered one wall, and a galvanized steel ladder led up to a hatch in the roof.

'What about the Dutch? They know anything about the job?'

However much you've been told, the guys on the ground always know a little bit more.

'Nothing. The police are really only here to liaise with the Muslim community. They keep an eye on the drug situation, of course. Ironic, really, given what you can get your hands on legally in a bog-standard Amsterdam coffee shop – but they're trying to keep a handle on it. The violence, the people smuggling, the prostitution all follow in its wake.'

Fluorescent lights flickered into life above us as we moved into the room at the end. Bicycle hooks protruded from the wall opposite another push-bar fire escape.

A brand new kettle, a box of tea bags and a couple of cartons of milk were spread out on the work surface beside a stainless-steel sink with exposed pipe-work beneath it. A large cardboard box sat on the floor with a sleeping bag and one or two other bits and pieces bundled inside.

'I bought you a few essentials. I didn't know what you were bringing. There's an airbed in there and some toiletries, pens, paper, that sort of thing.' He opened the milk. 'UHT, I'm afraid. There isn't a fridge. And of course the tea bags aren't as good as English.'

He flicked on the kettle and pointed towards an archway in the partition wall. 'Shower and the like. All the plumbing works.'

I poked my head round the corner and made admiring noises about the unopened multi-pack of toilet paper. He'd thought of everything.

Bradley unwrapped a couple of mugs.

I ran a finger along the push-bar on the door. 'Do the alarms kick off if I open it?'

'I don't think so.'

I shoved against it and emerged onto a cast-iron staircase that led past the door from the landing below us and down to the wasteground. No alarm sounded. I couldn't see any contact points on the doorframe; no sign of a circuit.

'I'll check downstairs. Can you do the roof?'

The other door was the same.

I returned to see Bradley giving the roof-hatch bolts the good news with a rubber mallet.

I fixed the brews while he finished the job.

7

Bradley reached for the blue plastic folder and tipped its contents onto the brown carpet between us. I shuffled through a printout of Slobo's Facebook picture and a couple of A4 Google Earth images. One was a straight satellite view of the target, the other a hybrid with street names superimposed. We were less than two K from where the possible and her companions were being held.

I held up the shot of the square, flat-roofed building. The image was fuzzy, but the tower was identifiable from the shadow it cast across the ground. 'Any idea what's inside?'

He hadn't.

'What about the outside? Cameras?'

Bradley looked like he was having a tough time in the *Mastermind* chair. 'I don't know, sorry.'

'Do you know what this job is all about?' I jabbed at the picture, pressing the paper into the carpet. 'You know about these two?'

He flashed another of his special smiles. 'No. And I don't want to know.'

There are lots of people like Bradley. They range from retired civil servants to company CEOs, all of them out in what they like to think of as the real world. Some help with information.

Some are in it a lot deeper, and I had the feeling he was one of them, despite his attempts to distance himself. Maybe he was on the Firm's payroll. Maybe they had something on him and he had no choice but to play ball. Maybe he was one of the weirdos who liked doing this shit because it fulfilled some fantasy.

'Do you have secure comms? How do we talk?'

Bradley looked sheepish. 'I'm afraid people like me aren't trusted with that sort of thing. I'm not complaining. I'd be at their beck and call, wouldn't I?'

'Tell you what, Brad. I have to stay here and crack on. Come back, on foot, tomorrow morning at ten?'

He took a final sip of his brew and put it on the drainer. 'Ten it is, Mr Smith.' He dusted down his jeans and threw me some keys.

'Who else has a set?'

'Just me.'

That probably wasn't true. The locks weren't new. There would have been quite a few sets in circulation over the years.

'Good. Tomorrow, be precisely on time and use your keys as if the place was empty. Just let yourself in, then stay right there. I'll come and get you.'

'OK. Whatever you need me to do . . .'

I could tell by his expression that he wasn't thrilled to be given chapter and verse.

'And don't ever come into the building with no warning. If there's an uninvited body in here I'm going to react first and ask questions later. That make sense?'

'Perfect sense.' He fingered his miniature shotgun cartridges.

'So can you see yourself out now, mate? Make sure you close up after you.'

I packed everything back into the folder, and added my credit card and ID. As the shutter gave its final squeak I moved to one of the front windows and watched the shit-covered Golf head towards the main.

8

I leant against the wall and slid down onto my arse to finish the brew. It was nearly half eleven and I was knackered. The last few days were catching up with me.

My body told me to get my head down, but years of training told me to cover my back first. I made my way through to the mailroom and climbed the ladder.

The hatch lifted. It was still miserable outside. There were puddles everywhere on the flat roof, and the clouds still hung heavily in the sky. From my vantage-point I had a panoramic view of the area I'd been looking at on the map. To the south, across the bay, was the distant neon glow of the city. A set of navigation lights lifted from Schiphol to the south-west and almost instantly disappeared.

I scanned the road below me. The dark silhouette of the ship was still visible at the water's edge about two hundred metres away to my left. A couple of cars were parked outside the porn shop to my right, which showed no sign of closing for business. Two women hung around under the canopies, on the look-out for customers who fancied some live action.

I got on with checking out my escape route.

There was open ground to the rear. If anything kicked off, I'd be in plain sight there. The houses on the other side of the vacant office block next door would give me some cover, but there was an eight-foot height difference between the two rooflines.

Apart from the front entrance and fire escape to the rear, it was my only way out of this building. If I couldn't go over the top, I'd have to get myself across the road and into the sprawling estate alongside the market. I'd get lost in there, no drama. Then I'd try and hook up with Anna.

I stared into the darkness. It had been a night like this when she'd first told me about Grisha.

Now I was going to die on her too.

This was alien territory for me. I guess I'd always assumed I'd be killed in action, hopefully without much fuss, and with nobody close enough to give a shit. Now I was starting to think that I'd do anything for a couple of months with her. At least we'd have time to say goodbye.

The skies opened once more. Rain fell on me like 7.62 rounds and brought me back to Planet Earth. Kleinmann's diagnosis had pulled the ring back on one big can of fuck-with-your-head, and I had to cut away from it.

I headed back to the hatch.

I had to put all that shit to one side, and focus on the job in hand.

I had to get myself on-target.

9

I pulled the wooden pigeonhole unit far enough from the wall to slip the blue folder behind it, then wedged a small piece of paper between unit and wall, about six inches up from the carpet, as I eased it back. If anything was disturbed, I'd be able to tell at a glance.

As always when going on-target, I had to be sterile. All I carried with me was cash: my run money. Everything else was in the folder. I didn't rush the drill even though I'd done it a thousand times. I found myself wanting to enjoy the ritual. If this really was going to be my last job, I wanted to savour every moment.

I folded another couple of pieces of paper and wedged them between the frame and the door of the fire escapes and the roof hatch. I trousered Brad's mallet and went downstairs. He might be the most obliging lad on the planet when it came to dodgy tea bags and shower gel, but I didn't trust him an inch. I eased a little sliver of paper into each of the three locks on the front door.

I did my best to bang out the dent I'd left in the Panda's roof. Rubber hammers are better than steel ones for panel beating, thumping in wooden tent pegs and dropping humans. Steel imparts a blunt trauma on soft material like bone, but rubber or wood conveys all its kinetic energy without penetration. It can take someone down much more effectively. And if you hit a skull too hard with a steel hammer it can become embedded and really mess things up.

I backed the car out into the rain. As the shutters came down I pretended to check that I'd locked the front door properly. I wanted to make sure I could see my telltales if I looked directly into the keyholes. No drama: it all worked.

I got into the Panda and headed down the road. The rain had calmed down but there was more to come. I put the wipers on intermittent. FilmNoord XXX was still open, but the girls had decided to call it a day.

Despite being closed, the market was still brightly lit. The kebab shops and one or two nearby stores were still open. Mopeds buzzed around the place like wasps and one or two lads were busy spraying a beard and glasses on a Geert Wilders poster. For a moment it felt just like home.

I paralleled the main until I got to the small roundabout and turned onto Distelweg. Before I went on-target, however, I had one final bit of business to take care of.

10

I crossed the canal and looked for somewhere to park. The windscreen wipers kicked off again as another squall blew in. I spotted two truck cabs outside a tile warehouse with a massive glass front. I pulled up between them.

The entrance was decorated with a row of oversized concrete plant pots. As anti-ram-raiding precautions went, these ones looked good, but the plants themselves had died long ago. Making it look like I was busy taking a piss, I tucked the safe-house keys in the one nearest the door and scooped some wet mud over them. Two minutes later I was on my way to the target.

I checked the gates as I drove past the stretch of waste-ground. Still chained and locked. And still no light from the building.

I parked up between a couple of petrol tankers just short of the bend and got out to check the ferry point. The timetable by the little glass shelter told me it only ran during business hours.

I went back to the car and sat in darkness, engine off, as the rain hammered on the roof.

11

I took a couple of minutes to get my head in gear. Then I got out, locked up and hid the keys in a patch of scrub by the fence. Zipping up my bomber, I headed along the fence line, looking for a way in that didn't involve climbing. If the possible was Lilian, and I had the chance to lift her, I'd need to get out quickly. The rain had calmed down a bit, but my jeans got soaked in the high grass and clung to my calves.

Eventually I found a gap where a couple of railings had been uprooted and the muddy track between them had been pounded by plenty of feet. It looked like a rat run.

I followed the trail for about twenty metres, then turned to face the way I'd come. I needed to have a clear picture of my route back. Three pinpricks of particularly bright light – cranes standing guard in a construction site, perhaps – hung like a small constellation over the edge of the city across the bay. The gap I'd be aiming for was almost directly in line with them. That was my marker.

The flour silo was about two hundred metres away, exactly as Anna had described it. I picked my way round waist-high chunks of broken concrete and dodged a couple of twisted steel reinforcing rods that arched up at me like bull's horns.

More and more mud stuck to my Timberlands. They were beginning to feel like divers' boots.

The ground dipped into a hollow the size of a bomb crater. I slid down into it and skirted more lumps of rubble. A circle of rocks surrounded a pile of ash that had once been a campfire. So many discarded syringes were scattered beside it that it looked like the entire junkie community had been playing their own version of pick-up-sticks. I was glad it was raining. They weren't going to be coming back for a rematch tonight: they'd all be competing with the working girls for space under the shop canopies instead.

Anybody out here would have to be totally off their heads. If I got challenged I'd pretend to be a drugged-up dickhead. It was pretty much how I felt right now.

That thought triggered a memory of my old mate Charlie. He'd been on his last legs about five years ago, and he'd done one final job to earn his family a wad before he keeled over. But I already had the money. I had what Charlie had been after. Why the fuck was I still doing it?

Fuck it – it must be the rain making me miserable. I knew why I was here, and it wasn't just to have one last crack. It was also about Lilian and those poor fuckers in the green house in Copenhagen, and the rest of them who'd been fucked up and fucked over by those shaven-headed bastards. I couldn't clear my mind of the sounds and images of what had happened above our heads while Anna was posing as the world's most uncompromising trafficker. The guys in that house were animals, and someone had to stop that shit happening. I wasn't going to be saving the world single-handed: I was small fry and hadn't got much time left to go on a crusade. But I could get one girl out, and maybe free the others, even if it was just a pinprick in the shit-pile.

There was less than a hundred metres to go now. I still couldn't see any cameras or motion sensors. That didn't mean there weren't any. If the intention was to detect people rather than deter them, they might have gone for concealment.

I pulled up about twenty metres short, looked and listened. The silhouette of the silo tower rose into the night sky; it dwarfed the remaining two-thirds of the building. I could make out two windows on the ground floor to the right of it, and two more one storey up. The arrangement made sense of Anna's description of the interior: two doors each side of the front entrance and a staircase on the left. There were no lights that I could see, and no movement.

A concrete strip ran from the front of the silo to the chained gates on Distelweg. The dock was less than thirty metres away from other side of the tower.

The silo was the only old building in the area. Maybe it was some kind of historical monument. Or maybe it just hadn't figured in anyone's regeneration plans yet. Everything else I'd seen had been thrown up with new brick or metal sheeting.

I found a slab of old concrete to sit down on and cocked an ear towards the target. I stayed like that for five minutes. Only then did I look around me, giving my unconscious the chance to take in as much as it could.

My jeans clung to my legs. My boots weighed a tonne. I didn't have to fake it too much when I swayed towards the silo, hands in pockets. If someone was watching me, I'd look as though I was doped up to the eyeballs.

I mooched along to the left, to the silo tower. The closer I got, the more obvious it was that there were no cameras. It looked as though they'd decided not to draw attention to themselves by throwing up surveillance equipment.

I liked doing this part of the job, just as I enjoyed going through Passport Control on fake documents and all that shit. Beating the system always had given me a buzz, ever since I was being a total arsehole on the Bermondsey estates.

The silo was square and about sixty metres tall. The bricks were rotting and most of the pointing had fallen out. The only things that seemed to hold it together were the old steel reinforcing plates that ran up the sides, and a thick layer of graffiti.

There was no entry point on the gable end. I moved to the corner on the side nearest the water, and sank slowly to my knees. I craned my neck gently round at muddy ground level.

There was no light whatsoever here. The concrete stretched all the way down to the dock, interrupted only by weeds pushing up stubbornly through the cracks. A big section of hard standing lined the water's edge, where a crane had probably once stood. A conveyor-belt ran down to it from the top of the silo at a forty-five-degree angle, supported by a steel framework made from the world's biggest and rustiest set of Meccano.

Noord 5 was five hundred metres away on the other side of the water. Its street-lighting and the intermittent sweep of car headlamps did nothing to help me. I put my ear to the brickwork to listen for a generator, but heard nothing.

I moved along the front of the building, covertly now, until I reached two large steel doors big enough to drive a truck through. Yet more weeds grew right up against them, looking like they were intent on forcing entry. None of them had been trodden on or driven over. Two padlocks were covered by security cups so you couldn't cut through them, and the huge rusty crossbars looked like they hadn't been shifted any time this century.

I carried on towards the far gable end. More windows: two up, two down, all boarded up with metal anti-vandal sheeting. I put an ear to the one I hoped the girls were still behind. There wasn't a sound.

I found the door Anna had gone in through. It had two locks. Going by the shine on the brass inserts, they were almost brand new. I sat against it, switching back into dosser mode, and had a look around. The next nearest building was a two-level warehouse or factory about three hundred metres away on the perimeter of the wasteground. Again: no light, no noise, no movement. This silo was a good place to hide people.

I put my ear to the lower keyhole. Nothing. I stuck my nose against it and inhaled deeply. I might be able to smell cooking or a cigarette, anything at all that would give me an indication of life. But all I got, as Anna had said I would, was the aroma of cake shop.

I got to my feet and gave the top and bottom of the double doors a push. They didn't give an inch. They were bolted from the inside. Somebody had to be in there.

There was no other entrance apart from this one and the large steel doors, as far as I could tell. But that didn't mean it was the only means of access.

I walked back to the conveyor-belt and started to climb. I only had to scale four or five metres of Meccano, but the junctions I used as hand- and footholds were awkwardly spaced and the steel was rusty and wet. By the time I heaved myself over the top, I felt like I'd completed an assault course.

The conveyor-belt itself was just over a metre wide. Its rubberized fabric was rotten and frayed and a lot of the steel banding was exposed. I raised myself slowly onto my hands and knees and started to crawl. Almost immediately, the rubber between the rollers gave way with a loud, tearing sound. I dropped flat, listened and watched. Then I decided not to fuck around. If they'd seen me, they'd seen me. It wasn't as if I could do anything about it. I might as well carry on until I heard the shouts.

The belt led up to a pair of rusty metal doors each about a metre square. A gentle push and they opened.

The brickwork was four courses thick. If there was still any flour in there, it would be bone dry. I edged forward on my elbows until my chest was on the lip of the hatchway and peered down. Right at the bottom, the faintest flicker of light showed through what looked like a tunnel connecting the silo with the rest of the building.

A vertical access ladder was fixed to the wall. I curled my body until I was able to reach my boots, unlace them and tug them off. I scraped off the worst of the mud on the top edge of the Meccano, tied the laces together and slung them round my neck. I eased myself back through the hatch, feet first, until I made contact with the top rung. I took a breath and started down.

After about twenty metres I stopped to look and listen. My feet hurt without the boots to protect them, but that was better than leaving mud on the ladder or having clumps of it fall off and land below.

The further down I went, the stronger the smell of flour and the brighter the light. I paused again just before reaching the ground. The edges of the silo were lined with flour two or three feet high.

I stepped down onto a concrete base. I didn't need to worry where I trod. There were plenty of disturbances in the flour, including footprints.

The opening into the rest of the building was about the size of a garage door. Steel shutters above it were locked in the up position.

Very slowly, I moved my head around the corner. A brick wall stood immediately opposite me, in the middle of which was a door. Two windows either side of it were in darkness. There were also three windows on the second floor of what had probably once been offices. Light spilt from the one on the right – enough for me to see its haze reflecting off the remains of what had once been hundreds of tonnes of flour dust piled up against the walls.

A body moved across the window.

I froze.

Male, early twenties. Both forearms dark with tattoos; cigarette in mouth; bare-chested and overweight. His bitch tits wobbled as he moved.

He shouted something to someone and gestured at his crotch. A young girl shuffled into view. Her hair was dark and frizzy. She sank slowly to her knees in front of him. Her head disappeared below the sill. Bitch Tits soon had a slack smile on his face. He looked down at her, took a deep drag and flicked some ash onto her head.

I stayed where I was. If there was just one of them, maybe I could take him now, then get Lilian and the rest of them out.

I heard screams from the ground floor, along with some very pissed-off male shouting.

The door to Bitch Tits's office burst open. The new arrival wore a lot of black leather. His head was shaved, neo-Nazi style. His face had multiple piercings.

Bitch Tits wasn't impressed by what he was hearing. 'Well, fucking find her! Don't you dare fucking lose her!'

He was a Brit – a Scouser. It was beginning to sound like a family business.

The ground-floor office door was also thrown wide. This time the yells were Dutch.

I didn't see any of the bodies. I was too busy climbing back up the ladder as fast as my legs would carry me.

12

I lay on my side at the top of the conveyor-belt and pulled my boots back on. I gulped in mouthfuls of air. The smell of decayed rubber made me gag.

The shouts below me – now in heavily accented English – echoed round the tower.

'There is nothing.'

'She is not here.'

More shouts from the Dutch guys outside. Bodies bomb-burst from the door. Bitch Tits screamed with anger – or it could have been fear. His voice was high-pitched, out of control. 'Fucking get out there! Fucking *find* the bitch!'

I finished tying my laces and started reversing carefully down the conveyor-belt, keeping as low as I could. A few metres below me, fucked-off men tried to organize themselves for the hunt. It wasn't working. Bitch Tits was going completely ballistic in Scouse. *'Yous cunts! We'll all be in the shite! Get out there!'*

By the time I was about two-thirds of the way down, the shouts had begun to fade. I stared into the darkness. The search party had spread into the wasteground. I jumped the last couple of metres and ran for cover.

I legged it in the direction of Distelweg, making each big

chunk of concrete a single bound. I checked the ground ahead as best I could, straining my ears for the shout that would signal they'd found her. She'd be terrified. Maybe she'd got stuck trying to get over the fence – desperately wanting to, but having lost all control because she was so scared.

I heard nothing. Total silence. The Dutch must have gone out via the gate or jumped the fence. Keeping in the shadows, I used my three-light marker to navigate back to the gap. Someone else had been through here since I last had. Someone in bare feet. I could see the mark of my boots in the mud, and also the imprint of small, frantic toes.

I slipped through and kept to the edge of the road, almost hugging the fence. The search party would be moving up and down Distelweg by now, checking every bit of cover, flapping more and more as the minutes ticked by.

I came level with the Panda and felt around in the scrub for the keys. Once inside I powered down the window and had one last listen before I fired up the engine.

Lights extinguished, I moved off slowly, following the road on the bay side of the dock. It started to rain again.

There was a massive thump on the front of the car. I braked hard.

A face flew up out of nowhere and banged against the windscreen. For a split second, all I could see was a mass of wet blonde hair and a pair of big scared eyes.

I threw the engine out of gear. Fuck the handbrake. I jumped out to grab her.

By the time I got round to the front of the car the girl was already scrabbling along the tarmac. There was blood on her face. Her jeans were soaked. Her feet were bare.

'Lilian?'

She was swallowed up by the shadows as quickly as she'd appeared.

I stopped and listened.

Nothing.

I jumped back into the Panda. There was a streak of blood on the windscreen. If it was Lillian, I had to get to her before those fuckers did.

I moved off, nice and slow, windows down.

13

I drove across the canal and into the prefab estate. A left took me back towards the Distelweg bridge. I parked up about a hundred metres further on and tucked Brad's mallet into the waistband of my jeans. I'd move back onto the target on foot and start searching again from there. I didn't want to take the car through the area twice that night. It was bad drills. Bitch Tits and his mates might still be out there.

The shop lights splashed across the wet pavements. I was hungry and thirsty, and it was going to be a long night. I went into a mini-mart and bought crisps, pitta bread and a bottle of water. I managed the whole transaction without a single word to the guy behind the counter. I just grunted and paid.

I jammed the crisps into the bread as I walked past a line of graffiti-covered boathouses. I kept close to the walls and fences of the industrial units, ready to dodge oncoming headlights. I threw the last of the crisp sandwich down my neck as I approached the tile warehouse.

I heard a cry.

Then male laughter, followed by grunts and curses, monosyllabic and aggressive.

I took a couple of steps.

And heard it again.

There was a blur of movement from beneath the canopy. The girl ran from the shadows, naked and sobbing. Two guys appeared behind her. Too fast, too powerful. They grabbed her and dragged her back into the darkness.

It wasn't hard to work out what they were doing to her. I just needed to know how many of them were doing it.

Another cry. Part pain, part despair.

It looked like Bitch Tits was the only one allowed to sample the merchandise on site, and this lot fancied a taster before they dragged her back to him.

14

Rhythmic sobs continued to come from under the canopy. I inched forward, fingers closing around the handle of the mallet.

I heard more grunts and a couple of slaps. There was a muffled, anguished scream followed by a chorus of laughter. The air was heavy with cannabis.

There were four of them, all fully paid-up members of the neo-Nazi club. Crew-cuts, tattoos and plenty of face metal were the order of the day. The girl was on her knees. Three of them stood around her with their jeans halfway down their thighs. A fourth lounged against the door with a stupid grin on his face, smoking a joint. It was either his turn to chill, or he preferred to watch.

The girl's bloodstained face was rounder and younger than the image I had of Lilian. Much younger. She took a couple more slaps to the head to make her work harder.

A million years of training told me there was nothing I could do. I couldn't intervene. Bad things happen. This shit went on a million times a day, all over the world. I was here for a job. I wasn't the UN. I needed to let this run its course. Four guys here raping this girl meant four fewer guarding Lilian. I needed to stop fucking around and get back to the silo.

But there was another voice in my head. Anna's voice. *What about* this *girl? What about her parents, her sisters, her brothers? How would you feel if this was happening to someone you cared for, if this was happening to me?*

I looked round for something heavier than the mallet. A bit of scaffolding would have come in handy. A wheel-brace, maybe . . .

Then I checked myself. What family? Every scrap of experience and years of fucking up screamed at me: I had to let this one go.

I turned and headed back the way I'd come. I'd have to pull my finger out if I wanted to get this job done by first light.

When I'd covered about twenty metres I straightened up and shoved the mallet back into the waistband of my jeans.

Another heartbreaking scream pierced the darkness.

Fuck it.

I pulled the mallet out again and turned back.

I was in auto mode, en route to a possible nightmare. I'd need to be quick and hard – just take them down and run. After that, the girl would have to sort her own shit out.

I got within a few metres of them. She was still on her knees. The one in front of her looked up just in time to see me jump into the air and bring the mallet down hard a couple of inches above his eyebrows. He didn't say a word. He couldn't. All I heard was a loud pop as the toughened rubber worked its kinetic shit and he crumpled to the floor.

I spun round, swung back my arm and zoned in on the guy to my right. He got the good news just above the temple. He groaned and collapsed onto the girl.

She whimpered and tried to kick him off.

I turned to the other two. The one with the spliff was still some distance from Planet Earth, and instead of rushing me, the other stupid fucker was pulling up his jeans. I barged against him. He staggered back under the canopy, arms windmilling, and crashed into his mate.

I didn't give them a second to recover.

Mr Windmill's jeans had slipped back round his knees.

I swung the mallet from right to left, demolishing his cheek-bone and part of his jaw. He howled with pain. It didn't make up for what he'd done to the girl, but it was a start.

Mr Spliff threw up his arms to protect himself, but he still wasn't up to speed. I cannoned into him. As he went down I gave him two more quick hits. He'd managed to cover his head, so I snapped his wrist with the first blow and banged the second into his bollocks. That opened him up big-time. I brought down the mallet right on top of his closely shaven nut. Hard rubber smashed into soft bone with a dull thud. He wasn't going anywhere fast. He wasn't going anywhere, period.

I dug the keys out of the plant pot. The girl held her jumper against her breasts, watching me.

Two of the bodies stirred.

I grabbed her arm and dragged her out from under the canopy. I gathered up her jeans and thrust them at her.

'Go! Go on! *Fuck off!*'

She stood there shivering, clothes held up in front of her, knees trembling, like the child she was.

I gave her a shove. 'Go! *Run!*'

Two sets of headlights swept down the road from the direction of the bridge.

She was so tiny it was easy to pull her out of sight. I pushed her against the wheel of a trailer loaded with pallets as the engine got louder. She struggled, trying to escape. She probably thought I fancied a bit of what the neos had already helped themselves to. I grabbed her by the back of her head, wound my fingers through her hair and pushed her against the tyre.

The car came into view: a green Passat, two up. It slowed but didn't stop. I caught a glimpse of long, greasy black hair and matching shirt but couldn't see their faces. Ten seconds later a blue-and-white did the same. I dragged the girl to her feet the moment it had passed and we started moving in the opposite direction.

We'd covered a couple of hundred metres when I heard the whoop of a siren, just one quick hit. Blue lights strobed the darkness, glinting off the puddles, then they stopped just as suddenly.

We kept going.

She had to come with me now, even though I knew I was giving myself a very big dose of drama. I couldn't let her get lifted. Tarasov and his box of tricks had better be worth all this shit.

I flung open the back door of the Panda and shoved her down into the footwell. Then I jumped in behind the wheel.

'You understand English?'

The only response was some laboured breathing and a cough. She was crying quietly to herself.

Ten minutes passed. There were no more wailing sirens or blue flashing lights. What the fuck was going on? One of the neos was probably dead, and the others couldn't have legged it. A broken jaw makes you think twice about doing that. It makes you want to stay very, very still instead.

A set of headlights appeared in the rear-view. I felt between the seats to make sure she was still hidden. The green Passat rolled past, still two up. I got a better look at them this time. They'd completed my circuit, down past the ferry, up the bay road, then back.

I waited five more minutes, but there was no sign of the blue-and-white. I switched on the ignition.

'Stay down . . .'

I threaded my way through the housing estate until I came out onto a main. I didn't know where the fuck I was, but I'd work it out soon enough. There was a lot of trouble by the back seat, and I needed to think.

15

I killed the lights and engine the moment I'd nosy-parked in front of the shutter.

'You – stay there.' I still didn't know if she spoke any English, but she didn't move a muscle.

I pretended to fumble with the keys while I checked my paper telltales. All three were still in position.

I didn't hit the light switch inside, just pressed the shutter button. As the car came into view, I could see that she was now sitting next to the child seat, her jumper on. She tilted her head and pushed back her blood-matted hair so she could watch me through the windscreen.

I got back into the car and gave her a smile. She pulled her jumper down self-consciously over her thighs, but if her face showed any emotion, it was relief.

I drove into the bay and hit the button again. She remained motionless as the shutter ground its way down. I only hit the light switch when we were in total darkness. The two fluorescent tubes flickered and hummed.

She looked around her. I tapped on the slightly dented roof and bent down to her level. 'You're safe here.' I gestured with my hand. 'Come on.'

She didn't budge. She looked at me like she had a choice

about this and had decided to stay put.

I pushed down the front passenger seat, leant in and grabbed her arm. She stumbled out onto the cold concrete, clutching her wet and muddy jeans. 'Let's try again. What is your name?'

Nothing.

'Russia? Ukraine? Moldova?'

Her goosebumps were the size of shirt buttons. She tried to cover herself up.

I pointed to the stairs at the back of the loading bay and gave her a gentle push. 'Let's go. Up there.'

She stopped at the first landing, awaiting my next command. I steered her all the way to the top floor, keeping behind her so I could check the telltales without her seeing what I was doing. She stood stock still in the middle of the floor, waiting to be told what to do.

I got a much better look at her now. She was no more than five feet tall and could have been anything from fourteen to eighteen years old. Her dyed blonde hair was thick and wiry, and brushed her shoulders. It needed about a week's worth of shampooing. She was a skinny little thing: not through lack of food, there just wasn't anything of her. With high cheekbones and huge dark brown eyes, her face looked bigger than her delicate shoulders and graceful neck seemed capable of supporting. She had no eyebrows. They'd been plucked or shaved. It made her look like a porcelain doll. Or a ghost.

I pointed to the shower room.

She looked at me and shivered.

'Let's go.' I took her hand. She offered no resistance. She probably couldn't have even if she'd wanted to. She felt like she weighed less than the mallet.

I turned on the shower. The cubicle filled with steam. I pointed at the bottle of gel and mimed washing my hair. I showed her the towel, then closed the door and let her get on with it.

I filled the kettle and flicked it on.

I was tired, and pissed off with myself for breaking a life-time's rule. But there was no point beating myself up about it. Even if it hadn't been the right thing to do, she was here now. I had to deal with it. I threw a couple of Smarties down my neck with a cupful of cold water.

The kettle clicked off and I made myself a brew with plenty of milk and sugar. I dragged the sleeping bag and airbed out of Bradley's box. He hadn't lashed out on the electric-pump option. I didn't have the energy to inflate it; she'd have to, if she wanted a comfortable night.

I dug around in my day sack, stripped off and put on a dry sweatshirt. I threw my spare jeans onto the sleeping bag; hers were in shit state. I added a long-sleeved T-shirt, a clean pair of socks and some boxer shorts for good measure.

Brew in hand, I went into the mailroom. I checked the tell-tale and pulled out the folder. I wanted to show her Lilian's picture.

I sat near the sink with my back against the wall and checked my watch. After 02.00. Fuck, I hadn't even been here six hours and I was already in rag order.

I put my mug down and rested my head against my knees. The next thing I knew, I was woken by the sound of her coming out of the shower. I looked up. The towel was wrapped under her armpits. She caught sight of the sleeping bag and all the gear and very nearly smiled. Or maybe I was just kidding myself.

'Drink?' I pointed at the kettle and made a brew sign with my right hand.

She looked down at my mug, which was still half full. I took a sip. It had gone cold. I must have been out of it for at least half an hour. She raised a non-eyebrow.

'Yeah, I'll have one.'

She brushed past me as she leant down to collect my mug. She smelt of shampoo. Her knees cracked, and she still had chicken skin because of the cold.

I stood up and stretched while she got busy with the kettle. I wiped the dribble off my chin stubble and pointed at the gear. 'That is for you. Dry clothes.' I went through the motions of putting on jeans. 'Blow up the airbed.' I made a trumpet out of my hands and puffed through it. 'For you to sleep ... All right?'

She passed me a steaming mug. The tea was black, with half a kilo of sugar. I fished out Slobo's Facebook picture and pointed.

'This girl. Her name is Lilian. Was she in the building? Have you seen her?'

I couldn't read her expression at all.

'Have you seen her? Lilian. Her – name – is – Lilian . . .'

She nodded.

'You *have* seen her? Today?'

All of sudden she was scared. I didn't blame her. It must have taken her back to the last place she ever wanted to be.

'You sure? Lilian – with you?'

She examined the picture more closely. Her brow furrowed, and she nodded again.

I dug about in Brad's goodie box for the packet of cheap biros. On the back of the picture, I sketched the internal layout of the silo complex, based on what I'd seen and Anna had told me. I traced a line into the main entrance and then right, into the first room. 'Lilian – is she in there? In there with you?'

She took her time before giving me another nod. I don't think she needed to think. It was more that she didn't know what the fuck was going to happen to her next.

'The guards? The bad guys?'

I treated her to my cartoon gorilla impression, complete with the hands-under-the-armpits thing. It didn't even get a flicker of a smile.

'The guards, there are four?' I held up my fingers. 'Four?'

She didn't answer. She burst into tears.

'It's OK. No one will hurt you now. It's OK . . .'

I went back to my wall, slid down it and took short sips of brew. I didn't want to crowd her. She calmed herself down, got dressed and started blowing up the airbed.

She avoided eye contact. I didn't know for sure what she was thinking, but I could guess.

I finished my brew and went back into the mailroom for the BlackBerry. I sparked it up as I returned to the loading bay. I didn't yet know whether the girl could speak, but I knew that she could hear.

The ringing tone went on for longer than before.

'I've found her.'

'Excellent.'

'I don't have much darkness left but I'll get back there now and try to lift her anyway.'

Tresillian did his usual party trick. 'No, you will not, Mr Stone.'

Not even a 'well done' this time.

'But it has to be tonight.'

There was an uneasy silence at the other end of the line.

'We have a . . . complication . . . Once you have lifted the girl I want the building and anyone inside it destroyed. No one who has had contact with Lilian must get away.'

'Destroyed?'

'I want an explosion. I want a spectacular. I want to see it on *News at* fucking *Ten*. Do I make myself clear?'

'You want me to blow up a building in a major European city?'

'Is there an echo on this line?'

I fantasized for a moment about blowing up the silo with Tresillian inside it. 'No, there is not.'

'Very good.'

'But first I need you to attend to another matter. It appears we have a little competition. Stand by, Mr Stone. But don't move a muscle. Your contact will explain.'

The line went dead.

By the time I got back upstairs, the girl was tucked up in the sleeping bag with her hands wrapped around her mug. She looked me in the eye, and I finally got the slightest of smiles.

I sat back down against the wall and rested my head on my knees once more.

16

Thursday, 18 March
06.27 hrs

I woke up face down on the carpet. The sleeping bag was
draped over me. I opened my eyes to see a pair of bare feet
peeping out from under my rolled-up jeans. She leant over me,
her hair frizzed almost into an Afro after sleeping on it wet. She
had a brew in her hand. Her expression softened as she put the
mug down beside me.

I tried to focus on my watch. At least I'd got a couple of
hours in. I looked up at her groggily. 'You OK?'

She didn't reply. She looked even more like a waif with my
clothes hanging off her.

I sat up, stiff and sore from sleeping on the floor, but I'd
got used to that over the years. It's just a matter of how you
position your head and shoulders and spread your legs to
distribute the weight.

I tore a blank strip off the bottom of the A4 sheet that held
Lilian's picture, grabbed one of the biros and wrote down an
address.

I took a sip of the extra-sweet black tea and gave her a grin.
Didn't they have any fucking cows east of Poland?

She retrieved her brew from the sink and went and sat on the airbed. Her knees came up to her chest. Her arms went round them. Her face was expressionless once more.

I had to get this thing moving. Bradley would be here at ten. By then I needed to have dealt with her, sorted myself out, and worked out exactly what I wanted him to do for me to get this job done.

As soon as we'd finished our brews, I pulled myself to my feet. 'Come on, let's go.'

I draped my bomber round her shoulders and coaxed her up. I took her hand and, gently but firmly, steered her to the door.

At last there was a reaction. Her eyes were like saucers. She was scared.

I opened the door for her and shooed her out. I let her go downstairs in front of me so I could check the telltales.

She stood shivering on the pavement in her bare feet while I locked up. I didn't replace the telltales in the door. I wasn't going to be long, and the less time I was exposed with her on the street, the better.

We started down Papaverhoek towards the main. I almost had to drag her. We passed FilmNoord XXX. The white tarpaulins lining the market flapped and billowed in the distance. The morning traffic buzzed across the junction ahead of us.

I dug into my jeans for the wad and counted out about a hundred euros.

She looked at me blankly. I had to prise open her hand and shove the money into it. 'Take this. You've got to go.'

I handed her the strip of paper and made sure she focused on what I'd written. 'Go to the Radisson Hotel, Schiphol airport. Taxi – take a taxi, yeah?'

I ran my finger under the address and slowly repeated it.

'Radisson Hotel. Airport – Schiphol airport. You take a taxi, yeah?'

I pointed to the road that led to the nearest taxi rank. 'Taxi, that way . . .'

I hadn't a clue if she totally understood me, but she got the general drift.

'A woman . . .' I started signing like I thought she was deaf. 'A lady – with short blonde hair – will meet you. She will help you. Help you go home, yeah?'

Her eyes welled up. I could see she was trying not to, but she couldn't help it. The tears eventually fell.

I took off my Timberlands and dumped them on the ground next to her feet. She didn't move. I had to get hold of each of her ankles in turn, lift it into a boot and lace it up.

'OK, you've got money and shoes – so go!'

She stood there.

'Go – it's time!'

'Where am I?' Her accent was heavy enough for her to be Brezhnev's daughter, but her voice was clear. 'What country is this?' She looked and sounded like the lost child she was.

I didn't want to hear any more. There wasn't time. I needed to be back at the safe-house ASAP. 'You're in Holland. Amsterdam. You have money. Get a taxi to that hotel. The blonde woman, short hair – she'll be there to meet you and help you.'

'I come with you?'

'I'm leaving tonight. I'm not staying here. The woman will help you.'

I pulled out another couple of hundred. 'Take a taxi to the airport. And make sure nobody sees you with all this money. Just go.'

I turned away from her.

'Thank you.'

'It's OK. Use it to get home.'

'No – not for this money. For what you did. For what you did last night.' She shuffled towards me in the Timberlands, raised herself onto the tips of her toes, and kissed me lightly on the cheek.

I patted her awkwardly on the shoulder and headed off in

the direction of the larger of the two roundabouts, not wanting to look back.

Chucking a left, I walked for maybe two hundred metres until I spotted a phone box. Anna answered immediately. It was as if she was on stag. Her iPhone only rang once.

'Listen – one of the girls from the building is heading to you right now, in a cab.'

'Does she have a name?'

'Probably. This has to be quick, I have to get back. She's got dyed blonde hair and no eyebrows. Maybe call Lena and see what she can do for her. I need you able to move at a moment's notice in case the shit hits the fan.' I didn't tell her that it already had.

'Are you planning on bringing them out one by one?'

It was a half-arsed attempt at humour but it made me laugh anyway.

'Nicholas?'

'What?'

'Be careful.'

17

From where I stood in the shadows by the middle office window, I had a good view of the front door and along about ten metres of road back towards the main. I'd be able to see Bradley coming – and anybody who was behind him.

My watch told me he should be here within the next ten minutes. I'd showered and shaved. I'd been to the market and bought everything I was after – for now, at least. I had new jeans, a ready-faded pair like the ones I'd seen the East European lads sporting in Moldova club land. The sweatshirt was so cheap it felt like a carrier bag, and my brown padded nylon coat wouldn't be on the catwalks any time soon. The trainers I'd selected to replace my Timberlands didn't even have a name, but fifteen euros wasn't going to take me all the way to Niketown.

The sky was grey. The sun occasionally made it through the clouds, but never for more than a few seconds. I tried to concentrate on the street below but I couldn't get the girl out of my head. That wasn't good. I hoped things would turn out OK for her, but this wasn't helping me with my next task. I was writing a mental list of gear I'd need to put the silo on CNN and the BBC – and how to divvy up that list with Bradley. There were a few things I could ask him to get for me, but one or two others I really had to get hold of myself.

I tried to cover all the options. Best-case scenario was that the girls would be kept in the silo until they were due to be moved. Would the Scousers accelerate the process because their neo mates had been given a malleting and a piece of merchandise had done a runner? These lads were in a tough business. They'd be looking over their shoulders big-time, but I doubted they'd flap every time there was a bit of a drama. And I doubted they'd call the police to report an assault. The burst of lights and siren had puzzled me last night, but now I wondered if the boys in blue had just thought the neos were dossers and given them a quick blast to move them on.

As for the lads in the Passat – fuck knows what was going on there. Fuck knows what Tresillian was up to either. Why destroy the building? Bricks don't talk. If it was just a plain search-and-destroy job I'd probably have binned it now and done a runner with Anna. But the girls – I couldn't leave those poor fuckers. Which meant I had two days and two nights left to get the job done.

Bradley saved me from my thoughts. He strolled into view, hands in his pockets, dressed exactly the same as yesterday. He reached the door and I heard the buzzer. I looked as far along the street as I could to make sure no one else was with him.

I headed downstairs in time to watch him step inside.

'Morning, Mr Smith.' He gave my new clothes the once-over. 'I've got you a present.' He undid his jacket to reveal a box of Yorkshire Tea. 'It's a great shop. Even sells baked beans.'

His smile disappeared. 'I have some news. There's been a change of plan.'

I turned for the stairs. 'No rush, mate. I know. Tresillian told me last night. We'll talk in a minute.'

Sometimes people can get so sparked up about putting the information across that they get ahead of themselves. Better a trickle than a torrent.

He went straight to the sink when we reached the top floor.

He couldn't have missed the mountain of aspirin packets on the draining-board. I'd bought three packs from each of four shops. But he eyed the mallet.

I shrugged. 'It fell down last night.'

He filled the kettle and I ripped the cellophane off the tea.

'The guy you took the video of? He's called Michael Flynn.'

'Who is he?'

Bradley showed me a black-and-white printout on a sheet of A4. I could see this really was a family business. The Flynn gene pool hadn't been blessed. Both sons had the same fucked-up eyes as their father. Robot looked a year or two older than Bitch Tits, who had put on a few pounds since this was taken.

Bradley stuck a finger on each of the boys' heads in turn to indicate. 'Mick Flynn has two sons – Jimmy, the elder, and Ray. Jimmy moves these girls on to the UK and all over mainland Europe. He's a major player on the drugs scene as well.' He hesitated.

'Very nasty people, the Flynns. The police found two girls in a rubbish skip three years ago. They'd been beaten and burnt so badly it took months just to discover who they were. Mick and Jimmy are rumoured to have tortured them for trying to escape from one of their holding houses. It was Ray who'd let them go. He took such a beating from his father that he was in hospital for weeks.'

'So where's the complication?'

'You may not be surprised to hear he's not the only game in town. Some new boys want in. Moldovans. If they succeed, things could get very messy for us. And for you.'

'Why? I'm not here to fuck about with some tin-pot gang war.'

He pursed his lips. 'I'm way down the food chain – but I think Mission Control is worried that they might hit the silo before you do.'

'What can you give me on these fucking Moldovans?'

'I have an address.' He turned back to the kettle. 'You'll need to write it down. The names here are as long as the roads.'

I pulled a Bart Simpson notebook out of Bradley's goodie bag.

I wasn't surprised he hadn't written it down for me. He wouldn't be leaving anything to link him to the job. If I was in his shoes I'd be making me do the writing as well.

'It's on W-e-s-t-e-r-s-t-r-a-a-t, number 118. It's just short of the junction with Noordermarkt, in the western part of the city. It's quite a smart area. There's a café with striped canopies on the junction.'

'You know anything about the house? Is it alarmed? How many occupants?'

He handed me a brew. 'We know the main man drives a smart green—'

'Passat?'

'How do you know?'

'Because my nan's Gipsy Rose Lee. What does he want doing to, this Moldovan?'

'Killed, Nick. That was all he would say.'

'I'd rather be doing the Flynns.'

'Mr Tresillian didn't say anything about the Flynns.'

'Yeah, anyway. Any idea where he parks the Passat?'

'That's all I was told. I thought you knew how to find out stuff like that.'

Fair one. He was sounding more like Tresillian by the minute.

'So I take care of things in Westerstraat before they make a play for Lilian and her mates, then turn the silo into a hole in the ground?'

He nodded. 'Life never ends well, does it?'

'What?'

'No matter who we are or what we do, we all die.'

'Tell you what, I need you to get me some gear.' I walked towards the door. 'I've got to get a move on.'

He fell in behind me as I headed for the stairs.

'Can you get me shotgun cartridges?'

'Yes.'

'Birdshot, solid shot, whatever. I need at least two hundred rounds.'

We reached the bottom of the stairs.

'No need for receipts.' I grinned and held out my hand. 'Lock up, so real people still think the place is empty.'

We agreed that he'd come back at the same time tomorrow, and I headed back up the stairs. I waited by the first exit onto the fire escape until I heard his key in the top lock, then legged it three at a time to the top floor. I grabbed the mallet, ran to the mailroom and scrambled up the ladder. I twatted the bolts and lifted the roof hatch.

I'd wanted my new best friend on foot today not just because of security but also because I wanted to start finding out what the fuck this guy was all about. Making him walk was a way of slowing him down. It might give me the chance to see what he did next.

I kept low to minimize exposure as I headed towards the top of the vacant office block.

Yesterday Bradley had claimed he didn't know what was going on – and didn't want to know. Yet this morning it seemed like he knew everything. He claimed he didn't have comms, yet he'd been talking with Tresillian. It was all a bit too foggy for me. And having comms didn't mean they 'had you'. That was bollocks. If it were true, I'd have dumped my comms on day one. No one will ever call when you're not expecting them to: it could compromise the job. The only danger lies in passing on mixed messages – like this fucker had been doing. Maybe he'd made the mistake of thinking I was a knuckle-dragging gorilla from London who should be kept in the dark. And maybe Tresillian had too.

I reached the next-door building and moved to the edge. I poked my head slowly over the parapet and looked down onto Papaverhoek. Bradley was almost level with me, hands in his pockets, heading for the main.

I slid back, took a bit of a run-up and jumped towards the higher roof. I managed to hook my hands over the raised brick-work at its edge and scrabbled with the tips of my fifteen-euro trainers to continue my upward momentum. One elbow followed, then the other, then my right knee as I swung my legs to the side like a pendulum. Ten seconds later I was lying on my stomach on the tar-and-gravel surface. I got to my feet and ran past the entrance to the central stairwell to the far side of the block.

Bradley had a BlackBerry in his hand. He was taking too much time just to dial. The fucker was waiting for secure comms. He finally raised it to his ear. I watched his back as he walked down towards the junction. His free hand was cupped around the phone. Whatever Tresillian was saying, he had Bradley's full attention. His head was down, and he kept close to the wall, as if it was giving him a bit of protection, and preventing him from being overheard.

So he had comms after all, and he was bullshitting. I'd been correct not to trust him, and not to say a word about the girl.

I watched him veer right at the junction and disappear. There was a gap through which I could see the main drag between the big and small roundabouts. I waited for a while, in case he came back into view.

If I'd had more time I might have followed Bradley to see what the little shit got up to, but I had more important things to do. I gave it another ten minutes.

18

I sheltered under the little ferry's glass canopy and watched the city grow slowly bigger as we crossed the bay. It looked more like a Second World War landing craft than anything a tourist would leap onto. But, then, who in their right mind would want to visit the decaying docks and warehouses of Noord 5?

The other seven passengers all had bicycles. A couple in workmen's overalls munched their lunchtime sandwiches. The rest were in jeans and trainers, like me. They all had day sacks.

On the other side of the scratched glass, boats of all sizes zigzagged between the big cargo vessels nudging their way east along the waterway into Europe or west out towards the North Sea. High in the air, and so far away it was scarcely visible, I could just about make out the pinprick of a helicopter. Not many people would have noticed it. Even fewer would have known the reason it was static. There was probably a surveillance operation on. More than likely, it would be something to do with drugs.

I could picture what was going on up there. Somebody would be sitting in the co-pilot's seat with the world's most sophisticated optics at their disposal. The heli was an eye in the sky. These things could hover kilometres from the target area and still get a grandstand view.

Even back in the nineties, when I was doing surveillance in places like Belfast and Derry, the gear was phenomenal. I once lost the target in a crowd in the Segments, a shopping area protected by turnstiles and security fences. I didn't have to panic. The boy was obsessive about his trainers and bunged them in the washing machine most nights with a scoop or two of Daz. The optics were so good I could just rattle around looking at feet rather than bodies, waiting for a pair of spotless white trainers to appear – which they did.

Nowadays helicopters were used to track vehicles that have had small GPS devices hidden on them, or to support covert police surveillance teams on the ground. The eye in the sky means the surveillance team don't have to be right up the target's arse all the time; they can go where the heli operator tells them to, only closing in when they're about to be unsighted. If he goes into a building, they can stay back: they don't have to have the trigger on the house because the helicopter can do that.

My walk from the safe-house to the ferry had taken me past the tile warehouse. I had the mallet with me. It always felt better having a weapon. The parking spaces were filled with shiny but battered Transits – Distelweg's factory units were doing a roaring trade. Almost every one of the bays was full. I'd kept my hands in my pockets as I mooched past the flour silo, head tucked down inside my new nylon padded jacket but eyes up. The gates were still chained and padlocked.

I'd passed the hole in the fence without giving it a second glance. The oil tanker that had been parked up yesterday had gone. The lads waiting for the ferry leant against their bikes, smoking or chatting on their mobile phones.

The Panda, for now, was static and hidden. I wasn't going to take it back to a place I'd been honked at. I wanted to check out the silo without being pinged by the neos.

The ferry was now about halfway across. The sky was still

trying to make up its mind whether to rain or shine. Now and again a shaft of sunlight broke through, but it was soon beaten back. I stared out of the window, yawned and checked to see if the pinprick was still above us. There'd be a lot of covert ops going on in the Costa del Clog. This city sold a whole lot more than red cheese and tulips. It was the world's drugs hypermarket and the United Nations rolled into one.

The Russians and Turks controlled the heroin, the South Americans the cocaine. The Moroccans, Jamaicans and Africans ran weed. The challenge for British gangs was transporting the stuff home. Most tried to ship it as bog-standard cargo, but there were other ways. The East Europeans helped them out. A mule can swallow about a kilo of coke packed into condoms. Fuck *Dragons' Den*. The big-time drug tsars could eat the men in suits soft-boiled for breakfast. If only these lads could apply their skills to the real world, we'd be out of recession in no time.

Deals were done here because it was a perfect distribution hub, east and west, and not just for drugs. For Brits like Flynn, the UK was only a ferry ride away, or less than an hour on a plane. Friends and family could pop over for the weekend. The Dutch all spoke English and they looked like us, so it was very easy to blend in. No wonder a third of all British fugitives were tracked down in this neck of the woods. One Brit was lifted by the Dutch police with a £125 million haul ready for shipment to the UK.

The landing-craft ramp came down at the end of Tasmanstraat. The bikes trundled off first and I followed. The road was dead straight, built on reclaimed land. I wanted to get hold of a map, but I wasn't going to find one here. The smart apartment blocks on my right looked like they'd been built in the thirties. On my left, the road was lined with trees and bikes. The canal was wide, with more apartment blocks on the opposite bank. They were Gucci too, and there wasn't a scrap of litter or an election poster in sight. This must be where the professionals

237

lived. Perhaps they were all so rich they didn't need shops. They had everything delivered.

I carried on towards the west end of the city. Daffodil buds poked through the ground, searching for sunlight. It was trying really hard to be spring, but it wasn't happening yet. What was going on here? I was on a job, not a nature trail.

I finally came across a shop on the ground floor of an apartment block. It wouldn't sell maps but the green cross meant it would have something else I needed. I went inside. Maybe a pharmacy in the building gave some indication of the age group of the people who lived here. I bought three packets of aspirin in tin foil and a bottle of water. I washed down a couple of Smarties and moved on.

The road became busier and wider still. I came to a bridge at a T-junction. Traffic lights were strung on cables across about five converging roads. The apartment buildings looked more sixties now, but were still upmarket. One to my half-right was arranged in an open square. A shopping plaza filled the ground floors. I headed over. There was another pharmacy, a newsagent and a café with chairs and tables outside.

There's something magic about the number three. If I tried to buy four packs the pharmacist might get sparked up – it just tipped the scale. If they balked even at three, I had my excuse ready. I took one a day to keep heart attacks at bay.

The newsagent fixed me up with a shiny new postcard-sized tourist map. The target road was about a kilometre away, at the start of the narrower canals. I'd soon be in *Van der Valk* country again.

Heading back towards the main to get my bearings, I noticed a bunch of daffs around the base of a tree that had managed to leap out of the mud and burst into flower. Either the plaza had its own microclimate, or the bulbs hadn't paid any attention to Mother Nature's timetable.

I went and sat outside the café and waited for someone to come and take my order. I admired the daffodils again, and then I found myself looking at all the people around me, doing everyday stuff like going into shops and walking around with mobiles; mums pushing prams; a couple of old men sitting on a bench under the tree, reading newspapers as they waited to die. I looked at the tree. It would also be budding soon, I supposed.

I'd never really bothered with this sort of stuff. When I was a squaddie, I only knew three types of weather: wet, hot, and cold. Even as a kid, I didn't understand about seasons. I didn't know how it all worked. Council estates were grey all the time, so what was the point?

I made a decision. I didn't want to die without living. Once this job was over, I needed to have a look at the real stuff. I'd head for Moscow with Anna and go and see some paintings I'd read about and try to work out what had got everyone so excited. In the meantime I'd sit here for a while and let my unconscious soak it all up. This could be my one and only chance at a bit of normality. Maybe I'd thought of it as shite all my life because I couldn't be bothered to get off my arse and go and have a look. Then again, maybe it was because I was scared of getting too close to what these people did – going to work, having a mortgage, raising families, looking in the mirror, being real.

19

A group of toddlers played in the square, watched over by their mums. The weapons-grade buggies they were pushing had probably cost more than my first car. I watched them for a while, then sat and stared at the speck hovering high over the eastern side of the city for so long it almost hypnotized me.

I was woken from my semi-daze by the arrival of coffee and a sticky bun. Good. I had to start concentrating. The job was the thing that mattered, not some daffs sticking out of the mud or me wondering what the view was like from the eye in the sky.

I drank my coffee, then fished out my map. The streets and canals became narrower from here on in. Westerstraat lay at the base of a triangle of land, with canals framing the other two sides. A road ran down from the apex, and vertical streets either side paralleled Westerstraat, forming a grid of sorts. I hadn't taken much notice of this yesterday. I'd just con-centrated on Anna's directions and getting to the meet on time.

Anne Frank's house, another place I should add to my bucket list, was a bit further down. I'd walked past it a few times when I was a squaddie, but never gone in. It hadn't offered strippers or beer.

I headed back to the junction with my pockets full of aspirin. I'd get a whole lot more later on: I'd need a Bergenful to achieve what I had in mind.

I crossed a bridge over the west-side canal. As I walked down it, I scanned the roads parallel to Westerstraat; they were narrow and one-way. I was coming into the Amsterdam I knew best, in *Van der Valk* country: canals, trams, cyclists weaving between pedestrians, cobbles, narrow one-way streets. Centuries-old houses leant out over the brick-paved streets. Bikes were parked everywhere. Pedestrians were segregated from cars by lines of bollards. The buildings were immaculately kept and predominantly residential. Even the houseboats looked expensive. A James Bond villain would have looked completely at home among their timber and glass.

I remembered reading somewhere that a couple of hundred years ago these houses were taxed according to how much land they occupied. Surprise, surprise, the Dutch went narrow and high. There were at least four or five storeys to all these places, with big, warehouse-style winches sticking out of their attics so anything large and heavy could be hauled up to the higher floors.

It was going to be a nightmare to recce in these narrow roads. There was no cover and no reason to be here. I couldn't just stand in the middle of a lane and study my target. I'd be able to do one walk-past, maybe two at a push, as long as I came back in an hour or so from a different direction.

There was the odd shop, and yet another pharmacy. I went in for more aspirin but also discovered something else I was after. Pure alcohol. Well, 95 per cent pure. It wasn't for drinking, but the sort old people use as an antiseptic. I bought two 500ml plastic bottles of the stuff and crossed it off my mental shopping list.

Eventually, I turned left onto Westerstraat. It seemed out of place somehow, an eighty-metre-wide boulevard among the lanes. There was even a central reservation big enough for two cars to park nose to nose.

A lot of the expensive-looking seventies and eighties apartment blocks boasted shops on their ground floor. They were independents rather than chains: a bike shop, a couple of small supermarkets, an Internet café next to a mattress store, a newsagent.

118 was down at the end of the street, as Bradley had promised. I saw a sign for an Internet café that turned out to be more of a 7/11. There were four or five banks of screens. You paid in a slot machine and could order food and drink, even buy music CDs.

I logged on with five euros for thirty minutes, then hit Google Earth and Street View for my virtual tour of the target. I could see the striped canopy that ran outside the café. The target house's pitched roof was immediately to its left. It was narrower than those on either side of it. It backed onto a square, with four similarly proportioned terraces lining each side. I clicked the arrows anti-clockwise along each of them, looking for a gap between the buildings. I finally found an archway. I could imagine a coach and horses rattling through to the stables after dumping the good burghers of Noordermarkt outside their front doors. The whole area had now been segmented, with fences and walls bordering private parking spaces and places to store industrial-sized wheelie bins.

I soaked up the imagery. This was the only known location for the target, and not a bad one. At least it wasn't exposed to the real world, unlike the café next door. Whatever went on inside was kept inside. For a while, anyway.

I wanted to get into 118 later today, to work out the best access route when I came back later to finish the job. I needed to check out the alarm system, and might even be able to adjust a window or door lock to make re-entry a whole lot easier. Once I'd sorted the competition, I'd have bought myself the time to get everything in place to hit the silo. My number-one priority was still the girls, whatever Tresillian had in mind.

I Googled Anne Frank's house and a couple of galleries to mix the session up a bit, then deleted my history and closed down, making sure the log-off really did log off.

20

The white café with striped canopies and a blue door was open for business on the junction ahead. The canal was less than a hundred metres further on. White plastic sheeting protected a run of stalls in a small, brick-paved square between the two. There were no green Passats in sight.

I crossed the road opposite 118 so I had the clearest possible view of its front elevation. A small glass porthole protected by a metal grid was set into the solid wood front door. The windows on all three floors were wooden-framed and double-glazed. I couldn't see lights or movement behind any of them.

I spotted two keyholes: Union cylinders, probably with night latches. They wouldn't normally be a problem to defeat; I could just buy a couple of other Unions and doctor the keys. But the road was constantly busy, and I didn't fancy fucking around with them in front of an audience: people were having a beer and a pizza just a couple of metres away. With any luck they'd have the same kit on the back door as well.

The entry point into the square was about a hundred metres up Noordermarkt. The street was much narrower, with houses and shops on both sides. Most of them seemed to be selling candles, linen and anything else that was white. The good burghers' coaches would have been rolling in and out of here pretty much all the time back in the eighteenth century, but these days they were a bit more reluctant to welcome uninvited visitors. A pair of wrought-iron gates now stood guard a few metres in. They were surrounded by vines and flowers, but weren't just there for decoration.

To the left of the archway, within arm's reach of a driver, was a bank of buttons on a steel box and a numbered keypad. To the right of the main gates was a smaller one for pedestrians, with its own digital entry box mounted on a steel panel on the latticework frame. There are ten thousand possible combinations to a four-figure code. I'd be here all week trying to find the right one; that was the whole point of them. I needed a simpler solution: I needed to find out how the guys on the inside of the square – and their welcome guests – managed to get out.

I pulled the map out of my pocket and gave my head a bit of a scratch as I pretended to get my bearings. The main exit would be triggered from the inside by a detector as a car approached the gate. But how did they open the pedestrian gate from the inside? It wouldn't need a code: they'd have a simple push-button arrangement of some sort. Was the button on the back of the electric lock? Was it set back, on the wall? I couldn't see much in the shadows. I gave the steel panel behind the entry keypad another look. It had to be there for a reason. It had to be there to stop anyone on my side of the fence getting access to the exit button.

I couldn't risk going any further in – I might just as well be wearing a striped T-shirt and a stocking over my head. I wandered back onto Noordermarkt and took the first left. I wanted to do a complete 360 of the square. There might be a less secure route in. I hung another left and was soon back on Westerstraat. I'd found nothing.

I crossed the road and carried on back towards the target, keeping my eyes open for a newly parked Passat or any change on-target. Was an extractor flue knocking out steam perhaps, because somebody had come home and jumped in the shower?

Nothing.

It was only two o'clock and another three or four hours until last light.

I carried on towards the canal, following signs that showed a little man walking towards Anne Frank's house. Not that I was going to see it – not yet, anyway. I was heading for the centre, the area of town I knew well, the bit that was full of bars and whorehouses, backpackers and tourists. That was where I'd blend in best, and where I could buy what I needed to get this bit of business done without anyone remembering me.

I crossed the canal and stopped at an ATM. I drew out three hundred euros on Nick Smith's MasterCard, as you would do if you were bumbling about the city centre, planning a bit of souvenir shopping and maybe a mooch around the red-light district.

I carried on to Damrak, the main drag from the central train station. It was a blur of trams and cars. Bells jangled. Cyclists wove between pedestrians. The place was packed, mainly with drug-dealers whispering, 'Weed? Cocaine?' to anyone who came within reach.

There were a couple of camping shops. A lot of the visitors here were backpackers. I went into the biggest, and therefore with luck the least friendly, and bought myself a black fifty-five-litre Bergen. Into it went a hard plastic knife-fork-spoon set any Scout would have been proud of and a Russian-doll type assortment of cheap aluminium cooking pans of the kind he'd make rehydrated stews in that nobody wanted to eat.

I also bought a twenty-litre plastic water container, the sort that concertinas down to save space, and a roll of silver gaffer tape big enough to stick the world back together. The last bit of kit I bought from this place was a portable stove in a plastic briefcase, fuelled by aerosol cans rather than Camping Gaz canisters.

At the checkout I paid with cash and picked up a novelty

mosque-shaped dual-zone digital alarm clock that was on special offer. I only needed Dutch time, not Mecca's, but it had a big speaker at the back of the green plastic casing. That meant it would have a decent battery pack to power it.

I shouldered my Bergen and headed deeper into the city centre. I still had a lot of shopping to do. I needed two tool sets, rubber gloves, three thick 500ml drinks glasses, small halogen light bulbs, a couple of metres of tubing and a shedload of aspirin. I needed some bits and pieces from a hardware store too, and a roll of freezer bags – not the zip-tight ones, which still let in air, but ones I could twist shut and seal with a wire twist. They were the only kind that would stop air getting in and causing an explosion before I wanted one.

21

By the time I got back to Westerstraat my Bergen was filled with nearly everything I was going to need. It wasn't dark enough yet for me to infiltrate the square and do my stuff. I might as well sit, look and listen. I made my way down to the café and took a table under the striped canopy. From here I could keep eyes on the target door. When the waitress arrived I ordered a pizza and a big bottle of water.

There was still no sign of life on-target. No light, no movement. There was plenty happening outside it, though. Little kids skipped past, hand in hand with their parents. Some stopped at the café for juices and ice creams and all sorts of other stuff that had to be cleaned off their faces with a pressure washer. Then there were shop deliveries, people like me just mincing about, and others engrossed in phone conversations. I sat back and watched, taking in some more of this real-life shit while I waited for my Margherita to make an appearance.

I glanced down at the Bergen. The business end of a red plastic G-clamp poked out of the side pocket. I'd bought it, along with a basket load of other stuff, in Amsterdam's equivalent of a pound shop. I pulled the flap back over it – nothing to do with being covert; everything to do with neatness. Having things sticking out of a Bergen was a big no-no in the army. They could catch or get pulled out, and make all sorts of noise. 'That's what fucking flaps are for,' our instructor had yelled at us zit-covered boy soldiers. 'So fucking flap the fucking flaps over.'

This was the second or third time recently that I'd found myself thinking about all the strange and funny stuff from way back. 'What's in the past belongs in the past' had always been my mantra. What was happening to me? Was this part of the process when you knew you were about to die? Was I going to spend the next two months digging all this stuff up and reappraising what I'd done and said? Or was the thing in my head growing and pressing the access buttons on Memory Central?

I dug a hand into my jeans and dragged out four Union keys. I'd thrown away the locks themselves, in four separate bins. They weren't the first four I'd picked up. I'd had to hunt for ones that didn't have exaggerated variations in their peaks and valleys. These were as even along the teeth as I could find. I wanted to spend as little time as possible filing them down.

The pizza arrived. I ripped off the crust and rolled up the rest. I'd never seen the point of cutting it up with a knife and fork or one of those little wheels that flick tomato sauce all over your shirt. This method was much more efficient.

As it got darker, I pulled the plastic G-clamp from its pouch and unscrewed the adjuster until it came off completely. I was left with something more like a C than a G. I chucked the bit I didn't need back into the Bergen.

One last check of the target front door and windows. Still no lights. I paid my sixteen-euro bill with a twenty and slung the Bergen over one shoulder. I wandered around the corner, not looking too purposeful, and up between the candle and stationery shops on Noordermarkt.

With the clamp in my hand, I pulled the second Bergen strap over my free shoulder and turned under the arch. This time I went straight up to the gate. You can't hesitate. You have to look like you do this most days; you have a reason to be there, and it's not just to make off with the good burghers' flat-screen TVs. I stood in front of the lock so my body and the Bergen masked my activity, as you would if you were about to insert a key or tap in a few numbers you didn't want anyone else to see.

I focused on the steel plate behind the keypad and worked the open end of the clamp between the wrought ironwork so that the jaws of the C looked set to take a bite out of the panel. The top pad was now poised on the inside of the plate. I scanned the wall to check I hadn't missed a button on my recce, then eased the clamp back towards me so that the pad could make contact with the electronic lock release. There was nothing I could do now but move it back and forth and hope to connect.

I heard footsteps behind me, but passing by on the pavement, not turning in through the archway. Nobody paid me any attention. I manoeuvred the C clamp another five or six times and suddenly heard a gentle buzz. The gate was open. I pushed my way through and closed it behind me.

Sure enough, the archway opened onto the square. I walked with purpose. I was a householder returning home. I always got a bit of a spring in my step after a successful infiltration, but this one felt particularly special. In all probability, I didn't have many more of these to go.

22

I took cover behind a group of over-sized wheelie bins and got my bearings. The area had been carved up by a good few more low walls and fences since Google Earth had taken its snapshot.

Lights shone at all different levels from the backs of some of the houses. Bodies moved around in one that looked like it had been converted into offices. There were no faces at any of the windows.

I bent down and pulled a pair of dark blue washing-up gloves from a side pocket of the Bergen. I'd ripped them out of their packaging when I'd bought them and thrown it away. I pulled them on and felt around in the Bergen for the mini toolkit. China's finest had set me back ten euros in a hardware store and came neatly packed in a black plastic box.

The set consisted mainly of screwdrivers, but I'd been after the tiniest Leatherman rip-off on the planet. It contained every tool I needed, including a knife and a saw.

'You're only as sharp as your knife.' Another instructor's voice from way back, as clear as a bell.

I shoved all the kit I needed into my jeans pockets, then took off the nylon jacket and left it on top of the Bergen. It could hang out behind the bins for a while instead of rustling on my body.

I jumped up and down to make sure I hadn't left any coins in my pockets, or anything that was going to rattle or fall out. I did one last check that all the other bits and pieces were good and secure in their pockets. I headed for the target, toolbox in my left hand.

I ran through the what-ifs. What if the Passat came in as I was approaching the target? What if another vehicle did? Where would it look natural for me to move to? What if it came in while I was working on the door, and caught me in its headlights?

I had no idea whether any of the doors ahead of me might suddenly fly open. There was a chance the café's might. They were bound to have lads coming in and out with deliveries and bin bags. Fuck it, I didn't really care. I was just going for it. If anything, I was upbeat. I was doing what I wanted to be doing. I got a kick out of covert entry and going in and doing things when people didn't know you were there. I always had.

As a kid, I used to break into the local fruit and veg shop and hole up in a corner while I ate their bananas. I wasn't hungry: it was all to do with the fact that I knew I was there and they didn't. When I couldn't sleep, I used to hide under the table in the kitchen. I sat listening as my mum and stepdad smoked themselves to death on Embassy Golds in front of the telly.

The target's parking space was separated from the café's by a two-metre-high wall. It was empty. The café's space was chock-a-block with wheelie bins and empty crates. Ahead of me were a couple of doors. A few lads were busy knocking up even more pizzas behind steamed-up windows.

There was nothing on the ground floor of the target building except a door, and the same pattern of windows on the higher floors that I'd seen at the front. As I moved closer, I could see that the door was slightly raised. A short steel staircase led up to it. Closer still, and I saw a basement well, with maybe two metres of clearance between the house and the square. It would be my best bet for cover if I needed it.

First things first. I nailed my mindset. Plenty of people

would be walking up to doors in this square every day, and that was all I was doing. I looked for somewhere convenient to stash a spare key. There wasn't anywhere, not even a plant pot or a flat stone. It looked like the area was swept and cleaned every day. Either it was a Dutch tidiness thing, or they were ultra-cautious about security.

I checked the back-door lock. It was a Union pin tumbler, chrome, centre right, all very nice and shiny. Maybe they had one key for both front and back. I made my way very slowly down the steel steps into the basement well. I didn't want my feet to jerk across a window. I didn't know who or what was down there yet.

As my eyes adjusted to the deeper darkness, I lowered myself slowly onto my knees. I put one eye against the sash window. The glass was clean. The paintwork was pristine. The frame was wood and the panes were double-glazed.

I couldn't see too much of the room on the other side of it, but the décor looked smart. There wasn't any rubbish: no magazines lying about; no clothes flung over a chair; every-thing was in its proper place. Were the Passat team just tidy lads, or did they have a Dutch housekeeper? And, if so, was she a live-in?

I couldn't see any motion detectors in the corners. I gave the bottom rail of the sash a shove. You never know. It didn't budge.

I shuffled across to the next window, which looked into the same room. I tried again, with the same result. A pity, but nothing insurmountable. I needed to get in and sort out the locks. Down here in the basement was going to be my entry point when I came back.

The door alongside them was lever-locked and bolted top and bottom. It didn't move an inch. And there wasn't even a speck of dust down here, let alone a hiding place for a spare key.

It was time to go and deal with the back door. I pulled out the three Union keys that I'd tied together on a string. I gripped them between my teeth while I extracted the mallet from my waistband.

I headed up the stairs. I was going to be exposed, but there was nothing I could do about that. I wasn't going to hang around for the green Passat to pull up so I could try to hijack its occupants.

I gave the dark blue door an exploratory push top and bottom; they both moved. No bolts. I'd been counting on that, because it was closest to where they'd leave the car, but I felt the tension leak out of my shoulder muscles nonetheless. If they'd secured the back and just gone in and out of the front, I'd have been in trouble.

A pin-tumbler lock contains a row of spring-loaded pins. When you insert the key, its peaks and valleys adjust the pins, both upwards and downwards, until the cylinder can turn. Once the operation is complete, the cylinder returns to its original position and so do the pins. It was a tried and tested system and, until a few years ago, secure. Then somebody discovered how to 'bump' them with a substitute key.

You insert the bump key all the way into the lock, pull it out one notch, apply pressure in the direction of the turn, and give the end of the key a sharp tap. The key bangs against the end of the lock, and the kinetic energy travels back along it. The pins jump, and because of the pressure you're applying, the key will turn.

I shoved the first of my trio of keys into the lock, pulled it back one click, my finger and thumb applying the necessary clockwise pressure. I put an ear to the door to check for noise one last time, and gave the handle a short, sharp tap with the mallet.

Nothing.

I tried twice more.

Nothing.

I swapped keys. I tapped again, and on the second attempt my clockwise pressure turned into a full rotation.

23

I shoved the string of bump keys back into my jeans, stepped onto the mat and gently closed the door behind me. The place was in darkness. There were no winking lights on a console by this door or the one at the far end of the hall. There was no bleep of an alarm waiting for a PIN to be entered.

The house smelt as if its owner had emptied every boutique in Noordermarkt of its lemon-scented candles. I flicked on the deadlock. If someone did come back, they wouldn't be able to get in. They'd give it a few goes, thinking the lock was jammed, and that would give me enough time to exit from the front.

I let my jaw drop open, so all the internal noises like breathing and swallowing didn't intrude. I did nothing but listen for a minute or two. The house was completely silent. There wasn't even the tick of a clock. All I could hear was the dull rumble of the Westerstraat traffic.

I cocked my head and listened again. I wanted to make sure no one was reacting. I'd opened a door. Even when people are asleep, their eardrums can be sensitive to minute changes in air pressure. Grannies call it sixth sense, but more likely it was caveman-survival stuff. You needed a little advance warning if a brontosaurus was coming to visit.

I waited a few seconds longer. There was still no creak of a floorboard, no sound from a radio or TV.

As my eyes adjusted, I began to make out the streamlined cabinets to my left and right. The walls were white. Rugs covered the polished wood floor all the way to the front door. A small bowl that contained change but no keys was perched on top of a glass cabinet. The two men's winter coats hung on a rack above it. There were no handbags, purses, patterned umbrellas or a copy of the Dutch version of *Hello!* to suggest a female presence. Two doors were open to my left. Gentle light filtered through them from the street. There was no hint of cigarette smoke or stale cooking. All I could smell was furniture polish, lemon and more lemon.

I focused on the shape of the front door at the end of the hallway. Somewhere down there would be the staircase to the upper floors, but I wasn't going to use it. I wasn't going to check the rest of the house. There was no need. Everything I was interested in was downstairs. I wouldn't be long down there, with luck no more than ten minutes. All I had to do was study the windows and door, and work out which of them I was going to leave unlocked for when I came back.

I put down the toolbox and mallet and took off my trainers. The floor would show any grit or dirt in this show-home, and anyone as fastidious as its occupants would notice. I would also check my socks weren't leaving sweat marks. If they did, I'd give them a wipe when I did my clean-up recce on the way out.

I tied the laces together, put the trainers over my left shoulder, and picked up the little black box and the mallet. There were two doors to my right. One of them had to lead to the basement stairs.

I was reaching for the handle of the first when it opened and light flooded into the hallway.

24

The guy had greasy black hair that reached the collar of his black shirt. His sleeves were rolled up. There was a mug in his hand.

He spotted me and his jaw hardened. With not so much as a shout, he hurled the mug. It missed me but the hot stuff in it didn't.

I lunged for him, but I was too slow. He was gone, legging it back into the room he'd come out of.

I followed him, crashing past leather sofas and a table. On the table sat an empty plate and a small kitchen knife. He grabbed it. He had a weapon. He turned back towards me. His face was stone.

I spun and tried to dodge the stab but he was too fast. I felt a punch to my buttock. At first there was no pain at all. A split second later, there was a dull throbbing at the site. Then a burning sensation permeated outwards and turned into intense pain. My leg buckled under me. As I crashed to the floor, I vomited. A trainer smashed into the top of my head. A pissed-off voice screamed down at me in a language I didn't understand.

He kicked out at me again and I jerked back my head. My face slid in my own puke. I brought my arms up to protect my head. The top of my right leg felt like there was a blowtorch playing on it.

He yelled something, either to me or to someone else in the house.

I brought my knees up to protect myself, trying to get into some kind of foetal position, but the pain in my leg prevented me. I had to jerk my right leg out to keep it straight, and curl up the left one as best I could. I got a kick to the stomach for my trouble. Thank fuck they were trainers not boots, but it still hurt. I was going down here.

My left eye was blurred. I tried to wipe it on the side of my arm. He walked around me and kicked me in the back. I took a deep breath. I felt his hands and knees pushing against my back, then his hands digging into my pockets. He dragged the cash out of the front of the jeans and I knew I'd never see it again. I hoped he'd count it – anything to give me some time to recover.

The pressure left my back. I watched as the trainers moved round to face me. He carried on to the door, and closed it to contain us both. The next thing I heard was the bleep of numbers being punched into a mobile phone. He was breathing like a porn star, but when he spoke, his voice was calm.

There was a pause.

I opened my eyes. The tattoos running up his forearms were tribal. They looked like the Pizza Express logo, and were very dark and new. He closed down and the phone went back into his pocket. He walked past me and disappeared to the other side of the room. Then he came back over and I sensed rather than saw him reach out. Pain shot through me. I realized the knife was still sticking into me, and he was sawing it backwards and forwards.

He leant down and shouted words I didn't understand. He played with the knife some more. All I could do was take the pain.

I gritted my teeth as the knife came out. My right buttock was on fire.

He screamed it down into me, jamming it back in.

He had to push a cushion over my face to muffle my yells.

25

The cushion came off and the kicks rained in.

I curled up. I flexed my leg even though I could feel the blade still stuck in my buttock.

There was nothing I could do. Sometimes you've got to accept you're in the shit and ride it out. He wasn't going to kill me. He was waiting for someone. I was still in with a chance.

The kicking continued until he finally lost his breath and beads of sweat poured down his face. Then there was silence. I heard window blinds being opened and closed, and the slam of vehicle doors outside. Black Shirt grunted something as he fought for breath. For all I knew he was talking to himself.

The back door rattled. Not once but twice. That was supposed to be my signal to leg it out the front. Black Shirt took a long, hard look at me and decided I wasn't going anywhere fast. He whipped along the corridor and did the business with the latch.

I heard another voice, deeper, stronger. He didn't like what he found. He started yelling. A pair of legs edged around the vomit. I saw immaculate jeans over smart brown brogues.

My arms were still protecting my face. The blue rubber gloves were covered with vomit. I lifted my elbow. He, too, had black hair and a dark complexion. He had his hands in the pockets of a short camel-hair coat. He bowed from the waist to try and get some perspective on my face. I smelt a mixture of cologne and cigars.

He straightened up and turned to Black Shirt. His hands swung between me and the pool of sick.

Black Shirt hung his head. It looked like Brogues was his boss, and he'd let him down badly. And, going by the concern on his face, Brogues didn't dish out that many second chances.

Brogues shouted as hard as he pointed. My body screamed at me in pain, but the longer his rant, the longer I had to recover.

Black Shirt muttered something and tossed him the container of Smarties.

Brogues threw up both his hands. It clattered to the floor. He didn't want his prints on it. He leant down to me and shouted a question in my ear. I moaned and groaned as if I was out of it on drugs. I wished right now that I was. At least it would dull the pain.

Brogues didn't bother asking again. He looked up and down the hallway, rubbing the designer stubble on his face and then the back of his head.

He pointed at Black Shirt like an inquisitor, his tone lower, more threatening. I still couldn't understand a word he was saying, but was pretty sure he was asking him to solve a problem, and that problem was me.

A moment later Brogues decided the time for questions was over. His jaw jutted and he started issuing orders. Black Shirt was looking for a little sympathy and understanding but getting fuck all. Brogues didn't wait for a reply. His shouts faded down the corridor and I heard my door slam.

26

I waited for Black Shirt to get close. I coughed and snorted the sludge from my nose, trying to make it sound like I was suffering, but in fact trying to get as much oxygen into my lungs as I could.

He picked up a cushion and kicked me. He knelt carefully behind me so his knees weren't in the puke, and pulled my head back and up. I took a deep breath just as the cushion came down.

Both his hands pushed against my mouth and nose. I gripped his wrists. He grunted with effort. My nose was compressed to breaking point. I knew I could hold my breath for maybe forty-five seconds. I struggled for twenty, and then I let my hands fall from his as he kept pushing. As my right hand dropped I wiped as much puke off it as I could onto my jeans. I jerked my head backwards and forwards to make it look like I was in the final throes of suffocation. I was, but I was also trying to grab another lungful of air while my hand closed round the knife handle.

My chest was going to explode. I could feel my face bloating and burning as I gripped the weapon more tightly. Now was the time. I jerked the knife out of my arse and swung my arm high. I rammed it back down in as wide an arc as

I could manage. If it missed him, I risked stabbing myself.

It made contact. He screamed. There was resistance. It didn't go straight in. I had to force it. The skin finally buckled and the blade sank between the bones.

I didn't pull it out. I might not get it in again. I pulled it down towards me as hard as I could and twisted my body as he came down on top of me.

I sucked in air. I saw the blade in his neck. There was no blood. It had missed the artery.

I kept digging, twisting and pushing, swung my left knee and came up astride him. The serrations faced the back of his neck. I got my left elbow onto his shoulder, pinning him with as much of my body weight as I could. His face was turned to the right. I twisted the blade until the serrations faced his windpipe and started to saw. The knife wasn't sharp enough. I had to bring it out and plunge it in again. I kept my arm solid, moving it up and down using the top of my body to get some weight behind it to help it rip through the tissue.

He screamed again. I grabbed the cushion and held it over his face with my free hand as I tried to cut into him.

I forced the cushion down harder. The knife was firm in my hand and my arm was rigid. I rocked and used body weight to move it up and down.

It wasn't long before he gave up. He had no choice. His body was giving up for him. It wouldn't be long. I would just have to leave him to die. It wasn't him I was here for. I now had to grip Brogues.

I lay there, trying to recover. I took deep breaths, snorting and gobbing to clear my nose. Black Shirt was fading fast. The rasping and gurgling noises became fainter and fainter.

I put my hand in his pocket and retrieved the money he'd forgotten to tell his boss about, and then put my trainers back on. I yanked the knife out of his neck and gripped it in my left hand.

Slowly, I opened the door. The hall lights were on. The

clink of bottle on glass came from my left, the other end of the hallway. I walked towards it, picking up the mallet on the way.

Brogues started gobbing off as soon I opened the door. I couldn't see him immediately but I could hear him. He thought I was Black Shirt. He took a swallow of something and walked round the corner towards me when he didn't get an answer. He had a tall glass of light brown stuff in his hand with ice floating on top. This boy was sharp. He charged towards me. No hesitation; no fear.

I stood still. There was nothing I could do about this. His eyes were locked on mine. He knew exactly what he was going to do when he got to me.

I had to do the same. I tried to focus. I could feel the blood warm and wet on my leg. It was ripping me apart but I had to get into the zone where it all became slow and defined in my head. He was coming to kill me, to do the job that Black Shirt had failed to do.

He finally got his head down. He was going to body-charge me back into the hallway. Once he'd done that, he was going to jump on top of me and finish the job.

I raised the mallet and waited. I concentrated on the back of his head. My whole world was focused on the blurred shape barrelling towards me.

When he was less than half a metre away I swung the mallet down. In the same motion, I twisted my body and dropped like a matador to get more energy behind the hardened rubber.

As my knees bent, he crumpled. His head fell onto my thighs and he came down with me. By the time I hit the floor his head was wedged between my thighs and chest. I checked his pulse. There wasn't one.

I scrambled to my feet. Keeping the mallet with me, I raced as fast as I could to the first floor. Unlike the hallway below, the rooms were all spotless.

There was no point looking for a weapon. Brogues seemed

too switched on to have anything that might compromise him in the house. He didn't even have an alarm system that could bring the police running if tripped.

I pulled a white satin duvet and the bottom sheet off a bed and staggered back downstairs. I checked Brogues's pockets for the Passat keys. They were empty. I had to stop and take a breath to calm down. Of course: the bowl by the back door. I wrapped him in the sheet. He wasn't bleeding, so wouldn't need anything thicker to soak it up. I turned off the lights, picked up the mallet and tool-box, and left him in the now darkened hallway.

I went outside and retrieved my Bergen. I threw on the padded nylon coat to cover the mess on my jeans and sweat-shirt. I climbed into the Passat. It was automatic, top of the range. I turned it round and reversed back in towards the door. I hit a button and the boot clicked open. I did one last scan. The square was in darkness. All the neighbours were in their own perfectly manicured little worlds. Nobody was rushing to investigate.

I couldn't lift them. I was going to have to lug each one down the steps and load them one at a time.

I wrapped Black Shirt in the duvet and dragged and pulled it towards the back door. I bumped him down the first couple of steps. The second was level with the Passat's boot. It took all my strength to lift and push him in. I brought down the lid in case someone above me suddenly got curious.

I repeated the process with Brogues, then got behind the wheel and gunned the engine. The Passat rolled towards the gates. I didn't have a clue how they opened, but I'd find out soon enough.

I drove slowly. Now wasn't the time to look like I was in a hurry. I travelled twenty metres into the square and turned right into the archway. I stopped about three metres from the gates and they began to open.

I turned left up Noordermarkt. My arse was still sending

Mayday signals to my brain, but I was breathing and I'd removed another couple of traffickers from the landscape before they could make a play for Lilian and her mates. Right now, that was all that mattered.

PART SIX

1

I turned left onto Papaverhoek and passed FilmNoord XXX. The window blinds were up and bright blue-and-white rope lights shone their welcome onto the pavement.

I'd used the same route as yesterday from Westerstraat, taking even more care than usual not to become the focus of any attention. I kept the sun visor down even though it was dark. There weren't as many speed and CCTV cameras here as in the UK, but I wasn't taking chances.

I passed the German office block and nosy-parked in front of the shutter, exactly as I'd done with the Panda. Headlights off, I climbed out and limped over to the door. The telltales were intact. I went to put the key into the top lock. Pain shot through my buttock as I raised my arm. The congealed blood felt cold on my skin. I'd been sitting on the warm leather of the Passat's driving seat and now the air was getting to it.

I leant on the door with my left hand as I started on the last lock. My leg spasmed and bile flooded into the back of my throat. My nostrils stung as the puke acid launched another attack.

I wrestled the door open. I wanted this wagon under cover as soon as possible, and then I wanted a brew, a shower, and some first aid.

The footsteps behind me were heavy. I spun round. She emerged from the dark interior of one of the doorless garages and headed straight for me, arm outstretched. She was still in my boots and clothes.

'What the *fuck*?'

'Please, *please* . . .'

She had a wad of euros clutched in her hand.

'Please, the money. Take it. I—'

I grabbed her and bundled her over the threshold, then followed her in. She fell against the stairs. I shoved my face right into hers. 'Wait here!' I needed her off the street, as well as the Passat. I'd get rid of her later.

She shut up. She was going to do what she was told. She wanted me to help her. She was going to be compliant.

I moved as fast as I could into the loading bay and down the metal steps towards the shutter. I banged the button and it started to grind open. I didn't turn on the lights. As soon as there was enough clearance I bent down and eased myself underneath it. It still stretched my wound and another jolt of pain shot through my body.

I slid behind the wheel. There was a smear of blood on the driver's seat, but there wasn't a pool of it. The capillaries withdraw after the initial trauma and the deeper muscle mass closes the wound. After a while the site is just gooey, not running with the stuff. But there was still one fuck of a hole in my right buttock and every move I made felt like I was sitting on a red-hot poker.

I drove in and parked alongside the Panda. As soon as the shutter came down I went back through to the front door and closed that too.

As the lights flickered on, she clambered to her feet, the cash still in her hand. 'Take me. You leave tonight, yes? Help me. Please.' Her eyes had filled with tears.

I stood with my back to the door. 'Why the fuck didn't you go to the airport? The woman, the blonde woman, my friend, was waiting for you.' I dug into my jeans, dragging out more cash.

She slumped to her knees and threw her arms around my legs, squeezing them tight. The red-hot poker got busy again and I pushed her off more vigorously than I'd meant to.

She saw the blood smeared on her hands from round the back of my jeans and must have smelt the bile. 'Let me help you. I will help you.'

I leant against the door. My mouth tasted of puke. My leg throbbed excruciatingly. I clenched my teeth and breathed deeply through my nose. 'Right – go upstairs. Get the kettle on.' Fuck it, it would all be over in twenty-four hours.

'Kettle?' Her face relaxed. She didn't know what it meant, but she knew I wasn't kicking her out.

'Boil the water.' I mimed drinking. 'For tea.'

She nodded and jumped up, eager to please. She bounded up the stairs.

I turned and locked the front door. I didn't bother with any new telltales.

Pushing myself off it, I shuffled back through the fire door and into the loading bay.

I took off the Passat's fuel cap. There was nothing to tell me if it took diesel or petrol. I gave it a sniff. Good: it was petrol. I'd need an extra bit of accelerant for what I had in mind.

I retrieved the Bergen from the front passenger seat and hauled myself upstairs to what I hoped was going to be a brew.

2

I checked the remaining telltales as I made my way gingerly up the stairs. I did all I could to avoid bending my leg. They were all in place.

The girl was standing with her back to me as I hobbled into the room. She seemed to be preparing the brew as if it was a three-course meal. Anything to look indispensable, I supposed. The roll of cash I'd given her sat on the drainer beside the open box of Yorkshire Tea.

I shrugged the Bergen strap off my shoulder and let its weight drag it down my arm. I didn't have the strength to lift it off properly. I leant against the wall in a vain attempt to relieve the pain. I didn't want to sit down and stretch the wound site any more. I was fucked, and I was glad to be here.

I let the Bergen drop to my feet and spoke to the back of her sweatshirt. 'What's your name?'

She didn't turn. Perhaps she still thought I was going to show her the door. She really was just a kid, doing the brew-making version of dragging the duvet over her head.

I didn't know if she hadn't heard me or if it she was ignoring me. I said it louder. 'What is your name?'

Her hands flew around in front of her as if she was

conducting the Philharmonic rather than just squeezing out a couple of tea bags. 'Angeles.'

'Like the city?'

She finally turned and smiled.

'Where are you from, Angeles? Nationality? Your country?'

'Moldova.'

'Why didn't you go to the airport, like I said? You could be safe now.'

She turned back and mumbled something into the draining-board.

'What?'

She got stuck into the sugar bag and finally came towards me with two steaming mugs of the black stuff.

'But I am safe. I want to stay with you.'

It wasn't much more than a whisper. Her hair fell across her face. I found it even harder to understand her now I couldn't see her mouth.

I was desperate to sit down, but leant my weight against the wall instead. She stood in front of me.

'How old are you?'

'Fifteen. I will cook for you. I will look after you. Anything. Please let me stay . . .'

I nodded and started drinking. The brew was hot and sweet and right at that moment it was as good as anything I'd ever tasted.

She sipped hers like a bird, then started waffling like a madwoman. 'I will help you, yes. Will you take me away from here? I can go with you tonight?'

I raised a hand to encourage her to slow down. 'I want you to do something for me. Get that towel and tear it into strips.' I held my thumb and forefinger about three inches apart. 'Like a bandage, yeah? I'm going to go and clean myself up.'

I started to move, but winced as the pain shot through my arse.

'Please – let me help. What happened?'

'Don't ask. Don't say anything. Just do what I say and I'll help you, OK?'

'Yes. Thank you.'

I staggered into the shower. As I turned on the water and waited for the steam, I struggled to peel off my trainers and jeans.

3

I almost screamed with pain as the hot water hit the puncture sites. But it was the only way. I had to get them clean.

I cupped my hand below the wounds and scooped the water over them. It was the best I could do for now. I'd get it sorted when I'd lifted Lilian and waved goodbye to Flynn and his silo.

Once the important stuff was done, all I wanted to do was get the smell of puke off me and brush my teeth. I could almost feel where the acid had burnt into the enamel.

I stuck my head out from behind the curtain. 'Can you bring me those bits of towel?'

I ducked back under the trickle of water and worked shampoo into my hair. It wasn't long before the door opened and in she came. I turned to face her. I didn't want her to get the wrong idea, but I didn't want her to see the stab wounds either.

I climbed out of the shower and used the part of my sweat-shirt that wasn't covered in puke to dry myself. She stood there with the door open, staring at the 'blunt trauma', as Kleinmann had called the knife, bullet and dog-bite scars that covered my body.

'Get your clothes off.'

She stared at me.

'Take them off. I need them.'

I tried to work the strips of towel around me like Gandhi to give my arse some kind of dressing. It wasn't happening.

Angeles handed me my jeans and sweatshirt before leaving. I put them on, then folded one of the strips and shoved it down the back of the jeans as best I could to get some protection over the punctures. I'd seen lads in Africa with much bigger wounds, big machete cuts that had taken chunks out of their arms and thighs, and they were still going strong. All I had to do was crack on for another couple of months.

As I pulled the sweatshirt over my head, I realized that in a curious way the pain felt good. It was from a proper old-fashioned wound, not some cancerous growth that I hadn't asked for and couldn't do much about. It was the sort of pain I could handle, and an aspirin or two would help. I wasn't going to run short of them any time soon. Perhaps the Smarties would too.

And then I realized something else: I'd left the Smarties at 118.

Fuck it, I'd be with Anna soon and I'd sort it then. Right now I'd just have to crack on.

Angeles was sitting on the airbed with the sleeping bag draped around her shoulders. The rest of my clothes were wet with blood or covered in vomit. I'd bin them eventually, but for now I was going to put them in one of the spare offices. The smell was making me want to gag even more. I started to gather them up. She jumped up to help. She grabbed whatever she could and wrapped it all in the brown nylon coat.

'Are you going home to your family? Your children?' She smiled. 'You have a baby seat.'

'I said no questions, remember? Don't ask. Do you understand?'

Her face fell. I kept forgetting she was only fifteen.

'Yes. I'm sorry.'

276

I took the bundle from her and reintroduced my feet to my Timberlands. 'I'm going out for a little while.'

Her world was falling apart once more. 'Please – can I come? Please don't leave me. You are coming back?'

I scrabbled about in the Bergen for a couple of aspirin. 'I'm going out to get some food, all right? I'll see if I can get you some clothes too. What do you want to eat? Meat? Bread?'

'Anything. Thank you.'

'Just sit down and rest. Do not leave the room. Understand?'

She wrapped herself up once more and settled on the airbed. She started to shiver.

'Look, I will be coming back. All my gear's here. I'm coming back. It's OK.'

In an ideal world it would be better if she came with me so I had control of her all the time, but I didn't have enough clothes for her. And I had a phone call to make.

I dumped the Bergen in the loading bay and locked the door. I headed down past FilmNoord XXX towards the market. I felt a lot better with my boots back on. The market itself wouldn't be open just yet, but some of the shops would be.

The all-night store I landed up in could have been anywhere in the Middle East. Big sacks of spices sat alongside crates of weird fruit and veg. The Arab version of *Starsky and Hutch* blared out from a TV mounted over the counter. Behind the checkout a young guy, with shaved sides to his gelled jet-black hair, munched pistachio nuts and watched the car chase. Half a souk's worth of bling hung down the front of his T-shirt, and the Iranian flag hung proudly behind him.

I walked up and down the aisles and filled a basket with pitta bread, cans of salmon with ring-pulls and cartons of UHT milk that sat alongside 25-kilo bags of rice and huge aluminium cooking pots. There were cheap plastic buckets, dustpan and brush sets, ironing boards and, more importantly, kids' clothing – cheap cotton shirts and jumpers, most of them with old Disney themes like *Lion King* or anything else that had passed its sell-by date. There were a few things that I thought would fit her and I threw them in the basket as well. I couldn't see any decent bath towels, just small ones the size of dish-cloths, but they'd have to do.

I got back to the counter as the cars drew level and bad guys with seventies haircuts and spear-pointed collars drew their weapons and fired at each other. The soundtrack sounded like belly-dancing music on steroids. A dozen or so phone cards were displayed in clear plastic wallets behind the boy with the bling. The point-of-sale poster showed little arrows aiming at all the different world flags, and a sentence or two in Dutch that I guessed told me it only cost two euros to call Iran or the USA. I grunted and pointed, as most people do if they can't speak the language, and managed to end up with a fifty-euro one.

I headed out with my shopping in thin carrier bags that dug into my fingers. The good thing about poor areas of any city, especially those with a migrant population, is that most of the phone boxes are still working. The mobile-phone network hasn't taken over completely because the locals don't have the cash.

I went into a call box and scratched the strip off the back of my brand new if slightly grubby card. I dialled the company number, and then the code. Finally, I dialled her mobile number.

I got a ringing tone, and then her recorded voice in Russian. I waited for the bleep.

'Anna – it's Nick. I'm going to keep trying to get hold of you.' I hit the receiver and rang straight back. If I'd woken her, she might have been too slow to pick up. After three rings I got the Russian version of hello.

'It's Nick.' I only told her as much about the girl as she needed to know for now. This wasn't the time for a full run-down and you never know who or what is listening. 'Her name is Angeles. She won't leave me. You have to come and pick her up.'

'She is scared, Nick. She's scared of everything and everyone – except for you right now. You're probably the only friendly face she's seen for months. I can get a cab and pick her up, but she could still run. Why should she trust me? She's probably been handed from person to person, and each one has made her situation worse. Can't you hand her over to the contact with Lilian?'

'No. I'll explain later. Could you lock her in the room?'

She thought for a few seconds. 'She is young, yes?'

'Fifteen.'

'Jesus. There's no saying what she will do. You are her only friend. Just think, Nick – chances are, the reason she is here is because of strangers. I have already called Lena. She will be able to help. She has contacts in the city. But you'll have to take her, Nick – you're the one she trusts.'

I stood with the phone to my ear while I tried to forget the pain in my arse and do some thinking.

'Nick? What do you want me to do?'

'OK, I'll keep her with me. Can you set up the meeting with Lena's people at your hotel, say three hours before the flight?'

'What flight?'

'Our flight to Moscow. We need to be away from here as soon as we can on Saturday. You should book the flights. Still got my card details?'

'Yes. But—'

'But what?'

'The other girls. What about them?'

'Don't worry. I have that sorted.'

4

My fingers were numb and throbbing from the carrier-bag handles by the time I got back.

She jumped off the airbed to grab them, the sleeping bag still gathered tightly around her. 'I help you.'

I let her. Why not give her the chance to feel she was earning her keep?

'Here are some clothes for you. Take a look.'

I went over to the kettle. I could hear the rustle of plastic behind me.

'My friend, the blonde woman, is going to help you – in a couple of days. But I'll be with you to make sure everything is OK, yeah?'

There was more rustling as she ignored what I'd said, pulled the gear out and tried it on.

'You must never tell anyone you were here, or tell anyone anything about me. You understand?'

I turned to see Angeles splitting open one of the carrier bags to make a kind of tablecloth. She spread it on the floor by the airbed and started tearing into the bread and opening the ring-pull cans.

'Angeles, do you understand what I said?'

All I wanted was for her to say jack-shit until I got tucked in with Anna in Moscow. After that, so what?

She looked up, her big eyes focused on mine, and nodded.

'OK, good. Start eating. Don't wait.'

She shook her head. She sat on the carpet with her legs tucked under her and waited while I poured water over another couple of Yorkshire Tea bags and added too many spoonfuls of sugar. I took the brews over and motioned her to take the mattress. No way was I going to sit down.

'Will you put some fish in the bread for me?'

She looked disappointed I wasn't joining her, but made me a salmon wrap and handed it to me. She didn't mess about after that. She gulped hers down, sucking her oil-stained fingers after each mouthful.

'Angeles, why have you got no eyebrows?' I wasn't going to tell her I'd seen what she had to do with an eyebrow pencil.

She stopped eating, mid-mouthful. Her hands, still holding the food, fell onto her lap. Her eyes followed. 'They raped us and then they held us down and shaved our eyebrows. They told us that the customers like their girls to look like that.'

'Just painted on?'

She nodded slowly, her head still down, as her mind took her back to wherever that place was.

I grabbed one of the cartons of UHT and sat down carefully beside her. She liked that.

I passed the milk over. 'What happened? How did you get here with the other girls?'

'I was walking home from school. Men came in a car when I was outside my village. Ukrainian men. They hit me, and put me into the trunk.' She looked up. Her face was a mask. 'They drove me to Odessa and locked me in a garage. In the trunk.'

She tried ripping at the carton's edge to release the milk but she couldn't do it, and it wasn't because she hadn't the strength. A tear welled in the corner of her eye and ran down her cheek. She put the carton onto the carpet as she tried to fight back. I picked it up.

'I was a virgin. I wanted to wait until I married, like my mother. But the men . . .'

I handed her the open carton and gave her a moment or two to gather herself. 'How did you get here?'

'I escaped from the garage. I went to the police. But they arrested me and sent for the Ukrainian men. They handed me back to them.'

I waited while she wiped her eyes. She took a swig of milk, her hands rigid with anger and distress. I was beginning to understand why Anna had felt so strongly about me not just handing her on.

'The men took me on a boat. I was on it for a long time. I had to . . .' She turned away, overcome by shame once more. 'I had to pay my fare . . .'

'You came here, to Amsterdam?'

'No, Copenhagen. Your picture, the girl – she is here now. She came here also. She told me Copenhagen. The men there . . .' She rubbed an index finger over where her eyebrows should have been. 'The men there did this.'

'You both stayed at a house there, an old, cold house?'

She nodded. 'A week, maybe ten days, I do not know.'

'And Lilian, the girl in the picture – she stayed there with you?'

She nodded. 'For maybe three or four days, with three other girls.'

My mind went back to the meeting with Robot, and what had been happening above us.

'Then they put us into a truck with lots of furniture and brought us here. But I escaped. I climbed up the tower.'

She wasn't celebrating.

'Angeles, how many men are there in the building? Where do they stay, what do they do? Do you think you could do me a drawing of the layout?'

She shook her head. 'I'm sorry. It was dark when we arrived and then we were kept in the room.'

'Did you go out of the room to eat, use the toilet?'

She shook her head. 'There is bucket in the room and they bring food from a takeaway. I don't know what else, I—'

'It's OK. Don't worry.' I didn't want to put her through any more of that shit than I had to. 'What about your parents? Brothers? Sisters? Family? Did they try to find you?'

She shook her head. 'My father? The Ukrainian men said they have given my father money. If he says anything or I go home they will burn our farm down. No one will help. My mother? What can she do?'

'The men, maybe they lied . . . Maybe they just said that so you wouldn't run home. You know what? My friend has people in Moldova who will help you. One of them was like you, taken away and all alone. But she is safe now, like you will be. They can find out if it's true what the Ukrainian men told you. Whatever happens, they can help you go home. Would you like that?'

She nodded. The tension was starting to ebb out of her face and neck. She gave me a small, shy smile. 'My brother . . . he looks like you.'

'Poor guy!' I gave Angeles as much of a grin as I could manage and left her to finish her picnic. The Bergen was in the loading bay, where I'd left it. I dragged out the twenty-litre plastic container and went back upstairs. I was going to need a lot of water for what I had in mind.

She watched me as she tidied empty cans into a bag.

'Stay here. Get some sleep. I've got to fill this, then do some work downstairs.'

She looked scared again.

'I'm not going anywhere, but do not come down, OK? Just stay here. Do you understand?'

She nodded.

'It's not long now. Then you'll be safe.'

She took a breath. 'What is your name?'

'Nick.' I turned away quickly and disappeared to fill the

283

container. My head had filled with images of what had happened to her and Lilian in the green house. I had to cut away.

I took the showerhead off and used it like a hosepipe. It was easier than fiddling around in the sink.

I hobbled down the stairs again with the full container and the bundle of vomit-soaked clothing. I laid out the kit at the back of the loading bay, behind the two vehicles. The fluorescents flickered uneasily. It didn't matter. I didn't need much light.

I took out the camping stove and screwed in the fuel, then opened the Russian-doll nest of pans.

The bulkiest item of all was the aspirin. I'd picked up 320 tablets of the stuff, and was going to use them all – minus the two I'd already taken, the two I swallowed now, and a couple more for luck.

The red-hot poker perked up again, but I found myself grinning like an idiot. I was going to sort out the bastards who'd done those things to Lilian, Angeles and the kids I'd spotted in the green house, and I was going to use 314 aspirin to give those fuckers the world's biggest headache. The kind of headache you got from an Improvised Explosive Device.

5

I didn't need much high explosive to totally fuck up the silo and anyone in it. CNN and the BBC were going to end up with some great footage. Two lumps would do it: one of about a kilogram, to produce a kicking charge; and one half that size to produce a firebomb.

Picric acid is magic stuff, but a fucker to make. To get there, I was going to have to separate the acetyl-salicylic acid in the aspirin from its bulking agent, add a couple more ingredients, and do a bit of mixing and distilling. The trouble was I only had the kit to make it in small batches. The whole process was probably going to take me all night.

I knew it better as Explosive Mix No. 7. As part of my anti-terrorism experience, I'd had to learn to be a terrorist. A lot of the time I was doing pretty much the same as they were, infiltrating a country, buying everything I needed in corner shops and pharmacies, and mixing those items with others in my basket so I wouldn't get noticed by the guy on the checkout. Then, like a terrorist, I'd go back to my hide, make and plant my device, and get out of the area before it went off.

The big difference nowadays is that we're in the age of the suicide bomber. They go in and stay with the device to make sure it goes off. Sometimes they're even wearing it. Neither of those things featured in my plans.

The first demolitions course I did when I joined the Regiment had lasted twelve weeks. I loved every minute of it. Even as a kid, I'd been fascinated by the TV footage of Fred Dibnah dropping power-station chimneys, and tower blocks imploding within their own perimeter. The principal task I trained for back then was to fuck up an enemy's industrial base.

Their troops might be giving us the good news at the front line, but no army can function if it can't get supplies. We might want to drop a bridge, railway line, hydroelectric power station or crude-oil refinery – or render docks useless, open floodgates, destroy military or civilian aircraft. So much damage can be done with just two pounds of plastic explosive. Why send in an air force to destroy a big industrial complex when the same result can be achieved by taking out its power source? It might be easier for a four-man team to infiltrate as civilians, do the reconnaissance, then buy ingredients over the counter to make the devices.

Destroying something doesn't necessarily involve removing it from the face of the earth. A large factory or even a small town can be neutralized by taking out an electricity substation. It might just mean making a small penetration of about half an inch with explosives into a particular piece of machinery. That might be all that's needed to disturb the momentum of the moving parts inside it. The machine then destroys itself. The skill is in identifying where the weak point is, getting in there to do it, and getting away again.

The problem is, you're not going to have a notebook in your pocket with all your formulas and bomb-assembly instructions. We'd spent the first few weeks of the demolitions course having to learn them by heart. There were nine basic mixes: nine different types of explosive for nine different types of job, from low explosive – a lifting charge if you want to make a big crater in a runway or blow up a road or vehicle going along it – to high explosives, which can be used with enough precision to cut steel if you want to destroy a power station or drop a bridge or a couple of pylons. It's horses for courses, different explosives for different attacks. High explosives were going to be perfect for me on this job.

I pressed forty aspirin tablets out of their foil and crushed them in the first of the three 5mm-thick juice glasses I'd bought in the market. I used the hard plastic spoon from the knife-fork-spoon camping set. It couldn't be metal. I was making picric acid because it's easy to detonate. The downside is that the slightest friction or percussion can set the stuff off. What's more, it attacks metal, creating salts that are just as explosive. It can only be safely in contact with wood, glass or plastic.

I opened the little tap at the bottom of the container, poured some water into the largest of the cheap aluminium pans and put it on the gas. While I waited for it to come up to the same temperature as a hot bath, I added a little water to the powder in glass number one to make a paste, then added a splash of alcohol. I stirred until it liquefied.

Only now was there time for my stab wounds to get a little TLC. I pulled my jeans down and poured some of the alcohol between the wound and towel padding. It was like my skin was on fire.

I left the mix on the concrete floor and hobbled over to the Passat. Brogues wasn't in complete rigor mortis yet. Everything but his eyelids was still soft and pliable. The process normally starts two to three hours after death and it can take maybe another four for all the muscles and organs to stiffen. It was cold in the loading bay, which would speed things up. The eyelids are among the first bits to go rigid, along with the jaw and neck. His eyes were no longer closed; he stared dully out of the boot. That was why the poor used to place coins over them to keep them closed.

His skin was already pale. The blood had settled in the parts of the body closest to the ground and had drained into the larger veins. The back of his head didn't look as beaten about as I'd thought it would. I pulled off his handmade brown suede shoes. I needed the matching socks.

I tried to sit down while I shoved a sock over glass number two, but my buttock wasn't at all keen. I had to stand and lean down instead. I poured the aspirin mix into the sock sieve. Cloudy liquid trickled through. After a while I removed the sock and wrung out the dregs. I didn't want the rubbish that was left – that was just the bulking agent. What I needed was in the glass – or, rather, what was going to be left after I'd evaporated the water and alcohol out of the liquid. But that was still a few steps away.

Glass number two went into the simmering water. It was going to take about twenty minutes for the alcohol and moisture to evaporate and leave a residue of white powder.

The next stage was to add the acid. Concentrated sulphuric was a lot harder to come by, these days, because of anti-terrorist legislation. Unless you're an industrial chemist, buying it arouses suspicion. My original plan had been to drain some of the Panda's battery acid, but the Passat was a bonus. Or so I thought. There was more of it, but it was a fucker to get out. Everything under the bonnet was covered and sealed to make it look all nice and Gucci. Nobody serviced these things any more: they just plugged them into diagnostic machines.

I poured out a third of the contents of each cell into one of the smaller cooking pots. Even depleted, the battery would still work. The battery acid had to be boiled until all the white fumes had disappeared. It had to be seriously concentrated.

The method for making picric acid hadn't changed for years. It was discovered in the late 1700s, and initially used as a yellow dye for silk and wool. Its explosive potential was discovered a hundred years later. The problem was, this stuff was so strong it attacked common metals like lead and copper to create even more dangerous salts, which were sensitive to shock. During the Boer War, the artillery boys threw shells into their guns and blew themselves up. There were some massive explosions in factories and ammunition ships. Tin and aluminium were the only metals picric acid didn't corrode. Millions of tons of the stuff were used in bombs and grenades in the First World War. They were all coated with tin to prevent the acid contaminating the metallic shell. Even so, munitions factory workers were nicknamed canaries because of the way it stained their skin.

Then they discovered that picric acid was only a nightmare in powder form. Even these days, if the powder is stored in a glass or plastic bottle, you have to take enormous care not to trap grains of it in the threads of the bottle and cap. It's so volatile that just unscrewing the top will make it detonate.

I was going to miss the kick of being able to get shit like this together and see the results. The payoff would be sitting on the flight to Russia with Anna on one side and somebody tapping away on his laptop on the other and me thinking, When you watch the news today you'll see what I've been up to.

I could see the white powder starting to settle in glass number two as the water simmered gently around it. I took the pan off the cooker and replaced it with the one holding the battery acid. It wasn't long before white haze was rising and wafting round the lock-up. Once it had stopped, I poured some of the concentrated acid into glass number three. Then, using the plastic knife, I slowly shifted the white powder out of glass number two and added it to the other so it became a white liquid.

All I had to do now was add a bit of potassium, before placing glass number three in the water and letting that boil down until the mixture turned a yellow-orange colour.

The final stage would be to filter it through a second sock placed over glass number four. But this time it wouldn't be the liquid I was after. I wanted what stayed behind in the sock. The yellow and – thankfully – wet lumps that remained were what this process was all about. Once dried, they would turn into one big fuck-off unstable explosive that could be detonated very easily by heat or an electric charge. For now, however, it would be stored wet in a double layer of freezer bags, twisted, folded over and fastened with the wire retainer to keep the air out and the acid wet. I would keep filling the bags until I had enough.

6

Friday, 19 March
07.20 hrs

I'd fallen asleep in Brogues's camel-hair coat, lying on the footwell carpets from the Passat. I'd spread them out on the floor alongside my four bags of explosive.

I forced myself up off the concrete. There was plenty more to do.

The first thing was to empty the water container to prepare it for its next payload. I opened the tap and let it run out on the floor. Next I got hold of the set of blister-packed halogen bulbs. The plastic packaging was so rigid I had to use the Chinese Leatherman to make any headway.

These bulbs were just what I needed. They were small, they banged out a huge amount of instant heat, and for their size they were more robust than normal bulbs, which were increasingly hard to find anyway because of EU green legislation. These ones would probably be banned as well when the law makers found out they could be used as detonators.

I pulled one out. It was about the size of the tip of my little finger. It had two loops of metal at the bottom for terminals.

The mosque digital alarm clock was next out of Santa's Bergen. I shoved in four AA batteries, then yanked out the leads that connected the power source to the speaker at the back. I twisted the bare wires around each of the bulb loops and set the clock to 08.00. Then I set the alarm for 08.01. Bang on time, instead of me getting the muezzin's wail, the bulb lit up. After three seconds it was hot to the touch – not enough to detonate anything, but that didn't matter for now. I was going to do something else to the bulb to bring it up to speed. I turned off the alarm clock to save the batteries and put it down.

The twenty-litre container had emptied. I picked it up, together with the length of clear plastic tubing I'd bought from a shop that sold tropical fish, and headed for the Passat.

I opened the fuel cap and shoved the tube down into the tank. With the empty container by my feet, I put the other end of the tube to my lips and sucked. My lungs filled with petrol fumes but I kept going. A few seconds later, the tube darkened. As soon as the fuel had risen to within an inch or two of the tip I slid my thumb over it and took it out of my mouth. I pointed it down into the container, pulled my thumb away and the fuel flowed.

I remembered all the times my stepdad had sent me out nicking petrol from other people's cars during the fuel shortage in the seventies. I was only about twelve. After that, he said there was a sugar shortage, so I used to get sent out to pocket the sugar shakers from cafés. There wasn't a sugar shortage, of course: it was my stepdad's way of saving a few pennies, and fuck the fact that I might get caught.

I left the tube where it was and let the siphon do its stuff. It was time for a brew. The flow would stop as soon as the fuel in the container reached the level of the tube, which was about twenty centimetres below the neck. That would be plenty.

I had a quick look at my G-Shock. Bradley was going to be here soon. I needed to have Angeles tucked away by then.

I had a quick check of the telltales on the way up to see if she'd been having a nose around. They were all in place, and so was the one behind the pigeonholes. I realized I felt nowhere near as bad as I thought I would without the Smarties. I made a mental note to stab myself in the buttock next time I felt a headache coming on.

The moment I opened the door she leapt up from the mattress and cut across the room. 'Nick! I make tea?'

I gave her a big thumbs-up. 'Madness not to.'

I looked at the sink. The mugs had been washed. Everything was laid out neatly. The milk stains and tea circles where I'd been making brews had all been cleaned. 'You had anything to eat yet?'

'No, Nick. I wait for you.' She looked worried. 'I touch nothing.'

I let her get on with it while I dug around in the plastic bags for a piece of pitta. It had started to go hard. What little scabbing I had on my arse had cracked with my exertions and was starting to hurt again. I leant on my good leg and gnawed on the crispy bits around the edges of the bread.

'Listen, Angeles, someone is coming to see me soon.'

She handed me my brew. She didn't look happy.

'This one must not know that you're here, OK? You understand?'

It didn't seem to register.

'He must not see you. I'll find you somewhere to hide. You've got to stay out of sight, yeah?'

She seemed to like the thought of not being seen. Maybe it meant she wouldn't be moved on.

'Stay hidden until I tell you to come out. You've got to be quiet. He's going to get really pissed off if you're here. He's only let me use this place because he thinks I'm on my own. If he thinks anyone else is here he'll be very angry with me. You understand?'

She nodded. 'Yes, yes, Nick. We still leave tonight?'

'No drama. Tonight. We'll meet the friend I told you about and she will ask her friends in Moldova if what the Ukrainian men said was true.'

I dunked my bread in the tea to soften it.

She almost skipped back to the sink to pick up her brew.

7

I had an even better vantage-point from the shadows beside the window of the middle office. I could see the front door as well as back along the road towards the main.

I checked my watch and gulped down my last couple of aspirin. They weren't helping much with the pain in my arse, but I thought I'd try one more dose just in case. The sky was still overcast. The sun hadn't quite given up trying to fight its way through the clouds, but it must have been tempted.

Bradley came into view, still in exactly the same clothes, but this time gripping a heavy and expensive-looking leather overnight bag in his right hand. I watched him to the door, then headed for the stairs.

By the time I'd got down to the fire escape on the first landing and turned to look down to the front door, he was inside and beginning to lock up.

'I have everything you asked for.'

'That's great, mate. Thanks.' I went down to meet him. 'Half the job's already done.'

'What do you mean?'

He followed me up the steps to the fire door and into the loading bay. His head bounced around the place, taking in the smell of vomit and petrol and the mess of pans and sock-covered glasses in my preparation area. The last of the sulphuric acid was still in its glass. But mostly his eyes darted between me and the Passat.

He was desperate to know what was going on but didn't want to ask.

'He's in the boot.'

'In there? You're sure it's him?'

'You tell me. Whoever it is, I got his sidekick as well. Don't ask.'

I fished out the key fob from my pocket and pressed the button. The bodies had hardened up completely. They were both curled up like Pompeii victims. Their puke- and blood-stained white shrouds only half covered them.

I went and picked up Brogues's camel-hair coat and extracted a slim crocodile-skin wallet. I produced a credit card with an unpronounceable name on it and tried to pass it to Bradley.

'Very good.' He didn't want to touch it. 'How did you do it?'

'Like I said, don't ask. That's my job. I'm more interested in what you've been up to. You get the cartridges?'

'Yes, of course.' He put the bag down and started to unzip it.

I talked to the top of his gelled-back hair. 'Have you spoken to Mission Control since we met up yesterday, last night, whenever?'

'No, not at all. Why do you ask?'

He was still hunched down by his bag, his eyes on the cooker. Mine were on the boxes of shotgun cartridges.

'How many did you get?'

'Twenty. When are you going to the silo?'

'Tonight.'

He nodded slowly as if the message had to sink in. 'I think I need to know what time you will be leaving here. I need to be ready to pick up the girl.'

'I'll drop her here as soon as I've got her, and then I'm heading straight off. I'll gaffer tape her up so she won't go anywhere.'

'What about the Passat?'

'Like I said, everything here will be clear. I don't know what time – nine, ten, eleven o'clock – but it'll definitely be clear tonight and the girl will be waiting.'

He knelt down to unload the cartridges. 'Excellent.'

He picked up the empty bag and we headed for the fire door.

'I suppose I'll never meet you again, will I, Mr Smith?'

'No, mate, never.'

If only he knew the real reason. Both of us would be dead really soon. I was coming to terms with that myself, but I almost felt sorry for him. He was a two-timing little shit, but all in the name of queen and country. Sadly for him, people like Bradley didn't realize that his queen had no idea he even existed, and his country didn't give a shit in return.

We went back down to the front entrance. Bradley stretched out his hand. 'Good luck, Nick.'

'Thanks, mate. And you.'

I unlocked the door and he stepped onto the road. Empty bag in hand, he carried on walking without looking back.

8

Back in the office, I threw open the cabinet doors. She was curled up like another Pompeii victim. Her face was creased with concern. It wasn't about being tucked into a filing cupboard and doing her own little Anne Frank, it was more to do with winning approval. 'I was quiet, yes? You did not hear me?'

'Yep, you were quiet. Now I have to go and work, so you have to stay up here again, OK? Go back to the airbed, rest, keep warm.'

'OK, Nick.'

I followed her into the back room. 'Not long now. We'll go out and buy you some real clothes for when we go to see my friend. I'll stay with you, don't worry, and we'll get some more food, OK?'

She nodded.

'You stay here.'

I closed all the doors behind me and headed back to the loading bay.

There were twenty cartridges in each of the twenty boxes, which was more than enough. In fact, it meant I could make my devices a bit bigger and a lot better.

Laying out my ingredients as before, I got back to work. The gaffer tape was a standard two-centimetre roll. I pulled out about two metres and placed a pan on each end so it didn't curl.

I opened the knife bit of the Chinese Leatherman and cut the top off the first cartridge. They were old. The red waxed-cardboard body cut far too easily, and the small pellets that dropped out were lead. They've been steel for years now.

After the front two-thirds of the cartridge was empty, I dug out the cotton wad that separated the shot from the propellant. I tipped the grains of propellant onto one end of the gaffer tape and an inch or two along it. I was doing pretty much the same as my stepdad used to do when he rolled his own fags, only this one packed a bit more of a punch than Gold Leaf did.

It took just over an hour to cut and pour the full two metres. I needed to make sure that whatever propellant was touching the tape was actually stuck to the adhesive. That way, there would be continuity in the burning even if there was a break here and there among the loose stuff if the fuse got bent. Once I'd done all that, I rolled the gaffer tape nice and tight until I had two metres of fuse half a centimetre thick. I put it to one side with the picric acid, well away from where I was working.

The next job was to make sure my bulb detonator was going to do its stuff. With the pliers part of the Chinese Leatherman, I crimped off the glass nipple to expose the insides of the bulb. I poured in propellant from one of the sixty-odd cartridges I had left over. Then I turned on the clock, set the alarm for one minute's time, and waited. The element lit up. Within three seconds the propellant ignited in a burst of bright flame. A small cloud of cordite was left hanging in the air.

I shook the residue off the bulb and reset the clock. I tried it again, this time without the propellant, and the light came on. I now knew the wire connections to the two terminals of the bulb were good, and the bulb itself was still working. Why use a new bulb and run the risk it was a dud?

I moved the assembly away from everything else. The clock

was the initiation device, and the bulb was the detonator. Now that they were joined, I had to make sure they didn't do their jobs until I wanted them to. I took the batteries out and laid them to the side.

There was just one more manufacturing task, and that was to pour the remaining propellant into two of the freezer bags, one for each charge. It took me just over an hour. When I'd finished, the bags went alongside the picric acid and the fuse.

I was almost done. All that was left was to retrieve the bags of damp picric. I cut them open and spread the yellow, clay-like substance on plastic to dry. Then, making one final check that Brogues's coat, credit cards and wallet were back in the boot of the Passat, I headed up the stairs.

The market would be open now, and we both needed clothes for our exfil. I needed to look as clean leaving the country as I had when I came in. And Angeles, well, she just needed to look dressed.

9

The food stalls were piled with all kinds of products you'd
normally find in a souk, from dates and spices to bags of rice
and pistachios. The next one along sold nothing but second-
hand clothing. Both of us blended in well. Angeles didn't get a
second glance in her gear from the House of Bling.

I was going to keep her with me now, regardless. No way
was I was going to let her stay in the safe-house with the
Moldovans downstairs and a roomful of volatile explosive
mixes. If she nosed around and found the bodies she might
lose it completely. If she found the mix and fucked about with
it she could take down the building. Only by controlling her at
all times could I be sure that I knew where she was.

The first priority was a coat each, not only to keep us warm
and dry, but also to cover our existing clothes if we had to do
a runner before we bought anything else. All the voices around
us were Dutch, Arabic and Turkish, so I did my normal grunt
and point. Next came a couple of sets each of trainers, jeans
and sweatshirts. I also bought her a hairbrush to sort out the
bird's nest on her head.

I was pissed off that I was still going to be in-country when
the place went up. The timer had to be set for two or three
hours at most. That way, the batteries had a good chance of

staying charged. Once I left the silo, I had no control over the device. I wanted it to be exposed for the least possible time, yet still able to give me enough to get out of the area.

I also couldn't control the space that the device was placed in, so would have no way of knowing if it had been discovered. I had to factor in getting back to the safe-house afterwards, not just to pick up Angeles, but also to shower and scrub the DNA and cordite off me, then get rid of the clothes I'd worn on-target. The last thing I wanted to do was to turn up at the departure gate, and have security sensors detect traces of explosives on my clothes or hands.

We moved away from the clothing stalls and she got changed in one of the coffee shops that lined the market while I slid into my nasty new black coat. I bought kebabs and coffees, and she shovelled everything down like a girl possessed.

'Nick?'

'What?'

'Your friend, what is her name?'

'You will find out soon enough.'

Even with just a few weeks left, I couldn't force myself to change the habit of a lifetime. I'd found over the years that giving out my own name was OK because it belonged to me. I could decide what I did with it, and what lies I was going to attach to it. But divulging the names of others was a different matter. That had to be up to them. In either case, you don't give out information unless you have to. The less she knew about me, Anna, Flynn and all the rest, the better. I didn't want to have an in-depth conversation about what I was doing here and where my family was. The only thing that was important was to get us both out of this situation. And as long as I kept her away from the loading bay, she'd know nothing and I could sort her out.

As we passed FilmNoord XXX, I scanned the road ahead. The ship still blocked the view of the waterway but apart from that there was nothing out of the ordinary, not even a car parked on the pavement.

We got to the door. She saw me checking the telltales in the locks.

'This is a bad area. You have to make sure nobody breaks in.'

The keys ripped through the little slivers of paper and I opened up. Angeles went through with the bags. I followed and turned to close the door.

The two bodies that bomb-burst out from the garages came at me in a blur of leather jackets, shaved heads and face metal. They were already halfway across the road and closing on me fast.

I jumped inside and tried to slam the door shut.

She looked at me, terror-struck, rooted to the spot.

'Run! *Go!*'

They kicked and pushed, jarring me backwards and forwards. I couldn't hold it any more.

The door crashed open.

10

I pulled her through the fire door and into the loading bay. That was where there were weapons. Where there were weapons, there was a chance.

There was nothing else I could do for her now.

I let go but she grabbed my hand again. I had to push her out of the way. The pulse in my neck surged as my body built up to the fight. She screamed somewhere behind me but my focus was on the glass of acid sitting on the concrete.

One of them was so close I could hear his laboured breathing. I dropped to my knees. They banged against the concrete. The pain shot up my thighs. I grabbed the glass and some of the liquid spilt. It burnt my right hand. As I turned, all I could see was jeans and boots.

I jerked the glass upwards and let go of it a split second later. I rolled away to escape the splashback.

The bearded neo screamed and his hands clawed at his face. He fell to his knees level with me. I jumped up. I wanted the Leatherman. I wanted one of the glasses. I wanted anything that was a weapon for the next man, who now blurred into my vision from the left. The grunts and screams continued from the lad below me. He was still on his knees as he took the pain.

The thud as the other guy's body hit me full-on was as hard

as if I'd walked into the path of a moving car. The momentum hurled me against the opposite wall. The back of my head hit the blockwork. Stars burst in front of my eyes. Hollering and screaming was coming from everywhere: from me, from them, from Angeles.

I scrambled onto my hands and knees. I had to stand. I had to keep on my feet. Go down and you're finished.

Neo number two was back and at me. He leapt on top of me. We grappled like a couple of scrappers in the schoolyard. I tried to head-butt him, bite him, anything to get him off me. I kicked and bucked. Both of us screamed. He had a week's bristle on him that rasped against my cheek. The boy stank. I could smell booze, cigarettes and unwashed skin. My face was stuck into his neck. I tried to get my hands up to squeeze against it. He snorted with exertion and snot fired from his nose.

He finally opened his eyes and I could see them bouncing around, out of control. He was in a frenzy. He managed to get his hands around my neck and squeezed. I tried to shake left and right. He started to snarl like a pit-bull.

He was on top of me, on the floor. I wrapped my legs around his body. My arse felt like I'd sat on a branding iron, but there wasn't a whole lot I could do about that. If I could get him closer he couldn't exert the same pressure round my neck as he leant in to me.

He lifted his head and snarled. It gave me a chance. I tried to head-butt him, tried to make contact wherever I could. I tried to bite into his cheek. He jerked his head away. I could taste his week-old sweat.

His mouth opened as he threw his face down onto the top of my head. He bit into my scalp. I could hear the skin break as his teeth sank in, and then the sound of him straining to bite harder.

I managed to get my legs tighter around his gut as the fucker started to pull his head back. I could feel the snorting from his nose as his teeth dug into my scalp and scraped along the bone.

I shoved my hands up in front of his face as my capillary bleeding sprayed the ground and ran down the back of my neck. My thumbs searched for his eyeballs and found the cheekbones and then went on from there. I pushed them down into the sockets. He jerked his head back. His teeth had to lose their grip. He needed to scream.

I moved my right hand so I had a flat palm underneath his chin, then switched my left to his ear. I didn't have much choice. If he'd had a fistful of hair I'd have grabbed that instead. He howled at me through clenched teeth.

I wanted to break his neck. To do that I had to screw it off, like I was turning a tap. I had to take the head off at the atlas, the small joint at the base of the skull. It's not so hard if you're doing it against a body that's standing. If you get them off balance as they're going down, you can twist and turn at the same time, so their own momentum works against them. But all I could do was keep my legs around him and try to hold him in one place.

I managed to get my boots interlocked, and at last I could squeeze and push down with my legs, at the same time twisting up with my arms as hard as I could. I kept on turning. We both screamed at each other. He bit my hand, trying to jerk his jaw left and right. This wasn't so much about him trying to kill me. I didn't know what he was doing. He was totally out of it.

I slid my left hand round the back of his head. I kept the palm of my right under his jaw and pushed up and round. His neck went with not too much of a crack. He slumped down without making a sound. His body didn't even twitch. He just went very still. I rolled over and kicked him off.

My vision was blurred. Pain seared the top of my head. Blood ran down behind my ear. But scalp wounds always look worse than they are. They're seldom serious. All there is on top is skin and bone.

My lungs were bursting. I sucked in oxygen as I rolled over onto my front. I forced myself up, ready for the next wave. But the drama wasn't what I was expecting.

Angeles was kneeling over the other body. He was lying on his back. Her arm moved up and down, up and down, into his body. Blood covered her hands and face as she stabbed and stabbed into his chest.

'It's OK – stop!'

I staggered over to her and caught her arm in mid-air as it headed down for another strike. I eased the Leatherman from her fingers and threw it on the floor. My right hand had a bright pink oval shape where the acid had etched into the top layers of skin, exposing the sensitive stuff beneath.

The area round the other guy's right eye had swollen so much it swamped the eyeball. The left one was open and dull.

Angeles convulsed with sobs, maybe from relief, maybe from fear. Maybe it was just happiness at getting back at these fuckers. I didn't know, and right now I didn't care. All I had to do was make sure we were secure.

'Wait here.'

I staggered through the fire door and down to the entrance. I locked up. When I returned to the loading bay she'd hardly moved from her kneeling position next to the body.

I stood over her and lifted gently under her armpits. 'It's OK. Let's go.'

I'd sort all this shit out later. For now, I needed her to get out of here before it all sank in and she started howling at the moon.

I helped her to her feet. She turned and put her arms around me and sobbed quietly into my chest.

In theory, the immediate priority was to get her cleaned up, and after that, to do the same to the loading bay. But she needed comforting. I put my arms around her and rocked her from side to side. 'It's OK, you're safe. It's all over. I'll look after you. Everything's going to be OK.'

11

I took her straight over to the shower and turned it on. There was a hum of electrics as it kicked off. Five minutes later she was still standing there, arms down at her sides, shoulders dropped.

'Get in there. Clean yourself up. Get some clean clothes on. You'll feel better.'

She didn't move. She just stared down at the blood on her hands.

She had to wash it off her quickly if she was to have any chance of putting this behind her. The longer you smell it, the longer you see and feel it, the deeper it digs into you. Every time she smelt blood in a butcher's shop, she'd think about today. Every time she had red ink or paint on her fingers, it would take her straight back. It didn't matter that the fuckers deserved it, or that she'd exacted some kind of revenge. If she kept being reminded of what had just happened, she'd be haunted for the rest of her life.

Steam billowed out of the shower and into the room. I dabbed at a pearl of blood that ran down my forehead. It would stop soon. I coaxed her towards the door. 'In you go. I'll take care of everything. Just get cleaned up, yeah?'

I wasn't getting any reply.

'Angeles, do that now? Please?'

I took her face gently in both my hands and bent down to try and get some eye-to-eye. There wasn't just blood on her hands now, but blood on her cheeks as well.

Finally she looked at me. 'Is he dead?'

'Yes.' There was no point denying it. 'But you did nothing wrong. You did a good thing. They would have killed us. You have saved your own life – and you have saved mine. Do you understand?'

Her eyes dropped.

'You understand that what you've done is good, don't you?'

Her head nodded slowly.

I kept my voice low and soft. 'Angeles, take your time. Clean up. But first, give me your clothes. I'm going to go downstairs, and I'm going to sort everything out. Do you understand?'

She gave a nod and I let go of her face. She started to undress and I went to the sink. The cold water on my hand felt almost as bad as the acid had, but I knew it was the only way. In a perfect world I'd have kept it up for at least half an hour, but that wasn't going to happen.

She came out with her bloodstained clothes in a bundle. Her shoulders were hunched. Her skin was goose-bumped all over. She looked like she belonged in a horror movie. Her skin was so white it was almost translucent, but her hands and face were crimson.

'That's great. Now go and have a shower. I'm going to bring the shopping up.' I gave her a smile. I pointed to her hair. 'You'll be needing the brush, won't you?'

I didn't get a smile back. There was nothing I could do for her apart from get things sorted and try to make her as physically comfortable as possible.

She loitered by the shower door.

'It's OK, Angeles. I'm not going anywhere except downstairs. I have to sort everything out. You've got to help me and I've got to help you. Everything is OK. Go, go.'

She nodded slowly and stepped into the steam.

12

The bags lay ripped and trampled on by the front door. I shoved whatever I could into the ones that were still intact, and scooped the rest of the gear into my arms. I headed back up and dumped the lot on the brown carpet. The electric shower hummed away on the other side of the stud wall as Angeles went through the horror of watching someone else's blood drain away by her feet.

I almost fell down the stairs in the rush to get back to the loading bay and start the clean-up. First into the rear footwell went the jeans with the stab punctures. I bundled up my vomit clothes and shoved them on top.

Next was my neo. I hauled him by his feet and pushed and heaved him on top of his would-be competitor. I'd never been a great one for poetic justice, but this came close.

Both neos were fucking idiots as far as I was concerned, but I needed to give myself a good kicking as well. They'd probably pinged us at the market, when I was paying more attention to cheering Angeles up than thinking about who might be looking over our shoulders.

They should have reported back to Flynn once they'd IDed the safe-house instead of taking things into their own heavily tattooed hands. Whatever, the fact was that in the next couple of hours whoever was back at the silo was going to be flapping and making some calls. But I had no control over that; all I could do was crack on with the plan.

I had to wedge Angeles's neo as far down the rear passenger footwell as I could. The boot was already full. I'd cover him with her sleeping bag before leaving.

The effort left me wet with sweat and gagging for breath. I leant against the vehicle and felt the top of my head. The wound was crescent-shaped where his top set had been able to rip into the skin. It would scab up soon enough. The sweat down my back started to cool and I felt myself shiver. My arse was hurting again, and so was my hand.

I had to grip the situation and make sure Angeles and I got out of here in one piece, simple as that. She'd only just started her life and I wanted mine to end with Anna. That was pretty simple as well.

I forced myself off the vehicle and carried on collecting together all the device-making paraphernalia and tucking it around the bodies. There was no easy way to erase my prints from the wagon, let alone the DNA. I could burn it, but even thirty years after an event, blood can still be identified. The only way I could to deal with this was to get all the evidence together and make sure it was never found. Not while I was alive, anyway.

I didn't touch the neos' wallets or ID. If I did my job correctly, the wagon would never be found, and all my problems, and some of Angeles's, would be packed away inside.

I lugged the battery back into the Passat and connected it up. Thank fuck it still worked. I didn't have jump leads.

I turned my attention to the devices. First into the Bergen was the water container with about four litres of fuel. Then I carefully curled the gaffer-tape fuse into a couple of loops and laid it on top. I took the roll of gaffer tape over to the alarm clock, gave the bulb a generous protective coating, made sure

311

the batteries were still in the wrong way round, then it went in as well.

Next was the picric acid. The yellow mush had crystallized on the plastic, and was ready for bagging. I placed it carefully in two new freezer bags, which I tucked into the left-hand pouch of the Bergen. The two bags of cartridge propellant went in the other side.

I put the Bergen into the front passenger's footwell of the Passat and climbed behind the wheel. I sat there, working through exactly what I was going to have to do tonight. I visualized my actions as if I were a camera lens, watching my hands assembling the devices, going through everything step by step. I didn't want to forget any detail that would stop the device detonating once I'd left.

The fire door opened. Angeles appeared in her new jeans. She had the brush in one hand but hadn't even tried to get through the knots in her hair. She looked about her. All that remained of the drama was a pool of dark red, almost brown, blood that had been smeared along the concrete as I'd dragged the body of her neo towards the Passat.

I climbed out. 'I need to clean that up before we leave.'

She wasn't listening. 'We will tell the police?'

'No, we won't tell the police anything. We just leave, and we never say anything to anyone at any time about anything. Is that OK with you?'

Her head juddered, maybe out of fear. 'I wanted to kill him.' She pointed at the blood on the ground. 'I wanted to make him pay. Make them all pay.'

I was expecting her to start crying again as I walked over to her, but she didn't. The tears had gone. She was pleased with what she had done. Fair one, I would have felt the same.

'Angeles?'

She kept her eyes on the blood.

'Angeles, look at me.' I went over to her and bent down so I could get eye-to-eye again. 'I've got to leave for a while tonight, but I'll be back.'

Her eyes widened.

'Just for a while. I have to get rid of the car. When I come back, we will leave here and go to my friend who is going to help you – help both of us.'

She gave a brisk nod. It was as if what had been left of the child in her had gone, which I supposed it did pretty quickly once you'd stabbed a man to death.

'Nick, why are you here? What are you doing for – what do you call it? – your job?'

'Remember what we said before? You ask no questions, because I'm not going to answer, OK?'

She looked at me for a couple of seconds, and nodded.

13

I stopped the Passat, jumped out and went back to hit the shutter button. A few moments later I was heading down the road towards the roundabout and then on to Distelweg, shoving the contents of Bradley's briefing folder into the glove compartment as I drove.

I was going to the silo sterile. My passport was still in the mailroom. The heating felt good around my body as the Passat glided towards the canal. It stank of bodies and vomit, but that didn't matter. I crossed into the world of darkness the other side of the water and was soon approaching the tile warehouse. I pulled into the car bays and killed the lights and engine. I sat, watched and listened. The sky was clear tonight; at least there would be no rain.

There were no lights, no voices, no traffic.

I waited another five minutes, then fired up the wagon and carried on down Distelweg. Not too fast; not too slow. I didn't want to be noticed for doing either. I couldn't see much, but I checked for anything that might have changed since I was last here.

The target was in darkness.

As I passed the two-level warehouse or factory immediately before the wasteground, an external door opened and there was a burst of light. It was closed again quickly. No drama. It was three hundred metres from the target. If somebody was working late, and staying inside, they wouldn't get hurt. There was nothing happening on the outside, for sure. There were no lights. What was about to happen would be something to tell the kids, but not much more.

I drove down to the sharp left-hand turn by the ferry point, and the city lights glowed at me from across the water. I followed the road, looking down the steep drop from the reclaimed land of the dock into the bay, for about two hundred metres. On my left, the land side, there was a clutch of small industrial units. A small brick path and a thin strip of grass ran away to the right, stopping at the water about three metres below. I found a gap between the wire-mesh fences of two units and reversed into it. I closed down once more but left the ignition on. This time I sank into the seat, nice and low, letting my arse slide down the leather. I kept my weight on the left cheek. As long as I didn't move, nobody walking past would see me.

I powered down the window to listen for vehicles or footfall and checked the luminous hands on my watch. It was nearly 20.40.

I switched the internal light to off, so that it wasn't triggered by the opening door, and stepped out of the car. I went round to the passenger side, took out the Bergen and put it down against the fencing. Then I got back behind the wheel.

I turned the ignition key and leant over and pressed the button to tilt the back of the passenger seat as far as possible to wedge Angeles's neo in place, then did the same with the driver's. I opened the door and took a quick final look outside.

I positioned my right foot on the sill, which made my stab wound throb as I strained to keep myself upright. My left hand gripped the edge of the roof. I changed it to my right, and then pushed myself in against the door hinges for support. I needed my left hand and left foot free.

I leant in, pressed my foot on the brake pedal, and selected

315

drive. I let go of the brake as the engine started to take the Passat gently forward. I held on, leaning back into the hinges, and once it had travelled about halfway across the road I pushed my left foot down on the gas and we lurched forward. I held it there a bit longer, but no more than two seconds because it was really starting to roll.

Hanging half out of the car, I pushed off with my feet and the Passat lurched on towards the water. As my feet hit the tarmac I curled up to accept the landing. I was only moving at about twenty m.p.h. but it felt like fifty.

I rolled a couple of times as the wagon disappeared from view, then heard a loud splash.

14

My arse had taken some of the hit on my right hip and I was in agony. I staggered to my feet and headed for the water's edge. I didn't bother looking left or right. The deed was done. If I'd been seen, there was fuck-all I could do about it.

I got to the edge just as the tailgate disappeared under the water. It looked like the last throes of a torpedoed ship. I'd only left one window open. I wanted the vehicle to fill with water to make sure it sank, but I also wanted it to keep the bodies entombed.

After three days, under normal conditions, the intestinal bacteria in a corpse produce huge amounts of gas that flows into the blood vessels and tissues. Large blisters form on the skin, and then the whole body begins to bloat and swell. The gas turns the skin from green to purple to black, makes the tongue and eyes protrude, and often pushes the intestines out through the nearest orifice. This process is speeded up if the victim is in a hot environment, or in water.

As a young soldier, I used to be on the beach patrols in Hong Kong, looking out for what was left of Chinese illegal immigrants. The illegals travelled in overloaded boats and many of them drowned. They'd make it to Hong Kong, but after floating there for three or four days they looked like aliens from *Star Trek*.

When this happened to Angeles's neo, I didn't want him to escape as he bloated and floated. With luck, the seats were going to restrain him, and if not, at least he was unlikely to come out through one window and bob to the surface. I just hoped my door had slammed shut when it hit the water and hadn't been forced open.

I looked down. The water was dark and solid. Fuck knew what was down there. Hundreds of years of bodies and secrets. The Passat was already becoming part of history. Or so I hoped.

I pulled out the BlackBerry and flung it as far as I could into the bay. I didn't want that thing banging in my ear when Tresillian went ballistic – which he was sure to do when I got those girls out.

As long as Anna was safe, I wasn't worried about reprisals. What was he going to do? Kill me? If so, he'd better get his finger out or the monster in my head would get there first and do the job for him. That would really piss him off.

I hobbled back to the Bergen. The pain subsided in my hip, though not so much in my arse. I remembered the last time I'd tried to dump a car in a reservoir. I was a young soldier, years before I was sent to Hong Kong. My old Renault 5 was a wreck. I'd have had to pay to have it scrapped, so a mate and I came up with a great idea in the pub one night. We'd drive to the Talybont reservoir in Wales and not stop when we got to the water. We'd go down in two cars on a Saturday night, and Sunday I'd report it nicked from the town centre.

We drove down to Talybont, and things were looking good. I revved the engine, jumped out, and watched the Renault going into what we assumed would be at least sixty feet of water. Instead it settled in what looked like about four feet, visible for all to see. It turned out there were so many cars dumped in that same spot that mine had landed on top of a pile of others. We had to make our way down, climb over the other rust buckets, and rock the thing until it toppled off into deeper water.

All this reminiscing was probably par for the course when you were running out of road ahead. Or maybe there was a little voice telling me that though I'd thought some of these things were pretty shit at the time, perhaps they hadn't been.

I shouldered the Bergen and kept in the shadow of the buildings that lined this side of the road. No more thinking about the old days. I had to concentrate on the job. That was what I was here for – and this was the part I really wanted to do. It wasn't about the killing, however much that was for the greater good, or however Tresillian would justify it. At the bottom of this pile of shit, I was never going to save the world. But it would be nice to think that getting Angeles and Lilian and the other girls out would make it – for them at least – a better place.

As I headed towards the ferry point, the only sound came from the four litres of fuel sloshing about in the container between my shoulder blades.

I slowed down as I neared the ferry point and then stopped. I rested my hands on my thighs, listening and looking. The weight of the fuel made me wobble a bit as I leant down and it levelled off in the top of the container. Apart from my breathing, the only noises came from the other side of the bay and the shipping in between. There was nothing going on over here. I turned the corner, crossed the road and headed along the fence line towards the gap.

The factory beyond the target, where the light had come from, was as dark as everything else now.

I stopped at the rat run between the railings to check for signs of movement. Then I dropped the safe-house keys in the weeds to the right of the gap. I was on foot now, so I wanted them near to me. Sweat gathered where the Bergen rubbed against my back. I leant forward and bounced on the balls of my feet so the Bergen bounced too. At the moment the pressure

319

on the shoulder straps was released, I pulled down and adjusted them so they were nice and tight.

I looked out for the glow of a campfire in the hollow. The junkies must have been having a quiet night in.

Bending low to ease the Bergen through the gap without having to take it off my shoulders, I wormed my way through into the wasteground.

Still there were no lights, no signs of life, just the forbidding outline of the silo in the darkness ahead.

15

I was about twenty metres short of the target. The tower dominated the night sky. I still couldn't see any lights. There were no obvious changes since I'd last been here two nights ago.

This time, I leant against a slab of concrete instead of sitting down and cocked an ear towards the target. I heard nothing but the distant honk of a ship getting pissed off with another ship in the bay.

I tried to swallow. My throat was dry from humping all the kit. My boots were heavy with mud. I moved off. There'd be no cutting corners. I had to carry out the recce. I might be doing a lot of work for nothing.

I moved along the gable end until I reached the waterside corner. There was nothing new on the hard standing. No boats tied up alongside.

Bergen on my back, I moved slowly along the bay side of the building. I got to the metal doors. They hadn't been tampered with. The grass and weeds were standing to attention.

There was still no light.

I reached the far gable end, passing the window to the office where I hoped the girls were being held. I turned right, and followed the wall to the door. It was still locked. I put my ear to the frame and could hear a faint noise. It was impossible to tell what was making it. I put my nose to the keyhole. It still smelt of cake shop.

I walked round to the back of the building, and carried on to do a complete 360 back to the conveyor-belt. Did anyone have eyes on me? Unlikely. Where would they be? Fuck it, so what? If it was happening, it wasn't going to change anything I was going to do.

I climbed the Meccano as close to the silo as I could. It made for a longer climb, but I didn't want to be struggling along the conveyor-belt with all this gear on my back. I wasn't exactly Spiderman, but even he would have had his work cut out with pains in his arse, hip, head and hand, and the unstable weight of the Bergen with a couple of gallons of liquid moving about inside it.

I took the rusty, flaky struts one at a time, maintaining three points of contact: both feet and hands firmly gripping, then one hand up to the next strut, and then a foot. I stopped and listened every two or three bounds. I was sweating, but it certainly wasn't from fear. I was doing what I wanted to be doing. I was having my one final kick.

And, anyway, this time I knew I was dead. I had an inkling of what it must feel like to be a suicide bomber. Like me, they had fuck-all to lose. It almost felt liberating.

I got to the last strut and hauled myself over the top. I lay flat on the rubber belt. The fuel sloshed as it levelled out. The hatch was slightly ajar, exactly as I'd found it and how I'd left it. I crawled forward. A jet took off from Schiphol in the distance and climbed quietly overhead.

The conveyor-belt creaked under my weight. To me, it felt like I was making enough noise to wake up the whole of Noord 5. It couldn't be helped. All I could do was take my time and not fuck up by dropping anything or falling off.

I slowly pushed the hatch open, just enough to get my head through. As before, my nose filled with the smell of flour. As before, there was the faintest glimmer of light through the gap at the bottom.

I loosened the Bergen straps and lay on my side to wriggle out of them. I had to work my way through the hatch and onto the ladder feet first. It would have been a nightmare with a Bergen on my back. I wrapped a hand around one of the straps in case the thing decided to fall.

I lowered my feet and found a rung. Once I had a firm footing, I dragged the Bergen towards me and hauled it back over my shoulders. No worries about muddy boots this time.

Slowly but surely I made my descent. By the time my boots were on the concrete and adding to the prints in the flour, my hands were caked with mud. I wiped them on my jeans. It was warm down here. I took off the Bergen and rested it against the wall. I eased my head beneath the steel shutters and into the main part of the building.

At first, everything looked exactly the same as before. The top right-hand window was the only one that had a light on. The two windows to the left of it were dark, as were the two either side of the door below into the office block. A TV flickered, but I couldn't hear any sound or movement. A haze of cigarette smoke filled the room.

I bent down and grabbed the mallet from under the top flap of the Bergen. The mush of TV waffle reached my ears and got louder the closer I got to the door into the main entrance hallway.

16

I knelt down and checked for light the other side of it. There was a soft glow. I put my ear to the door. The TV was still going strong; I couldn't hear anything else.

I tried the handle. It opened into a gloomy hallway

There were two doors on the left and two on the right. Ten fire extinguishers were lined up between them like sentries. At the far end of the corridor was the outside entrance. Light spilled onto it from up the stairs.

Light also seeped from under the second door on the left. I leant as close as I could to the top panel. There was a faint murmur of childlike voices. Someone was crying and being comforted. The Chubb-style key was still in the lock and a bolt – thrown back – had been newly fixed just above it.

I turned the key just enough to confirm that it was locked, then removed it to keep them contained. I could still hear nothing above the TV upstairs. I knew the voice. Horatio Caine was being *über*-smooth in *CSI: Miami*.

The external door hadn't been bolted. The deadlocks were on. No one was getting out unless they had the keys. There were three to undo so it would take them a while. I eased the bolts into place. Now it would also take a while for anyone to get in.

I turned left towards the stairwell. I only had one chance to make this work quickly and quietly. The light on the landing above me came from two naked fluorescent tubes. The steps were solid concrete. Their coating of red paint had faded over the years and the concrete had worn. There had once been a handrail but now only the fixing holes remained.

I clenched the mallet in my right hand. I swung my arms as I took each step, head up, sucking in deep breaths to prepare for my attack. Two neos were now at the bottom of the bay. I had no idea how many of the four I'd introduced myself to at the tile factory were up and about. But I assumed that Flynn and Bitch Tits would be looking after the shop. By the time I was halfway up I could smell cigarette smoke. The kind that makes your eyes water and takes the skin off the back of your throat. Whoever was up there wasn't paying much attention to the government health warning.

I reached the top landing. I was in auto-mode. I felt blood surge into my hands and legs, preparing me for fight or flight.

Then, just when I needed him most, Horatio stopped waffling.

The door to my half-left was open. I had maybe one second's advantage on whoever was in the room, no more. I could hear everyone in Miami loud and clear.

There were other doors: two to the right, three to the left. All closed. Notice boards peppered with rusty drawing pins but no paper lined the walls, punctuated by steel spikes that had once supported fire extinguishers. Faded hazard warning signs still hung above them.

I took three steps across the corridor and over the threshold. Arm raised, I was ready to take on the first part of any body that came within reach.

There was nobody in there apart from Horatio, but the last inch or so of an untipped cancer-stick still glowed in the ashtray.

A cistern flushed and the door opened at the far end of the

room. Robot came out, still doing up his flies. He was dressed in the same brown overcoat he'd been wearing in Christiania.

He patted the zip into place and raised his head. There was no surprise on his face when he saw me, no shock, no fear, no hesitation. He launched himself straight at me.

I brought up the mallet. His arm chopped up and blocked it easily. His other fist punched into the side of my head and his leg kicked out. It connected with my thigh and I buckled with pain.

My head hit the floor. Stars burst in front of my eyes. Pain coursed through my body. More kicks landed. I could feel myself starting to lose it. I couldn't let that happen. I worked hard to keep my eyes open, curling up as a knee went down onto my chest.

His face displayed the same lack of emotion as it had when he'd talked about Mr Big's fringe benefits in the kitchen of the green house. Calmly and efficiently, he was just getting on with the job of killing me.

17

I had to pull myself together or I was dead.

I tried to twist my head out of the way as the fists came down. I felt one brush my ear as it missed and carried on into the concrete. He didn't flinch.

I bucked like a madman to present a moving target. All I could hear was a voice in my head telling me to keep him close.

I grabbed him with my arms around the back of his coat and pulled him in to me in a big bear hug. I tucked my head into his neck so he couldn't butt me. If I kept hugging him I might be able to control him for long enough to work out what the fuck to do.

I wriggled as much as I could. I wanted to roll on top of him. I was heavier than him. Maybe that would work. But he wasn't having any of it. He tried to expand his arms so he could break out of my grasp. His head jerked down the side of mine, right onto my ear. It popped and burnt with pain. I rolled over, but not in the direction I'd wanted. We were both side on to the ground.

He got his mouth to my ear. 'Give up. You're just going to die fucked.' The Scouse was as precise and unhurried as it had been at the negotiating table.

I writhed again to try to get on top of him, but we rolled together and hit the wall.

My hands were pinned behind his back. All I had left was my head. I butted him in the temple.

His arms flailed. My hands broke free. I was going to have to be quicker than him. Or just better.

I kicked and he let me go. It was pointless running. I had to stay here. He was the target. I had to carry on.

Somehow I got to my feet, my body side-on to him, crouching, legs nice and stable, arms up.

He stood up too. Dusted off his coat. I half expected him to shoot his cuffs. We were about three metres apart. Our eyes locked.

I mirrored his pose, knees bent to protect my bollocks, arms up, head pushed down so my chin hit my chest. I stared at him, ready to grab or punch or otherwise react to whatever he did. I hated this. I'd rather a short, sharp frenzy without any controls.

Robot bounced on his boots a little, as if he was looking for an angle of attack. He was almost enjoying it. Maybe he was rehearsing his attack in his head. A lot of martial-arts lads visualize what they're going to do before they actually do it. That's why they stand there squaring up to each other for two minutes before there's three seconds of action and it's all over and done with. It's all about pre-work. I knew that and appreciated it. I just didn't want him to do it on me.

I kept my feet planted firmly on the ground, muscles gripped, everything tightened, ready to take the hits. I wanted him nearer. He was still out of range. But I knew he'd close in when he was ready.

In he came. A high kick flew towards my ribcage. I kept my arms up and tried to block it. It hit my left bicep. The force of it made me punch myself in the forehead.

I rocked back. Another kick to my other side. I took it on the wrist and opened up my arms. I knew another kick was coming. He launched it and I grabbed his leg with both hands. His calf was almost on my shoulder. I had hold of his thigh and could feel the kneecap through the fabric of his jeans. I pushed down, trying to control it, gripping hard with both hands. I moved into him, my hips between his legs like the foreplay was over and we were going to have sex.

With my right hand on his kneecap, I grabbed him round the top of his leg with my left, pulling him closer, trying to lift him. I kept the forward movement and almost bounced him towards the wall. He crashed against it and arched his back as he felt the fire extinguisher spike. His eyes opened wide. His muscles tensed, desperate to resist the impact of the steel rod. He tried to push me back. Flecks of spit landed on the side of my neck.

I leant into him, my legs almost at forty-five degrees as I pushed and pushed, my body weight hammering him into the spike.

His coat gave way first, then all seven layers of skin. He didn't scream. He took it, breathing heavily but not panicking, trying to work out what the fuck he was going to do. A rib cracked under the pressure and the spike gave him its full six inches. His hands flew back against the wall like he was breaking a fall. He pushed himself off it, grunting with pain, and sank down onto his knees. He kept his eyes on me. He was going to get up. He was going to fight on.

I pivoted on the ball of my left foot and swung round, volleying a kick into his face that pushed his head back into the wall. There wasn't much noise, just a sound like splitting wood as his skull made contact. He jerked, and then he was very still.

I felt his carotid. There was nothing. He'd gone. I collapsed beside him, my back against the wall. Next door, Horatio and his *CSI* mates cracked yet another case and the music blared.

A mobile rang in the TV room. I jumped up and headed towards it. A fist pounding on the main entrance stopped me in my tracks.

18

Chest still heaving, I staggered down the stairs. I bounced from wall to wall, almost falling, then somehow staying on my feet.

'Open the door! *For fuck's sake!*'

The mobile rang again upstairs. I stumbled to the door and pressed my ear to it. A vehicle was ticking over. Then I heard the clank of keys in locks.

There were more bangs, exactly where my head was.

'Fucking – open – up!'

The accent was the same as Robot's.

The door shifted under his weight until the bolts took hold. He knew someone had to be inside. He yelled behind him. 'Call him again! What a bunch of cunts!'

I could make out another voice, cooler, more measured.

I got my eye to the centre keyhole. Bright headlights, then a body blocked the view. The lights had been above knee height. An MPV maybe, or truck to take the girls away.

The guy was apoplectic. 'Call him again, Dad. Where the fuck is he?'

I finally recognized the first voice. It was Bitch Tits. Whoever he was with, I couldn't let them leave. I'd lose control of what they did next. I turned and focused on the fire extinguishers. I picked up two and positioned them on the second stair. I plunged the hall into darkness and used the chinks of light spilling from the keyholes to find my way to the doors. I put on my best Van der Valk accent. *'Ja, ja, komm.'*

Bitch Tits threw a terminal wobbler as I pulled the first bolt. *'What the fuck are yous up to in there?'*

I freed the last bolt and ran towards the stairs. I picked up the first fire extinguisher as the door burst open and light flooded the hallway. Shadows danced across the concrete as Bitch Tits stormed in. The man behind him was big enough to block out the headlamp beams.

'Get the fucking lights on, then!'

I heaved the fire extinguisher above my head and hurled it at Bitch Tits. I didn't see where it made contact, just that it hit him with a thud and he went down in the direction of the girls' cell. I was already heading to the main door with the second extinguisher.

Flynn was three steps into the hallway. I'd burnt his image into my memory: a well-fed body with a shaven head. I knew from my BlackBerry video that the crow's feet around his eyes gave away his age, but he was in good nick.

I slipped behind him. He was still taking a second to react to what had happened to his son. I pushed against the door with my shoulder and it was dark once more.

The second extinguisher came down hard on the back of Flynn's head. He grunted and buckled. This time I kept my grip on the top of the cylinder but let go of the bottom and brought it down on the blurred shape below me like a pile-driver, again and again. I didn't care where it made contact, as long as it did. One time it hit bone. There was a crunch but no screams, just subdued groans, then heavy slobbering as he tried to breathe through the mess I'd made of his head.

I moved up the hallway and repeated the process a couple of times on Bitch Tits. I was tempted to finish him then and there, but I had something else in mind.

My face was covered with sweat by the time I dropped the

extinguisher and headed outside. The Lexus was ticking over smoothly. I turned off the ignition and lights and pocketed the keys. Back in the hallway, I slammed the door behind me and bolted up before hitting the light switch.

Flynn and Bitch Tits lay prone on the concrete. They'd taken a battering but their chests still pulsated.

I gave them both another slam into the back to keep them immobilized before checking for weapons. They were clean.

Legging it as best I could, I went through the door into the silo to retrieve the Bergen. I lifted it on one shoulder. My feet were heavy. I was fucked. I gulped huge mouthfuls of air. Adrenalin was going to keep me going here. Adrenalin and blind fucking rage. I had to get back to them before they had time to recover. I needed to control them.

Dutch voices had taken over the TV above me now. I dropped to my knees beside the bodies and took off the Bergen. I unpacked the gaffer tape. The one eye that Flynn could still open was fixed on me.

They gave no resistance as I grabbed their hands. I taped them behind their backs, and then I did their ankles. I wrapped a strip over their mouths. I kept it as tight as possible. I wanted them to have to fight for every molecule of oxygen.

I taped open two out of the four eyes that weren't broken or swollen. I didn't want them to miss a thing.

19

I slid down the wall and sat there, totally fucked, fighting for breath. The two of them were starting to recover a little. They tried to beg and reason with me via muffled, gaffer-taped moans.

I didn't want to get up. But I had to.

I staggered to my feet and opened the windows and doors of the two ground-floor offices that faced the silo, then did the same in the three upstairs. The news was still on. A female anchor with sculpted blonde hair was getting highly excited about the football results. Robot hadn't moved an inch.

I stumbled downstairs. Grabbing Flynn's bound feet under my arm, I dragged him into the silo. He kicked out as best he could, but his weight was more of a problem. I dropped his feet just past the door and kicked into both of them. It wasn't about control: every time I looked at these guys I kept thinking about the green house.

Picking up his feet once more, I finished dragging him into the centre of the main building. I left him with his back against a heavy desk, then went back and fetched Bitch Tits.

I put my ear to the girls' door. They'd heard the fight. Their voices were high and agitated. Some of them cried. I heard one of them speaking only centimetres from my head. She was probably doing the same as me, ear to the door, trying to work things out.

I hit the light switch by the main entrance and checked the Facebook picture, then unlocked the door and pushed it open.

'Lilian Edinet?'

The girls were all wearing jeans and sweatshirts. They had nothing on their feet or above their eyes. They cowered by their mattresses, some holding hands, expecting the worst.

'Lilian?'

I looked at each face, the blonde ones first.

'Yes, I am Lilian.'

The girl who stepped forward had been standing in the far left-hand corner, by the slop bucket and piles of grease-stained pizza boxes and plastic sandwich wrappers. Her hair was longer than in the picture, and matted. Her expression was defiant.

I moved towards her, my hand outstretched.

'Come on. Move!' I knew I should be treating her to the full Mother Teresa number, but I didn't have the time. None of us did.

I had to grab her arm and pull her all the way out of the room. I slammed the door shut and threw the bolt.

Under the lights in the hallway, her resolve crumbled. Tears cascaded down her cheeks. She was trembling. She tried to hide it, but wasn't having much success.

'Please, please . . .'

I took her face in my hands and moved it up towards the light.

It was her all right. The Goth vampire look had faded, but you couldn't mistake the fire in her eyes. Whatever they'd done to her, they hadn't yet broken her spirit.

I let go of her and pressed the picture into her hand. 'Who is that? What is his name?'

The paper shook in her hands. Teardrops hit the page. 'Viku.'

I grabbed her by the arm once more. 'I'm taking you home.'

I dragged her to the office opposite and pushed her inside.

'Turn the light on. Stay here. I'll come back soon. Do not leave this room, OK?'

She nodded.

I closed the door. This one also had a key in it. They probably all did if this place was being rented out. I gave it a turn. It would put the frighteners on her again, but I didn't want her to see what I was getting up to next.

Everything I needed was squared away. All the girls, and the two fucks next door, were contained, and I had Lilian. Now I could sort out the device.

I hoisted the Bergen onto one shoulder and headed back into the silo. Flynn and Bitch Tits thrashed their legs about, their heads jerking in unison as they tried to shout out at me through the gaffer tape. The pleading had stopped. They were just pissed off big-time.

Three thick, cast-iron heating pipes ran from beneath the concrete, through evenly spaced brackets up the wall, all the way to the floor above us. I gave them an exploratory tug. They didn't give an inch.

My body ached, my feet were getting heavier and I was gagging for water, but nothing could detract from the glow of knowing these two were going to watch my every move and then work out exactly what was going to happen to them. And to make sure that happened unimpeded, I dragged each of them across the floor and ran the gaffer tape around their heads and the pipes, and then did the same with their chests and waists. Their legs stretched out in front of them. They were going nowhere. The show was about to begin, and I wanted them to have ringside seats.

The offices above me spilt enough light for me to see what I needed to see and do what I needed to do. Whatever was on the TV, it was now in Dutch.

I removed the freezer bags: two with the yellow picric acid crystals, and two with the shotgun propellant. The fuel container came out next. I laid them all in a line. I had to do this methodically or I might fuck up and forget something.

The pair of them had stopped moving about. They had one good eye each and they were fixed on me like laser beams. They were trying to work out what the fuck was happening. They'd know soon enough.

First I had to assemble the two explosive charges. I unsealed a bag of picric, inserted an open pack of dark grey propellant into the middle of the yellow crystals, and put them to one side. I exposed one end of my home-made fuse with my teeth and shoved it into the second pack of propellant, then gaffer-taped the two securely together before repeating the process. I taped the second picric bag too.

I moved across to where the remnants of the flour had drifted like snow against the wall that joined the silo to the admin building. Dropping onto my hands and knees, I scooped as much as I could of it to one side so the twenty-litre fuel container could sit directly on the concrete. My nose and mouth were soon full of fine white powder, and so were my eyes.

I placed the container in the space I'd cleared, and taped the second IED on top of it. The fuse snaked off to my right.

The flour began to mix with the sweat running down my cheeks and gathering at the back of my neck. I must have looked like a cross between the world's most enthusiastic coke head and the Pillsbury Doughboy.

I grabbed the components of the first IED, which was to be the kicker charge. I dug deep into the flour that I'd just helped bank against the wall. I had to make sure of two things: first, that I placed the kicker charge higher than the firebomb; and second, that it went as deep into the flour as I could manage. These bags still weren't sealed. It wasn't their time yet.

I checked the fuse leading from the petrol bomb to make sure it was within easy reach of the kicker charge, and that it didn't touch the fuel at any point. That was why the kicker had to be higher – so the fuse flowed easily into the picric.

I picked up the Bergen and moved away from the two devices. The TV news was still blaring away. They'd have something right on their doorstep to talk about in a couple of hours.

I took out the mosque alarm and the bulb, lifted the batteries out of the back of the clock and reinserted them the right way round.

20

I unwrapped the gaffer tape protecting the bulb and gave it a quick test. Perfect. I closed it down before the filament got hot. I set the alarm for two hours. That would be enough for me to get back and shower all this shit off me before I went anywhere near the airport.

I moved back to the device and gently pushed the bulb into the open propellant bag of the kicker charge. I bit away the free end of the fuse and shoved that alongside. I made sure both were sunk deep into the propellant before sealing them in place. I wrapped some more tape around both the wire and the fuse and made sure it was all nice and tight.

The timer gave a gentle green glow as I started scooping flour on top of the kicker charge. The clock would spark up the bulb. That, in turn, would set off the propellant in the bag, and at the same time ignite the fuse. The fuse would start burning towards the firebomb. The propellant inside the kicker charge would generate a fuck of a lot of heat. The picric acid would explode. And since it was against the wall, the force of it would push up, down and forwards into the building.

The pressure wave would force out the flour in a fine mist at supersonic speed. There'd be a massive amount of pressure, because this place was so enclosed. There were no windows, and the building itself was sealed. The pressure wave would have nowhere to exit. So as it bounced and rattled around the building, it would take the cloud of flour and dust with it. The cloud would fill the building.

All the while, the fuse to the kicker charge would be burning down to the propellant inside the main charge. It would also explode, and detonate that lot of picric, creating another massive pressure wave. That was why there had to be an air gap between the fuel and the explosive. You need to give the wave a little time before it hits the fuel. If it's physically touching, it can sometimes just explode and kick out fluid at supersonic speed instead of flame.

What I wanted was flame. It would ignite all the particles of flour, and that would create even more pressure. The wave would burst its way round the entire building in a couple of seconds.

Flynn and Bitch Tits looked like they were going to explode all by themselves.

I finished burying the kicker charge and laid the Bergen next to the fuel but kept the remaining gaffer tape in my hand. I'd almost done it. The last bit was the hardest of all, and that was the wait. But it had benefits, I supposed. Flynn and Bitch Tits also had to wait.

They'd gone noisy again. I wasn't sure if they were begging, trying to cut a deal, or just giving me their final thoughts on my mother's sexual history.

I knelt down beside them and rolled all the remaining gaffer tape around both sets of legs.

I fished around in Flynn's smart leather coat for the main door keys. Flynn fixed his eyes on mine. He knew what I was thinking and accepted he was going to die. Bitch Tits wasn't following his dad's example. He continued to flap. That was good for me.

I turned and went out, leaving the door to the hallway wide open.

21

She was standing in the far corner of the empty office, her back firmly against the wall. If she could have burrowed her way into it, she would have done.

'Come on, hurry!'

She didn't budge.

I ran across the room. Her arms came up to protect herself.

'For fuck's sake, calm down. I'm not here to hurt you.'

She wasn't responding.

I touched her on the shoulder as gently as I could. She recoiled like I'd hit her with a Taser. I lowered my voice, kept it as calm as possible. 'Listen, Lily. I'm here to help you. But you must help me, OK?'

I took her arm and headed for the main door.

'Mister – my friends . . . ?'

I turned to see her pointing at the only remaining closed door.

'Mister . . . ?'

I opened the front door just enough to check outside, then closed it again.

I turned to face her. 'Listen in. You tell them that they are going to be free, OK?'

She nodded, concentrating hard to make sure she understood every single word.

'Tell them that I will show them a way out. And they *must* not come back here. Do you understand?' You didn't need even two brain cells to know that this was the last place on earth they should be, but the big wide world might have seemed an even more frightening prospect.

'Yes – but where do they go?'

'They are in Amsterdam. I will show them, once we get out of here.'

She wasn't with me.

'Fuck it, just get in there and tell them to follow me.'

I opened the cell door and almost threw her back in. 'For fuck's sake, hurry up.'

They gathered by the main entrance.

I moved outside and held them there while I locked up. I still had Flynn's fob. But I wasn't touching the car. We couldn't all fit inside, and it was another bit of kit to connect me with the job. I didn't want any last-minute complications. We were all better off on foot.

I turned right, and switched into Pied Piper mode. I started across the wasteground towards the rat run. I had to stop every now and then to give the girls time to catch up. Their bare feet weren't making life any easier. I took them around the edge of the crater so they didn't fall foul of the junkie pick-up sticks.

About ten minutes later I shepherded them, one by one, through the gap in the railing. I held them on the other side until everyone was through, then headed along the fence line. I passed the ferry point and followed the road towards the canal, throwing both sets of keys into the bay to join the Passat.

I pointed in the direction of the lights across the water. 'Amsterdam.'

Lily passed on the message and there was a murmur of understanding, dread and excitement.

341

22

I moved at a steady jog, pulling Lily behind me. The rest followed like a gaggle of refugees.

There was no time to talk – no reason to either. When the silo exploded, they'd throw up cordons. I needed to be away from here and on my way to Russia. That was the only thing on my mind now. I brushed my clothes as I went. The Doughboy look was not what I was aiming for.

I slowed to a walk as we approached the bridge. I gathered up the girls and told them to be quiet. Lily translated.

We were soon in the land of the white prefabs. The girls were out of breath. Lily pulled at my arm. 'Please, slower . . .'

I gripped her hand and pulled a little harder. We had to make distance.

The housing estate was alive. TV screens glowed behind net curtains. Kids played football under street-lamps. All the shops were open, their bright lights flooding the pavements.

I was gagging for water but it was going to have to wait. I checked my watch. Thirty minutes had gone. I had to get a move on here. With luck I could have the wheels turning by about 22.15. The device would kick off just after 22.30. By then we'd be on the A10 to Schiphol.

I stopped short of the roundabout and waited for my ragtag

band to join me. We got stares from passing drivers, but I was past caring. There were more important things to think about.

I pointed down the road towards the taxi rank. 'Lily, tell the girls to cross the road and keep walking. Tell them to go to the Islamic cultural centre, the mosque – you get that?'

She nodded, then gobbed off at the frightened faces.

'Tell them the people there will help them.'

She did as she was told and I started to move them on.

'Tell them not to say where they've come from. They don't know – it was near the motorway.'

She gobbed off again and I had to physically turn them in the right direction.

'Go on, fuck off, *go!*'

Lily started to move with them.

'Not you.'

I hooked her arm and guided her across the roundabout towards Papaverhoek.

That was me fucked with Tresillian yet again, but so what? I was fucked anyway. He'd have to find me to grip me. As for the target building, fuck it. It was going to be a while before they found out where the girls had come from, even if they told the truth straight away.

I couldn't get Lena's friend involved. It was too complicated, and there wasn't time. But at least the girls were safe. They'd be fed and watered and given warm shoes and a place to rest before someone remembered to ask the police if they might like to find out where they'd been held, or about the man who'd saved them. By then it would be too late.

Lily was hobbling now, but she'd live. FilmNoord XXX was doing a brisk trade. Four cars were parked up, their drivers browsing the shelves. A woman in her late forties and not exactly box fresh smoked a cigarette and scoped for business. She didn't give us a second glance. She was more interested in the lads with back seats than a guy who'd already found what he was looking for.

I approached the safe-house from the opposite side of the road. Everything looked OK. I checked the telltales, unlocked and closed the door quickly behind me. I hit the lights and locked back up.

I stood there for a while, composing myself – allowing myself a moment or two of satisfaction for a job well done.

'You will be taken home, Lily. Soon.'

As I opened the fire door and we moved into the office corridor, I could see that the door to the mailroom was open. But it wasn't Angeles who emerged from it to greet us, and the dull light was clear enough for me to see he had a shotgun at his shoulder. The barrels were pointing at me. Bradley had both eyes open. His finger was inside the guard, and its pad was resting on the trigger.

23

'For fuck's sake . . .' My shoulders slumped. I shook my head slowly as Lily jumped behind me for protection.

At that moment I realized that if it wasn't for Anna and the two girls, if Angeles was still alive, I'd just let him get on with it – and feel happy that it would be over and done with.

Bradley looked at me, weapon still up. 'What *have* you been doing, Nick? Starting a collection? This other young lady should still be in that building.'

The barrel moved left to right. 'Follow me.'

He walked slowly backwards, barrel facing us, until he reached the door to the back room.

'Both of you – *inside.*'

Angeles was sitting by the opening to the shower, blood pouring from her nose. Her hands were red with the stuff. She'd been packing. Most of the gear was gone, but now the mugs lay on the carpet and tea bags from the box were strewn by her feet. She recognized Lily at once and started to beg Bradley in Russian. Tears rolled down her bloodstained cheeks. Was it a bluff? Had she gone straight into her native language so she didn't give away she understood English? Or was she so shit scared she couldn't force any English out?

Bradley tried to appear calm, but I could tell he was

flapping. The plan had probably been to enter the building, wait for me and Lily, and simply drop me. Now he was going to have to think on his feet, with another body to sort out.

He looked behind me.

'Lilian?'

'Yes.'

He immediately looked a lot more cheerful. 'Then who on earth is this one, Nick?'

'Just a whore. From the porn shop. She knows fuck-all.' I moved sideways and leant against the wall. My arse was killing me. 'Well, she knew fuck-all until you decided to come in here like Wyatt fucking Earp.'

'Stand *fucking* still.' Bradley was in command mode now he had Lily.

'Why? What are you going to do if I don't? You going to shoot me?' I nodded at Angeles. 'Look at the fucking mess you've made of her.'

'Who else knows about you being here?'

He moved the weapon up a couple of inches, as if that was going to make me flap. Fuck him.

'You had anyone else here?'

'Why the fuck should I tell you? You're going to drop me anyway, aren't you?'

Angeles was quiet now, her eyes flicking between us. The weapon was still in his shoulder. I couldn't see if the safety was on or off. It was on top of the weapon, just in front of the stock.

I looked at his eyes. They were flickering. They weren't cool and steady. Maybe it was OK killing men, but young girls . . .

I knew the feeling.

His finger was still curled inside the trigger-guard. I watched his eyes. Whether by action or default, he could still drop me. The end result would be the same. He blinked. Then again. He had the tools to do it, but had he the intent? Execution without reason or emotion is for psychos, and unfortunately for him, he wasn't one. I knew; it was easy to tell. It was probably why I'd fallen for this whole stitch-up in the first place.

'Bradley, you don't have to do this. You do this, mate, you're going to have nightmares for the rest of your life. It fucks you up for ever, believe me. You can't sleep. Your head will fill with my face and hers every time you close your eyes. Don't do it. We can sort something out. We can make it work for both of us . . .'

He was weirding out. The fingers of his left hand started to jump about on the barrel like he was playing the trumpet. He adjusted his grip on the weapon and squeezed it more firmly, as if it was going to run away.

'Once you do me, they're going to do you – you understand that, don't you? Someone will be coming for you. They won't leave loose ends, mate. You've seen how they work. We're all tools here. We're all used and abused.'

I had to get on with this shit one way or another. There was less than an hour to go. If we were still here at that point, we were all in the shit.

I noticed beads of sweat forming on his forehead. I kept eye-to-eye. 'Mate, you'll be next. It's what they do. I can help you make that not happen. I've been doing this shit for years. They don't like people like you and me, mate. They—'

A mug flew left to right and made contact with Bradley's head. I dropped beneath his line of sight.

'Fucking *bitch*!'

Angeles hurled another mug-shaped missile and ran towards him in a frenzy. I focused on the barrel. I lunged and grabbed it with my left hand, moved it straight down towards the carpet, trying to keep the muzzle out of harm's way. Angeles lashed out at him as he slumped to his knees. Arms windmilling, screaming like a banshee, she rained blows on his head, eyes closed, then leapt on him.

They both fell, the barrel between them. The weapon kicked off, the lead shot peppering the wall beneath the sink and blowing a hole the size of a fist through Angeles's tiny chest.

I pulled the shotgun away from him as I dragged him free of her, then jumped on him. I wanted to keep him on the ground. I wanted him alive. I wanted to find out who, where and when.

He kicked out like a madman. 'Leave me alone! *Leave me alone!*'

I shoved my left arm onto his chest, punched into his face and shouted down at him: 'Stop, Bradley. For fuck's sake, *stop*!'

His face was red with fear or rage. He wouldn't stop moving. *'No! No!'*

I felt the gun barrel cold against the side of my head. It made contact with Bradley's cheek. The loose flesh creased and folded around the muzzle.

'No, Lily! *No!*'

I jerked back, but felt the pressure wave of the blast against my face. A fine, liquid mist coated my skin, and I didn't need a mirror to tell me what it was.

There was a massive oval-shaped hole just below Bradley's eye. Through it, I could see a patch of red and glossy carpet.

She showed no emotion as she stared down at him. I got up and took the weapon off her. She looked at me. 'He tried to kill you.'

There was no time for waffle. We had to get out of there.

I dropped the shotgun on the floor. I didn't need it. And the rounds I hadn't used for the IED were at the bottom of the bay.

I pulled off Angeles's trainers and handed them to Lily. Then I took the cash from the back pocket of her jeans. I couldn't bear to look at her face.

I had the notes in my hand when someone gave the front door a good pounding and a megaphone sparked up outside.

24

'Wait here!'

Crouching low, I scuttled into the middle office and took up position at my Bradley-spotting vantage-point. I wasn't about to stand there and wave. Blue lights flashed all over our bit of Noord 5; uniforms, police cars, guys taking cover behind ballistic shields. A four-man team with an enforcer were hammering away at the door.

I ran back into the mailroom, grabbed my docs from behind the pigeonhole and climbed the ladder to the roof hatch.

I wrestled with the bolts. She appeared at my feet.

'Get up here, *quick.*'

I jiggled the bolts up and down and tried to pull them back at the same time. The more I struggled, the less purchase I had with my sweat-covered fingers. I pulled my sleeve as far down as I could, and used it as a glove.

The front door caved in. Shouts surged up the stairs.

The bolts shifted and I pushed open the hatch into the night sky. Cold air hit me as I climbed out. I pulled Lily up behind me before dropping it back.

Keeping low on the roof, we scrambled towards the rear of the building. Blue flashing lights were piling in front and back.

Headlamps bounced across the wasteground. The air was full of radio squawks and shouts.

'Just stay with me, OK?' I gave her arm an encouraging squeeze. I didn't want her to flap any more than she already was and fuck up.

We aimed for the three-metre wall that would take us across the top of the next-door office block. There'd be no second attempt.

My throat was parched and I couldn't get enough oxygen. Adrenalin took over. I sprang up and my hands gripped the edge of the parapet. My legs scrabbled against the brickwork. I repeated the elbow trick. I heaved and kicked until my stomach reached tar and gravel. I clawed my way a couple of feet further, then swivelled round and stretched my hands over the edge.

'Come on.'

She jumped and I grabbed her hands. She slipped from my grasp.

'Again!'

This time I gripped her with my right hand and flailed around with my left, hoping for something to grab. I got a fistful of sweatshirt and heaved her up onto the lip. She swung her legs sideways and came the rest of the way.

More shouts drifted up from the street. More loudspeakers barked either side of the building. Blue lights sped down from Distelweg.

I didn't bother checking the entrance to the central stairwell. Even if we could get in, we couldn't stay there. We had to make distance. We needed one big straight line out of the immediate danger area.

We ran past it to the far edge of the roof. FilmNoord XXX shone like a beacon. I knew Lily was behind me; she coughed and I felt her breath on my sweat-soaked neck. I edged along the parapet until I was directly above the galvanized-steel platform I'd seen the last time I was up there, slid my legs over and dropped. I landed with a clang like a bass gong, but noise wasn't a problem. They were making enough of their own.

Her feet dangled above my head. I cupped my hands beneath them to give her some support.

More sirens and blue lights swept down Papaverhoek and screamed to a halt. They were throwing up a road-block. Why else would they stop so close to the main?

We hit the ground and headed right. I wanted us to be able to lose ourselves among the maze of brick walls and wooden fences that surrounded those back gardens. We found a muddy track that ran between them and crossed a strip of rough land. Brick walls reared up in front of us, but there was always a way round. I didn't have a clue what lay the other side of them. I just wanted to get within reach of the roundabout and then the estate.

I caught a glimpse of the main at the far end of a narrow alleyway. I moved swiftly along it and glanced left. I couldn't see the police cars but I knew where the road-block was. Blue lights strobed all around the incident area, bouncing off the low cloud, but up here it was as dark as any other night.

'We slow down now, Lily.'

Her shoulders were heaving, her eyes wide. She leant forward and rested her elbows on her thighs.

'Deep breaths – come on now, calm down, sort yourself out.'

I wanted her looking as normal as possible. I put my hand on her shoulder. 'You OK? We've got to go.'

She was still gulping air, but she nodded. I hooked out my arm for her to take. 'Girlfriend and boyfriend?'

She raised the skin where there had once been an eyebrow.

'OK, daughter and dad . . .'

That earned me my first smile. It gave me a bit of a lump in my throat. I pictured another little girl who'd trusted me and died. I was fucked if I was going to let it happen this time around.

We stepped out and followed the pedestrian crossing to the

351

right of the market into the warren of streets behind the parade of shops. We hadn't gone more than a hundred metres when I had to pull her into a doorway as yet another blue-and-white zoomed towards the incident.

And in that moment, from about a K and a half behind us, came a loud, dull bang. A jet of flame shot into the sky like the gas flare above an oilrig. It only burnt briefly. After that, the raging inferno would be contained by the silo walls.

25

I looked at the glow in the sky above Noord 5.

Lily tugged at my arm. 'What is it?'

'I don't know. Let's keep going.'

The less she knew about everything the better. But Lily stayed still, watching the flames, then turned back to me. I knew she wanted an explanation. She wasn't getting one. That job was done. I was already thinking about my next one.

We passed the Islamic centre. Checking left at the junction, I could see the girls standing in a huddle with two police cars holding them together. They, too, were staring towards the site of the explosion. The police must have been all over them as quickly as they had been with me. They were the victims; it didn't matter. The reason the police had come calling at the safe-house also didn't matter right now. Thinking about it didn't achieve anything. The only thing that did was making distance from them.

In the meantime, I'd put that whole side of things on the back burner. It was getting more crowded by the moment.

We walked for another thirty minutes. We crossed wider waterways and parks, and under elevated dual carriageways. Our surroundings became increasingly residential. Trendy apartment blocks sprang up, with cycle lanes and neatly parked cars. We were back in civilization but there was no way I was taking trams, buses or taxis. Municipal transport had CCTV. Taxi drivers might remember something. The police operation that had almost netted us was not going to shut up shop for weeks.

A shiny green phone booth materialized in front of us. At last I could make the call.

Anna answered immediately. I could hear the tension in her voice. 'When will you be here? I—'

'Stop, stop! I need you to come and pick us up. Can you do that? There's been a drama. Can you get a car?'

'Yes.'

'Get a car with sat nav, and meet me.'

'Do you still have her?'

'No, it was a fuck-up. But I have Lily. You got a pen?'

I waited a few seconds as the information sank in but she stayed completely switched on. She knew now wasn't the time to go wobbly.

'Go.'

'I'm at the junction, and I'll spell it, of H-e-t new word D-o-k and K-o-p-e-r-s-l-a-g-e-r-i-j. The street names have one zero two one on them – that must be the area code. It's on the north side of the bay. You got that? It's full of smart flats, grassy open spaces and a smart green telephone box.'

'Got it.'

I listened as she read everything back. I checked the road sign again, making sure the spelling was correct. 'Quick as you can, Anna, without speeding.'

'Is she OK?'

'She's fine. The other girls are safe. But you need to call off Lena's friends. No need to meet up. Angeles won't be needing them.'

The silence hung between us as she realized what I'd just said.

'OK, sure. I'll call.' I could hear her moving now, the door to

354

her room closing behind her and her voice beginning to echo in the hotel hallway.

'It's probably going to take you about thirty minutes this time of night. I'll call you to check how you're doing. OK?'

'See you soon.'

'Anna . . .'

'Yes?'

I hesitated. 'I can't wait to see you.'

She thought about it for a second. 'So get off the phone.'

26

For almost the whole hour and a half that we waited under the dual carriageway sirens wailed along the tarmac above us. The park was deserted.

I'd called Anna from a phone box when I said I would. She was on her way.

We sat shivering against a tree and I had to hold Lily in my arms to keep her warm. Her head was on my chest.

'Lily, what happened? Why did you leave home?'

She didn't move. Maybe she felt safe where she was.

'I had to get away.'

'Had to?'

She shrugged. 'It seems so stupid after what has happened. My father betrayed me. And he betrayed the protest movement.'

'After the election?'

Her head moved on my chest. 'You have to realize how wonderful it was for us to finally know democracy. For one day, for one bright shining day, it seemed as though the power was in the people's hands. We, the students, were going to be part of the solution. Not part of the problem, like my father.'

'He liked it just the way it was?'

I felt her head nod slowly.

'The Communists rigged the election. They bought everyone

off – using money from people like my father. He just thinks of himself and his business. I wanted to leave – I wanted to hurt him just as he hurt me.'

'Why Christiania?'

'I read about it for a sociology class last year. Communal life. Utopia. It sounded like a good place to escape to.'

She dug into her jeans and brought out the Facebook picture. She opened it up as if I'd never seen it before. 'But he changed that.'

'Was he your boyfriend?'

'Sort of.' She paused. 'He wanted sex but I wanted to wait until I married.'

Her hand dropped and let go of the paper. I had to grab it before it blew away.

'He said he knew someone in Copenhagen, a friend of his father's. He said he would talk to him and he would help me there.'

I folded the picture and shoved it into my jeans.

'Viku *sold* me . . . How could I have been so stupid?' She craned her neck to get eye-to-eye. 'I met the old man. He was kind to me. He bought me something to eat and we talked of how wonderful Christiania was and how happy I was going to be there. But then he took me to a house where he said I could stay.'

She didn't cry, just stared down at the ground, trying to close her mind to what had happened next.

'It's OK, Lily, I know the rest. But you are safe now.'

She replaced her head on my chest. I felt her jaw clench. Safety was something that belonged to another life.

'My father, did he send you?'

'Your dad knows nothing about it. One of his friends did.'

She scoffed. 'One of his murderer friends?'

'What makes you say that?'

'He and all the others who make weapons, they are killers.'

'I thought your father was in electronics?'

357

It was worth confirming what I thought I had worked out.

'I don't just mean missiles and tanks. Computers and radar are weapons too, any equipment that helps to kill and maim.' She sat up. She was getting quite animated. 'A military computer is as lethal as a bomb. Making military computers is a trade in misery.'

'The people your father sell his computers to – isn't he just meeting a demand?'

Her eyes blazed. 'A *pimp* meets a demand. A *drug-dealer* meets a demand. What is the difference between trafficking heroin or women and exporting weapons, except that weapons are more dangerous? They're all merchants of death. My eyes were opened to these things at university. I do not want to profit from his trade any more. That is why I left. Look where it got me.'

I thought she was going to cry.

'Please do not tell him what has happened to me.'

I gave her a hug. 'He'll get nothing from me.'

'Thank you. What is your name?'

'Nick.'

'Thank you, Nick.'

We lapsed into silence. Lily was either asleep or almost there. Her breathing was slow and stable.

Another couple of sirens buzzed along the dual carriageway at warp speed. I consulted Mr G-Shock. 'We've got to go.' I stroked the top of her head.

She stirred. 'She is here?'

'Should be by now.'

We walked back out across the park, the traffic still zooming backwards and forwards overhead but now behind us. What I was looking for was a silver Opel estate. The start of the reg was 62-LH.

I spotted it parked just past the junction, and then the silhouette of Anna's head. There was no time for casual contact drills. I wanted to get in the car and go.

358

As we got nearer, I heard the clunk of the central locking. I opened the back door for Lily and I got into the front. Anna backed out and moved off without saying a word. The sat nav gave her a string of English instructions. I caught a hint of Bulgari that made me feel a whole lot better.

Anna checked her rear-view. She didn't want to talk yet. She wanted to get out of the area. I looked at her face and gave her a smile. It wasn't returned. She wasn't impressed with life right now.

It was only when we hit the dual carriageway that Anna broke the silence. 'Lily . . . Can I call you Lily?' She didn't wait for a response. 'My name is Anna.' She gobbed off in Russian.

Lily gasped, and then almost choked with emotion. Her hands whirred like she was signing for the deaf. She leant in towards the front seat, her lips on overload. The only word I could understand was 'Angeles'.

'Stop, Lily. Stop.' I turned to Anna. 'All she knows is that Angeles is dead. I'll tell you everything as soon as we get to the hotel. But not now, yeah?'

27

We parked in a multi-storey at Schiphol. Lily had crashed out on the back seat. I felt like doing the same. The heater had been working overtime.

Anna showed me her Radisson door card. The room number was scrawled on its folder. 'Fifth floor.'

'Which way are the lifts when you walk into Reception – left, right, straight?'

'Turn right as soon as you go in, past the reception desk.'

'I'll give you and Lily fifteen minutes, yeah?'

Lily yawned, stretched and sat up. She must have sensed that we were no longer moving.

I looked over my shoulder. 'We can't all go in together. Anna and you go first. I'll come after.'

Her hand was already on the passenger-door handle.

'Lily, it's OK.' I reached over and gripped the leg of her jeans. 'You stay with me. We'll go together.'

Anna cut in: 'You two go in first, and I will follow. Is that all right with you, Lily?' She passed me the door card.

We climbed out of the Opel and headed down the stairs of the multi-storey, arm in arm again. The stairwell didn't stink of last week's piss like it would have done back home. 'Walk normally, Lily. Smile at me if I smile at you. It's just like we're staying here and we're heading back to the room for the night. Is that OK?'

She knew as well as I did that the desk staff would think she was a whore I'd picked up for the night. I was banking on the night shift not expecting to recognize any faces, and not wanting to embarrass me by checking. This was Amsterdam, after all.

We walked into the empty foyer. In case there were eyes, I fiddled conspicuously with Anna's door card and turned immediately right, as if I knew where I was going. I strode towards the lifts and pressed the up button. I studied the card again for good measure.

It was after midnight and a few people still propped up the bar. Flat-screen TVs above the optics showed pictures of fire fighters at the silo. The roof had collapsed. Two fireboats pumped water over the smouldering ruin. It was drenched in spotlights from police boats alongside. People in high-vis clothing swarmed all over the area.

I held Lily close as we waited. She'd seen the screens. A tear finally did roll down her cheek.

'It's OK, Lily. You're safe. Everyone is safe.'

The lift pinged open and we shot up to the fifth floor.

With its twin beds, walnut veneers, TV and mini-bar, the room could have been in any chain hotel anywhere in the world. I threw her chocolate and a carton of orange juice. She ripped the wrapper off the Milka bar and got stuck in. 'Thank you, Nick.'

'Go and have a bath. Anna will give you some clothes for tomorrow. I'm not going anywhere. Leave the door open if you want.'

She padded into the bathroom. I dug out the folder and threw it onto the bed.

'Lily?'

I heard the sound of running water. She came to the door.

'Anna will look after you, I promise. She won't let anything happen to you – you understand that, don't you?'

361

She nodded. 'Yes. Thank you.' She closed the door behind her.

I sat on the end of the bed and shoved cashews down my neck. According to the price list they cost the best part of a euro per nut. I washed them down with the world's most expensive can of Pepsi and channel-hopped with the remote. The silo fire was on all the local stations, as well as CNN and BBC News 24. Kate Singleton was showing the world her gravitas.

There was a knock on the door. I checked through the peep-hole and opened up.

'No problem with the desk, Nicholas?' She nodded past me, towards the sound of running water.

'Everything's fine.'

I led her into the room. She sat next to me, pointing at the screen. 'Why?'

'Fuck knows, but it's just the tip of the iceberg.'

28

I told Anna everything about the Flynns and the neo-Nazis, the Moldovan competition and Tresillian changing the plan and wanting all the girls dead. Then I told her about going back to the safe-house to find Bradley waiting for me, Angeles getting killed, and the police bursting in.

'The police? How did they—'

'Bradley maybe – fuck knows what else he got up to in that house. Or the neos – who must have followed us from the market? Who gave a fuck? What pissed me off more was what happened to Angeles. She wanted to protect me.' I pictured that shy smile again, and the endless steaming, super-sweet brews. 'She got fucked up by doing it and that's down to Tresillian – and, of course, Jules.'

She wouldn't believe it. 'But he is a friend.'

'You reckon? I want to think so, but I don't know what the fuck is going on.'

Then I told her what had been clawing away at me ever since Bradley pulled the shotgun. 'Everything and everyone connected with Lily is being taken out. This can't just be about a favour to a friend. It's something bigger, and Tresillian is tying up all the loose ends . . .'

She looked at me. She knew where this was leading. She was too smart not to.

I nodded. 'If he doesn't know already, he'll find out soon enough that you were in on it too.'

She didn't answer. She just let everything sink in.

Lily emerged from the bathroom, freshly scrubbed and fragrant, wet hair scraped back from her face. She curled up on the bed, in her own private world, eyes glued to the flickering TV screen.

I couldn't wait around. We had things to do.

'The Panda is going to flag up Nick Smith. The flight to Russia is history. Lily is the key, and I'm starting to think I might know why. As long as we've got her, they won't get us. You must take her somewhere safe. I need both of you out of harm's way.'

She sparked up. 'I know people in—'

I put a hand over her mouth. 'Stop. I don't want to know.'

It was safer for both of them. If I fucked up and Tresillian didn't see things my way, he'd want to know where Lily was. Whatever he did to me, I couldn't tell him what I didn't know.

Anna understood. 'What about you?'

'I'm going back to the UK. That's where all this shit started.'

The TV rolled the same mobile clip of the explosion, over and over again. At least it was somebody's lucky day.

'All three of us could leave, right now.'

I shook my head. 'I've got to go back. If Lily is safe, Tresillian won't touch us. He needs her. I have to sort a few things out.' I gave her a slightly crooked smile. 'Then we can spend whatever time I've got left watching the geese fly over the Moskva River.'

We stood only a few centimetres apart.

She took my hands in hers, unable to speak. She looked like she was going to break down at any moment. She held my hands to her face and kissed them. She gazed into my eyes.

I'm not sure what she saw there, but she wasn't smiling back.

29

I pulled a can of Pepsi out of the mini-bar and offered it to Lily. She shook her head. She was sitting on the edge of the bed, still in the bathrobe, watching Anna do stuff with her iPhone.

She'd opened up Google Earth. I needed to check out the coastline. The mother of all canals headed north-west out of Amsterdam's bay, cutting through the forest of oil and gas containers that stretched the length and breadth of the industrial landscape. A system of locks governed entry to and exit from the mouth of the canal before it opened out, in the shape of a flue, into the North Sea. Just beyond the locks was a marina, and that was what I was looking for.

The photographs of the marina showed long pontoons packed with sailing vessels and gin palaces.

Anna took Lily's hands in hers, murmuring words of comfort.

I pointed at the screen. 'That's where I need to be.'

'It'll take an hour or so to get there.'

'Can you look up how far to the Brit coast?'

I checked the Smith passport and credit card. They'd be good if I was spot-checked for ID, but I wasn't going to get through Customs and Immigration with them.

I shoved the £400 in sterling I'd brought over with me back into my jeans.

Anna carried on working her magic with the iPhone. 'It's just over a hundred and fifty kilometres due west. You'll hit the UK somewhere on the Norfolk/Suffolk coast.'

I switched on the crooked grin again, this time for Lily's benefit. 'Come on then. We'd better get moving.'

Alarm immediately clouded her face. 'Where to?'

'You're going to drop me off somewhere. I'm going home for a while, but I will come back.'

Anna gave Lily some of her clothes.

'OK, Lily – you and I will leave first. Anna, we'll meet you by the car.'

I helped Anna throw the last of her stuff into her wheelie.

Lily hadn't moved a muscle. 'What is happening, Nick?'

I put my hands on her shoulders and bent down to get eye-to-eye. I'd been doing quite a lot of that these last few days. 'I'm going home, but just for a while. Anna will take you somewhere safe. Then I will come and meet you both. But I have to go home first. There are some things I need to do to make sure you're properly looked after. Is that OK?'

She nodded slowly but I could see she wasn't impressed.

'Come on, let's get to the car.' I tried to make light of it. I crooked my arm out again. 'Remember, daughter and dad, like last time.'

She didn't laugh.

We headed for the door.

30

The drive took longer than I'd expected but the sat nav brought us smoothly onto Kennemerboulevard and no one in a blue-and-white paid us the slightest bit of attention on the way. The road formed the base of the large marina triangle. The North Sea chopped and churned at its apex.

The road was ruler straight and built on top of a retaining wall of enormous chunks of rock. The seabed was ten metres or so below it. Bobbing up and down in the water were two or three hundred boats of all shapes and sizes, parked up in very neat rows along several wooden pontoons.

Where the canal widened, the marina opened onto a ferry port. A blindingly bright arc of light banged into the sky above a ship being loaded with cars and trucks. I was eight hundred metres away, and could still hear the clank of ferry doors being opened and closed and trucks rumbling to and fro over steel ramps.

It was pointless just driving around. I needed to be on my feet to do my job. 'Anywhere along here . . .'

As Anna pulled in to the side of the road, I turned to Lily. 'I'll see you very soon, yeah? Anna's going to take good care of you.'

The gentle glow of the ferry's lights reflected off the water welling in her eyes.

'It'll be OK. Really. I'll be back soon.'

She nodded, but she didn't quite believe me. I couldn't blame her. I didn't quite believe myself.

I turned back to Anna, feeling quite pleased with myself. I had a plan. 'I need you to get everything onto a hard drive as soon as you can. The whole story from your side, OK?'

She studied my face. 'Be careful, Nicholas.'

'I will. And when I catch up with you guys, I'll add my stuff. Don't forget: no emails, bin the phone, no electronic tags. Open a Facebook page and call it . . . Lily Vampire-Girl. I'll contact you with a pass number of . . .'

I looked at Lily. 'You're twenty, right?'

She nodded.

'Twenty it is.'

We needed something that would definitely not be forgotten. The system was simple. Anna would set up the page via Lena or by messing about with ISPs so her location couldn't be traced. I would open a gmail account, then sign on to Facebook and search the Vampire-Girl pages. I'd email the newest one, the one with no shit on, and offer up the first part of the pass number. We'd then have made contact.

She leant across and kissed me on the cheek. Lily squeezed between the two seats and did the same. 'Thank you.'

Anna gave me a hurry-up smile. She was right. There was too much goodbyeing going on here.

'You've only got four or five hours until it's light . . .'

I nodded and looked back at Lily. I gave her one last smile before getting out of the car.

Anna had her foot on the accelerator almost as soon as I closed the door. The Opel moved off and I stepped into the darkness. The North Wind started attacking my face. G-Shock told me it was just after 02.00. First light would be in four and a half hours max.

I needed something fast. I wanted to be able to dump the boat in the dark and make as much distance from it as I could.

Getting back into the UK wouldn't be that hard. Smugglers were doing it on a daily basis. During the Second World War, all the Resistance lads fucking about in Bradley's safe house were probably getting in little boats and rattling over with downed aircrews and SOE agents. I couldn't understand why so many illegals risked their lives hanging off lorries from Calais when all they had to do was follow their example.

I'd done a similar trip in a little Gemini when I was stationed with the Regiment in Belize. The only power was a 25hp outboard on the back and a couple of paddles in case we fucked up.

Three of us got on the river by the airport camp and navigated down to the coast. Our destination, the island of San Pedro, was so far away it wasn't visible from the mainland. For navigation we had just an ordinary 1 in 50,000 tourist map. San Pedro was a little speck in the middle of the Caribbean; we took a compass bearing and off we went.

After a few hours we passed a ship en route to Belmopan. They hailed us and asked if we were all right. 'No drama.' We waved. We must have looked like narcos.

'Where are you going?'

'San Pedro.'

He threw his hands in the air and went back into the wheelhouse.

The first place we were trying to find with our map and Silva compass was called Hick's Island. From there we took another bearing, and four hours later, with just one fuel bladder left, we motored into San Pedro for our long weekend. Good times.

I walked along the concrete dock. Most of the boats were covered with tarpaulins and lashed down and locked up for the winter. Hardly any were attached to the grey plastic boxes that fed them fresh water and electricity.

It was going to be easy enough to get into one of these things

369

and start it up. The problem would be fuel. I had about eighty miles to travel. These pleasure craft were no good. Their tanks wouldn't be left full over the winter. There would be only one kind of boat in a place like this that would be gassed up all the time.

31

I headed up a pathway that ran along the left side of the triangle. The sea lapped against the rock wall. A cargo ship cast off its mooring ropes and pulled away from the docks. The glow of arc lamps and vehicle lights at the ferry port filtered across the water and cast weak shadows on the concrete below me.

At last I found what I was looking for. The Coast Guard here had two RIBs, monsters, well over thirty feet, both with twin 115 h.p. Yamaha outboards. At least, I assumed they were the Coast Guard. They had the word *Kustwacht* plastered everywhere, which sounded about right. Whatever it meant, it looked official, which in turn meant it belonged to an organization that would have demanded full tanks before binning it for the day.

The *Kustwacht*'s land base was a boring-looking cube of a Portakabin with loads of little signs and notice boards outside. I ignored it for now. There was no blaze of lights to suggest anyone was home.

I jumped on the first RIB and pulled up the wooden flooring planks by the engines to expose the fuel-tank cap. It was locked, just like on a car. The two 115s had motorcycle-type locks securing them to the boat.

I checked the centre console, which was basically a steering-wheel with a Perspex shield in front to protect you from the wind and water. There were no keys tucked away inside, and no compass or sat nav either – just an empty cradle.

I climbed out and walked towards the Portakabin. The windows were covered with something that looked like chicken wire. It was screwed in from the outside, so was probably intended to protect the glass from passing yachties rather than stopping people like me gaining access. No one in their right mind would rob a police station or a coast guard's – unless they were deep in the shit to start with.

A couple of minutes of ripping and tugging was all it took. I left it hanging from the frame and slid the window to one side.

I pulled myself up until my stomach was on the sill and wriggled inside. The smell of cigarettes and rubber hit me first – the place smelt like a garage. There was just enough ambient light to make sure I didn't crash into anything.

I moved to the rack of orange dry-bags hanging neatly by the door. These Gore-Tex overall things had integral rubber boots and hoods, and gloves that you zipped on and off from the cuffs. I riffled through them until I found a suit my size and zipped it up as far as my stomach.

I looked around for the RIB keys. They wouldn't be lying in a designer bowl. There would be a log book with them, noting who'd been on board, how much fuel was used, how long they were out, all that sort of stuff. You sign in and sign out each time you use them.

Two thick plastic folders with serial numbers stencilled on the front lay at the top right-hand corner of the desk. I flicked one open. Of course the RIBs had been filled up. Both were done at 19.00 tonight. Bean counting is the same anywhere; it doesn't matter what language it's in. The admin god decrees it. They'd each been out for two hours during the day. One had been topped up with sixty-eight litres, the other fifty-two. The tanks had to hold more than a hundred. They'd want to get five operational hours out of them.

The keys were in the folders too. Both had rubber covers, like jam-pot lids, to protect them from the weather when the RIBs were up and running. A yellow spiral cord clipped them to the driver, acting as a kill switch if you crashed or fell. I took both. I couldn't find a compass, but still left the sat navs. The last thing I needed was a great big electronic arrow pointing at my exact location.

I left via the door. I bounced over the side of the first RIB I came to, slid down to the console and inserted a key. No luck. I tried the second and both Yamahas fired up. The pointer on the fuel gauge immediately showed full. A cloud of smoke belched from the exhausts. The propellers were still low in the water so, for now at least, I didn't have to work out how to sort the hydraulics. I untied the mooring rope, hit the power lever to the right of the steering-wheel, and eased the nose gently out towards the sea.

As I emerged from the apex of the triangle a ship's navigation lights glided past me into the canal. I left the protection of the sea wall. Wind buffeted my face. I zipped up the rest of the dry-bag and donned the hood and gloves as well.

When I'd put a bit of distance between me and the shore, I slipped the lever into neutral. I kept the engine running, but powered right down. The boat bobbed in the swell as I moved back to check the fuel lines. One 115 h.p. engine was more than enough for me to piss it to the UK. Two engines would burn twice as much.

I twisted the cut-out on what I thought was the left-hand fuel line but the right-hand one cut out instead. I found the button for the hydraulic ram and lifted it out of the water. I didn't want any unnecessary drag.

Next priority was navigation. There was no ball compass. This boat's direction-finding devices were all Gucci. As I came out into the sea, I was more or less heading west, so north had to be to my right. But before I went much further I was going to need Polaris.

373

The Pole Star is the most accurate natural guide there is in the northern hemisphere. As all the other stars appear to move from east to west as the earth rotates, this one stays stock still, directly above the Pole.

First I had to find the Plough, seven stars grouped in the shape of a long-handled saucepan. Draw a line between the two stars that form the side furthest from the handle, extend it upwards by about five times its length, and the star you get to, all on its own, is Polaris.

Once I'd found it, all I needed to do was make sure I kept it to my right until I bumped into the UK. Exactly where, I couldn't predict.

I looked west and picked another star to aim for. I opened the throttle again and the bow lifted. The wind tugged at my hood. I sat on the cox's seat behind the screen, glancing back and forth between my star and Polaris. I'd waver left and right; the wind and the single engine would make it impossible not to. But that didn't matter, as long as I was going west.

I powered down until the bow dropped and I was bouncing over the surface of the water.

I thought about Robot – my mate from the battalion, not the one I'd hung on the extinguisher hook. We were posted in Gibraltar, so it wasn't easy for him to get to Millwall on a Saturday. He came up with a plan. One Friday night, he stole a speedboat from the harbour; he reckoned that as long as he turned right and followed the coast, he'd soon reach France. Once there, he'd chuck a left to the Den. Being Robot, he had no idea how far he had to go. The boat ran out of fuel in the Bay of Biscay. He never made the game.

Shit, I was doing it again . . .

PART SEVEN

1

Spray blasted my face. My arse wound was sore from four hours of constant sitting and standing. My arms ached from gripping the wheel. I was exhausted and hungry. But soon none of that mattered. Lights twinkled three or four K ahead, some high, some low. I focused on the low ones, near the water. I didn't want to end up steering towards a cliff. The biggest concentration was south-west of me. I turned the wheel and headed for the darkness about a K to the left of it.

The more I thought about this shit and the closer I'd got to the coast, the more worked up I'd become. I needed to control myself.

It was nearing first light. For some reason, that always made me feel even colder. But apart from my injuries I was feeling all right. Even the acid burn wasn't that bad. The lack of Smarties hadn't had any effect at all.

Half a K out I powered down, keeping the bow pointed towards the land. The tide was out. I'd have about three hundred metres of beach to cover.

About five short of the water's edge I heard the Yamaha scrape along the bottom. I gave it a quick burst of reverse and then swung the wheel so it faced out to sea again. I unclipped the kill cord from my dry-bag. Making sure the engine was facing dead ahead, in line with the bow, I tied the wheel to the console with the wires from both keys.

I sat on the edge of the RIB with my legs spread and my right hand gripping the grab loop. I leant out towards the console, slapped the throttle lever and jumped. The engine revved and the bow came up. The boat roared off, back the way I'd come.

I was waist deep in water. Some had made it down the neck of the Gore-Tex but otherwise the suit had done its stuff. Daylight was breaking behind me as I waded onto the deserted sand. I moved across it as quickly as I could, heading for the cover of the dunes. I needed to wriggle out of the dry-bag before the place was crawling with early-morning dog-walkers.

As I approached the edge of the town a van came past, and then a milk float. They drove on the left and had British plates. Thank fuck they weren't Belgian or French. Or, worse still, Norwegian. I'd read about a guy in Kent who'd bought himself a little boat. With only a road map for directions, he'd set off from a town on the river Medway, en route for Southampton. He ran out of fuel, then drifted onto a sandbank. He told the rescue team he'd been careful to keep the coast to his right. He'd ended up going round and round the Isle of Sheppey.

I passed a boatyard. A sign said, 'Welcome to Aldeburgh'. The road became the high street. It was a typical east-coast town, with old houses painted in pastel colours and local shops trying to compete with the big chains.

A Budgens was open. I picked up a litre of milk, some crisps and Mars bars, and a couple of packs of egg-mayonnaise sand-wiches. A woman was sorting the morning papers at the counter. I added a copy of the *Sun* and had a quick chat with her about the weather.

Back on the street with my carrier bag, I passed an old butcher sorting out his shop front. At last I found what I was after. The bus stop near the tourist information centre told me I could get a 165 to Ipswich railway station, or I could get the

164 to Saxmundham. The first to arrive would be the 6.59 to Ipswich.

I only had about ten minutes to wait. I sat on the bench in the bus shelter and munched and drank over the morning paper, as you do on your way to work. The early edition carried nothing about an exploding silo in Amsterdam.

2

Chelmsford
Saturday, 20 March
11.16 hrs

Liverpool Street wouldn't be too far now. I was at a table seat with my back to the engine. My head rested against the window. My eyes were closed and the motion of the train made it harder not to sleep.

A bunch of squaddies had got on at Colchester and taken the table across the aisle. All four were in jeans and trainers, and 2 Para sweatshirts so we knew who they were. Four regulation-issue black day sacks sat on the racks above them.

I caught snatches of banter between dozes. It sounded like they had a weekend off and were looking forward to a night on the town and a cheap room at the Victory Services Club at Marble Arch. I'd stayed there once as a Green Jacket, off to Buckingham Palace to get a medal from the Queen.

I would have been about the same age as these guys, but not half as excited. They'd got discounted tickets to the Chelsea game on Sunday from a new website just for squaddies.

I jogged myself awake. "Scuse me, lads – Chelsea are at home, aren't they?'

The one nearest to me answered. 'Yeah, against Blackburn.'

'What time's kick-off?'

'Four.' He pointed at my head. 'But you'd better leave that at home, know what I mean?' He didn't actually tell me I was a wanker, but I could see he was tempted.

I smiled. I had a Man U baseball cap on. It wouldn't be the cleverest thing to wear anywhere near Stamford Bridge, but it went very nicely with the baggy brown raincoat and geeky reading glasses I'd kitted myself out with at the British Heart Foundation shop in Ipswich. They rattled against the window as I watched the scenery become more built up. The baby Paras got more excited with every passing minute. They planned to drink the city dry tonight and then shag it senseless before watching the Blues hammer Blackburn.

Until I got back to Anna, I was going to change my appearance at every bound. I'd ditched my Timberlands in favour of a pair of plastic-soled shoes that were already half dead when I'd handed over the two pounds for them.

I had to shed my skin twice a day. This country has more CCTV than the rest of the world put together. That was why I was wearing the glasses and the cap with a big brim. They've got facial recognition and software that can analyse the way you walk.

Once I'd got to London, I'd take on another look. And this was the last time I'd be using buses and trains. They all had cameras. I'd pay cash for everything and stay away from my flat, my car, my London life. They must know by now that I'd dropped out of sight, and that Bradley wasn't delivering Lily on a plate. The voice-recognition gear and all the Tefalheads' other toys at GCHQ would be whirring away looking for the shape, sound or PIN of Nick Stone.

I watched rows and rows of thirties bay-windowed houses flash by as we hit the suburbs. My head started to hurt, but only where the bite on top of it vibrated against the window.

I closed my eyes again as the Paras got even more lairy about the weekend ahead. Another four cans of Carling came out of a day sack.

3

London
13.23 hrs

I legged it the fifteen minutes or so to Brick Lane. I'd never understood why people liked Ye Olde East End, the area rubbing up against the financial centre. I'd spent my whole childhood in a shit hole like that, trying to dig my way out. But today I was glad it was so close to Liverpool Street. It had loads of charity and corner shops.

Walking back from Brick Lane towards Shoreditch, I kept my eyes open for somewhere to change into my new clothes. I found the Hoxton Hotel, a monument to glass and steel. I looked like Tracey Emin's unmade bed, but so did many of the *über*-trendy lads round here. This was jeans-hanging-round-your-thighs territory.

I went into the toilets, quickly washed my face and splashed my hair to smooth it down. I emerged wearing a green parka, brown cords, blue baseball cap, and cheap Timberland rip-offs that were so scuffed and knackered they looked the height of Hoxton chic.

I made sure the blue cap shadowed my face, dumped my train clothes in a bin and turned towards the City again. A café selling salt-beef sandwiches took another few quid off me. I munched as I walked and tried to work out my plan of action.

The later editions were already showing colour pictures of the burnt-out silo and blaming Muslim fundamentalists. 'Reliable sources' said the local Muslim population had had its fill of Amsterdam's decadence, and Iranian-funded extremists had stepped in to take direct action. The papers said that, in response, the Brits, along with the rest of Europe and the US, had taken their own threat matrix up a level as the UK waited to see if it would be next on the attack list.

I got my salt beef down me and felt better than I had at any time since the Vietnamese with Jules.

I passed a pound shop and picked up a shrink-wrapped pack of steak knives with plastic handles pretending to be wood and the world's biggest fuck-off pair of pliers. Back out on the main I hailed a cab.

'Regent's Park tube, mate.'

He was happy. It was a good fare. And I was happy because the cab had no cameras. I got my head down and pretended to sleep. We moved slowly towards the West End. We were caught in stop-start traffic on Marylebone Road.

I leant forward. 'I tell you what, mate, quick change of plan. Can you go down Harley Street and drop me off near John Lewis?'

'No drama.' He looked around, both hands off the wheel, as we ground to a halt yet again. 'I blame Ken Livingstone. Them fucking bendy buses fucking everything up.'

We turned left into Harley Street and followed the one-way system south towards Cavendish Square, Mercs and Rolls-Royces parked up every few metres with their four-ways on.

'Some fucking money down here and no mistake.'

I looked from side to side and nodded. But I wasn't admiring the cars or the shiny brass plates: I was scanning the street for a stakeout on the clinic. It was a known location. Being paranoid pays dividends in this business.

I wasn't expecting to see anything as obvious as a two-up in a smoked-glass MPV or guys hanging around in Ray-Bans. If anything, it would be somebody in the building, or camera surveillance. The Firm could have requisitioned a CCTV camera a kilometre away and zoomed in on the entrance on twenty-four-hour soak.

The clinic was on the first floor of the building to my left as we carried on south. I looked up at it through my new thicker-rimmed glasses. The chandelier burnt away in the consulting room. The lights were on; I hoped somebody was at home.

We got to the bottom of Harley Street and turned left into the square.

'Just here will be fine, mate.'

The fare was twenty-six pounds. I gave him three tens and told him to keep the change.

It looked like I'd made his day. 'Hang about . . . here you go, mate. For you.' He passed me a couple of clean receipts.

I smiled to myself as he drove away. Maybe I'd fill them in and present them to Jules as expenses.

I brought up my hood as I crossed the bottom of Harley Street and headed back the way we'd come. I must have looked like the guys at the Bender checkpoint. The clinic was now across the road, to my right. I'd done the drive-past, and now I was going to do the walk-past.

I hoped he was there. I hadn't called ahead. The only time you ever make contact with the target is when you either grip him or drop him.

The sky had been threatening rain, and it finally started as I drew level with the clinic. I kept my hands in the chest-height pockets of the parka, head down but eyes up, trying to catch a glimpse of Kleinmann thrusting a fistful of leaflets at a new victim. There was no one in sight.

Unless there was an exit at the rear, he could only go left or right. There were cars parked outside, but mostly with uniformed drivers. Chances were, he'd turn left and head for Oxford Street.

Scaffolding shrouded a building in the process of renovation about sixty metres further on. A working platform had been constructed halfway up the basement well, skirted by plywood sheets to stop debris falling onto the pavement. Stacked against it were a neatly folded furry blanket and some flattened cardboard boxes. Its occupant was currently not in residence.

I jumped the railings, ducked beneath the window sill and got comfortable under the blanket. I had eyes on the target door. Sleeping rough was part of the city landscape. Passers-by wouldn't give me a second glance. These bundles only came to life at last light; heads appeared, wary of muggers, the protection racketeers who charged them for good cover, out of the wind and the neos' British wing who'd just fill them in for the fun of it.

It was just after half three. I kept my eyes on the target and tried hard not to fall asleep.

4

I lay there for about an hour and a half. I was getting ready to bin it and start staking out the Vietnamese when the unmistakable haircut of Max Kleinmann emerged from the doorway. He walked down the three marble steps and chucked a left towards the square. I pulled off the blanket and refolded it exactly as I'd found it.

Hood up and hands in the lower, bigger pockets of my parka, I started south again. I fingered the blister-pack, bending it over the sharp ends of the knives until they pierced the plastic. I hadn't opened them before now, in case I got stopped and searched. An open knife is an offensive weapon. One still in its packaging is a birthday present for your mum.

He was walking quickly but he wasn't aware: he was too busy waffling away on his mobile. His head was down, his shoulders hunched against the drizzle. Rain glistened on the pavements as the street-lights flickered into life.

He dodged the traffic on his way to the green area at the centre of the square. He was either going to carry on towards Oxford Street, or head for the entrance to the underground car park.

He passed a red phone box and disappeared. I followed him into the stairwell, no more than five seconds behind. I slowed down almost immediately and heard a door bang.

I ran down the first flight of concrete steps, turned on the landing, then down another. The smell of stale piss made my eyes water. I didn't know if there were cameras down here, but I had to assume there were. I pulled one of the knives out of my pocket and held the pretend wood in my palm with the blade against my wrist. I went through the door into the basement.

The smell of exhaust fumes took over. Cars lined the concrete walls. There was movement to my left. Kleinmann was in a black jacket and matching jeans. Ahead of him, lights flashing, was a new red Volvo two-door hatchback.

'Hey, Doc! Am I pleased to see you!'

I waved. Big smile, big surprise. I still couldn't see any cameras

His eyes narrowed, trying to make out who I was.

'Fancy seeing you here, Doc!'

I got nearer, looking down so my face was covered by the baseball cap.

He cocked his head to the side, trying to get a better look at me. 'Do we—'

'Know each other? Yeah, course we do.' I grabbed his hand with my right one, making sure he felt the weapon dig into him, and embraced him with my left. 'Fuck me about and I'll cut you.'

His body shuddered as he tried to step back. I gripped him and dug deeper.

'Please, take what you want. I won't say a word to anyone, I promise.'

'*Shut up!* Get into the car!'

He nodded, wild-eyed.

I pulled away from him, my right hand still gripping him and my left hand on his shoulder, controlling him.

He was flapping big-time.

'Don't look at me. Look at the floor.'

A car mounted the ramp to my half-left, its tail lights glowing red as it made its way to the exit.

'Just stay calm, all right? Don't do anything. You got kids? Think of them.'

He shook his head, which made him more of a dickhead. I would have said yes, to make my assailant think he had the leverage.

'Then think of your wife. Got one of those?'

I let go as another car swung towards us. 'Go to the driver's side.' I made sure I stayed level with him, the far side of his Volvo as a Prius glided past us. We got in together. I jabbed the knife against his crotch as he went to put his seatbelt on. 'Not yet. Don't look at me. Face the front.'

We were inches from a bare concrete wall, with his reserved parking sign drilled into it at head height. His nostrils flared as he breathed. I knew what was going through his head. He was working hard at not fucking up here. He wanted to get this nightmare over and done with.

By the look of him, he hadn't shaved since I last saw him.

'Give me your phone.'

I could hear a couple talking behind us. I saw them in the wing mirror. They didn't notice us. Even if they did, they'd probably do the city avoidance thing and not want to get involved. They'd rather walk past and see if their suspicions were right when they watched the ten o'clock news.

He passed over an iPhone. I took it with my left hand, and kept the other holding the knife to his bollocks. 'Lean forward. Head on the wheel.'

I tapped the calendar icon. He had loads of appointments today until three forty-five, and then it went blank. On Sunday evening he had a chess game. I assumed that was what it was – it just said, 'Chess'. Maybe it was the musical. I didn't care. There was still no indication of what or with whom. No dinner parties booked, nothing else going on.

'Please, just take everything. I won't say anything.'

'*Fucking shut up!*'

I hit the number list. 'Who's Gillian? You made a call to her at ten oh eight this morning.'

'She's my receptionist. I was a little late and . . .'

The only other call was the one he had just made. 'Who's M?' I pressed a +1 310 number, Los Angeles.

'My mother, she doesn't sleep so well and—'

'Give me your wallet.'

'Now you've got to let me go. I have nothing else. Take the car!'

I opened the slim brown leather folder. Besides cards, there was about £150 in crisp twenties and tens, straight from the ATM. There were no family snaps. He should at least have had a baby picture in there, even if it wasn't his. It gives you far more chance of having your wallet returned.

His driver's licence gave an address in Stanmore Hill in North London. The house number was followed by a B. He lived in a flat.

'Get the keys, left hand. Turn on the engine.'

'Just take everything.'

I pressed the knife harder into his crotch. 'Turn on the engine.'

His left hand fished for the key and the diesel was soon ticking over. I powered down the window and smashed the phone onto the concrete. I kept his wallet. It joined the other steak knives in my pocket.

'Now sit up, and belt up.'

Breathing heavily, he did as he was told. Sweat ran from the back of his head down the front of his face and nose, and was now trying to make its way onto his chin. He glanced across and got his first view of me as I pulled down my hood. When he saw who it was under the glasses and cap it was like the opening of a floodgate.

'Oh, my God! They made me do it! I'm so sorry, I—'

'Who? Who made you do it? Tresillian? Julian?'

'Who – what? Look, I don't know. Two guys visited with me. Heavies. They said this was your scan, and they gave me the drugs. I swear. I had no choice. Please—'

He lost it. His hands came up, pleading with me. 'They made me! Please believe me! I don't know anything . . .'

I pressed the knife down further. 'Calm down.' I pointed at his face. 'You got no wife or kids over here? You on your own?'

'Yes.'

'Well, whatever – you don't know it yet, but you're in deep shit. I can't lose control of you until I've finished what I'm here to do. That means either killing you . . .'

'No! Please!' He was almost hyperventilating.

'Calm down, for fuck's sake. Or it means keeping you with me all the time, making sure you can't tell anyone what's just happened.'

If I was right about him, he was in as much shit as I was. He just didn't know it.

'Take deep breaths. Come on, that's better.' I took the knife away and held it up between us. 'But don't go mistaking kindness for weakness, all right? You tell me what you know and do what I say and you'll get out of this car alive.' I pointed the blade at his face. 'OK, a couple more deep breaths and then you're going to drive us both to Fulham.'

5

Kleinmann was a good prisoner.

We sat at a window table in TGI Friday's. A far too cheerful waitress bounced over and announced she'd be looking after us tonight. Kleinmann was happy for me to do the ordering, as long as it was chicken.

My eyes never left the restaurant front on the other side of Fulham Broadway. Getting something to eat and keeping out of the rain were secondary. We were here for the stakeout on the Vietnamese.

Passing buses obscured the target for a couple of seconds now and again. The junction was busy. High-sided vans sometimes got stuck at the lights. Most of the footfall had their heads down, collars or brollies up, orange Sainsbury carrier bags alongside them, en route to a ready-meal for one and a bottle of wine in front of the telly.

Our food turned up, with another round of Diet Cokes. I knew Kleinmann was scared, but he probably felt secure. If people have control, you feel safer. You're being held for a reason, and they're not going to do anything rash.

So far he'd done exactly what I'd told him to do. He'd shut up, driven us here, parked up, and even offered to buy dinner, which was good of him considering I had his wallet.

'The shadow on the scan, the big red Smarties . . . It's all bull-shit, isn't it?'

He nodded miserably.

I dunked a chip in the dish of tomato sauce. 'Why are you mixed up with all this shit? What have you been doing to get so fucked up?'

He wiped his forehead with the paper napkin. His liquid brown eyes glistened with anguish. 'These guys came in. They made me do it. I had no choice. I don't know who they were. I don't know why they wanted me to do what I did, and I don't know why I'm sitting here. I just know I'm scared . . .'

He stared at his untouched food. I picked up another chip and poked it at him.

'What is it they've got on you? Or did they simply come in and say they were going to kill you?'

His hands came up. 'Please, I'm doing everything you say. Please don't use those words.' He rubbed his beard and took a shuddering breath. 'Well, it's kind of—'

I dropped my chip on the plate. 'Look over there. See that restaurant – the Vietnamese? Do you know him? The black guy at the door, going in? Was he one of them? The guy now inside, taking his coat off, waiting for a seat. You see him?'

Kleinmann adjusted his glasses. 'Who?'

'The black guy. Talking with the waiter now. You see him?'

'No . . .'

'The suit. The smart guy.'

'Yes, I see him – but it wasn't him. They were both white. Sounded like you – that London thing.'

Jules was shown to a table and sat with his back to the door. A waiter appeared. He didn't bother with a menu. He was a regular. He knew what he wanted.

Kleinmann fidgeted. 'Can I go now? I promise I won't—'

I picked up my burger and nodded at his. 'Better start getting that down you. We'll be leaving soon.'

He sat there and played with a couple of chips as I cleared

my plate. I asked for the bill and watched the top of Jules's head tilt back as he helped himself to a beer.

I paid with cash from Kleinmann's wallet, then stood up and pulled on my parka. 'Remember, don't mistake kindness for friendship or weakness. Just do what I say, when I say, and all will be well. OK?'

He nodded and stood up.

We turned left towards the tube station, walked about thirty metres and ducked into the doorway of a boarded-up book-shop. It was near a bus stop and a natural place to wait, especially in this weather.

I got hold of Kleinmann. I needed his full attention. 'When he comes out, he's going to head for the tube. We're going to follow him. Then I'm going to make sure he comes with us to your car.'

'Then what?'

'Don't worry about that. All you have to remember is that if you fuck me about I'm going to have to do you. You know that, yeah?'

He nodded.

We waited twenty or so minutes. People got on and off buses. Others huddled in doorways like us. My eyes never left the restaurant door.

I nudged Kleinmann. 'Here we go, stand by.'

I reached into my parka pocket and grabbed the pliers. Julian was going to come with me whether he liked it or not. And then he was going to tell me what the fuck was going on.

He stood on the pavement, pulling up his collar and looking up at the rain. He turned towards the Underground, and then double-checked behind him, further down the road, away from us. As I followed his eye line, I could see a cab approaching, its bright yellow sign a beacon in the gloom.

He stuck his hand out. Minutes later he was gone.

Kleinmann took it all in but didn't say a word. He was waiting for my reaction.

'Back to the car. You should have eaten that burger. Like I said, it's going to be a long night.'

6

Rain pounded on the Volvo roof. The windows were steamed up and the car stank of my farts. The burger was taking its toll. We were parked in a sixties housing estate somewhere near Baron's Court. I didn't know exactly where it was, but I'd seen the name on road signs. All that mattered was that it was near Fulham, and it was out of the way of mainstream roads.

I'd tied Kleinmann's right hand to the steering-wheel with his belt. He couldn't get his seat to recline because his arm wasn't long enough. He'd assumed the position he had in the Cavendish Square car park, head on the wheel, but this time because he was knackered.

I was stretched out on the fully extended passenger seat. There was a slight risk in using the car. It was a known location if someone phoned the police to say Kleinmann hadn't turned up somewhere tonight, but it was a chance I had to take. It was better for me to control him here. It was better for both of us than having a night out in this shit. He'd probably never slept rough. He'd be more of a drama out there than he was in here, and we wouldn't look like vagrants when I moved in on Jules tomorrow.

I turned the electrics on to lower my window a couple of

inches. Kleinmann was in a world of his own. Sometimes he mumbled.

I wouldn't sleep with him moaning to himself and the rain hammering on the roof, but I turned my back to him, trying to get comfortable.

He stirred. 'Can't we just go back to my apartment? I've got food – a shower.'

'No.'

'Who are you guys? Drug-dealers? Mafia? What is it?'

He waited for an answer. He didn't get one.

'It's drugs, isn't it? You guys fighting over drugs?'

I shook my head. 'Tell you what, you tell me how they got you to work and I'll tell you what's happening.'

He looked out of the window and rubbed his hair. 'I had a practice. Cosmetic surgery. Fat asses, droopy chins. Marlene was cool. Ten years younger than me, but I had everything she wanted.

'Then three years ago, when she was about to turn thirty-five, she had an affair with a twenty-year-old cowboy.' He shook his head like he still couldn't believe it. 'She went to an all-woman, arm-and-a-leg fancy dude-ranch retreat – on my dime. I say all women – except the young cowboys who were there to run the place. She spreads them for this kid and decides he's her soul-mate.

'The affair went on for a few months. Marlene started "volunteering" at this ranch and then she told me, immediately after our tenth wedding anniversary, she wanted out. Know why the tenth anniversary is significant? Because in fucking sunny California, without a pre-nup, a spouse gets half of *everything* for life if the couple are married ten years.

'I fought long and hard for two years to get us in therapy. I promised to change all the things she blamed me for. I was "controlling", she said, and kept too tight a fist on the money. She couldn't do all the decorating projects she wanted, for example, because I thought they were too expensive. Hello . . .

395

I was the only fucking one working to pay for this shit. But she said she was out the door. I think she was even screwing the therapist – on my dime again. She even said, "I have to get out now so I can snag a great guy while I'm still hot."

'So I said, "OK, I get it, I understand. We tried and it didn't work out. No hard feelings. Let me help. A couple of nips and tucks and you'll be ready for the world." So I carried out a procedure on her and that was the end of her . . .'

I sat up. 'You killed her?'

'No – I just fucked up her face a bit. Now she looks like she's sitting in a fucking wind tunnel.' He pulled back the loose skin on his face to show me. 'So the bitch divorced me and sued me for malpractice on the same fucking day. How fucking cool is that?'

Big fat tears were rolling down his cheeks. 'I came here. Used my original family name. Over there I was Klein. This country is great for locum work with hardly any checks. I worked hard to make a few dollars – I'm trying to tuck it all away before her lawyers find me. But I know they will. It's going to be a nightmare.'

'So that's what they've got on you?'

'Yeah. They came into my office one day. They told me my life story and that was it. Two white guys, nice suits.'

'They gave you the scans?'

'Yes. And the drugs.'

'What were they?'

'I haven't a clue. Nothing I'd ever come across before.'

'They might have been specially made?'

'Why not?'

'What did they say was going to happen next?'

'Nothing. They said they'd be in touch. Who gives a fuck? How could it be worse?'

I lay back down and took a breath. 'Actually, mate, it's a lot worse. You're mixed up with the intelligence service. You've seen the movies?'

He nodded slowly, taking the hit.

'That's what I'm trying to sort out. Help me tomorrow, and then you fuck off out of the UK as fast as you can. Even take your chances back in the States. These guys are a lot uglier than Marlene.'

'What about you? Why are they after you?'

'It doesn't matter. But they're never going to leave us alone unless I sort this shit out.'

7

Sunday, 21 March
17.55 hrs

A roar went up and the clapping and cheering started – but it wasn't as loud as I was used to when Chelsea won. The crowd began to surge out of the West Stand and past the merchandise van I was leaning against. I'd intended waiting further down Fulham Broadway, until I'd noticed the hundred metres or so of steel barrier that bisected the road from the tube station to the ground. It was to stop queue-barging and congestion in the station itself. Fans wanting the tube were channelled into it by mounted police more or less as soon as they exited the ground. I had no alternative but to wait further up.

Everyone in blue had a not-so-happy face on. 'Mate, fucking one–all against Blackburn? Nightmare,' somebody yelled into his mobile. 'Who'da fucking believed it?'

I scanned the crowd and pinged him almost immediately. He came level and passed me, looking like something off the cover of a menswear catalogue in his blue wool coat and pressed blue cords. He looked straight ahead, trying, like everyone else, to avoid banging into people or getting knocked over himself. The crowd was shoulder to shoulder.

I let him pass and get five or six paces ahead before I edged my way into the flow with a big smile on my face, like I was making my way over to a mate. Nine out of ten times, if you're friendly when you tell them you're coming through, people will move aside.

As they did, I reached into my right pocket and gripped the pliers, making sure the jaws were nice and open. Jules's hands were down at his side. He couldn't have swung them even if he'd wanted to. I focused on his left hand. He probably had a watch under that coat sleeve but that didn't bother me. It would just add to the pain.

My right hand was at the same level as his left and centimetres away. I pulled the pliers from my coat, jammed them against his sleeve and squeezed hard. I grabbed his arm with my left hand so I could steer him. He reacted like he'd been stung by a bee, but he still hadn't worked out exactly what had happened. It could have been a burn from somebody's cigarette. Then his eyes widened as he saw who it was and the pain really started to register. He tried to pull away but I squeezed the pliers into his wrist and manoeuvred him with my right shoulder.

'Don't fuck about or I'll drop you here and now.'

We stayed in the flow as the crowd spilled onto Fulham Broadway and the majority turned right. Jules almost hugged me in his effort to keep the pressure off his pinched wrist. He looked like a walking heart-attack victim.

'Not the tube. Left of the barriers.'

The street was still packed but we were no longer shoulder to shoulder. There were no words from him yet, but I wasn't expecting any. If he was able to talk, his one and only concern had to be the pain.

I steered him left at the junction with Harwood Road. The crowd started to thin and most of the noise was behind us. I scanned for the Volvo down on the left. I knew it was going to be there, but I wanted to see if the driver still was.

As we approached, he opened the passenger door and pushed the seat forward for me. Still gripping Jules, I jumped into the back. I pushed the passenger seat upright again and dragged him inside with the pliers. Kleinmann's trouser belt was beside me. The loose end was already threaded into the buckle to make a loop.

No one said a word as I threw the keys to Kleinmann. Jules fought the pain through clenched teeth. Kleinmann did up Jules's seat belt like I'd told him to. I didn't want the police making a routine traffic stop just because the passenger was unbelted. Jules's face was screwed up with pain. I looped the belt over his head and around his neck and the head restraint, and pulled.

Jules's left hand dangled between the door and the seat. I'd swapped the pliers into my left hand so I could keep control directly behind him. He pushed back against the head restraint and took several deep breaths, fighting the belt that was trying to stop him. It looked like he was going to start talking.

I pulled the belt tight to keep him in place. 'Not now. You'll have plenty of chance to waffle.'

I gave Kleinmann a nod. 'Let's go.'

The Cavendish Square car park was as good a place as any to head for. The car had a reason to be there because it had a designated space. It was also Sunday, so many of the business spaces around his were going to be empty.

It took us half an hour just to get away from the area of the ground, and another thirty minutes to get up behind John Lewis. He nosy-parked in his space.

Kleinmann unfastened his seat belt and opened his door. He was more than ready to get out. He left the keys in the ignition. He knew he had to return in thirty minutes. If he did, he did. I was beyond worrying about that at the moment.

As soon as the door closed I pulled tighter on the belt. Julian gagged and writhed his hips, as if that was going to help.

'If you think that hurt, you're not going to believe what's coming next.'

I released the pliers and swapped them back into my right hand. Then, with my arse in the air, I reached over the back of his seat and clamped them onto the bridge of his nose. I squeezed until I could feel bone against the steel. He jerked his head and I squeezed harder. 'Any more pressure and it's going to burst. You know that.'

I wanted him scared. But I also wanted him to talk.

8

Jules's breathing was fast and laboured. He tried to adjust his head to give his throat some respite. I felt the steel grind against bone. His hands gripped the sides of the seat to take the pain.

'Kleinmann, Anna and me –' I gave the pliers a squeeze '– we're trying to find a way out of this shit, and you're going to help us.'

I pulled some more on the belt. He arched his back and his legs jerked straight, his feet pushing into the footwell. His mouth opened to spray saliva onto the windscreen. My left forearm rested on the top of his head with the pliers still gripping the bridge of his nose.

'Why did you fuck me over, Jules?'

He didn't react. He'd probably thought about it and knew the best thing was to stop moving and start thinking.

I released the belt a fraction so he could speak.

'Nick, why didn't you stand down and come back when I told you?'

'What the fuck are you on about?'

I looked at him in the rear-view. His eyes were fixed on mine. Saliva ran down his chin. His eyes were wide, but fighting to keep control. He knew he was in the shit, and had to talk.

'The police. The Dutch. They were watching the silo. A drugs operation.'

I loosened the belt a bit more.

'We didn't know about it, Nick. They saw you when you did your recce. They pinged the car, got the plate, and started to follow you out – but they lost you when you left the building. We only got on to it when Nicholas Smith was flagged. That's when I told Bradley to stand you down. It was categorical, Nick. Come back, cut away. Why didn't you?'

I jolted the belt to let him know I'd heard enough.

His eyes had already done most of the talking by the time he answered.

I released the pressure on his nose.

He took deep breaths and raised a hand to the wound.

I stuck the pliers against his neck, clamped down, and twisted. He screamed as I pulled tighter on the belt. The windows were completely steamed up.

'Why send me on a job when you knew Bradley was going to drop me afterwards?' I twisted again.

Now he was really worried. He knew how dead he might be soon.

I loosened the belt.

'Please, Nick. You asked for the job. It got compromised on the first night and I told Tresillian to stand you down. Next thing I know, the silo's hit, and Bradley and a girl are dead.'

'What about Kleinmann? The drugs? The scan?'

His eyes flickered around, trying to process all this information.

'You kept telling me you were fine. I know nothing about the drugs. I know nothing about any illness.'

He twisted his head left and upwards. As our eyes made contact I told him what had happened.

He didn't move. The pliers had pinched into the skin and drops of blood coated the steel jaws.

'It all started after our meal, Jules. What am I supposed to think?'

He fell silent. Neither of us spoke for a while.

'You can do what you want with me, I know that. But I had nothing to do with what is happening to you or Kleinmann. Maybe I'm next. Have you thought about that? Maybe we need to sort this out together.'

Could he be telling the truth? Only one blue-and-white during the raid, and no back-up . . . Maybe I'd been followed, and they'd been sent just to break up the rape so they could keep me moving. They must have lost me. Then picked me up again when I planted the device . . .

The door opening on the factory next to the silo . . . maybe that was their OP. They didn't know what the fuck I was doing with those girls. They wanted to follow the trail to get more int. They'd obviously react as soon as the shotgun rounds went off in the building. Maybe I'd been the target of the eye in the sky. I didn't know. Maybe it didn't really matter what they knew.

I wanted to believe Jules. And I knew he was right about one thing: there was a much bigger picture.

And it was hanging on Tresillian's wall.

9

Jules drove us up the M5 to junction eleven, and then the A40 towards Cheltenham. Just before the town he turned off at the roundabout and got onto Hubble Road. We were in a company Prius from Thames House. Jules didn't have a car of his own and we weren't going back to get mine.

We'd been quiet all the way. It was only a little over a week since we'd last made this journey. A lot had happened since then. We were both taking stock.

Jules had called Tresillian and explained that I had Lilian and wanted to meet him.

I knew that Tresillian would take the meeting. What choice did he have?

Jules had some nice scabs forming on his neck. His nose was much the same and some bruising was just starting to show around his eyes. It would be weeks before he was box fresh again and back to catwalk perfection.

I thought back to the al-Kibar raid. I guess I'd always known that was the key. The rumours had run riot since the day of the attack. There were no hard facts out there at all. Nobody agreed about who knew what, or what people in the city had or hadn't seen.

The following day, after I'd spent the most boring few hours of my life admiring ancient water wells, Damascus-based Syrian news, the voice of the government, reported that Israeli fighter jets had violated Syrian air space in the early hours of the morning, but Syria's courageous defenders had triumphed. Two aircraft, they said, had been shot down. The others had been forced to leave, shedding their payloads in the desert without causing any damage whatsoever.

Nothing else was ever said. The Israelis denied the incident had occurred. The US State Department said they had only heard second-hand reports, contradictory at best. To this day, both Syria and Israel, two countries that had technically been at war with each other since the founding of the Jewish state in 1948, played down the raid, even though it had been an act of war.

The reality was much more interesting. Immediately Cody Zero One reported the target destroyed, I'd closed down the gear, sorted myself out, and gone down for a nightcap with Diane.

While I was doing that, the Israeli prime minister called the Turkish prime minister and explained the facts of life. He told him about the ten Israeli F-15s they must have tracked going out into the Med, and asked him to give President Assad of Syria a call. 'Fuck you, Assad,' was the message. 'We will not tolerate a nuclear plant. But no other hostile action is planned.'

Olmert said he was going to play down the incident, and was still interested in making peace with Damascus. If Assad didn't draw attention to the Israeli strike either, those talks could go ahead. The Americans wouldn't say a word – apart from relaying the message that they didn't want them cosying up to the North Koreans, or the Iranians. 'So, basically, Assad, wind your neck in. No one will say anything, and let's leave it at that.'

It was a final warning. The Iranians' reaction had been to

entrench themselves. Literally. Since the attack, many of the centrifuges in which they enriched uranium were relocated deep underground. Not even one of the bunker-busting super bombs the Pentagon was trying to get hold of, but was being denied on the grounds of cost, was capable of fully destroying the facilities that the Iranians had at Natanz. And that wasn't the only one. There were more than a dozen known nuclear facilities in Iran. The Americans and Israelis, and probably the UK too if we got dragged into a war with Iran, were going to be conducting air strikes for weeks.

Al-Kibar was protected by the same Russian-built Tor-M1 air defence system used to protect Iranian facilities. I'd often wondered if Israel's strike had been a test run to find flaws in Iran's air defences.

I leant over to check the dashboard clock.

Julian read my mind. 'He said he'd be there. You know for sure that Lilian's safe?'

'Totally.'

There was a barrier across the road ahead. Jules flashed his pass and we were waved on towards the Doughnut.

We pulled in alongside the black BMW again. The driver was on his own this time, in a sweatshirt, still behind the wheel, engine running. He said fuck-all. He just looked over at us and turned back to his DVD, probably pissed off that he'd had to work two weekends running.

We went into the building. A different woman was at the desk, but she treated Julian to the same smile. He handed over his ID and she swiped it through a reader.

'Good evening, Mr Drogba.' She tried but couldn't keep her eyes off Jules's wounds. 'A rough game this afternoon?'

She passed him a form to sign.

I was handed my red badge.

'Could you hand it back in when you leave, Mr Lampard?'

We went through the electronic version of a body search and came out onto the Street. We passed the night shift of

Tefalheads, doing whatever they did. They were probably still trying to find out what the fuck I'd been up to.

I followed Jules along the bright fluorescent-lit corridor and into the same room as before. This time there was no glow from the plasma screens on the walnut veneer above Tresillian's head. It was dark and gloomy. The air-conditioning hummed as I closed the door behind us. We crossed the deep pile carpet towards the big oval table.

Tresillian was watching us. He wasn't a happy bunny. But he soon cheered up when he saw the state of Jules.

'Mr Stone, I now see why Julian was so eager for us to meet this evening.' He sat back in his leather swivel chair, elbows on the arms, fingers steepled beneath his chin. He was in a scruffy jumper and trousers. Maybe he had his pyjamas on underneath. 'Sit.'

Jules and I took the same chairs as last time.

Tresillian didn't look worried or concerned. Not even angry or anxious. I liked that. I wanted to hate him, but couldn't.

'Let's not fuck around, Mr Stone. How do I know that you really do have Lilian, and that she is still alive?'

'When I'm ready, I'll throw her up on Facebook. She'll be called Lillian Vampire-Girl. I'll make sure there's proof of life up there at the same time. But that's not going to happen until we have a deal, I get a pass, and you answer some questions.'

He leant back again. 'Go on.' He was almost smiling.

'It was the Vietnamese food, wasn't it? That was what fucked me up. The fake scan, the fake drugs?'

'Of course.' He was surprised I'd even had to ask.

'Why go to all the fucking effort of getting me to believe I was dying? I took the job because of it, but you could have got someone else with far less effort.'

'You were a test, Mr Stone. A simple exercise to find out how good our technology is. We collected your DNA, and we carried out a field trial. And it was a fucking good one, don't you think? No one else who ate in that restaurant was contaminated. It was designed to target just your DNA. Now, if we'd wanted to kill you, we would simply have used a different compound.

'At first you weren't even being considered for the task. Since the Russians killed Litvinenko by garnishing his sushi with polonium-210, we thought we'd see how well our concoctions would work in the field.'

He was feeling very pleased with himself.

'I think we can safely say our activities in that department put us among the leaders in the field.'

Jules wasn't happy. 'Why wasn't I informed?'

Tresillian turned to face him. 'Because you would have disagreed.'

'The scan, the drugs?'

'The scan was faked, and the drugs, very shiny red placebos. A chalk compound, I believe.'

'So you decided to fuck me over with a plate of rice, then send me on a job and kill me afterwards?'

He raised his hands, palms upwards. 'Why worry about being killed when you're already dead?'

'And you were pretty fucking sure you'd get two for the price of one.'

'Julian kept telling me how shit-fucking-hot you were. But I think it's safe to say that even you would never have found the girl in time if it hadn't been for that incredibly intelligent Russian woman of yours.'

'And you had to find Lily before Tarasov did. So maybe he's not such a great mate after all. He must have been pretty pissed off when you rubbed out his two lads in Amsterdam. Rival traffickers? He just wanted his daughter back. I knew Bradley was talking shit.'

Tresillian was enjoying every minute of this. He was like a magician who couldn't wait to explain his best conjuring trick.

'You were never trying to find her so you could hand her over, were you? You were going to keep her. She's leverage.'

409

He looked at me like I was the village idiot. 'Just as you are now using her against me. Hector Tarasov is not yet a friend of ours – but he does have a rather important role in our immediate future. The deal we have in mind will take two more weeks to complete.'

'Just before a certain shipment leaves his factory for Iran.'

His expression clouded, just for a moment – but long enough for me to know that I'd pulled off a conjuring trick of my own.

'Our aircraft may well have to infiltrate Iranian air space to destroy their nuclear power plants. We might have to fight alongside the French in Algeria to defend our oil and gas interests. We might have to fight alongside the Americans in West Africa to safeguard our energy supply against Muslim fundamentalism in the Niger delta. We need those motherboards . . . adjusted. Very simply, Mr Tarasov needs to do as he is told if he ever wants to see that child again.'

'But you don't have Lily. I do.'

The light went out in his eyes. 'You are welcome to keep her, Mr Stone – as long as she doesn't go near her father. Can you guarantee that? If so, I may be able to accommodate you and your not only intelligent but very attractive Russian friend.'

'And Kleinmann, of course. He gets a pass. This time tomorrow he'll be back in LA with his mother, trying to dodge his ex-wife's lawyers.'

He raised a hand and slapped it back on the table. 'I imagine they'll deal with him rather more brutally than I would have.' He leant forward again, his forearms resting on the table. 'But you should be in no doubt, Mr Stone, I have a lot more plates than Mr Tarasov's to keep spinning, and I will do whatever the fuck it takes to meet my objectives.'

'So you keep saying. But what about fucking up Amsterdam? You didn't even know I was going to end up there.'

His eyes burnt into mine. 'Read the papers, follow the informed debate. The attack on the silo was carried out by

Iranian-backed Muslim extremists. A number of innocent young girls would have been killed – if you hadn't suddenly turned into the Scarlet fucking Pimpernel – strengthening our country's resolve to fight and defeat them.

'The only truth that matters, Mr Stone, is the one that people want to believe. Am I right?' He didn't give me a chance to answer. 'My job is to attack them from every angle, at all times, with all means. There is no quarter for courageous restraint, Mr Stone. We are at war, and you are – or were – a casualty. Finding the girl was the objective, but along the way I saw an opportunity target and I attacked it. If the trail had led you to the centre of fucking Cheltenham and the same opportunity arose, I would have taken exactly the same action. I will always use everything in my power to protect the UK, its territories and dependencies, wherever I can, and whenever I can.'

'Which includes ramping up anti-Muslim rage?'

He wagged his finger like a headmaster. 'No, no, no. Don't be so naïve. It's there to ensure the pro-Iranian factions understand the dangers we face. It was an opportunity that you brought to me and it worked.'

The leather squeaked as he sat back into his chair.

'Tell me, Mr Stone. Why did you save those young women? It served no purpose.'

I hesitated, but only because I'd just realized the answer to his question. 'Your DNA experiment did me a favour. It put me through a moral carwash. I wanted to sleep at night, particularly since I didn't have that many of them left.'

He didn't miss a beat. 'And having gone through this moral-fucking-carwash, I take it that you will not be serving your country again?'

'Correct. I'll leave it in your capable hands.'

'Do not underestimate me. If my operation against her father doesn't succeed because of you, I will retaliate.'

It was my turn to lean forward.

'No, you won't. I'll keep my end of the deal, but I have

411

everything documented, and it's sitting on a cloud. Everything – and I mean everything – will be there for anyone to download should anything happen to me, Kleinmann or the girls. So get on with your Tarasov stunt, but be quick about it. Lilian is pretty angry with her dad right now, but she might want to go home on day fifteen. Who knows? And by then that fucking cloud will contain a few more goodies – including this meeting.

'You'll deny it, of course. But everyone in our world knows there's no smoke without fire.'

If I had got to him, he didn't show it.

'Will that be all, Mr Stone? I need to get on with my life now. I want to go home – and I'm sure you want to do the same.'

Jules shook his head in disbelief. 'And you just let me stumble around in the dark?'

Tresillian stood and brushed a loose thread off his sleeve. 'There were certain things you simply did not need to know. If you ever get to sit in this chair, you can decide who knows what. Until that day, I will.'

It wasn't the answer Jules was after. He controlled his anger, but only just. 'You had me put my friend's life at risk. You were going to have him killed, for Christ's sake.'

Tresillian sat and stared. His voice was low and even. 'Julian, man up. What do you think we do for a living?'

I stood as well, to relieve the pain in my arse wounds. 'I know I'm pond life, on the shit side of the fence, but isn't Jules supposed to be one of yours?'

Tresillian chuckled. 'Well, Julian, what side of the fence *are* you on?'

Julian stayed put, his eyes fixed on the tabletop.

I turned and went outside. The smaller of the two heavies greeted me with a smile. 'We'll escort you to the station, sir. The first train to London on a Monday morning is in about six hours.'

412

Epilogue

Wednesday, 14 June
11.15 hrs

It wasn't supposed to be this way, but this time I didn't give a shit.

I leant against the triple-glazed floor-to-ceiling windows of the penthouse apartment and looked out over the river. But the view from the flat I'd rented was over the Moskva, not the Thames. To the right was the Borodinsky Bridge, and behind that the Russian Federation's government buildings. It was a great place for me to do much the same as I'd done in London a few weeks ago – just sit and gaze out at the city, especially at night.

Anna had been right. Moscow had looked great in the spring, and looked even better now in early summer. I must have walked in every one of the city's ninety-six parks. Of course, Gorky Park had been the first. It was the only one I'd heard of. Then I discovered there was more green stuff here than in New York, and New York had more of it than London. It almost made me glad I'd left.

As the days got longer and warmer, Anna and I had headed for Serebryany Bor, an island just a trolleybus ride away. It

413

could be walked at any time of day, but it was especially great in the evening when the late-setting sun bathed the *dachas*, woods and river. I checked out the spring buds and flowers, kids on bikes with stabilizers, all the normal shit that now made sense to me. These were people who were getting on with their lives. I was getting on with mine too. It was all right. It wasn't as if I jumped up every morning and ran outside to kiss the flowers and hug the trees, but I'd been taking the time to stand and stare. For a week or two, anyway. Then I'd started to get itchy feet.

The sound of a plate smashing echoed round the open space. I turned to see Lily steaming with frustration. 'For fuck's sake!'

I pointed at her, bollocking style. 'Oi, less of that!'

It was just about the only new bit of English Lily had learnt, and it had become her catchphrase.

Anna had taken her to Dresden. They'd stayed with some Romanians she knew. I'd kept well out of the way, in case Tresillian reneged on his side of the deal.

When the two weeks were up, Lily decided not to go back to Moldova. She contacted her father and apologized. She couldn't agree with his views but she understood them. She wanted to stay in Moscow and continue her degree at Moscow State when the new academic year started.

It was like a refugee camp in here sometimes, with Anna's mates bringing her girls they'd rescued from the meat markets and Mafia nightclubs in the city. Anna then turned them over to the Lenas of this world.

It wasn't all about saving the world and appreciating the green stuff. Anna and I had been hitting the galleries and museums. My favourite was the Tretyakov. I found myself getting well into Russian icons.

The doorbell rang. 'For fuck's sake!'

I walked towards her. 'I'm warning you!'

Anna checked her watch as she came out of the bedroom. 'He's early. You said he'd be here at five.'

I flicked the kettle on.

She opened the door. Jules stood there with a black wheelie, his face once more a vision of perfection.

They kissed and she ushered him in.

I'd said no at first to a meeting. He'd made his choice. I'd made mine. Lesson learnt. But Anna was right. If he wanted to come over, fuck it, he could.

Jules stared at me from the hallway. He held out a hand. 'Hello, Nick.'

He looked apprehensive, but he needn't have. I didn't care that he knew where we were, or even if Tresillian did. Anna had written up her version of what had happened, and together with mine and Lily's, it was floating on the Apple MobileMe cloud, ready to be discovered as soon as any of us had a drama.

Anna took his wheelie and rested it against the cloakroom door. He wasn't staying.

I went and shook his hand. 'Tresillian sorted?'

He nodded. 'It all worked.' He glanced at Lily as she made the brews. 'Our Moldovan friend came on board.'

Lily came out of the kitchen area. She walked up to him with a smile and an outstretched hand. 'Hello, my name is Lilian. Nick says you're staying in the city for a couple of days?'

Jules looked a bit uncomfortable. 'Yes, I've got something I want to talk to Nick and Anna about.'

Lily got it. 'I've made the tea. It's British, not Russian.' She turned to Anna. 'OK if I go?' She'd made some friends in the building.

The tea was weak and shit. I turned on the Nespresso machine. Julian and I sat at the black marble breakfast bar but Anna remained standing. She tapped Jules's hand. 'What is it you've come to talk to us about?'

I dropped a capsule into the machine and sparked it up.

'I've resigned.'

Anna's jaw dropped.

415

'A month ago.' Jules turned to me. 'Remember what you said about a carwash?'

I pushed him a brew. Things went quiet for a while. I didn't know what to say.

Anna tugged her cigarettes out of her jeans. I pointed to the balcony. There's no smoke without fire.